D0497825

MEG

NIGHTSTALKERS

*Published by Tom Doherty Associates

MEG

NIGHTSTALKERS

STEVE ALTEN

TOR

A TOM DOHERTY ASSOCIATES BOOK ||| NEW YORK

MEG: NIGHTSTALKERS

A Tor Book
Published by Tom Doherty Associates, LLC
175 Fifth Avenue
New York, NY 10010

www.tor-forge.com

Tor® is a registered trademark of Tom Doherty Associates, LLC.

The Library of Congress Cataloging-in-Publication Data is available upon request.

ISBN 978-0-7653-8796-7 (hardcover)
ISBN 978-0-7653-8797-4 (e-book)

Our books may be purchased in bulk for promotional, educational, or business use. Please contact your local bookseller or the Macmillan Corporate and Premium Sales Department at 1-800-221-7945, extension 5442, or by e-mail at MacmillanSpecialMarkets@macmillan.com.

First Edition: June 2016

Printed in the United States of America

0 9 8 7 6 5 4 3 2 1

This novel is dedicated to my friend
BELLE AVERY,
whose incredible dedication, hard work, and belief
will bring the MEG series to the big screen.

ACKNOWLEDGMENTS

It is with great pride and appreciation that I acknowledge those who contributed to the completion of *MEG: Nightstalkers.*

First and foremost, many thanks to Tom Doherty, Whitney Ross, Amy Stapp, Sean Agan, and the great team at Tor/Forge. Thanks as well to my longtime literary agents, Danny Baror and Heather Baror-Shapiro at Baror International, and my dear friend and MEG movie producer, Belle Avery.

Very special thanks to Tan Ngo, 3D modeler and 2D artist (www .tan-artwork.com) whose brilliant interior images add to the reading experience, along with forensic artist William McDonald, who contributed with his amazing submarine designs. To graphic artist extraordinaire Erik Hollander at Hollander Design, Mario Lampic, and underwater photographer Malcolm Nobbs (www.malcolmnobbs .com) for the cover art.

Thanks as always to the tireless Barbara Becker for her editing and her work in the Adopt-An-Author program, as well as Robert Nash. And to my webmaster, Doug McEntyre at Millenium Technology Resources, for his excellence in preparing my monthly newsletters.

Last, to my wife and soul mate, Kim, our children, and, most of all, my readers: Thank you for your correspondence and contributions.

Your comments are always a welcome treat, your input means so much, and you remain this author's greatest asset.

—Steve Alten, Ed.D.

To personally contact the author or learn more about his novels, go to www.stevealten.com.

MEG: Nightstalkers is part of Adopt-An-Author, a free nationwide program for secondary school students and teachers.

For more information, go to www.adoptanauthor.com.

The Adopt-An-Author program recognizes the generous contributions from the following MEGhead VIPs:

PROLOGUE

||||||||||||||||||||||||||||||||

Dr. Timothy Schulte
Family Wellness Center
Monterey, CA.

PATIENT: Taylor, David
AGE: 21
DATE OF SESSION: 26 September

PATIENT SESSION 3

(Transcribed from audio)

TS: David, I'd like to begin today's session by talking about the girl who died . . .

DT: Kaylie.

TS: Yes, Kaylie. How long had you two known each another?

DT: Eight weeks . . . the summer. What difference does it make? I loved her.

TS: You never told me how she died. I know—from what little your

parents have said—it was very traumatic. I think it might help if
you—

DT: She was eaten.

TS: My God. Was it Bela and Lizzy? Did this happen after the Megs
escaped from your facility?

DT: It wasn't the sisters, it was a *Liopleurodon*. A freak of nature; it
was bigger than Angel.

TS: I don't understand. Where did it—

DT: They discovered a prehistoric sea located beneath the Philippine Sea Plate . . . an ecosystem that's been around for hundreds of millions of years. Kaylie and I were hired as submersible
pilots by a Dubai prince to help capture these creatures for his
new marine exhibit. We'd enter the Panthalassa Sea through a
borehole and bait whatever life forms chased our submersible up
into the nets.

TS: That's . . . incredible. And obviously incredibly dangerous. How,
uh . . . did—

DT: Kaylie and I were trapped at the bottom of the Panthalassa
inside a titanium sphere. The sphere was anchored to the ocean
floor; it had been used as an observation post and docking station by Michael Maren, the scientist who discovered the hidden
sea. My father rescued us; he freed the anchor and guided us
back to the surface using Angel as an escort.

TS: Angel? Yes she'd certainly make an intimidating escort. But I
thought I read somewhere that she had died.

DT: She was netted as she surfaced. The *Liopleurodon* eviscerated
her while she hung suspended along the side of a tanker. Kaylie
and I were in the water; there was blood everywhere. We were
holding on to my father's submersible; Kaylie on one side, I
was on the other . . . as close to each other as you and I are
now—that's when that thing came up from below and took her
from me.

TS: That's . . . a lot to live with.

DT: You think?

TS: When did you cut your wrists?

DT: I dunno. Maybe a week after I got back to California.

TS: After all the two of you had been through, do you think Kaylie would have wanted you to end your life like that?

(1:45 sec elapsed time)

TS: David?

DT: It hurts. I can't . . . think. I hate being in my own skin. I want to scream . . . I want to punch my way out of this nightmare. She was so beautiful. I see her in my dreams, and then . . .

TS: Your mother says you're drinking.

DT: Weed makes me paranoid.

TS: What about the new meds I prescribed?

DT: They leave me with brain fog. Plus they dry out my nose and eyes.

TS: Give them another week. Adjusting one's brain chemistry takes time. And the night terrors . . . do you still wake up screaming?

DT: Yes.

TS: Every night?

DT: Unless I'm drunk.

TS: And how often are you drunk?

DT: Lately? Every night.

TS: A bit excessive, don't you think?

DT: Adjusting one's brain chemistry takes time.

TS: David, therapy means very little unless you're a willing participant.

(1:22 sec elapsed time)

TS: Your mother mentioned to me that you and Monty moved into an apartment together. He's the bi-polar fellow.

DT: Is that a problem?

TS: You tell me.

DT: He babbles and I scream. We make a nice couple.

TS: And the two of you get drunk together.

(00:45 sec elapsed time)

TS: I understand your father's been in touch with Kaylie's parents. He said they wanted to meet you. It could be a good thing. Sharing grief can sometimes ease one's sorrow.

DT: Sorrow's a funny thing. There's the sorrow one feels when a loved one dies, say, of cancer; that's a pretty bad sorrow. You feel empty inside. You share that grief with others. Eventually you move on. Then there's a different kind of sorrow . . . like, say, I shoved a gun in your wife's mouth and blew her head into a million fucking pieces. That sorrow's a little trickier to deal with. Basically, you have three options. The first is to take the easy way out. That's where my head was when I got back.

TS: What changed?

DT: I lived. When I came to in the hospital I realized my actions were selfish, that I was pulling my family into the same hell hole I'm wallowing in. Not cool.

TS: You mentioned three options to deal with a traumatic death. Suicide was the first—

DT: The second is to go numb while you talk about shit with professional sorrow sharers like yourself, as if anything said in this room's going to change a thing.

TS: I see. And the third option?

(00:25 sec elapsed time)

TS: David, where are you going?

DT: This'll be our last session. Me and Monty, we're going away for a while. Call it a business trip.

TS: Do you think that's a good idea? You've only been out of the hospital three weeks.

DT: Yeah, well, it beats the other two options. See you in my dreams.

(End Session 3)

Jonas Taylor handed the transcript of his son's last therapy session to his wife, Terry. "He's not going after Bela and Lizzy. He's going after the *Liopleurodon.*"

PART ONE

THE
SISTERS

1

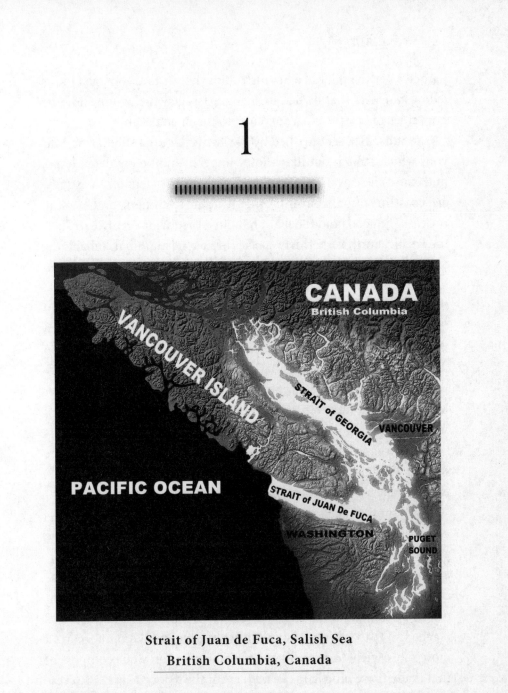

Strait of Juan de Fuca, Salish Sea
British Columbia, Canada

The Salish Sea (pronounced SAY-lish) is an intricate network of waterways located between the northwestern tip of the United States and the southwestern tip of the Canadian province of British Columbia. The entrance into the Salish Sea from the Pacific is the Strait of Juan de Fuca, a hundred-mile-long deepwater channel named after the pilot of a Spanish ship who, in 1592, bragged to his fellow mariners that he had located a passage which connected the port cities of Seattle and Vancouver to the open ocean.

The Salish Sea is nourished by the Pacific Ocean's submarine canyons which stretch out like knotty fingers, channeling dense, cold, nutrient-rich seawater toward land. The deep waters off the southern coastline of Vancouver Island are home to chinook and salmon, rockfish, lingcod, and the giant halibut—the major carnivore fish of the Pacific Northwest. Thirty species of marine mammals inhabit the Salish Sea and its barrier islands, including sea otters, sea lions, and harbor and elephant seals—a favorite delicacy of the great white shark. Humpback whales forage the strait for plankton funneled in through the tides. Gray whales follow an annual migration pattern that routes them south from the Bering Sea past Vancouver Island on their way to the Baja Peninsula.

Situated atop the Salish Sea's food chain are the region's killer whales. Several hundred transients pass through these waters each summer, gorging on salmon. Resident orca pods patrol the straits like lions roaming the Serengeti, their black dorsal fins rolling the surface with each *chuff* of breath, the mammals shadowed by tourists in whale-watching boats and thrill-seekers in kayaks.

Now, another apex predator has made this waterway its home— two female siblings born into captivity to a parent whose sheer size and brutality had forged the sisters' bond of survival.

Carcharodon megalodon: the most ferocious species ever to inhabit the planet. For most of the last thirty million years these giant prehistoric great white sharks had ruled the oceans. Adult females reached sixty to seventy feet and fifty tons, their male counterparts a more subservient forty to fifty feet. But size was only one component that made these monsters the menace of the Miocene era. The creatures possessed an upper jaw that unhinged when hyperextended, yielding a bite radius that could engulf a small elephant while delivering a force of forty thousand pounds. Its triangular teeth were lethal; serrated along the edges and as large as a man's hand. The lower teeth were more pointed and used for gripping their prey while the wider uppers were used to saw through flesh and bone. As hard as diamond, the ivory cutlery was backed by replacement teeth set in rows beneath the gum line.

Megalodon was far quicker than the cetaceans it hunted; its powerful caudal fin able to accelerate its torpedo-shaped body at bursts of thirty knots. The sharks' enormous girth also functioned as an internal heat factory, its moving muscles channeling gobs of hot blood into its extremities through a process known as gigantothermy, enabling it to adapt to even the coldest Arctic temperatures.

As if size, speed, and the deadliest bite ever to evolve weren't enough, Nature had endowed its ultimate killing machine with senses that gave it the ability to see, hear, feel, smell, and taste its prey for miles in every direction.

And yet for all its advantages, the creature had vanished from the paleo record approximately 1.8 million to 100,000 years ago—roughly about the time primitive man had learned how to use fire. Perhaps God or nature or evolution had not wanted these two dominant species to mix. Perhaps that is why those Megalodon that managed to survive the last ice age did so in the oceans' deepest abyss.

Seventy percent of our planet is covered by water. Modern man has only explored five percent of the oceans and less than one percent of its extreme depths. We know more about distant galaxies than the abyssopelagic and hadalpelagic zones—habitats whose depths exceed 13,000 feet.

The deepest location on our planet is the Mariana Trench. Located in the Western Pacific near Guam, the gorge plunges 36,201 feet—nearly seven miles. The 1,550-mile-long, forty-mile-wide canyon was forged by the seismic activity generated by the Philippine Sea Plate subducting beneath its behemoth neighbors. And yet as unlikely as it seems, this isolated abyss became home to a prehistoric food chain—thanks to the very process which had created its extreme depths.

As cold water seeped into cracks along the Philippine plate's fracturing ocean floor, it was heated by molten rock in the Earth's mantle. Exposed to oxygen, magnesium, potassium, and other minerals, this superheated elixir was forcibly ejected back into the trench by way of hydrothermal vents. Once this hot mineral soup met the cold depths of the Western Pacific it generated hydrogen sulfide, which in turn fueled bacteria—the foundation of an abyssal chemosynthetic food chain. Tube worms fed off the bacteria, small fish off the tube worms, and bigger fish off the smaller fish. But it was the formation of a hydrothermal plume—a ceiling of soot coagulating a mile above the vent fields—that formed a warm water oasis, which attracted history's most dominant predator.

During the Pleistocene epoch, cooling seas decimated many whale species—the staple of the Megalodon diet. As its food supply diminished, hungry adults turned to cannibalism. This allowed pods of orca access into shallow Megalodon nurseries and the rein of history's apex predator was over.

It was the Megalodon nurseries located along the coastline of the Mariana island chain that preserved the species. Hunted by orca, the juvenile sharks went deep, discovering a warm water abyss that was stocked with food—albeit nothing as high in bio mass and fat content as whales.

Survival depends upon adaptation. Megalodon survived in the Mariana Trench by consuming squid instead of whales. The drop in fat content and protein lowered the sharks' metabolisms, affecting their ability to hunt. Further adaption came with the loss of their dorsal pigment, their albino hides better suited for attracting both prey and mates. Spawning was limited by the availability of food; when food was scarce they turned on their own.

For several hundred thousand years the species remained trapped in its warm water purgatory . . . until modern man showed up and everything changed.

Jonas Taylor wasn't looking for giant prehistoric sharks when he entered the trench's *Challenger Deep*; the navy's best deep-sea submersible pilot was escorting two scientists on a top-secret dive to vacuum manganese nodules off the trench floor.

It was on their third descent in eight days that disaster struck.

An excerpt from the recently released Defense Department files—courtesy of Eric Snowden—includes Jonas Taylor's testimony, where he describes *Homo Sapien's* first documented encounter with *Carcharodon megalodon*: "*The Sea Cliff was hovering about ten meters above the hydrothermal plume. Dr. Prestis was working the drone's vacuum and the soothing vibrations of the motor were putting me to sleep. I must've drifted off because the next thing I knew the sonar was beeping—an immense object rising directly beneath us. Suddenly a ghost-white shark with a head bigger than our three-man sub emerged from the mineral ceiling, its gullet filling my keel portal.*"

Taylor's first instinct was to jettison the sub's weight plates into the creature's mouth while executing an emergency ascent—a maneuver not recommended below 10,000 feet. The sub's pressurization system faltered, turning head wounds into fatal hemorrhages.

The two scientists died and Taylor was blamed. The physician-on-duty ordered a ninety day evaluation in a mental ward, after which the commander received a dishonorable discharge—a parting gift from his commanding officer, who intended to deflect his own culpability for ordering the exhausted pilot to make the dive.

His career over, Jonas set out to prove the albino monster he had encountered was not an aberration of the deep. Five years later he graduated from the Scripps Institute with a doctorate degree in paleobiology. A year later he published a book which theorized how ancient sea creatures living in isolated extremes could evolve in order to survive extinction.

Colleagues panned his work.

While Jonas struggled in the world of academia, world renowned cetacean biologist Masao Tanaka was completing construction of a new aquatic facility on the coast of Monterey, California. The Tanaka Oceanographic Institute was essentially a man-made lagoon with an ocean-access which intersected one of the largest annual whale migrations on the planet. Designed as a field laboratory, the waterway was intended to be a place where pregnant gray whales returning from their feeding grounds in the Bering Sea could birth their calves. Masao was so convinced his facility would bridge the gap between science and entertainment that he mortgaged his entire family fortune on the endeavor.

Rising construction costs forced Masao to accept a contract with the Japanese Marine Science Technology Center. The mission: to anchor sensory drones along the sea floor of the Mariana Trench, creating an early-warning earthquake detection system. To complete the array, D.J. Tanaka, Masao's son, had to escort each drone to the bottom using an *Abyss Glider*, a torpedo-shaped one-man submersible.

When several of the drones stopped transmitting data, Masao needed a second diver to help D.J. retrieve one of the damaged aquabots in order to diagnose the problem.

He sent his daughter, Terry, to recruit Jonas Taylor.

Jonas accepted the offer, desiring only to recover an unfossilized white Megalodon tooth photographed in the wreckage—the evidence he needed to prove the sharks still existed.

The dive ended badly; Jonas and D.J. coming face to face with not one, but two Megs. The first was a forty-five foot male, which became entangled in the surface ship's cable; the second was its sixty foot pregnant mate, which was lured out of the trench into surface waters teeming with food.

The Tanaka Institute took on the task of capturing the female. Jonas and Masao were determined to quarantine the monster inside the whale lagoon, with JAMSTEC agreeing to refit the canal entrance with King Kong-sized steel doors.

The hunt lasted a month, culminating in an act that would haunt Jonas's dreams over the next thirty years. All was not lost—the Megalodon's surviving pup was captured and raised in Masao's cetacean facility—and a monster shark cottage industry was born.

Angel: The Angel of Death.
Two shows daily. Always your money's worth!

Angel grew into a seventy-foot albino nightmare that drew crowds from across the world, earning the Tanaka-Taylor family hundreds of millions of dollars. She also managed to escape twice, birth two litters of pups, and devour no less than a dozen humans—five of them in her own lagoon.

And yet people still lined up by the tens of thousands to see her and they wept when it was announced she had died.

The public had an entirely different reaction when they learned "the sisters" had escaped.

Angel had given birth to five female offspring four years earlier, but two of the sharks were nearly twice the size of their three smaller siblings and far more vicious.

Elizabeth, or Lizzy for short, was pure albino like her mother. The voting public (swayed by various European blogs) had named the shark after Elizabeth Bathory, purportedly the worst serial killer in Slovak history. In 1610, the infamous "Countess of Blood" had been charged with the torture and deaths of hundreds, mostly young girls. Her cold savagery seemed to match the personality of the stark-white juvenile, who often took a calculated second position to her more ferocious twin, Bela.

Known to the staff as "the Dark Overlord," Bela was the only Megalodon offspring born with pigmentation. Though her head was pure white, the rest of her dorsal surface was a dark charcoal gray, giving her a rather bizarre, sinister appearance. Named after Belle Gunness, the infamous "Black Widow" who teased and killed fourteen of her suitors back in 1908, Bela was the brawn to Lizzy's brains—an aggressive predator that had to be separated from the pack during feeding time by trainers using bang sticks on reach poles to keep her from going after her smaller siblings—the blood in the water driving the forty-six-foot, twenty-one-ton killer into a frenzy.

As terrifying as the sisters were, they always feared their parent. For filtration purposes, the Meg Pen and the lagoon were connected by a five-foot-wide channel. Angel couldn't enter, but "mom" could smell her brood. Every once in a while Angel would slap her tail against her side of the grating, antagonizing her maturing pups.

The intimidation tactics forged a bond between Bela and Lizzy. The two juvenile Megalodons would circle their habitat in tandem—Lizzy in the dominant top position, the darker Bela below, the pigmented shark's albino head just behind her sibling's pelvic girdle so that the trough created by her sister's moving mass towed her effortlessly around the tank.

And then one day, their domineering parent was gone, drugged and transported inside a refurbished hopper-dredge on her journey back to the Western Pacific. The move was precipitated by pressure exerted by a rogue animal rights group and the fact that Bela and Lizzy were getting too big for the Meg Pen. Bela had already attacked the acrylic walls in the underwater viewing area and the sisters had to be moved into Angel's lagoon before the damaged glass shattered.

But the animal rights group wasn't satisfied and bribed one of Jonas's staff to release the sisters into open waters—and now every boater, diver, and fisherman from Baja California to Alaska was experiencing more than a bit of anxiety.

––––––––

Situated off the southeastern tip of Vancouver Island is the San Juan archipelago, a cluster of over four hundred islands, islets, and rocks, only a fourth of which were deemed large enough to actually name. The Salish Sea is littered with these oddly shaped landmasses, their forest-covered hills of evergreen and pine dwarfed by the snow-peaked Olympic Mountains which dominate the waterway's horizon.

There are no bridges linking the archipelago to Vancouver Island or the Canadian mainland; access being limited to boat or air. The island chain is surrounded by heavily used shipping channels, with swift currents and dangerous riptides fueled by the Strait of Juan de Fuca to the south and the Strait of Georgia to the north. Haro Strait serves as the western channel connecting the Port of Vancouver with other destinations in the Salish Sea. Rosario Strait lies to the east and is used as the major shipping channel for oil tankers originating out of the Cherry Point Refinery to the north.

San Juan Island is the second-largest and most populated land-

mass in the archipelago, its year-round residents numbering just below seven thousand. Its main hub is Friday Harbor, an Old World seaport with New World charm, located on the east side of the island. Built on a hill that overlooks the marina's crystal green water, the community is a tourist Mecca for vacationers looking to experience the unspoiled beauty of nature.

Eric Germata was an adventurous outdoorsman with a sense of humor; at least that is what the food and beverage manager from Chicago had highlighted in his Match-Date.com profile. He and Ashley Kuehnel had been Skype-dating for three months when the blond twenty-eight-year-old had suggested they plan a whale-watching vacation together. Rendezvousing in Seattle, they had taken a charter flight together to San Juan Island, arriving at the Friday Harbor Bed and Breakfast in the late afternoon—Ashley having reserved two rooms, just in case things didn't work out. Their first official date was a walking tour of the harbor's quaint shops, followed by dinner, drinks, dancing, and a carriage ride back to their B&B where they spent the night together in Eric's room.

Ashley had chosen the San Juan Islands because she wanted to kayak in open water with orcas. Eric was an outdoorsman; what he wasn't was a good swimmer. The thought of being in deep water surrounded by thirty-foot killer whales in a boat barely wider than his waist gave him serious trepidation, but if he wanted his second night on the island to end like the first, Eric knew that his girl-friend's wishes had to be honored.

They had checked out of the B&B after breakfast and had taken a bus across the island to Mitchell Bay, their destination—the Snug Harbor Resort and Marina. Eric secured the keys to their seaside cabin while Ashley went down to the docks to reserve two spots with Crystal Seas Tours for a six-hour kayaking adventure.

Their group was made up of two other couples. Natalie Baker and her friend, Vicky, were a lesbian couple from Britain. The Cunning-hams were a married couple from Houston. Nikki Cunningham was part Korean, part Italian, and with her brown hair, gray contact lenses, and freckles, looked neither Asian nor European.

Eric couldn't recall the husband's first name.

Their instructor was a Nashville native named Nic Byron. A fit, heavily tattooed man in his early thirties, Nic had vacationed in the San Juan Islands six years earlier and never left. He spent the first twenty minutes instructing the three couples on how to climb back inside their two-person kayaks in the event they tipped.

Their route would take them out of Mitchell Bay where they'd fol-low the western coastline of the island to the south, making land at Lime Kiln State Park at a place called Dead Man's Cove. After explor-ing the trails they'd enjoy a cookout before the return trip at sunset.

Because the water was cold, they'd be using sit-inside cockpits. There were two types to choose from. Recreational models—being shorter and wider with larger cockpits—were recommended for be-ginners. Touring kayaks were thinner, longer and not as stable but were faster in the water.

While the other two couples went for stability, Ashley lobbied Eric to go with the sleeker touring model used by their instructor.

It was nearly three o'clock by the time the trio of two-man kayaks followed their leader out of the docking births. Nic Byron gave his group free rein within the confines of Mitchell Bay, to get a feel for their boats. Situated in the stern cockpit, Eric quickly mastered the rudder pedals, his mind wandering as he stared at Ashley's muscular back and the pair of blue angel tattoos adorning her shoulder blades.

Once out of the harbor the tranquil surface became two-foot swells that had Eric silently cursing his male ego. On their left were miles of unspoiled coastline. Patches of rock yielded to arching Madrona trees that reached out like gnarly copper-brown fingers, their berry-filled branches providing relief from the sun for fish living in the crystal-green shallows. Birds flitted about by the thousands and Nic pointed out several bald eagles soaring above the pine trees, their stark white heads and chocolate-brown feathers easily recognizable.

On their right was a forty-mile stretch of sparkling blue water culminating in a spectacular horizon of snow-peaked mountain ranges looming in the distance like a mile-high tsunami.

Nic gathered his charges. "The waters around the San Juan Islands are nutrient rich, perfect for migrating fish. Our resident orcas come here every year to dine on their favorite delicacy: Chinook, the largest species of salmon. The killer whales consist of one clan subdivided into three pods—about eighty individuals in all. That includes Granny, whose age is estimated at one hundred and two. The first person who spots an orca fin gets a pass on cookout clean-up duty."

Nic led them into deeper water, keeping the group about three hundred yards off shore. Ashley pointed to a whale-watching boat moving south through Haro Strait while Eric fastened two more clips on his life vest, keeping his eyes focused on the water.

His pulse raced when Vicky yelled out, "I saw an orca fin!" She pointed fifty yards to the northwest where a series of black dorsal fins were rolling along the surface.

Signaling for the group to stop paddling, Nic scanned the surface using a pair of high-powered binoculars. "Good spot, Vicky, only those are Dall's porpoises. They're black and white and look just like miniature killer whales, only they're a lot smaller."

Ashley pointed to one of the whale-watching boats. "That boat just circled back; maybe they spotted something?"

Nic aimed his binoculars. "Congratulations, Ashley, you spotted members of K-pod. Guess you're excused from clean-up duty." He passed her the glasses. "Take a look. You can't miss the adult bull's big dorsal."

"Can we get closer?"

The Cunninghams chimed in. "Yes, let's get closer."

"We'll halve the distance, as long as there are no standing waves and the current cooperates. Stay together and be prepared to link up in case the whales want to get a closer look at us. Remember, adult males can weigh as much as six tons."

Eric felt the blood drain from his face. "Uh, exactly how safe is it to be kayaking so close to an adult male orca?"

"In six years, I've never witnessed a single act of aggression against a kayaker or boater by a killer whale. That's not to say they couldn't cause a kayak to tip—which is why we link up. Like their dolphin cousins, orca can be playful. Usually they'll just pass under the boats."

The group started paddling, their leader keeping the three double-occupancy kayaks on an intercept course for several dozen black specks moving south on the horizon. Ashley's back muscles flexed with her increased effort. Eric eased up, fearing his girlfriend wanted to beat the rest of the kayaks to the whales.

After a ten minute sprint, Nic abruptly raised his hand. "They've changed course. Everybody link up, you're about to have a once-in-a-lifetime experience!"

Eric's heart raced as he reached out to the Cunninghams' kayak. He managed to clip his bungee cord to their fast-line a moment before the British females' boat abruptly rammed his left flank from behind, nearly sending him head-first into Nikki Cunningham's ample cleavage.

Nic Byron clipped his single kayak to Ashley's bow and then all seven kayakers held their collective breath as the killer whales moved closer.

And then suddenly they were all around them, passing under the boats before breaching the surface behind them with powerful blasts of expelled salty air tinged with sea water.

Eric's fear turned to amazement as a mother and her calf swam straight towards him before diving directly below his kayak. They reappeared on the opposite side of the flotilla, the entire pod racing for shore.

And then something else passed beneath Eric's kayak—something infinitely larger.

Its head was bullet-shaped and pure white like the bald eagle's, and it was followed by a lead-gray torso as wide and as long as the commuter plane in which he and Ashley had arrived twenty-four hours earlier. A rigid expanse of pectoral fins spanned the entire width of the flotilla; the tail seemed to take forever to appear as the creature completed its leisurely trek beneath their boats before disappearing into the depths.

Eric's throat tightened, rendering his voice box mute. An orca moves through the water in arching north-south bursts as it surfaces to breathe. The creature that had just passed beneath his kayak swam in east-west undulations, powered by its half-moon shaped caudal fin.

Shark . . .

Megalodon.

Bela!

Unable to speak, barely able to move, Eric reached forward with his paddle to tap Ashley. She screamed as he connected with the blue angel on her right scapula, her expression aghast in terror as she pointed.

Ten feet in front of Nic's kayak, poised above the choppy surface like a white buoy, was the enormous triangular head of another Meg. The shark was spy-hopping, its blue-gray left eye clearly analyzing the flotilla and its human passengers.

The depths surrounding the forty-six-foot Megalodon glowed like a turquoise-blue island, identifying the albino monster as Bela's sibling, Lizzy.

Time seemed to stand still, life reduced to whitecaps and ten knot winds, the fading *chuffing* of the fleeing killer whales and the pounding pulses of the kayakers who shivered and waited while an inquisitive killer debated their fate.

Nic Byron broke the silence. "Slowly and quietly, detach your lines."

Eric's hand trembled as he struggled to unclip his bungee cord from the Cunningham's kayak.

As if sensing the disturbance, Lizzy's head slipped below the surface.

Now the real terror began.

"She'll come up beneath us!"

"Vicky's right; we need to go."

"No one's going anywhere."

"You're not in charge!"

"Keep your voices down; it can hear you."

"Listen to me," said Eric. "There are two of them; Bela, the dark one, passed under my kayak—she was after the whales. I think we need to get to that whale-watcher boat."

They turned in unison, locating the tourist craft a good mile to the west.

"We'll never make it," Nic said from behind his binoculars. "See those ripples? Those are standing waves, five feet high inside the trowel. They'll come right over our heads."

Ashley gripped the instructor by the Moby Dick tattoo covering his right biceps. "I don't want to be eaten."

"No one's being eaten," said Natalie. "These Megs were raised in captivity. Humans aren't on their menu."

"How do you know what's on their menu?" Eric demanded.

"I studied marine biology back in London. I think I know a little bit more about it than a food and beverage manager."

"Yeah? Well, Lana Wood was human and they ate her!"

Nic searched the mile-and-a-half of sea separating them from San Juan Island's coastline, then shoved the binoculars into a watertight compartment. "We'll head south, working our way back to shore. Nice and easy, no splashing. You see a big shark fin—break for land."

They set out, paddling quietly. Hearts raced, flesh tingled. The Cunninghams prayed aloud for God to watch over their three children. The British women whispered softly.

A shrill orca cry caused everyone to cease paddling.

Less than a mile to the northeast the surface erupted—Bela's upper torso rising out of the sea, a twelve-foot juvenile killer whale thrashing within her hyperextended jaws.

Eric gritted his teeth as the impaled orca and the Megalodon flopped sideways in an explosion of bloody froth, the sharp *clap* reaching them on a three second delay.

"Let's move!" Plunging his oar into the water, Nic set out on a brisk pace which forced the other kayakers to keep up. He counted a hundred strokes to the south, then cut the rudder hard and set out on a direct beeline for shore, targeting the Lime Kiln State Park lighthouse.

Now it was a race, every boater for themselves.

Ashley's shoulder muscles ached as she pulled great gouts of water, each stroke accompanied by a grunted word. "Aren't . . . you. . . . glad . . . you . . . listened . . . to . . . me . . . and . . . picked . . . the . . . faster . . . kayak!"

She was right, they were flying through the water, pulling nearly eight knots as they passed Nic Byron. Within two minutes they were thirty yards ahead of the others and had halved the distance to shore. The late afternoon sun reflected brightly off the lighthouse's lens; waves lapped along the shoreline of Dead Man's Cove—bloody waves.

The couple was less than fifty yards from the rock strewn beach when Eric saw the first dead orca . . . then the second.

And then he was airborne.

The twenty-four-ton albino had launched its upper body out of the water just ahead of the kayak, the underside of its lower jaws striking the deck of the bow so hard it flipped the plastic craft's stern into the air like a catapult, tossing Eric Germata out of his cockpit and over the outstretched jaws of the Meg into the shallows.

The fifty-six-degree water might as well have been electrified. Seconds after sinking, Eric was scrambling awkwardly to his feet, stumbling onto land past the eviscerated remains of a beached juvenile bull orca that was bleeding out in Dead Man's Cove.

Eric dropped to his knees in shock, the island spinning in his vision.

Then he remembered the girl. "Ashley?"

He stood, searching the cove. The shallows were littered with the bobbing, bleeding, butchered members of the orca pod, many still alive and squealing. Twenty yards from shore Lizzy's bloodstained dorsal fin cut slowly across the surface, her thrashing caudal fin frothing the sea pink.

Eric's eye caught movement. The others had come ashore a quarter mile to the south. He took a quick head count—Ashley was not among them.

Then he saw their touring kayak.

The craft had washed ashore, intact but upside down. Eric struggled to roll it over. He took one look inside the bow cockpit, turned his head and retched.

Ashley was still inside the watertight compartment, at least her lower torso was. Her body had been severed at the waist; her upper torso having been bitten in half as she was flung head-first into the breaching Megalodon's open mouth.

2

||||||||||||||||||||||||||||||||

Dubai Land Central International Airport
Dubai, United Arab Emirates

Located in southern Dubai, the Jebel Ali International Aerotropolis is an $82 billion complex comprised of five-star hotels and shopping malls, sixteen cargo terminals, over 100,000 parking spaces, and a high speed express rail designed to whisk upwards of 120 million passengers a year to their destinations within the UAE.

It was just after seven p.m. local time when the JetBlue commercial jet inbound from San Francisco International airport touched down in Dubai to a rousing applause from its passengers.

None were as grateful as David Taylor.

The twenty-one-year-old's nerves were shot, having spent nearly sixteen hours seated next to his friend Jason Montgomery. Monty was a former Marine Recon medic who had his brain scrambled from a roadside explosion while he was deployed in Iraq. It wasn't enough that the big chested, broad shouldered, heavily tattooed man with the shaved head and six inch "devils" goatee looked like he belonged in a biker gang, but the long trip in a confined space had exacerbated

Monty's bi-polarism, causing him to rant gusts of random observations almost nonstop.

"Hey Meg-Boy, did you know the word 'tax' comes from the Latin *taxo*, meaning 'I estimate'? Did you know ninety percent of people who hire housekeepers and babysitters cheat on their taxes. The Bible has about seven hundred thousand words. The Federal Tax Code has three million seven hundred thousand words. Are you eating your peanuts? Humans can survive longer without food than they can without sleep. Sorry, was I keeping you awake?"

It had taken three sleeping pills and a miniature bottle of scotch for the man with the words, "PAIN DON'T HURT" inked around his neck to finally pass out—at which point his snoring kicked in.

A grizzly bear made less noise taking down an elk.

David was exhausted but afraid to sleep, fearing a night terror and its accompanying "blood-curdling" scream. As bad as Monty was, the fit and tan athlete with the long brown hair and matching almond eyes could be more frightening to his fellow passengers than the ex-Marine, so he stayed awake, forcing himself to watch movies on his iPad lest his mind drift to memories of Kaylie.

The last time David had been in Dubai, he had been hired to care for two of Angel's "runts" while helping to tutor several dozen candidates competing for eight high-paying pilot openings on what turned out to be a sea monster hunt sponsored by the Crown Prince. Using submersibles designed by the Tanaka Institute, the Elite Eight would descend in teams into the Panthalassa Sea—a prehistoric refuge located beneath the Philippine Sea Plate—where they would attempt to lure history's most dangerous predators up through a crater into the surface ship's nets. The captured species would then be drugged and placed into watertight cargo holds aboard one of two refitted oil super tankers and taken back to Dubai.

In their first and only dive together, David and Kaylie had crossed paths with a mature female *Liopleurodon*—a creature whose size defied fossilized records. The Lio had killed both Angel and David's lover. Before the monster could flee into the Western Pacific, the expedition leader, Fiesal bin Rashidi had tagged the beast with a radio transmitter.

Two months after his attempted suicide, David had reached out to the Crown Prince, wanting back in the game. The Dubai billionaire had authorized two round-trip airline tickets, but the coach seats clearly demonstrated the man's hesitance to involve himself again with Jonas Taylor's only son.

Grabbing their carry-on backpacks, David and Monty filed out of the jet and into the concourse, following signs to the monorails. Framed posters advertising Dubai Land were everywhere, featuring water parks and roller coaster rides, global villages, space and science worlds, petting zoos, and safaris. Another series of posters, labeled *Phase-II* depicted an artist's rendition of twelve different aquariums, each holding an extinct nightmare of nature.

There was one with a pair of *Kronosaurus,* a crocodilian beast. *Thalassomedon,* a plesiosaur with a twenty-foot-long neck. *Shonisaurus sikanniensis,* a species of ichthyosaurus that measured seventy-five feet from its dolphin-like nose to the tip of its tail. *Dunkleosteus,* a heavily armored prehistoric fish possessing two long bony blades for teeth and *Mosasaurus,* a fifty-foot brute that dominated the Cretaceous seas.

Across the poster of *Liopleurodon ferox* was written, "the most fearsome creature ever to inhabit the planet."

David paused to gaze at the image of an albino Megalodon—one of two "runts" the institute had sold to the Crown Prince. Neither shark had traveled well; only one had survived.

"David!"

He turned to see Ibrahim Al Hashemi, the executive director of the aquarium, waving by the monorail concourse.

"Mr. Hashemi, good to see you. You remember Monty?"

The man dressed impeccably in the three-piece tailored business suit regarded the American wearing the untucked Dodgers baseball jersey, jean shorts, gray wool socks and hiking boots. "Mr. Montgomery, I see you've expanded your wardrobe."

"Yeah, I put on a few pounds. Did you know only half of a dolphin's brain goes to sleep, while the other half stays awake?"

David rolled his eyes. "Where's the Crown Prince?"

"He will see you at the aquarium. If you two would follow me." The director escorted them past several long lines of travelers to sliding glass doors labeled *Dubai Land-Phase-II: Coming Soon!* Inserting a key, he turned the lock, causing the double doors to slide open.

Ibrahim Al Hashemi led them out onto a covered platform, the glass doors sealing behind him.

They boarded an empty monorail train. The car pulled away from the gate, running silently as it accelerated beyond one hundred and sixty miles an hour above the magnetized track, streaking toward Dubai Land.

David glanced out the tinted windows at a flat desert before turning to face their host. "Mr. Hashemi, how has the Meg pup adapted to its new tank?"

"She is doing quite well, as you will see."

"She's probably relieved at not having to share a tank with the sisters. Lizzy and Bela killed one of the runts last summer."

"So we heard. We were more shocked to learn the two sisters had escaped. What will your family do now, with the institute having gone from six Megalodons down to none?"

"I don't know. Maybe we can purchase one of your Meg pups when your shark gives birth?"

The Dubai man offered a confused smile. "And with what male Megalodon shall we inseminate her?"

"My father never told you? The three runts—Angelica, Mary Kate, and Ashley—weren't conceived by a male Meg. Angel's eggs were internally fertilized by Angel."

Ibrahim Al Hashemi's dark eyes widened. "Parthenogenesis? The process has been well documented in hammerhead sharks, but we were never told the two Meg pups were conceived asexually."

"At the time we didn't know. My father hired a specialist to find out why Bela and Lizzy were so much larger than the three runts. Turns out those two were conceived with the male Megalodon,

Scarface, while the runts were perfect genetic clones of Angel. Even though the sisters are bigger, your Meg will catch up fast. In a few years she'll pop out a few more females and the institute will be back in business."

"Incredible. And what of Bela and Lizzy? Will they asexually reproduce in the wild?"

David shuddered involuntarily. "God, let's hope not."

———

The desert horizon gave way to the Arabian Gulf and a coastline of glittering skyscrapers. Turning away from the city, the monorail paralleled a six-lane highway which led into Dubai Land's grand entrance. Landscaped with palm trees, colorful gardens, and "Jurassic" lakes, complete with life-size models of sea-dwelling dinosaurs, the Phase-I facility was open for business.

Phase-II was still under construction.

Laid out like a clock, with twelve unique hotels situated in the hour positions along the periphery of the park, the design fed the park's visitors into the center attraction—the aquarium complex. A glass and steel structure, the facility featured a dozen 200-foot-high gold-plated "shark fins," which corresponded with moving sidewalks that linked each hotel to the stadium-size arena.

A 360-degree FanVision ringed the two-hundred-acre complex, welcoming visitors in six different languages.

Monty mumbled, "Welcome to Hell's Aquarium. Unruly guests will be eaten."

The monorail dropped precariously and suddenly they were underground, the car braking at a subterranean entrance. David and Monty followed Ibrahim Al Hashemi into the aquarium's northern entrance past empty ticket booths and a seven-story-high lobby.

Four wide corridors divided the twelve eighty-million-gallon tank destinations into quadrants. The facility director headed for the alcove that accessed Tanks One, Two, and Three.

T-3's gallery was dark, marked only by floor lights. Rounding a bend, they came face to face with a forty-foot-high wall of acrylic glass.

At first it appeared as if the tank was empty . . . then the shark approached.

"Recognize this fellow? I believe you were credited with the catch."

David shook his head.

The *Helicoprion* was seven feet long, its lower jaw composed of a tooth-whorl—a spirally arranged cluster of teeth resembling a buzz-saw. Born to the late Carboniferous period 310 million years ago, the species had survived in the open oceans for over sixty million years.

David turned away. "We found it in the belly of a ninety-foot Leeds' fish. It killed the biologist that was performing a necropsy on the dead giant."

"Big tank for such a puny shark," Monty commented.

"The exhibit will feature other prehistoric creatures," Al Hashemi assured them. "Come, let us visit your runt, who we have renamed Zahra."

They returned to the alcove and entered the arena of Tank Two.

David's eyes widened when he saw the Megalodon pup, formerly known as Ashley.

In just over six months the Meg had nearly doubled in size and had put on a solid ten tons. She was every bit as frightening as Bela and Lizzy—a mature juvenile version of her deceased seventy-four-foot albino parent.

"My God, she must be forty feet long." David approached the tank, his sudden movement causing Zahra to charge the glass. A second before impact, searing purple bolts of electricity ignited from nodes embedded in the acrylic, the voltage momentarily scrambling the shark's ampullae of Lorenzini, sending it veering away.

"Wow. She's hyperkinetic. When did she become so aggressive?"

"Zahra is very territorial. All her life she has lived under the threat of her larger siblings. Now she is queen of her realm. Queen Zahra, we call her."

Monty moved closer to watch the Megalodon circle the enormous habitat. "And if the queen should birth a litter of princesses? How will you get them out of her tank before she kills them?"

David glanced at the aquarium director, who had a perplexed look on his face. "This needs to be discussed with our new head trainer. Dr. McDonnell is waiting for us in the Devonian arena."

Occupying exhibit T-1, the Devonian annex featured six pillar-shaped million-gallon aquariums situated in the gallery leading to the main tank. Five were empty; the sixth was occupied by more than a dozen small sharks. The *Stethacanthus* were three to five feet long, with narrow bodies and a blunt head resembling that of a tiger shark. What distinguished the species from other modern-day sharks was an anvil-shaped crest which functioned like a dorsal fin.

Standing by the tank while speaking into a handheld digital recorder was a heavyset Mexican-American in his mid-forties; a former athlete who had traded the gym for the lab. He acknowledged the approaching trio with a wave.

"Beautiful, aren't they? We netted the mother last month. She died en route but we were able to salvage her eggs. These sharks are the first Panthalassa predators born in captivity." He offered his hand to Monty. "Matthew McDonnell; I'm the new marine biologist."

"Do you know forty-eight percent of smart-phone owners watch videos in the bathroom?"

The scientist looked to David. "Am I missing something?"

"No, but he is. David Taylor. What happened to Barbara Becker?"

"The Defense Department recruited her to head up a marine lab in Miami. Something about using shark stem cells to repair damaged spinal cords. Let's go inside the gallery, the Crown Prince is waiting for us by the main tank."

David's heart raced as he remembered the monster contained in T-1.

Dunkleosteus . . .

The four-ton predator swam in awkward lurches behind the aquarium's thick glass, its round eyes watching the Crown Prince, who was seated in the second row. The placoderm's thick, armor-covered hide appeared dark brown, its belly reflecting a silvery hue. The creature's head was rounded and blunt, its midsection barrel-chested and as wide around as a school bus. The tail was thick and upper-lobe dominant, capable of only sluggish movements. The Dunk more

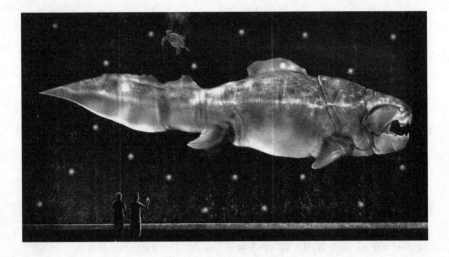

than made up for that with powerful jaws, which contained two long, bony blades instead of teeth. Cusped and deeply serrated from the shearing action generated by the double upper fangs constantly sliding past the lower incisors, the blades were backed by jowls possessing a bite force in excess of eight thousand pounds.

The Crown Prince turned and signaled his guests and staff to join him.

"I love this creature; I could sit and watch it for hours. I especially enjoy watching it feed. It's a rather slow swimmer, but its mouth opens in a fiftieth of a second, creating a powerful suction that literally pulls its prey into its gullet. The Dunk remains my favorite exhibit . . . at least until we capture the *Liopleurodon*."

He turned to David. "*Liopleurodon* fossils have been found throughout Europe, and yet these creatures were but half the size of the monster who stalked you in the Panthalassa Sea. Dr. McDonnell, tell him why our Lio is so much larger—so big in fact that I am forced to build an even larger arena to contain it."

"Bergmann's Rule," the marine biologist replied. "A century and a half ago, a German biologist by the name of Carl Bergmann observed that animals tend to be larger at higher latitudes than they are at the equator, correlating colder ocean temperatures with increased body size. The lower the ratio of body mass to surface area, the less heat loss an animal will experience."

The Crown Prince turned to David. "What was the water temperature in the area of the Panthalassa Sea where you first encountered the *Liopleurodon*?"

"Freezing. The Panthalassa was segregated into hot vent areas and cold seeps. The creature preferred a chilly habitat. You're saying the Panthalassa Lios grew much larger than their reptilian ancestors in order to stay warm?"

"Precisely," Dr. McDonnell said.

The Crown Prince stood, his movement eliciting a response from the Dunk. "David, no one knows that monster better than you. I would love to hire you and your friend to join my cousin in hunting down the Lio . . . only I can't."

David felt a knot in his stomach. "Why not?"

"Because you seek to kill this magnificent creature, just to avenge the death of this Szeifert girl . . . a girl you barely knew."

"I give you my word, I won't kill it."

"I don't believe you."

"Test me. Let me prove it to you!"

The Crown Prince stared at the San Francisco Giants sweatbands covering David's wrists. "There are two converted supertankers engaged in hunting down several predatory species that fled the Panthalassa Sea. The *Mogamigawa* is in the Western Pacific heading north toward Japan; her sister ship, the *Tonga*, is after the Lio, which is heading south. Prove to me your motives are pure aboard the *Mogamigawa*. Pilot one of the Manta subs and help the crew capture these creatures and I'll allow you to join my cousin aboard the *Tonga*."

David exhaled. "What about Monty? My friend needs a job."

"He can join the crew as a deckhand."

Monty shrugged. "Beats living in my cousin's garage."

"Dr. Al Hashemi will take you to your hotel. Spend a few days resting poolside. We'll fly you out on the next cargo plane bound for the *Mogamigawa*."

The aquarium director led David and Monty out, leaving the Crown Prince and the marine biologist alone to talk in private.

"Is he really worth it, Your Highness?"

"The girl's death was witnessed by both ships' crews. After seeing the size and ferocity of the *Liopleurodon* the other pilots quit, along with a third of the deckhands aboard the *Tonga*'s trawler. In the last three months we've recruited a dozen more submersible pilots from around the world—Navy SEALs, Air Force pilots . . . none possess the reflexes or skills of David Taylor. He's fearless, ready to put himself in harm's way to kill that monster."

"There's a difference between fearless and suicidal. The kid's as angry as Ahab, and that makes him dangerous. How do you expect to turn David's demons into something more manageable?"

The Crown Prince smiled. "Leave that to me."

|||||||||||||||||||||||||||||||||||||

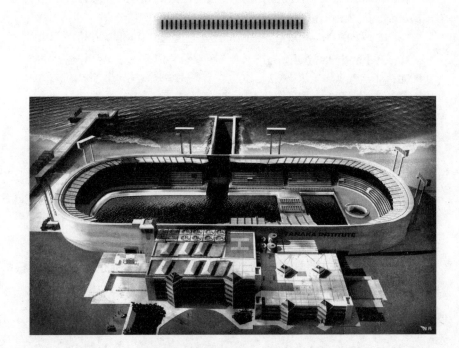

3

Tanaka Oceanographic Institute
Monterey, California

A steady wind howled through the concrete and steel bowl, ruffling canvas canopies and rippling the azure-green surface of the man-made lagoon. Sunlight warmed the aluminum bleachers. The Pacific was more aggressive, slapping at the mammoth steel doors sealing the ocean-access canal, causing the bells atop the warning buoys to toll.

The Tanaka Institute and Lagoon: once home to the most danger-ous creatures in the planet's history; now an empty fortress.

James "Mac" Mackreides exited the elevator on the third floor. He walked past rows of vacant desks to the executive suites. The office manager—a petite blue-eyed blonde in her early forties—was seated before a computer screen, her newborn son, Kyle, swaddled in a blanket in her lap.

Patricia Mackreides looked up at her husband. "The authorities on San Juan Island couldn't contain the story; it went viral about twenty minutes ago. Are you packed?"

"The gear's in the chopper."

"Mac, what are you doing?"

"My job."

"You're sixty-five years old. Do you really need to be chasing after sea monsters?"

"Hey, I'm a spry sixty-five. My loins just sprouted a kid."

"My loins did the sprouting; yours couldn't make it out of bed for his four a.m. feeding. And your pal Jonas is in worse shape, hobbling around on two bad knees. Terry said he was up all night again with his acid reflux."

"The sisters will do that to you. This is the life we've chosen."

"Don't give me that *GodfatherII* bullshit; you're not in the Mafia. Sell the institute and walk away from this nightmare while you still can."

"You don't think I want to? I spent two hours last night meeting with Tom Cubit. According to our lawyer, we're liable for any damages inflicted by Bela and Lizzy, even though they're no longer under our care."

"I don't understand. It was that radical animal rights group that broke in and released the sharks; the institute had no intention of letting them go."

"Technically, Virgil Carmen was still employed as the institute's assistant director of husbandry. As for the shark lovers at R.A.W., they don't have a pot to piss in. Cubit's right; the victim's family will come after us." Mac offered her his best Michael Corleone imitation, "Every time I think I'm out, they pull me back in."

"This isn't a joke. I didn't marry you to be widowed before our first anniversary. Don't you want to enjoy your son growing up? Look at what Jonas and Terry are going through with David. Is that Kyle's destiny . . . to be hunting these prehistoric monsters until one kills him?"

Mac remained silent, watching his sleeping child.

"Terry's had it, Mac. She's ready to leave Jonas. So I'm asking you again; what are you doing?"

————

The bay windows of Jonas Taylor's office looked out onto the man-made lagoon, the western bleachers, and the blue waters of the Pacific. Jonas adjusted the venetian blinds to filter out the reflecting rays of sunlight while he waited for the overseas call.

Like Jonas, Dr. Zachary Wallace was a marine biologist who had resolved the demons of his past by proving to the world that an ancient creature—in his case the Loch Ness monster—actually did exist. The two had met in San Francisco seven years ago while Zach was on a world tour promoting his autobiography, *The Loch*. They had become close friends and it was actually the Scottish intellect who had convinced Jonas to pen his own memoir—one of many projects he had never finished.

Three years later Angel had returned from her eighteen-year hiatus and the institute was back in business. With money to burn, the Taylors invested in a start-up alternative energy company founded by Wallace that his friend promised would one day manufacture clean energy machines designed to replace fossil fuels. Why a world-famous marine biologist like Zachary Wallace would walk away from his career to develop zero-point energy generators remained a mystery to Jonas, but he backed the brilliant inventor with $14 million in start-up costs without asking any questions—even after he refused to go public with his first line of prototypes, three of which were now being tested on the institute's second generation of Manta submersibles.

Jonas's iPhone chimed, chasing away his thoughts. "Zach, thanks for getting back to me."

"No problem. I jist read about the attack in British Columbia. Whit are ye going tae do? Nothing crazy, I hope?"

"I don't know yet. The authorities asked for my help in tracking down the sisters; I'm debating whether to recapture them or just kill 'em. What would you do?"

"Yer askin' the man who was once the single-most despised human being in all of Scotland whether tae kill two sharks and potentially save a lot of lives, or risk yer own life tae save a business that grossed close tae a billion dollars in the last four years? The irony would be laughable if the outcome wasn't so serious. So before I provide ye with an answer, assure me again that the new Manta subs the Crown Prince ordered are all equipped with air bags inside both cockpits."

"You ask me this every time we talk. Yes, Dr. Wallace, the subs have air bags. Any other recurring dreams I need to pacify?"

"I'll make a list. Which brings me tae David. Ye were right, yer son and his brain-bashed friend are in Dubai looking tae rejoin the monster quest. My source inside the aquarium tells me David leaves fer Japan in a few days, where he'll rendezvous with the supertanker *Mogamigawa*."

"The *Mogamigawa*? Then he's not after the Lio?"

"Word is he has tae prove himself first before the Crown Prince will allow him tae go after the big girl. I don't expect that tae last. Bin Rashidi's crew hasn't had a whiff of the *Liopleurodon* fer weeks and he's losing it."

"Good."

"Not good. It means David's going tae be on the *Tonga* sooner rather than later, so ye jist make sure those new air bags are workin' properly so I can sleep at night."

"When are you going to share this recurring dream with me?"

"When ye and yers stop chasing sea monsters. Which brings me tae the sisters. Many a night after my own near-death drama did I lay awake and question my actions, especially when the tourism industry shut down in Loch Ness and families were going hungry. My own father pointed the finger at me fer ruining his resort, and not his index finger if ye ken whit I mean. But we built our factory in Drumnadrochit and hired only Highlanders and now all is forgiven.

"So here's my advice, J.T.: Kill those bloody Megalodons. And when I say kill, I don't mean ye and Mac. Let the United States Coast Guard do the dirty work. Then go find yer son, sell the institute, and live out yer days happy, fat, and stupid."

"Thanks for the advice, Brother Wallace. But I'm already getting fatter and stupider by the day; I just need to work on the happy."

4

||||||||||||||||||||||||||||||||||

Dubai, United Arab Emirates

Ibrahim Al Hashemi was standing outside the entrance of the Dubai Land Hilton, waiting by the stretch limousine when David and Monty exited the five-star hotel. "Good morning gentlemen. You look refreshed. It appears a day in Dubai Land did you some good."

David handed his duffle bag to the driver. "Sun, pool, massages, and all the lobster and jumbo shrimp you can eat . . . yeah, I'd say it was just what the doctor ordered. Please be sure to tell the Prince thank you."

"You can thank him by helping him fill the nine vacant tanks at the aquarium. The driver will take you to a private airport where the Crown Prince's personal 747 jumbo jet is waiting. Flight time to Tokyo is ten hours."

David and Monty looked at each another. "We're flying out on the 747? I thought we were traveling with the cargo?"

"The nature of the cargo has changed. To promote the opening of the aquarium, the Crown Prince has agreed to an offer from the Discovery Channel for a new reality series that will document life on board the *Mogamigawa*. The two Manta subs have been equipped with night vision video cameras; you and your fellow pilots and crew members will be filmed while you attempt to capture these incredible prehistoric sea creatures."

The aquarium director opened his attaché case on the hood of the limo. "The contracts are fairly straightforward; you'll each receive three thousand U.S. dollars for every episode you appear on camera."

Monty snatched the pen and contract from Dr. Al Hashemi and flipped to the last page, scribbling his signature. "I was born to play this role. Did you know the new Rolls-Royce Phantom takes two months to build and comes in a choice of forty-four thousand colors?"

"Monty, don't you want to at least read the contract?"

"Why? Where else am I gonna earn forty-four thousand dollars for being myself?"

"It's three thousand an episode and . . . never mind." David glanced at the four-page document. "Can I read it on the plane?"

"Read it on the way to the airport, we begin filming on the plane. You'll be flying over with your co-stars—ten of the most stunning actresses and models in all of Arabia. These women are competing to become the three finalists that you, David Taylor, will select to join you aboard the *Tonga*. Be fair warned—our contestants will do their best to influence your vote. I do envy you, my young friend."

Monty punched David on the shoulder. "Women and a free Rolls-Royce . . . sign the contract, stupid!"

If it gets me aboard the Tonga . . .

Ignoring his father's voice in his head, David signed the last page of the contract, then handed it back to the aquarium director and climbed inside the back of the limousine.

———

Monty propped his hiking boots up on the opposite seat, stretching out. "Dude, what's with the sour face? Ten hot women, fighting to get inside your pants. Every guy watching the show will be wishing he was you . . . except for maybe the gay guys. Oh yeah, and when you're being chased in your sub by some giant fish trying to eat you . . . Know what? Forget about what I said, no one will want to be you."

"You don't get it, Monty. The Prince is manipulating me; he thinks he can cure my depression by dangling a bunch of beautiful women in front of me. It's not about sex. I hurt because I *loved* Kaylie. I wanted to marry her! My heart aches whenever I think about her. You just don't shut that down. You can understand that, can't you?"

Monty glanced at the thick sweatbands covering the freshly scarred wounds on the inside of his friend's wrists. "Yeah, man, I feel you. Kaylie was a thunderbolt, a girl so incredibly beautiful the closest you probably figured you'd get to being with her was inside your own head. And she really liked you. When you piloted her sub during the last day of competition . . . capturing a sea turtle on the hood of your Manta when your net malfunctioned—dude, you were her hero. Hearing you cry at night . . . I hurt for you. But David, you gotta move on, you gotta let her go. Look at me. When I left for Iraq I had a steady girl and a good job. Two tours of duty later my brains were scrambled, my boss lets me go, and the woman I loved was with another guy. You think there weren't nights when I didn't seriously think about swallowing the barrel of my gun?"

"What stopped you?"

"Two things. The first was God. I was raised to believe the man upstairs has His own game plan for each one of us and He isn't a big fan of suicide."

"And the second reason?"

"What second reason?"

"The second reason you didn't try to kill yourself."

"I didn't try to kill myself; an I.E.D. did this to me."

"Not the explosive . . . never mind." David watched as Monty grabbed a bottle of scotch from the limo's bar and crammed it into his duffle bag. "Really, dude?"

"Hey, it's not for me. That's for you, in case you want to sleep on the plane. The last thing we need is for you to go off into la-la land and wake up screaming from one of your night terrors."

"The new meds my shrink gave me seem to be working. Besides, I'm not tired."

"And what if you end up in the Prince's bedroom suite? Trust me, after you get lost between the sheets with three or four of those Arabian beauties you'll be nodding off like a newborn. Of course, if you can't handle it you can always call your old pal, Monty. The last woman I was with had to be inflated."

David smiled. "I have a better idea."

———

The driver stopped at two airport security checkpoints before following a private road onto the tarmac where the Crown Prince's 747-300 jumbo jet was in position to taxi onto the runway.

Standing on either side of a red carpet leading up the mobile staircase were ten women in their mid to late twenties. Each Arabian beauty wore a crème-colored Dubai Land blouse and a short gray skirt with matching stiletto pumps. Name tags written in English and Arabic identified the participants' first names.

David climbed out of the back of the limousine, only to be rushed by an American sporting a video camera and a familiar face. "David? James Gelet. We've never officially met, but I worked for your father aboard the hopper-dredge *McFarland*, when we transported Angel out to the Panthalassa Sea."

"Dude, I think you have me confused with the guy in the limo. I'm Monty, James Mackreides's nephew."

The documentary director looked confused. "But you look just like Jonas and Terry—"

David grabbed his arm, leaning in. "I'm Monty. Just go with it."

Monty climbed out of the back of the limo. "Hello, hello! David Taylor is in the house. Who's hosting this freak show?"

A petite woman in her early thirties with dark blond hair and a Texas accent hurried to Monty's side. "Amanda Silvernail, I'm the executive producer of the show. It's so nice to meet you."

"Of course it is. Introduce me to the ladies, Anita; I've got an important announcement to make." He whispered in her ear, motioning at David. "That's Monty. Don't waste a lot of air time on him, he's a little *meshugganah*."

They approached the reality show contestants. "Ladies, this is

David Taylor, the submersible pilot who will be selecting three of you as finalists over the coming weeks."

"You mean hours. I'll be rendering my decision the moment we land in Tokyo. Ten hour flight; ten ladies. Do the math, Wanita."

"It's *Amanda*, and this isn't what we agreed to."

"Hey sweet thing, that's the way David Taylor rolls. Every time I go down in my sub, there's no guarantee I'm coming back. Life's like that for us adrenaline junkies. Speaking of going down, I'll be conducting one-on-one interviews in the Crown Prince's private suite. Each of you lovely ladies will have an hour to persuade me to vote for you. So, who wants to be first? How about you?"

Monty approached the first woman on the right side of the red carpet, a Lebanese model. "And what's your name?"

"Hoda."

"Well, Hoda, I'd love to check under *your* hood-a." He winked, then turned to the dark-haired Egyptian actress on his left. "Zeina . . . how would you like to play my warrior princess?"

And on it went, Monty working his way from one Arab beauty to the next. There was Rana, a well-endowed Iranian actress and Jihan, a Dubai brunette with the legs of a swimsuit model. Nesrin was a Syrian university student with bedroom eyes; Ghada was born in Libya to a Syrian father and Lebanese mother. Saba was a Jordanian actress with a Botox lower lip. Ayisha was a model from the United Arab Emirates, sporting a knockout figure and western attitude. A sultry Moroccan with raven-black hair . . . a Qatar beauty with waist-length wavy brown hair.

Monty flirted and cracked inane jokes like a bad game show host, then led the procession of women up the stairs and onto the jumbo jet. The ten contestants dutifully followed him and a protesting Amanda Silvernail onto the upper level where they took seats outside the Prince's bedroom suite; a stewardess directed David down a circular staircase to the lower level.

Six rows of first-class seats were situated up front, followed by a cherrywood conference table, several private work stations, bathrooms, a dining area, and in back, a home theater, complete with padded lounge chairs and a fifty-two-inch screen.

Tears clouded David's vision. It was in this very cabin, six months earlier, that he had met the stunning blue-eyed woman who had captured his heart. She was a few years his senior, her brunette hair long and wavy and tinged with red highlights, her features resembling those of a young Stefanie Powers. She was wearing white shorts and a navy hooded sweatshirt, the name *K. Szeifert* embroidered in white beneath a Scripps Institute insignia. Her long tan legs bore the calf muscles of a sprinter. A pair of thongs dangled from her bare feet, which were propped up on the polished wood table top he was now staring at.

"It's pronounced 'See-furt.' Kaylie Szeifert."

"Hey . . . you okay?"

David turned to his right to find an apple-pie American girl in her early twenties in the window seat, her tan complexion unusual considering her strawberry-blond hair. It was shoulder length and pulled into a conservative ponytail, her blue eyes framed behind reading glasses. *Brown University Field Hockey* was printed across her gray T-shirt. Her knees poked through holes in her worn jeans, her bare feet were propped on the duffle bag beneath the seat ahead of her.

David casually wiped away the evidence of his tears. "Allergies. All this dry heat."

"Those looked like real tears to me."

"Shouldn't you be upstairs auditioning for the show?"

"Do I look like I just got plucked out of a harem, David?"

"No, David's upstairs. I'm Monty."

"And this Brown T-shirt came with my degree. You want to get your friend laid—go for it. But don't spray your can of bullshit my way and try to call it a fragrance. Ignorance can be worked with, stupid is forever and I have zero tolerance for either."

The *Fasten Your Seat Belt* sign lit up. "Good morning. This is Captain Michael Schallhorn in the flight deck. As you can see, I've just turned on the seat belt sign in preparation for takeoff. Kindly refrain from moving about the cabin until we've reached our cruising altitude. That would include any unscheduled activities apparently going in the Crown Prince's romp room."

The strawberry-blonde removed her backpack from the aisle seat and tossed it on the floor. "Sit."

Sit? What am I? A dog?

The 747 lurched forward, causing David to fall into the aisle seat. "Thanks. So, um . . . who are you and what are you doing here?"

She held out her hand. "Jacqueline Buchwald, my friends call me Jackie. My degree is in marine biology with certificates in shark awareness, SCUBA, underwater photography, and advanced open water diving. I was recruited for the hell's aquarium gig by Barbara Becker and promoted from associate to assistant director after she was transferred to a DOD facility in Miami. I've personally overseen the diets and care of every aquatic animal in the exhibit. Dr. Al Hashemi felt my expertise was needed in the field, where the mortality rates of captured specimens have been so high. You net 'em; I'll vet 'em."

"And how do you intend on vetting a hundred-ton monster nearly half the size of a football field?"

"The Lio is the *Tonga*'s mission, not ours. Focus on the task ahead and maybe we'll end up together on the big hunt. For now, we're after three pretty nasty prehistoric fish."

Jackie removed a manila folder from her backpack and handed David an artist's rendition of a sea creature with a dolphin-shaped mouth, a whalelike torso, narrow front and rear flippers, and a double-pronged tail. "*Shonisaurus*. A massive species of ichthyosaur or fish-lizard which dominated the late Triassic seas approximately two hundred and eight million years ago."

"I know. Kaylie and I barely escaped a pod of them."

"Those were *Shonisaurus populari*. . . . fifty-footers weighing about forty tons. The species we're after is a seventy-five-foot version classified as *Shonisaurus sikanniensis*. After the Lio followed Angel up through the borehole into our surface waters, three Shonis escaped from the Panthalassa Sea. Unfortunately, the two supertankers couldn't get their nets in place fast enough to capture these amazing creatures."

David hurriedly secured his seat belt as the 747-300 jumbo jet suddenly accelerated along the runway, its Pratt & Whitney engines providing 54,000 pounds of thrust until its massive wings gained lift, freeing the 300,000-ton aircraft from the Earth.

"It wasn't a borehole, Jacqueline. The gap was created by the USS *Indianapolis*. When she sunk back in 1945 her bow must have struck the sea floor like an anvil. Ten thousand tons of cruiser punched a hole straight down through the Philippine Sea Plate into the Panthalassa Sea—I know because I saw the wreckage. But the shaft was fairly narrow; how can you be so sure anything else besides the *Liopleurodon* escaped?"

She passed him the rest of the file. Inside were a series of satellite images taken at night, the ocean appearing dark green. A red circle highlighted three distinct florescent-olive images moving beneath the surface. In the next photo the circle was enlarged, revealing the three *Shonisaurus*—two larger adults sandwiching an offspring a third their size.

"These thermal images were taken two days after you were rescued. Like the Lio, the *Shonisaurus* are night stalkers, their eyes being nocturnal and sensitive to the light. Their cardiovascular systems aren't used to the higher oxygen content of our surface waters, rendering them a bit hyperkinetic. It's made it a bit of a challenge tracking them."

"What are they feeding on? Whales?"

"We're not sure. They only possess teeth in the front end of their jaw, which are used primarily for snatching prey, so whales are probably not on the menu."

"Where are they headed?"

"We think north, toward the Sea of Japan."

David handed her back the file. "It's a big ocean. How the heck are we supposed to find them?"

"Don't worry Junior, Mama has a plan." She pointed to his wrist bands. "Do you sweat a lot or are you just making a fashion statement?"

David's pulse pounded in his neck, his face flushing. "I don't like head games, Jacqueline."

"Who's playing head games?"

"You are, right now. You've obviously been briefed about me, which means you know all about the track marks on my wrists. Since you're neither ignorant nor stupid, that means you're testing me. Don't. I spent three days in the Panthalassa with these monsters—"

"And netted nothing. Don't confuse activity with accomplishment. I'm sorry about what happened to Kaylie Szeifert, but my job is to keep these animals alive, not to allow you to play Captain Ahab."

Jackie Buchwald cringed as David punched the overhead bin before storming up the spiral staircase, his tirade chasing off the Arabian beauties seated inside the Crown Prince's private lounge.

Opening her laptop, she composed an email.

TO: Dr. Al Hashemi
FR: Jacqueline Buchwald
RE: First encounter with subject.
Anger issues remain unresolved; temper easily provoked. Whether the subject's emotional instability will impact his performance is yet to be determined, however pairing him with a co-pilot at this time is not recommended.

5

||||||||||||||||||||||||||||||||

Dead Man's Cove, San Juan Island

For over a century, the Lime Kiln Lighthouse has guided ships across the waterways at the entrance to Haro Strait, a major shipping route that links Puget Sound to the Gulf of Georgia. Built atop solid rock, the lighthouse towered twenty feet above high tide, its lantern room encircled by a concrete observation deck. The only other buildings in the area were two original keeper's dwellings located at the edge of a wood behind the lighthouse, now used by park personnel.

The lighthouse overlooked waters that had been designated a whale sanctuary. Under the direction of the Whale Museum in Friday Harbor, scientists had equipped the lighthouse with webcams and hydrophones designed to track the movements and behaviors of the resident orca pods.

Jonas Taylor stood on the lookout deck of the lighthouse, staring at a tranquil sea. The remains of an early morning fog obscured the view of the Olympic Mountain range and the shores of Vancouver Island. There were no boats visible on the horizon.

Below, a team of marine biologists continued the Herculean task of photographing, measuring, and tagging each killer whale carcass.

Park officials had already hauled four of the beached mammals onto flatbed trucks using a winch and chain, now they turned their attention to the bloated, bleeding corpses floating in the shallows of Dead Man's Cove.

Mac joined Jonas out on the deck. "There are two head honchos we need to deal with. Captain Michael Royston is the U.S. Coast Guard sector commander; he's en route aboard an MH-65C helicopter. You're on the top of his shit list being that he had to shut down all whale watching and sport fishing tours over the last thirty-six hours. Then there's Nick Van Sicklen, head of the Whale Museum in Friday Harbor. As bad as Royston has it for us, Van Sicklen has it worse. Apparently this Whale Museum has an Adopt-an-Orca program, and the sisters decimated the equivalent of an entire orphanage. Van Sicklen is organizing a flotilla to protect the other resident orca pods, only he can't kill Bela and Lizzy as they're protected under the same marine sanctuary rules as the orca. Of course, if a bigger predator feeds on another predator, who's to say—"

"They weren't feeding, Mac. I've examined the wounds. The sisters bled them but these are not big bites, they took out the flukes and pectoral fins but left the meat. Orcas aren't even high on the Meg's diet; they lack the fat content of a baleen whale. No, I think this was more of a territorial dispute and the kayakers found themselves in the middle of it."

"The sisters are territorializing these waters?"

Jonas and Mac turned, confronted by an angry man in his mid-twenties, his short-cropped brown hair poking out beneath a University of Florida baseball cap.

Mac stepped between them. "Jonas, meet Nick Van Sicklen, head of the Whale Museum and director of the Sea-Sound Remote Sensing Network program. Nick's group has hydrophones anchored throughout the San Juan Island channels; he's fluent in orca."

Van Sicklen ignored the compliment, along with the offered handshake. "Your sharks butchered my whales."

"And a woman," Mac reminded him. "I'm just saying."

"Look, kid . . . if you want to blame me for what happened, get in line behind the victim's lawyers. For the record, and the story was in every paper, the animal rights wackos freed Bela and Lizzy, not us. Having said that, we're here to prevent any more attacks."

"How?"

"Yeah, how?" Mac asked.

Jonas shot his friend a glare. "We're going to help the Coast Guard track down the Megs and kill them."

"You can't kill them; the Salish Sea is a protected marine sanctuary."

"Why don't you let us worry about that. I saw the hydrophone setup inside; maybe you can give us an idea where the other orca pods are located."

Van Sicklen led them inside to three listening stations, each equipped with a computer hard drive, monitor, speakers, and headphones. "We can identify pods and their activities by the types of sounds we hear. Orcas are able to generate a wide variety of sounds by forcing air in and out of a complex network of passages and cavities located in their foreheads, or melons. Clicks are generally used to echolocate food and other underwater objects. Squealing sounds are what orca use to communicate with one another.

"The Salish Sea has three distinct groups of orca: resident, transient, and offshore killer whales. These groups are genetically quite different from one another and they possess unique vocabularies, which may be one reason why they don't interact socially. They also have different diets. Resident orca, better known as Southern Resident Killer Whales, or SRKW, are all derived from J-clan, then subdivided into three matriarchal lines. SRKWs are fish eaters with a preference for salmon. They use sonar clicks to locate their prey and communicate frequently to other resident orca. Your sharks attacked members of K-pod. There are still eleven members unaccounted for.

"Transient killer whales feed on other sea mammals—seals, sea lions, dolphins, porpoises, and the occasional gray whale; as a result they're much quieter when they're hunting. As far as we can tell, West Coast—or what we call offshore orca—are fish eaters like our residents. They usually hunt just outside the Juan de Fuca strait."

"Other than their vocabularies, how can you tell the three groups apart?"

"We've documented subtle differences in the shape of their dorsal fins, especially among the females. Resident dorsal fins have a rounded tip that ends in a sharp corner. Transient fins are more pointed, like that of a shark. Offshore orca have dorsal fins that are rounded on both ends of the tip. Pod sizes and locations among the three groups also vary. Offshore killer whales prefer the open ocean and travel in the largest pods—upward of forty to sixty individuals. Transient pods are the smallest with no more than half a dozen members moving in close proximity. Transients will swim anywhere, making their movements the most challenging to predict. Resident orcas are subdivided into genetically related clans which travel through established territories in pods numbering up to several dozen."

"Did your hydrophone system record the attack?" Jonas asked.

Van Sicklen typed in a command, causing a menu of recorded data to appear on screen. He selected one using the mouse and clicked on it. "You'll hear the warning cries from the bulls first, followed by the actual attack."

A duet of long, deep haunting chirps played out over the speakers, followed by intermittent clicks . . . and then the attack—a high-pitched, rapid, chaotic chorus of desperate squeals.

Nick waited two more minutes then shut it off, unable to listen. "It goes on for nineteen torturous minutes. Your damn Megs wiped out the entire Haro Strait clan."

East Sound, Orcas Island

Named after the viceroy of Mexico (and not the killer whales that inhabit its waterways), Orcas Island is a landmass of lush woodlands and country roads disrupted by snowcapped mountains. There are no major population centers on Orcas, just quaint villages.

Two waterways split the horseshoe-shaped island, each sound

harboring boat-filled marinas and seaside marketplaces run by local artisans and farmers that catered to tourists looking for a bit of solitude on their summer vacations.

In the wake of the Megalodon attack, all kayak adventures and whale-watching excursions in the Salish Sea had been cancelled by order of the U.S. Coast Guard. Sports fishing charters were limited to boats with lengths exceeding thirty feet, with a sunset curfew in effect.

Restrictions proved unnecessary. Well aware of the horrors Bela and Lizzy could inflict, tourists kept to land-based activities or cut their vacations short. Charter boat captains refused to leave their moorings.

Retired independent film producer Steven Lebowitz stood at the helm of the *Lebofilms,* a forty-one-foot Albermarle game fishing boat, the down payment for which had come from the profits of his last movie, entitled "*She*." The craft had a yacht-like feel with its oversized cockpit and galley, spacious forward stateroom, two heads with separate showers, and sleeping accommodations for three. Unfortunately, Lebowitz had taken a loss on the sequel, forcing him to part with either his Palm Beach condominium or the boat.

He had made the choice eight years ago and had never looked back.

Bottom fishing wasn't just one of Steven Lebowitz's passions, it also earned him a decent income. He had learned the island hotspots for flounder, halibut, cabazon, and greenling and made a few extra bucks on the side supplying red rock crab and shrimp to the local eateries. The outdoors agreed with him, but last winter had been harsh. This year he planned to head south to San Diego sometime in late September.

For the last twenty minutes, Lebowitz had been watching a tall, athletic man and his short brown-haired girlfriend work their way across the docks, receiving turn down after turn down from the other charter boat captains. When it became clear he was their next stop, Lebowitz covered what remained of his thinning salt-and-pepper hair with a *Lebofilms* baseball cap, and then stepped out on deck, busying himself with one of the rigging stations.

Thirty-year-old professional diver Lucas Heitman paused at the edge of the dock to speak with his business associate, Donna Johnston. "This is the guy I told you about. Do it just like we rehearsed."

The twenty-seven-year-old native of Edinburgh, Scotland, twirled a blue-dyed strand of hair while her eyes focused on Steven Lebowitz. "You'd better convince the ole *bampot*. My dealer's leaving for Frisco tomorrow afternoon and wants everything crated tonight."

They headed down the pier, Lucas waving as Steven turned to face him. "Morning, captain. Beautiful boat."

"She'll look even better when she's paid for."

"Maybe we can help. I'm Lucas. This is my boss, Donna Johnston. Donna flew in last week all the way from Scotland to hire me to film B-roll for her documentary."

"No kidding? I used to be in the business . . . Lebofilms." He pointed to the transom. "What kind of B-roll do you need?"

"Underwater footage," said Donna. "Kelp forests, a few shots along the bottom. Lucas found the perfect spot, only no one has the *bollocks* to go out."

"Who can blame them; did you see the news coverage? Just out of curiosity, were you going to shoot using a drone or a reach pole?"

Lucas grinned sheepishly.

"An open water dive? *Boychick*, you're crazy."

"The Megs were after orca; the attack occurred in the deep waters off the west coast of San Juan Island. We're shooting in the shallows. Are you familiar with Obstruction Pass?"

"Are you kidding? I could practically spit there from here. Still, it's too risky."

Donna removed an envelope of bills from her jacket pocket. "Here's five hundred dollars for about an hour of work. You'll receive another thousand when we get back to port."

She handed the envelope to the former movie producer, who thumbed through the cash. "An hour, huh? These hour shoots tend to be more like three. Where's your gear?"

Lucas pointed in the direction of the parking lot. "There's two crates on wheels in my pickup truck. We can be loaded in twenty minutes."

Donna rubbed the captain's arm. "I'd love to have a *peek* at your film. Maybe you can show it to me while Lucas is fetching his gear?"

Steven Lebowitz removed his cap to wipe sweat beads from his receding forehead. "Sure, I can do that. Grab your gear, Lucas. And make sure you don't have any open wounds."

The MH-65C Coast Guard helicopter cruised at a pedestrian thirty knots over the placid green waters of Haro Strait, its bright orange skin glistening in the late afternoon sun. Instead of a tail rotor, the search and rescue craft possessed a fenestron—ten blades spinning inside a circular housing at the base of its tail fin.

Two pilots manned the cockpit. The flight mechanic sat behind the 7.62mm M240B/H machine gun mounted by the open bay door. A spotter was harnessed next to him, his binoculars trained upon the surface glistening a hundred and sixty feet below. The chopper's rescue swimmer was assigned the 7.62mm shoulder-fired precision weapon which rested on his lap.

Captain Michael Royston, the U.S. Coast Guard sector commander out of Port Angeles tapped Jonas on the shoulder, then pointed to Mac, who was dozing in his seat. "War vet?"

Jonas nodded. "And a new father. His wife has him pulling three a.m. feedings."

"Poor bastard."

Jonas shrugged off the attempt at conversation, struggling to shift his weight in the jump seat. They had been circling the western coastal waters of San Juan Island for three straight hours. He was tired and hungry; his lower back ached and his knees were cramped. *This is a waste of time. . . . an exercise in futility aimed solely at appeasing the public. Bela and Lizzy could be a hundred miles from here or be swimming two hundred feet directly below us—either way we'd never know it. And shooting at them with a machine gun . . .*

The co-pilot signaled to starboard. "Sir, we sighted another pod of gray whales. Should we stay with them?"

Captain Royston glanced at Jonas, reading his pained expression. "How are we on fuel?"

"We can remain on this course and speed another twenty minutes before . . . stand by, Captain. We're receiving a report from one of the auxiliary units. A sighting . . . a white dorsal fin . . . three miles southwest of Obstruction Island."

Obstruction Pass

The *Lebofilms* cut a V-shaped wake of white water across the glassy emerald green surface, its captain maintaining a southern heading through the narrows of East Sound. On their port side was Obstruction State Park, its public boat launch closed. The channel ended up ahead, emptying into open water.

Steven Lebowitz called down from the helm to the lanky man in the dry suit. "Hey, shark bait, see those whitecaps? That's your destination."

Lucas Heitman waved, his eyes focused on his iPhone and the GPS map.

Obstruction Island came into view on their left, its forest-covered landmass concealing a private residential community. Donna Johnston observed the landmass from the bow, just as she had four days earlier in her lover's yacht. Alexi Alexandrovich Lundgard owned one of the island's seaside properties. She had met the Russian immigrant two years earlier in the United Kingdom where he ran a black market import-export company. One of Alexi's hottest commodities was pinto abalone, a San Juan Island seafood delicacy contained in a six-inch-flat, ear-shaped shell, the interior of which was an iridescent pearl coating set in swirling patterns of color that shifted with the light. Commercial demand for abalone was high, the polished shell pieces used in guitar inlays and saxophone keys as well as women's jewelry.

Abalone diving in the Salish Sea had been banned since 1994.

An avid SCUBA diver, Alexi had come across a large patch of abalone a week earlier while investigating a twelve-foot ridge hidden among a kelp forest along the bottom. While Donna kept vigil topside, he and Lucas had collected over two hundred live specimens, but could not risk hauling the heavy burlap bags on board as a Coast Guard chopper had been circling overhead. Instead they tied the bags and hid them beneath a shelf of rock in Obstruction Pass.

Alexi's movements were being watched. That left it up to Donna to secure the haul.

Lucas signaled the captain to stop. The boat listed beneath its own wake, its engines chortling blue-gray exhaust fumes. Lebowitz checked the depth gauge and dropped anchor, the line going taught in the currents.

Donna intercepted him as he climbed down from the helm. "You have a winch, yes?"

"A winch? Yeah, I have a winch. What do you need a winch for?"

She led him to the five-foot-long, four-foot-wide rectangular wooden crate Lucas had hauled onboard. Through gaps in the wooden slates Lebowitz could see a burlap sack held shut by a padlock. "What's in the bag? A dead body?"

"You are a funny man. These are props we need in the shot. One is a bust of Poseidon; the other is a statue of his rival, Hades. Best to leave them in the crate; Lucas will position them along the bottom."

Lebowitz tested the crate's weight, estimating it to be about a hundred and thirty pounds. With Donna's help, he rolled it across the deck to the starboard pulley. Clipping the end of the line onto the crate's O-ring, he reversed the winch, lifting the load off the deck. The Scottish woman swung it beyond the aluminum rail and the captain lowered it until it came to rest along the bottom.

Now it was up to Lucas.

The diver stood on the rocking transom, gazing at the churning water. Conditions were poor, the tide swift. He could see the tops of the bull kelp quivering just beneath the surface, his mind rationalizing the simplicity of the task before him against his own undercurrent of fear.

For the umpteenth time his eyes scanned the horizon. No orca, no giant six-foot white dorsal fins.

Donna nudged him from behind, jump-starting his already rapid heartbeat. "Forgetting something, lad?" She handed him the underwater video camera.

"Right . . . thanks."

Rubbing saliva inside his dive mask, he sealed it to his face, then held the camera to his chest and stepped forward off the listing boat, falling feetfirst into the sea.

The inflated buoyancy control vest prevented him from sinking. Bobbing along the surface, he reached for the valve and released air, sending himself plunging into an emerald green world entangled by towering strands of kelp.

He paddled into a clearing and continued his controlled descent, following the steel cable to the bottom. He felt the pressure building in his eardrums as he passed thirty feet and paused to equalize, pinching his nose while blowing out his cheeks. When the squeezing sensation eased he continued, his eyes wide as they focused on the curtains of deep green kelp and what they might conceal.

So engaged was Lucas with his surroundings that he was startled when his flippers struck the top of the crate, sending him tumbling backward. His air tank struck the rocky bottom with a loud *crunch*.

In a frenzy of movement he righted himself. *Which way was the ridge? The GPS had pointed southeast . . . which way was that?* He checked his dive watch, collecting his bearings.

First things first—empty the crate.

Flipping open the metal latches, he opened the crate and dragged out the burlap sack. Inside were two cheap plaster busts Donna had purchased at a farmer's market. Dumping them on the sea floor, he pushed away from the bottom, setting off at a brisk pace to collect the bag of abalone.

Lucas bypassed the denser sections of kelp, swimming over a reef. Large anemone and sea cucumbers bloomed into view, along with coon-striped shrimp, ten-armed sunflower starfish, and other colorful clusters of invertebrates.

The ridge was in a clearing up ahead—a slanted shelf of rock, twelve feet high at its apex and eight feet deep, serving as the local hangout for a variety of fish.

A school of kelp greenling hovered before the entrance like nervous deer, the males with their brown bodies and irregular blue patches seemingly a different species from their female counterparts with their reddish-brown spots and yellowish-orange fins.

A cluster of China rockfish darted out of his way, their dark blue bodies marked by a yellow stripe that extended around the third dorsal spine down to their lateral lines. As he neared the ridge opening he saw a lingcod hovering like a bulldog, its massive ninety pound girth spotted in shades of gray.

Avoiding the popular eating fish, he ducked inside the ridge, nearly stepping on a buffalo sculpin lying along the bottom, the bottom dweller no doubt attracted to the roiling abalone trapped inside the burlap bag.

Lifting the sack with both hands, he half-kicked, half-strode out of the crevasse of rock—only to be confronted by a ghost.

It was a great white, a six-foot, three-hundred-pound female, its hide as pure as the driven snow. The albino swam with frenetic movements, her back arched in an aggressive posture. Clearly agitated, she circled the area like a caged tiger, then abruptly darted into the curtain of kelp and disappeared.

Lucas remained beneath the ledge, his heart pounding in his chest, each breath panted. He checked his air gauge . . . *twenty-two minutes.*

He searched the surface for the boat and located its keel a good fifty yards away. The seventy-seven-foot ascent added precious minutes; he'd have to pause at least once to avoid ending up with the bends.

Lucas removed the diving knife that was strapped to his right ankle, but found it too cumbersome to wield while holding the bulky sack.

He considered leaving the abalone behind, but realized he could use it as a shield in case the shark attacked. *Get back to the crate as fast as you can, then ascend nice and easy. If the shark attacks . . . stab the fucker right in its gray eye!*

Adding just enough air to his vest to compensate for the sack's weight he set off, the burlap bag pressed to his chest. Keeping his head on a swivel, he cut north across the coral bed, his eyes continuously checking the position of the boat's keel.

That's when he spotted the great white. It was circling the kelp forest high overhead like a bird of prey, its silhouette lead-gray against the ceiling of shimmering daylight.

As he watched, a second shark joined the first.

Before Lucas could think, a third shark made its presence known. Unlike the others this predator was stalking him through the dense kelp forest on his left, its white albino head partially concealed behind fluid strands of vegetation, its lead-gray flank revealing a bizarre two-tone pigment.

Lucas's eyes caught movement and he turned—confronted by the shark's identical twin—which was now bull-rushing him! A pink band of gums opened into an expanse of needle-sharp teeth a split second before the diver raised the burlap sack in self-defense—

Whomp!

The concussive impact stole Lucas's breath, causing his regulator to pop out of his mouth as the burlap sack exploded into a gray oily cloud of shattered shells and raw abalone.

The shark shook its head like a pit bull in a game of tug-o-war, its head caught in the emptying sack, the burlap blinding the panicked creature.

Lucas fled, kicking and paddling across the sea bed until he ran out of air and was forced to shove the dangling regulator back inside his mouth. Kneeling by the open crate, he forgot to purge and sucked in a mouthful of seawater . . . puked it out, and gasped a breath of air.

He saw a flash of white and instinctively dove inside the crate, twisting around on his back into a fetal position in order to shut the heavy container's lid. He closed his eyes to the terror, then felt the impact of wood crushing against his right shoulder. He moaned into his regulator and waited for the insanity of the predator's fangs puncturing his flesh—only it never came.

Opening his eyes, he peered through a three inch slit separating the wooden slats. A swarm of moving bodies surrounded the crate, no less than four great whites positioning themselves for the anticipated feeding frenzy. Lucas saw a white-headed, gray-backed shark chase off one of the albinos—his body trembling in terror as another ghostly predator methodically moved through the chaos until its sea-snorting nostrils pushed between two wooden slats, homing in on Lucas's pounding pulse.

Unable to reach the protruding snout with his fist, the diver slammed it with his elbow, the impact unleashing a wave of pain down his arm.

The shark twisted its head sideways and swam off.

Lucas knew he was hyperventilating, the fear of being eaten un-leashing waves of anxiety. He checked his air and was actually relieved. I'll suffocate before the bitches can sink their teeth into me . . .

And then, miraculously, the crate began to rise.

———

Attached to the *Lebofilm*'s keel was an underwater camera. While Donna Johnston remained out on deck working on her tan, Steven Lebowitz had been watching Lucas Heitman's descent on the boat's closed circuit monitor.

The kelp had obscured much of his view until the diver had reached the sea floor. He knew Lucas had emptied the crate because the tension on the winch's cable had eased. Using the boat's fish finder helped fill in more of the missing pieces to the puzzle.

No one in their right mind would have dived within fifty miles of a Megalodon sighting unless there was a big payoff to offset the risk. That meant drugs or weapons. Having radioed his fellow charter captains, Lebowitz knew the girl was an associate of Alexi Lundgard, a reputed dealer in the black market. Weapons were easy enough to purchase in the States, so it had to be drugs.

They probably had to dump their stash overboard when the Coast Guard shadowed Lundgard's yacht.

Lebowitz was about to radio the authorities when the first shark appeared on his fish finder.

With the abundance of food available in the Salish Sea—including seals and sea lions, favorite delicacies of the great white—one might assume shark sightings were prevalent around the San Juan Islands. In fact they were rare. Great whites, it turned out, were an orca delicacy. While the offshore killer whales patrolled the entrance to the Juan de Fuca strait, the transient and local orca pods protected the kayakers and divers.

And yet the fish finder had identified not one but six juvenile great whites.

From their rapid movements, Lebowitz knew the sharks were

hungry and that they were aggressively circling his diver. He had tracked Lucas back to the crate when the first predator launched its attack.

The sudden stress on the winch's cable painted a clear picture of what was transpiring below.

Lebowitz ran out on deck, the .12 gauge shotgun in his hand startling Donna Johnston. "Captain?"

"We've got visitors."

"The sisters?" She backed away from the rail into Lebowitz, who was reversing gears on the winch.

"It's not the Megs, but there are an unusual number of great whites circling your diver."

"Is he okay? Is he able to surface with the crate?"

Lebowitz restarted the winch, the cable and pulley straining under the additional weight. "If I'm right, he's *inside* the crate."

"Inside the crate? But what about . . . ?"

"The drugs? Guess he had to leave them behind."

Donna moved to the starboard rail, catching sight of a gray dorsal fin. "It wasn't drugs. It was pinto abalone."

Lebowitz looked up. "You risked his life for a bunch of . . ."

The word *shellfish* caught in his throat.

Steven Lebowitz had experienced fear twice in his life—the first time at age eight when he was swimming in the ocean alone and found himself caught in a riptide; the second at age fourteen when he suddenly ran out of air while going for his SCUBA certification.

That was fear; this was terror—the shortness of breath, the rapid thumping in his temples, the sudden weakness in his legs . . . it all seemed like an out-of-body experience.

Gripping the winch to keep from collapsing to his knees, he stood by the starboard rail and gazed in awe at the spy-hopping albino goddess. The Megalodon's head was so incredibly large he felt embarrassed to have challenged the creature's authority, her gray-blue eye so close that he could have prodded it with the barrel of the shotgun had he the audacity to move. The peppered underside of the snout . . . the thick muscle set around a mouth so immense he could have climbed inside its trap door of a jaw—the silently jabbering lower hinge offering a hint of serrated teeth.

Queen Lizzy stared at her human subject as if she were debating its fate.

Donna Johnston's blood-curdling scream shattered the moment and returned Steven Lebowitz into his body.

Raising the shotgun, he fired.

The buckshot blasted a ring of lead pellets in and around the Megalodon's left eye, spraying blood and cornea bits across Donna's chest.

Insane with pain, the albino slammed its inflamed, gushing eye socket against the surface in looping east-west gyrations, scooping up great swaths of sea, which rolled the fishing boat.

Realizing he had just "poked the bear," Steven Lebowitz raced up the ladder to the helm and powered up the engines, slamming down the throttle.

———

For Lucas Heitman, the miracle of his rescue had turned into a nightmare.

Rising within the wooden crate, he braced for the impact of the swarming juvenile great whites—only to see them flee into the kelp forest. Elated, the diver whispered a prayer of thanks into his regulator, then wondered how his employer would react to the loss of the abalone.

Alexi's going to be pissed. No doubt Donna will blame it on me.

Looking up, he saw the boat's hull pass overhead—and realized, to his horror, it was one of the Megalodons. The monster's belly and pectoral fins resembled a small passenger jet, its tail methodically pushing it into an easy glide which ended with a ballet-like vertical ascent as Lizzy's head broke the surface.

Helpless and terrified, Lucas could only hang on and wait while his crate continued to rise alongside the Megalodon's gently swaying caudal fin, the half-moon-shaped appendage channeling a rush of water that pushed him beneath the boat.

Twelve feet from the keel all hell broke loose.

Blood splattered across the surface—which erupted in a maelstrom as the forty-six-foot albino beast shook its head to and fro beneath the frothing shallows, unleashing a tornado of kelp.

Seconds later the twin engines spun a dervish of bubbles and suddenly the crate—and Lucas—were bouncing along the surface.

———

The MH-65C Coast Guard helicopter chased its shadow over the emerald-green waterway, approaching Obstruction Island from the west. The co-pilot's eyes shifted from the white speck on the horizon to the airship's fuel gauge. "Captain, we're on fumes. One flyover, then we need to refuel at Shaw Island."

Captain Royston glanced at Mac. "Don't look so worried, *grandpa*. There's always a little reserve left in the tank."

"Really, douche bag? Because my wife says the same thing . . . just before she runs out of gas."

Jonas had moved nearer to the open cargo door, the shifting cabin making it difficult to keep his binoculars trained on the fishing boat up ahead. For a brief second he thought he saw Lizzy's head poised above the water . . . until the frame spun away as the craft beneath his feet started losing altitude.

———

He needed to head north for the safety of East Sound, only the *Lebofilm*'s bow was pointing south. As Steven Lebowitz accelerated and then pulled his boat into a tight portside turn, the former movie producer realized he had made a costly error.

The anchor was dragged thirty feet through the kelp forest roots, digging in tighter and deeper until it had become firmly entrenched between two rocks. The more Lebowitz gunned the engines, the higher his bow rose and the less his boat moved.

"Son of a bitch!"

Tethered to the bottom, they were sitting ducks.

———

The Coast Guard chopper hovered sixty feet above the rotor-blown surface, its crew mesmerized by the spectacle taking place below.

The fishing boat's twin engines were running at full throttle, yet the charter seemed frozen in place. Twenty feet to port was the Meg. Like the ship, the albino monster seemed stuck in place, its enormous head—easily the size of the ship's bow—whipping the sea as if the shark had gone insane.

"Captain, I've got the target sighted!"

"Hold your fire until that boat clears the area."

"Why isn't it moving?"

"Its anchor's hung."

Jonas focused his binoculars on Lizzy. "Mac, she's wounded."

"Good. Where's Bela?"

Jonas's flesh tingled. *Where was Bela?* "Captain, watch our altitude!"

The reflection of the late afternoon sun and the propeller-whipped whitecaps had camouflaged Lizzy's dark-backed sibling. Charging the surface, the twenty-one-ton Megalodon rose out of the sea, her snout coming within five feet of the chopper's struts before gravity compelled its return.

Twisting sideways, Bela struck the surface with a thunderous *clap*, the impact spraying water across the helicopter's windshield.

That was enough for the two pilots. "Captain, if we don't leave now—"

"Sir, there's a man in the water!"

———

Suspended three feet below the surface, Lucas Heitman knew two things—that the *Lebofilm*'s anchor was caught along the bottom and that he was out of air. Now he had to choose—drown or attempt to board the boat before the captain cut the line and left him to be eaten.

Releasing his grip on the crate's lid, he pushed himself out of the wooden container . . . and sunk.

Stripping off his weight belt returned him to neutral buoyancy.

Slipping out of his gear forced him to kick his way to the surface for a desperate breath of air.

His head emerged into a wind storm, the helicopter's rotors whipping his face with salt water drenched with carbon monoxide fumes. The boat's transom loomed ten feet away, only it was swaying to and fro so violently that Lucas hesitated to get near it lest he be sucked into the twin propellers.

Something blotted out the sun, causing him to look up seconds before the bright orange harness struck him in the head.

———

"He's in, Captain, we're reeling him up."

Jonas peered over the hoist operator's shoulder, watching the pace of the rising survivor, the pilot maintaining a static hoist evolution. "Captain, you can't keep us stationary like this, you're serving him up to Bela as lunch."

Royston knew Taylor was right. "Pilot, switch rescue procedure to a dynamic hoist and get us to Shaw Island."

"Not enough fuel, Captain. We'll have to set her down on—"

The pilot's eyes widened as the sea erupted beneath the fishing boat, flipping it out of the water. Twisting on the anchor line, it landed keel up, its twin propellers slicing air.

———

One minute Steven Lebowitz was shouting at the girl to grab the ax—the next he was leaving his feet, the helm controls spinning in his vision, the top of his head smashing painfully against the deck which was somehow above him.

And then he was underwater.

Disoriented, Lebowitz kicked away from an entanglement of aluminum ladder rungs and curtains of charts, his reeling mind recognizing that the boat he had called home for the last eight years was sinking on top of him and he desperately needed to move.

Swim to daylight . . .

Steven Lebowitz swam to what his eyes perceived to be the surface—his primordial fears igniting as the white surroundings suddenly rushed at him, inhaling him into a moment of excruciating darkness.

Lizzy did not swallow her prey as much as she chomped down upon its flesh until its blood and innards squished warm between her teeth.

Donna Johnston remained trapped in the submerged inverted galley, her mind freaking out as Bela gnawed her way through the cherrywood cabin to reach her. Refusing to be eaten alive, the Scot asked God for mercy, said goodbye to her family, and then inhaled the sea deep into her lungs.

Lucas Heitman was dragged inside the aft bay just as one of the Coast Guard helicopter's twin turbine engines coughed . . . and died.

Jonas and Mac looked at each another. A breath later the five ton aircraft pitched sideways as it lost altitude, its pilots fighting to reach Obstruction Island with their remaining engine.

"Hold on, we're going down!"

Jonas gripped the mounted hoist's boom with one hand, the door frame with the other as the emerald surface whipped past the open bay at a sloping thirty-degree angle, the chopper rapidly running out of altitude.

For extended seconds the pilots held gravity at bay—the depths marbling into azure shallows. And then the second engine seized silent and the airship fell forty feet, collapsing onto the beach.

6

IIIIIIIIIIIIIIIIIIIIIIIIIIIIIIIIIIIIII

Aboard the Supertanker *Mogamigawa*
77 Nautical Miles South of Japan

The converted Japanese supertanker, *Mogamigawa* moved through the dark waters of the Western Pacific, displacing 300,000 tons. She was as large as they came—a Malacca-max VLCC (very large crude carrier) designed with a draft shallow enough to navigate the Straits of Malacca, the preferred route between the Persian Gulf and Asia. A floating steel island, the *Mogamigawa* and her sister ship, the *Tonga* were 1,100 feet in length and 196 feet wide, with a superstructure rising out of the stern that towered twelve stories. But it was the converted crude holds that made these goliaths unique—six large seawater pens, each rubber-lined saltwater tank equipped with saline and temperature controls, along with jet stream breathers designed to tranquilize, subdue, and safely transport extreme aquatic life forms that were larger than whales and bore the ferocity of a tiger.

Accompanying the *Mogamigawa* was the *Dubai Land-II,* a 196-foot, 280-ton fishing trawler which held two Manta submersibles designed by Jonas and David Taylor. The pilots aboard the *DB-II* had been trained to use their subs to entice a targeted sea monster up from the depths of the Panthalassa Sea—a prehistoric purgatory isolated beneath the Philippine Sea Plate. That mission had shifted dramatically (to the sub pilots' relief) when several species had escaped into the Western Pacific.

The Boeing CH-47 Chinook twin engine heavy lift helicopter hovered above the *Mogamigawa*'s helipad. Fifteen restless passengers were seated in the cargo bay, exhausted from their ten hour flight into Tokyo. Upon landing, they had been ushered through customs and taken by bus to a commuter airport for the two hour helicopter ride south.

The Chinook touched down with a double *thud*. The bay door opened, venting the hold with a blast of cold air.

Amanda Silvernail, the executive producer, stood watch over Nichole Middelkamp, her petite green-eyed assistant, who passed out manila envelopes to each of the ten female contestants. "You'll find cabin assignments and a map of the ship inside. The local time is nine-fifteen p.m. Breakfast is in the galley at eight, followed by video bios. Get some sleep, ladies, tomorrow is a big day. If you need anything contact Nichole."

The women grabbed their suitcases and makeup bags and formed an exit line. As they passed Monty, two Egyptians and a Syrian model ceremoniously slapped the Iraqi War vet across his face—all to the delight of James Gelet, who was filming everything (the cameraman having sent a text moments ago that the man they had seduced aboard the 747 was not in fact David Taylor, but an imposter assigned to the tanker as a short order cook).

David winced as another dark-haired beauty smacked Monty atop his head, cursing at him in Arabic.

"Was it worth it?"

Monty rubbed his skull, his cheeks—swollen and red. "Well, that hellcat wasn't, but the other three . . . hell, yes. Did you know ancient Roman priestesses called vestal virgins were required to keep their hymens intact as proof of virginity until they were thirty years old, or they'd be buried alive. That'd be my dream job—hymen inspector." He nodded to Jackie Buchwald, who was seated four rows back.

"What's with the strawberry-blonde? You've been giving her the evil eye for the last hour."

"Her? Nothing."

"Studious type, but definitely cute. One of the reality show producers?"

"She's with the aquarium . . . a marine biologist who thinks she knows it all."

"Uh oh. You either like this chick or she makes you *Bushusuru.*"

"What?"

"*Bushusuru.* It's a new Japanese word for vomiting in public. It was created after George Bush Sr. vomited on the Japanese Prime Minister."

"She was playing head games with me, Monty."

"Big head or little head?"

"I gotta get some air." David grabbed his duffle bag and headed outside. "Amanda, do you have an envelope there for me?"

"Jason Montgomery . . . let's see—"

"His name is David Taylor." Jackie Buchwald pushed him aside, grabbing her envelope from the confused producer. "Wouldn't want you to get caught up in any head games, David."

Slinging her bag over her shoulder, Jackie jogged across the helipad and entered the tanker's looming superstructure.

———

He was struggling to keep his head above water, each incoming swell a five-foot mountain concealing Kaylie. She was up ahead, her long, lean body slicing across a surface slick with oil and blood.

Obliterating the sunset was the Tonga, *the ship's starboard flank towering overhead. Suspended from the tanker's reinforced steel net was Angel, the Megalodon's eviscerated lower torso gone, her innards a crimson waterfall which splattered into the Philippine Sea.*

He was swimming in it; the oil pouring from Angel's ruptured liver . . . her hot blood coagulating in the cold Pacific. It was getting in his mouth—he fought the gag reflex, fearful of losing the girl.

He paused to get his bearings, relieved to find her holding on to the buoyant escape pod.

"David, hang on to the other side."

Barely able to lift his arms, David paddled over to his father's submersible and held on, pressing his face to the glass.

His father was sitting up in his cockpit, shaking his head.

"Dad?"

"I told you not to join the expedition, son. But you never listen. You're just like I was—impetuous. Balls-to-the-wall . . . always thinking you can cheat death. There's a price to pay, David. Always a price."

He glanced at Kaylie, who waved at him from the other side of the escape pod. "Good-bye, David. I enjoyed our brief time together."

"Please don't go."

"Baby, don't be sad. We both knew this was never meant to be. I have my destiny; you have yours."

As he watched, the Liopleurodon *rose from the depths, its gargantuan crocodilian jaws widening around Kaylie.*

"Kaylie, wait! Will I ever see you again?"

Reaching out, she held onto a curved dagger-like tooth to keep from slipping down the monstrous gullet. "Every night . . . until you release me."

The monster's jaws closed, the beast returning to the depths.

———

"Ahhh! Ahhhh!"

David shot up in bed, his body trembling, his T-shirt drenched in a cold sweat. He was in the belly of the beast—a swaying, groaning darkness with no perceivable dimensions, and he needed to get out!

Hyperventilating, he fell out of bed onto a cold steel floor and crawled blindly until his forehead smashed into a ledge, the collision blasting stars in his vision.

A passage opened on his right, a figure looming in the gray shadows.

"David?"

"Yes!" He tried to stand and smashed his head even harder.

"Where's your light switch?"

A dull white florescent bulb flickered on high overhead, illuminating the eight by ten foot cabin. Steel bulkhead, no portal, bed frame bolted to the floor, small dorm-style refrigerator, metal toilet and matching sink.

Embarrassed, he crawled out from beneath the bowl of the sink, rubbing his head.

Jacqueline Buchwald helped him up. David's eyes lingered over her bare feet and smooth tan legs, the loose-fitting gray sleeping shirt offering tantalizing hints of her naked breasts pressing beneath the thin cotton fabric.

"What are you doing here?"

"My cabin's next door; you were screaming."

"Bad dream." He sat on the edge of the bed, shivering.

She searched through a pile of clothing, pulling out a clean shirt. "Put this on."

He pulled off the wet T-shirt, revealing an athlete's muscular upper torso . . . and the thick three-inch red scars embedded along the palm-side of each wrist.

He redressed quickly, covering the evidence of his attempted suicide with the wet T-shirt.

"David, there's no need to be embarrassed. It's just a scar."

"It's a little more than a scar, don't you think?"

"Only if you continue to dwell upon it. Give yourself a break."

"You sound like my shrink."

"Been there, done that. Antidepressants . . . alcohol therapy. You'd be amazed how normal you are compared to the rest of us. Back at Brown, all I cared about was filling out my resume—scared to death I wouldn't be able to find a job after graduating. I spent three years as a professional dancer while I was an undergrad, just in case the whole marine biology deal fell through. I think the Crown Prince chose me more for my legs than my grade point average." She stood on her toes, her leg muscles flexing as she assumed a ballet pose, her raised arms causing her shirt to ride up her hips, revealing a flash of her shaved vagina.

David's heart pounded in his chest, the blood rushing to his groin. "So, what was it about?"

"What was what about?"

"The nightmare. Do you get them often?"

"Yeah."

"I know a cure; guaranteed to get you seven hours of sleep a night."

"I don't like sleeping pills, they make me feel weird."

"Who said anything about a pill? I was talking about sex." In one motion, she pulled the gray shirt over her head, revealing her naked body.

"We work in a stress-filled environment, David, filled with very real scary monsters. At the end of a long day I need to let loose. I'm not interested in love; this is purely about preventing nightmares."

"By having sex?"

"No. By fucking each other's brains out before we go to sleep. Think you can handle that? Or would you rather take an Ambien?"

"Screw that." David stood, stripping out of his T-shirt and boxers—Jackie's hands groping his body as she slipped her tongue inside his mouth.

———

The supertanker's galley had been upgraded by the Crown Prince to accommodate the reality show cast and crew. Cafeteria-style seating and buffet lines replaced the vessel's third world "slop-stop" décor; while the usual breakfast selections of oatmeal and powdered eggs were upgraded with fresh produce and an omelet station manned by Monty.

David entered the galley with a spring in his step. He and Jackie had gone at it until two in the morning. Finally spent, the two of them had curled up like spoons and fallen asleep.

For the rest of the night there were no more bad dreams. When he awoke seven hours later, she was gone.

David headed over to the omelet station where Rana, an Iranian actress, was yammering in Farsi at Monty. She ended the exchange by grinding a tomato wedge into his friend's face.

"Hey!" David grabbed her arm. "Don't do that; he's my friend."

She turned to slap him, only to realize it was the *real* David Taylor. "Mister David, I am so sorry. What can I get for your breakfast, please?"

"It's okay, I can handle it."

"No, no, I insist."

"Okay. How about an egg white omelet with ham and cheese."

She turned to Monty. "Idiot, you will make him the best egg white omelet ever or I will slice open your ball sack and fry your testicles in that skillet. David, please go and sit, I will serve you your food when it is ready."

Monty winked behind the raven-haired beauty's back.

David glanced over his shoulder, realizing everything was being filmed. Spotting Jackie, he squeezed his way past three more contestants offering to serve him breakfast and hurried over to her table.

"Good morning."

She looked up at him from behind her laptop. "Can I help you?"

"No. I just thought I'd join you."

"These seats are taken. Why don't you sit with the members of your harem." She pointed to a table where Jihan, a Dubai brunette, and Saba, a Jordanian actress were waving him over.

"I'd rather eat here."

"David, you're interrupting my work. You're also late for the captain's nine a.m. briefing."

David sat down. Whispered, "Jackie, did I do something wrong?"

Rana joined them, carrying a plate with his omelet in one hand, a tray of muffins in the other.

Zeina set down two glasses of orange juice, the dark-haired Egyptian actress squeezing into the chair next to him. "Rana has failed to please you; your eggs are too hot to eat. Give them to me, I shall blow on them."

Shutting her laptop, Jackie stowed it inside her backpack and left.

"Jackie, wait—"

Rana wrestled the omelet back from Zeina. "Do not let this

Egyptian dog contaminate your breakfast with her rancid breath. If you knew where her mouth has been—"

"Enough!" David stood on his chair. "Ladies, can I have your attention, please. Everyone see the egg man over there? His name is Jason Montgomery and he'll be the one deciding which three of you will be finalists on the show, not me. Say something, Monty."

"I am the egg man, goo goo g'joob."

———

David climbed the five flights of stairs to the supertanker's bridge—a wide expanse of steel surrounded by large bay windows. Computerized instrument panels set on evergreen counter tops framed the command center.

Captain Steven Beltzer looked up from his chart table. "You're late, Mr. Taylor. Our meeting was scheduled for nine. Nick, tell Mr. Taylor what we do with members of the crew who don't show up to meetings on time."

"We feed them to the sharks." The command chair swung around, revealing a blue-eyed nineteen-year-old male with a mop of dirty-blond hair and an infectious grin. He was balancing on two stumps where his legs should have been, his arms extending just beyond his elbows.

"David Taylor, this is my son, Nick Porter. Nick's a big Megalodon fan; we took him to the institute when he was eight."

Nick smiled. "I used to tell everyone at school Angel ate my arms and legs."

David fist-bumped at the offered appendage. "I saw Angel take out a guy your age last summer; it wasn't a pretty sight."

The captain passed his son his prosthetic arms and legs. "Nick's been training with the Manta crews as a co-pilot. His sonar scores are tops on the team. We were hoping you might give him a tryout."

David tried to hide his discomfort. "I'm not sure that's my decision—"

His aluminum alloy legs attached, Nick slid off the chair—standing chest to chest with David. "If you're worried about my ability to operate the foot pedals, I can reach them fine with my prosthetics. I've been operating Xbox, Wii, and Playstation controllers since I was a kid and wrestled in middle school until my weight left me behind. As far as the decision goes, it's yours to make."

David stepped back, not wanting to commit. "It's only fair I meet the rest of the team before I choose my co-pilot, but I promise I'll keep you in mind. Captain Beltzer, about our briefing—"

Beltzer handed him a computerized map of the Philippine Sea Plate. "We've been tracking the three *Shonisaurus* on and off for months. The white dot marks the extraction point out of the Panthalassa Sea; the numbers correspond to our four confirmed satellite sightings. As you can see, the creatures were following the eastern

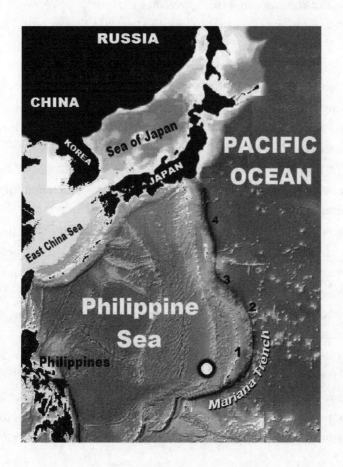

boundary of the Philippine Sea Plate. Two nights ago a fishing trawler was sunk two hundred and sixteen miles south of the Japanese mainland, two crewmen lost. The boat's captain told the coast guard that his deckhands were bringing up the nets with a big haul when two enormous whales with dolphin-shaped heads attacked the catch. One of the creatures struck the keel and split open the trawler's hull. Satellite thermal images confirmed the sighting and picked up the trio at four this morning as they continued north, closing on the Japanese mainland. This may be our best opportunity to capture the shonisaurs. My orders are to get you aboard the *Dubai Land-II* at thirteen hundred hours for a briefing on tonight's mission."

"What's tonight's mission?"

Captain Beltzer turned to his son, whose eyes lit up like a defensive tackle about to sack the opposing quarterback. "We want to net the juvenile so we can use it to bait the two adult shonisaurs."

The *Dubai Land-II* continued on a northwesterly course, its captain reducing the trawler's speed to three knots to allow the Zodiac motorized raft and its two passengers to board. The *Mogamigawa* remained a mile and a half astern. The difference between predator and prey among prehistoric marine life was often determined by size; the trawler's captain did not want the supertanker frightening off his intended quarry.

The Arab sailor piloting the Zodiac accelerated right up the stern ramp used to disperse the trawl nets and launch the Manta subs. Two crewmen held on while David assisted Nick Porter out of the craft. Weaving around trawl nets, winches, gallows, and towing blocks, the two made their way forward to the wheelhouse to find out where the mission briefing was being held.

Captain Inge Ehrenhard was from the city of Nijverdal in the Netherlands. David found the big man in his command chair surrounded by electronic displays that integrated the ship's navigation equipment, communications, trawl sensors, and fish detectors. A shark tooth necklace hung from the skipper's unshaven neck.

"Captain, I'm David Taylor. There's supposed to be a briefing—"

"*Ah, goedemiddag, Meneer* Taylor."

"Could you tell me where the meeting is with the other pilots?"

"Sorry, *ik spreek geen* English. *Goedemiddag.*" Smiling, he returned to his instruments.

David waited thirty seconds before heading back outside. "Nick, do you speak any Dutch?"

"*Ja, een beetje . . .* yes, a little."

"Congratulations, you're my new co-pilot. Get up there and ask Captain Gilligan where our meeting is being held."

Five minutes later they were below decks, entering the galley.

Jackie Buchwald was leading the briefing. Seven men, all in their late thirties to mid-forties, were seated around a wooden table. The elder among them was a blue-eyed, silver-haired pilot who greeted them with a drill sergeant's glare. "Mr. Porter, you know better than to be late to one of my mission briefings."

"Yes sir. We hit a rough patch on the crossing and—"

"It's actually my fault," David said with a sheepish grin. "We should have never stopped for sushi."

Jackie winced. "David, this is Commander Kenney Sills, a retired Navy SEAL submersible pilot and our mission leader."

"Ms. Buchwald left out the most important part; I'm also the ass-hole who determines whether you get to graduate to the *Tonga*. So take a break from the stand-up, *Mr. Comedian*, and park your *keister* on the fucking pine." He nodded to Jackie. "Continue, please."

The other six pilots seated around the table covered their grins.

Jackie returned to her power-point display of the trawler towing its net underwater. "As I was saying, in order to catch the juvenile *Shonisaurus,* the *Dubai Land-II* will deploy two parallel trawl nets. The first will remain deep while the bait trawl skims the surface, its net filled with scad and yellowtail."

"Excuse me, Ms. Buchwald," David interrupted, "but is scad and yellowtail what that Japanese trawler was hauling when it was sunk?"

"Probably not."

"Then why—"

Commander Sills cut him off. "We suspect the Japs were hauling dolphin—the mammal not the fish. Since we're not about to kill *Flipper* on prime-time television, Ms. Buchwald elected to go with scad and yellowtail. Is that all right with you?"

"You realize I'm half Japanese."

"I don't really give a shit what you are."

Jackie hurriedly advanced the projection. "The *Shonisaurus* travel in a staggered formation with the big male out in front. The first Manta sub must play a cat and mouse game to lure him away. The moment that happens, the second sub will engage the mother, allowing the deep trawl net to sweep junior up from behind. Once the calf is caught, the captain will circle back to the *Mogamigawa*, leading Mom and Dad into the tanker's big trawl nets. The two adults must be sedated before they're removed from the water and placed in their holding pens or they'll bash themselves to death." She nodded at Commander Sills, shutting off her laptop.

"Thank you, Ms. Buchwald. I've divided the night into two shifts. Colton Wright and Paul Rudd are in *Manta-One* from nineteen hundred hours to oh-one hundred; Chris Mull and David Taylor in *Manta-Two*. Second shift runs until dawn. I'll be in *One* with Chris Coriasco; Matt Evans and Eric Stamp are in *Two*. If there are no other questions—"

"Nick's my sonar guy," David said. "I promised him the gig."

The other pilots snickered.

Commander Sills's expression cut them off. "Mr. Porter is not on the duty roster, Mr. Taylor."

"You're in charge, Commander; put him on."

Sills stood very slowly. "Gentlemen . . . Ms. Buchwald, let Mr. Taylor and I have this room."

Jackie followed the pilots out of the galley, Nick Porter the last one out.

Commander Sills hovered over David and leaned in until the tips of their noses nearly touched.

And then both pilots cracked up in laughter.

"David Taylor, half Jap, one hundred percent kamikaze pilot. How in the fuck are you?"

"Good."

"Sure you are. Let me see those wrists . . . sweet Jesus, you meant business, didn't you?"

"That was a bad time; I'm better. What are you doing out here? Last I heard you were in Iraq. Aren't you a little old for that shit?"

"You sound like my wife and daughters. I was in the Green Zone solely as a trainer; you know, sittin' by the pool stuff, teaching rookies younger than you how to keep from getting blown up. Then the surge happened, and well . . . I couldn't handle worrying about my guys, wondering who'd come back in a body bag. I figured they'd be safer with me going out on patrol with them. One day we were in Tikrit and an RPG-7 hit a propane tank on a local's house. I ran in and dragged two kids out, only to be hit by hot frag during the explosion. My legs were badly burned, plus there was shrapnel that required surgery to remove. They shipped me to Guantanamo, then back to Kauai. Two surgeries and three months later this guy bin Rashidi contacts me and says Dubai needs a submersible trainer and lead pilot to capture live sea species. Easy stuff; good money. They sent me video footage of that Dunk and that sealed the deal. I had no idea the institute had sold them Manta subs until I arrived. Four months at sea and we've barely gotten wet."

"Just the same, please don't tell my father I'm out here."

"He already knows. When you skipped town, he called his Scottish pal, Zachary Wallace, who has connections in Dubai. Wallace told him you're on board. He also convinced your old man to reconfigure the *Tonga*'s two subs with *Valkyrie* lasers."

"Lasers? What the hell for?"

"Who knows? Your dad ordered me to restrict your activities and not to allow you to set foot on the *Tonga*."

"Screw that, Kenney. I'm the best pilot you've got."

"For the daredevil stuff . . . maybe. When it comes to staying within mission parameters you're a royal pain-in-the-ass. I'm giving you one mission at a time; take an unnecessary risk and I'm pulling you off the duty roster. And what's this stuff about Nick Porter riding shotgun with you?"

"I looked into his eyes; he's not afraid."

"Then he's stupid."

"His father said he graded out tops in sonar."

"Which would actually mean something if you were nine miles down in the Panthalassa Sea, covered by a rock ceiling. Here you've got a trawler and supertanker patrolling the surface, equipped with sonar and the best hi-tech fish-finders oil money can buy. I'll be in your ear telling you where to turn before Porter can utter a word. The kid's a gamer, but his prosthetics slide off the Manta's foot pedals. If you're exhausted or injured and he needs to take over—what then?"

"Give him one shift, Kenney, that's all I'm asking."

"One shift; but only if you answer me honestly. Buchwald—are you tapping that?"

David grinned. "How'd you know?"

"The way you were eyeballing her, with the emphasis on the *balling*." Kenney Sills shook his head. "You live to buck authority and she's a control freak. Where do you think that ship's headed? Ah, screw it . . . there's a million square miles of sea for these monsters to hide in, we could be at this a year and still not catch a whiff. Go on, find yourself an empty stateroom and get some shut-eye. But if this boat starts rockin' in calm seas I'm kicking down your door and putting you on trawl duty."

7

|||||||||||||||||||||||||||||||||||

Peace Island Hospital
Friday Harbor, San Juan Island

Terry Tanaka-Taylor waited for the cab driver to remove her suitcase from the trunk of his taxi before handing him a twenty dollar bill. "Keep the change."

"Thanks. Ma'am, are you all right?"

She waved, managing her way slowly up the handicapped ramp, wheeling her suitcase behind her.

Parkinson's Disease. Michael J. Fox had called it the gift that keeps on taking. Eighty percent of the neurons in Terry's brain responsible for secreting dopamine had shutdown before her first telltale symptom had appeared years ago, and now the degenerative disease was progressing. Resting tremors, slow movements that fell under the term Bradykinesia; postural challenges that affected her balance . . . worst of all the damn rigidity. The muscles on the right side of her body felt like they were coated in lead, especially where her quadriceps inserted into her hip, forcing her to shuffle and lean forward when she walked. A friend with advanced PD had once joked that Frankenstein suffered from Parkinson's, and now Terry found herself struggling to stay upright on leg muscles that felt like they were adhered to the ground.

If Parkinson's was a forest fire, then stress acted like gasoline, exacerbating her symptoms. The last six months things were as bad as she could remember. Her son had attempted suicide. The institute was shut down, its attractions gone. A fresh batch of lawsuits were being filed against her family and their business . . . and now Jonas was laid up in the hospital, having nearly perished in a helicopter crash.

And once more, these damn sharks were to blame.

Terry entered the hospital lobby, only to be swarmed upon by the media.

———

Considering the extent of the damage to the Coast Guard helicopter, Jonas Taylor's injuries had been minor—a concussion, bruised ribs, and a fractured left radius bone close to his wrist. Sitting up in bed, he held his arm out as an orthopedic tech wrapped florescent-orange gauze from his left hand up to his elbow, the wet material quickly setting into a cast.

Dr. David Thomas Ford entered his "celebrity" patient's private room, having just given a statement to the horde of reporters and news crews gathering in the lobby. An emergency room and hyperbaric physician, the former medical director of the Free Hispanic Mission had moved his family from Columbia, South Carolina, to the San Juan Islands because of his addiction to SCUBA diving. Dr. Ford's office walls featured photos of his dives with schools of hammerhead sharks, bull sharks, and his experience hitching a ride on the back of a whale shark. Like the other islanders, he was not happy with the recent ban on water activities, forced by the relocation of the Megalodon siblings.

Leaning on his patient's bed, Dr. Ford shined the ophthalmoscope's light into Jonas's left eye, examining the interior structures of his retina. "The blurriness should clear in a day. If it doesn't, I'll set you up with our ophthalmologist."

"The eye's fine; breathing's the challenge. Last time I bruised my ribs was playing football my junior year at Penn State. I remember it hurt for weeks."

"What was that . . . about a century ago?" Mac entered the room, limping noticeably.

"Mac, they told me you were okay."

"I jammed my left knee when we landed. Probably tore the meniscus. At least I was strapped in. Hey, doc, were you the one who treated the diver?"

"Yes." Dr. Ford shifted the scope to Jonas's right eye.

"Did the guy say anything to you before he went into a coma?"

"We induced the coma, Mr. Mackreides, and no, the brain trauma was too severe. But I know the patient; he's a local dive master."

Jonas shut his eyes against the purple spots remaining from the exam. "Doc, any idea why a dive master would violate an ordinance and risk his life to enter the water with Bela and Lizzy in the area?"

"Oldest reason in the book—money. Lucas Heitman spent a lot of time with a local Russian mobster by the name of Alexi Lundgard. Alexi's girlfriend was the woman aboard the charter boat your monsters sank. I'm guessing Lucas was retrieving something Alexi had stashed in the shallows. The water's not very deep coming out of the strait; Lucas probably didn't think the Megs would venture that close to shore."

Dr. Ford marked something on Jonas's chart. "You have a grade-2 concussion. I'm discharging you, but take it easy for a few days. If you were intending to fly home, I'd wait at least until Monday. That should give you plenty of time to game plan."

"Game plan?"

"Your two sharks have killed three people in the last week while shutting down the tourist trade. What are you two schmucks intending to do about it?"

Jonas looked to Mac, who shrugged. "I dunno, doc. The induced coma sounds nice. What do you think, J.T.?"

Before he could respond, Terry entered the room.

Mac took one look at her expression and rose from his chair to leave. "Terry, so good to see you. Dr. Ford, wait up—I have an in-grown toenail I'd like you to look at."

"Mac—sit." She turned to the physician. "Can you arrange transportation to our hotel without those reporters following us?"

"I suppose we can smuggle the three of you out in an ambulance. Just give the nurse about thirty minutes to process your husband's discharge papers."

"Thank you." Terry waited until he left. "Mac, you have a wife and a newborn son at home. Haven't you had enough of this cowboy stuff? And you"—she turned to her husband—"where is *our* son?"

"Last I heard, he and Monty were en route to the Sea of Japan to rendezvous with one of the Crown Prince's supertankers—not the one that's after the Lio. Kenney Sills is in charge of the submersible crews; he promised to keep David under control."

"Kenney Sills? Why does that name sound familiar?"

"He was one of our original Manta test pilots. You remember . . . the Navy SEAL?"

"I remember a *former* Navy SEAL who used to get shitfaced drunk every Friday night with Mac. Would that be the responsible adult you've entrusted with my son's life?"

"Maybe I should wait outside." Mac headed for the door.

Terry took the vacated chair. "You're a good man, Jonas . . . a good father. I've tried to be a supportive wife; but I can't take this anymore. The stress plays havoc with my Parkinson's, and I have no interest in giving your eulogy. My terms are simple; either you come home and let the Coast Guard handle Bela and Lizzy or I'm leaving you."

Taiji, Japan

The town of Taiji is located on Honshu, Japan's largest and most populated island. Thirty-five hundred residents occupy this small coastal village, where fishermen trace their ancestral roots back to the whaling trade.

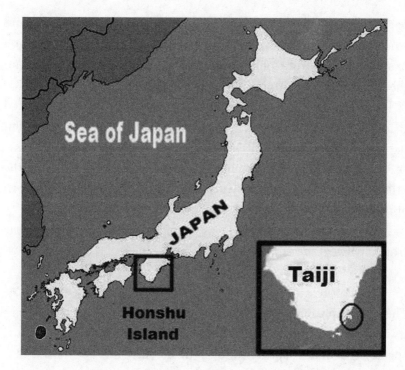

Enter Taiji today and one would get the impression that the locals have evolved into cetacean lovers. A life-size statue of a humpback whale and her calf greets visitors against the backdrop of Kumana-nadu Sea. There is a whaling museum that chronicles the town's history and an aquarium where live dolphins perform. Images of smiling cetaceans are everywhere; from the dolphin-shaped tour boats that circle Taiji Bay to the myriad of cartoons posted in local businesses and restaurants. To the casual observer it would appear that the people of Taiji truly love their dolphins—only for different reasons than one might think.

Each September through March, thousands of dolphins return to Japan's southeastern Pacific coast as part of their primordial migratory pattern. Every day, a dozen Taiji fishing crews head out to sea in "banger boats" to meet them. Hammering away at metal poles attached to the sides of their vessels, the fishermen create a noise barrier which panics the mammals and herds them toward shore where they are netted in one of Taiji's shallow lagoons. Thus begins a brutal two-step protocol long kept secret from the rest of Japan and the international community.

Phase one was slavery. Female bottlenose dolphins were selected from the group by dealers who sold them to marine amusement parks for upwards of $150,000 a piece. Divers in wet suits wade through the frenzy of frightened mammals, tying ropes around the tails of coveted specimens, which are hauled into boats in front of approving locals and protesting visitors.

Phase two of the enterprise was far more brutal, performed away from any eyewitnesses.

The two-man submersible was dark brown on top with a white belly, its nine-foot wingspan similar to that of *Manta birostris*, the aquatic species that had inspired its design. Its skin was composed of a

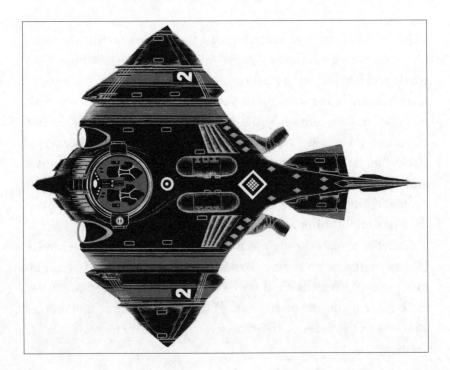

seamless layered acrylic, its interior cockpit sealed within a spherical escape pod that could withstand 19,000 pounds per square inch of water pressure. As an added escape feature, two hydrogen tanks were mounted on its back, capable of temporarily transforming the sub into a rocket.

David Taylor was feeling restless. For the last four hours the two Manta subs had led the trawler and supertanker on a slow journey of boredom through the deep waters off the southeastern coastline of Japan. The cockpit-cam had captured him relieving himself and picking his nose; the outer camera faring slightly better when they had joined up with a pod of dolphins. There was no sign of the fifty-ton ichthyosaur trio, nor was there much promise in the narrow swath of sea Kenney Sills had outlined twenty miles south of the mainland.

David continued testing the commander's orders, gradually distancing his submersible from the Manta piloted by Colton Wright and Paul Rudd.

Nick Porter knew what he was doing, but said nothing. Situated in the co-pilot's seat on his right, the nineteen year old was just happy to be included in the mission and openly reveled at David's piloting skills and the olive-green night-vision panoramic underwater view provided by the cockpit glass's nocturnal setting.

"This is amazing . . . you are an amazing pilot!"

"Dude, chill out, we're cruising on auto-pilot."

"*DB-II* to *Manta-Two*, you're drifting off course again. Mr. Taylor, I want you within six kilometers of *Manta-One*."

David winked at Nick. "Sir, I'm not up on the whole metric thing. How many miles is that?"

"Slightly more than three miles; you've pushed it to five. Adjust your heading to two-five-zero."

"Two-five-zero pushes us headfirst into an easterly current, Commander. I wouldn't want to risk losing the exterior camera; I'm not sure the housing could handle it."

"Very well. Maintain course and speed, Mr. Taylor, we'll come to you."

Damn. David watched his sonar screen as *Manta-One* altered its course.

He turned to Nick, who was doubled over, his prosthetic hand pressing the headset to his ears. "What is it? The shonisaurs?"

He shook his head. "I hear . . . screaming."

David switched his headphones from radio to sonar.

The sound was very faint, the source still a distance away. That Nick had heard it at all was impressive as it wasn't a reflection of their active sonar, but a haunting chorus of high-pitched squeals.

"Nick, get me a heading."

"Course zero-one-zero, range nine point seven kilometers—sorry, that's about six miles—due north."

David switched back to the radio setting. "*Manta-Two* to *DB-II*; Nick's detected an unusual disturbance on sonar—we're changing course to investigate." Without waiting for a reply, he pushed the joystick to the right and pressed his left foot pedal to the floor, sending the Manta banking hard to starboard.

Rising to within sixty feet of the surface, David accelerated to forty knots—the submersible's top speed. Nick braced himself as best he could with his four metal appendages, grinning from ear to ear.

Commander Sills did not share the young sonar operator's enthusiasm. "Mr. Taylor, return to course two-five-zero immediately; that is a direct order."

David turned to Nick. "Switch sonar to the external speakers so the rest of the world can hear what we're hearing."

"Belay that request, Mr. Porter! David, remember what we talked about—"

The sound of a hundred tortured squeals filled the cockpit, cutting off the enraged commander.

Nick shouted into his mouthpiece, "Range—two miles. I've got a fix on the target. It's a small town on the southeastern coast of Honshu Island called Taiji. The sounds are coming from a shallow waterway that cuts through a place listed on the GPS as Tsunami Park."

A text message appeared on the communication screen:

DAVID, DO NOT ENTER TSUNAMI PARK UNDER ANY CIRCUM-
STANCES OR YOU AND YOUR CO-PILOT WILL BE DISCHARGED
FROM THE MISSION AND SENT BACK TO THE STATES.

David glanced at Nick, the cries of distress cutting through both their souls. "Are you ready to lose your job over this?"

"Screw the job; I wouldn't be here if it wasn't for you."

David surfaced the Manta, the dark horizon of the Japanese mainland looming half a mile ahead. Nick guided him around a rocky coastline until they arrived at a narrow channel.

The waterway was only fifty feet wide, bordered on either side by steep cliffs. David reduced his speed to five knots and switched the cockpit glass from night-vision to normal—and suddenly they were awash in blood.

"My God . . . what is this place?" Nick whispered.

David felt queasy. "It's a dolphin slaughterhouse."

––––––––

Hours after the aquarium dealers had made their selections, the Taiji fishing boats returned to the lagoon. Dragging the nets holding several hundred remaining dolphins, they appeared to head out to sea—only to follow the coastline, where they entered a channel that led into a secret cove in nearby Tsunami Park. There, by bonfires' light under cover of tarps, the Taiji fishermen invaded the shallows, armed with spears and knives . . .

––––––––

The nose of the Manta pressed against the top of a thick brown net. On the other side of the barrier the dolphins wailed long agonizing squeals as their human oppressors, standing in the water in wet suits and pushing through the squirming masses in skiffs loaded with dead dolphins, hacked and speared and mutilated the mammals, adults and calves alike.

David gritted his teeth as he watched a Taiji fisherman coldly eviscerate a female bottlenose dolphin while its three month old infant attempted to leap over the top of the net, blood oozing from its blow-hole.

A primordial rage rose from David Taylor's gut. Gripping the joystick, he slammed both feet down on his pedals and rammed the net, driving it straight into the shallows until it collided with the skiffs, the sharp edges of the Manta's wings undercutting the divers' legs.

The dolphins rushed to the break in the gauntlet, the mortally wounded animals attempting to follow their fleeing brethren out to sea.

The bottom of the Manta skidded onto shore. Bright lights glared down upon the two young Americans inside the cockpit as armed policemen aimed their guns at the sub's bulletproof Lexan glass, yelling out commands in Japanese—every action recorded on film.

8

Friday Harbor, San Juan Island

The Bird Rock Hotel was more of a large house—like one might find on the Jersey Shore—than a hotel. Using a friend's credit card to hide their identities, Terry had reserved a suite with a king-size bed and a private balcony with a hot tub and view of the harbor. Any chance of Jonas enjoying a restful night was ruined by the pain he experienced while lying down and the agony of watching the sisters' latest attack, which still dominated Washington's evening news.

Heeding Terry's advice, Mac had flown back to Monterey to be with his family. Meanwhile, the Coast Guard announced it had deployed the *Active*, a 210-foot-long medium endurance cutter armed with a single 25 mm gun on the forecastle and two .50-caliber machine guns. It sounded like an impressive step except when one considered the sheer size of the Salish Sea, the unpredictable nature of the two juvenile Megalodons, and the reality that bullets fired at two hundred rounds per minute were only effective when the intended target surfaced.

By morning, the fog in Jonas's head had cleared. Donning a Seattle Mariners baseball cap and dark sunglasses, he followed Terry down their private outdoor staircase to take in Friday Harbor. After eating breakfast at the Rocky Bay Café they worked their way from one quaint shop to the next, the stress associated with the institute's mounting lawsuits momentarily forgotten . . . until they arrived at the wharf.

The Save-Our-Sharks society was established to stop the senseless slaughter of sharks by fishermen supplying Asia with fins for their soup. Sharks had the right to exist and served to keep the entire ocean ecosystem in balance. Like most conservation groups, S.O.S. lacked funding and publicity. A nonviolent faction of scientists and activists, they had come to San Juan Island seeking to turn the media's exposure of the Megalodon attacks into a rallying cry for their own movement. Marching on Friday Harbor, two dozen members of S.O.S. staged a peaceful protest before a small army of field reporters and their camera crews.

Opposing the group were the locals whose livelihoods depended on tourism and the islands' water-based activities—fishing charters, dive boats, whale-watching tours, kayaking, and Jet Ski rentals. For twenty minutes they threatened to toss members of S.O.S. into the sun-soaked bay waters until the police arrived to separate the two groups. Film crews desperate for any new angle on the story remained on the scene—until word spread that one of the local charter boat captains and his guests had encountered a Megalodon and were en route to Friday Harbor to hold a press conference that would "shock the world."

———

Paul Agricola believed in karma.

Thirty-five years ago, the only son of Canadian venture capitalist Peter Agricola was in the Philippine Sea aboard his father's 275-foot research vessel, the *Tallman*. The marine biologist and his team had been commissioned to gather data on NW Rota-1, a deep submarine volcano that towered twelve stories off the bottom of the sea floor in the Mariana Trench.

To explore the deepest location on the planet required special

equipment. Fastened to the *Tallman*'s keel like a twelve-foot rem-
ora was a gondola-shaped device that housed a Multi Beam Echo
Sounder (MBES), its dual frequency deepwater sonar pings designed
for mapping the abyss. Paul Agricola's biggest challenge in collecting data on a geological feature located 36,000 feet below the surface was the dense hydrothermal plume which coagulated a mile above
the bottom of the Mariana Trench like a swirling ceiling of soot.
The mineral layer effectively sealed in the heat percolating from the
seven-hundred-degree Fahrenheit waters spewing from thousands of
hydrothermal vents, but it also played havoc with the Echo Sounder's
sonar signal.

Paul's solution was to deploy the Sea Bat, a winged, remotely-
operated vehicle. Tethered to the MBES, the Sea Bat worked like a
charm, flying below the plume like an underwater kite, using its onboard sonar to relay signals back to the *Tallman* that identified every
object within its acoustic perimeter.

For three months the *Tallman* had circled the area above the un-
dersea volcano, gathering water samples while imaging a thriving
chemosynthetic ecosystem spawned by the hydrothermal vents. Having completed its mission, Paul's crew were set to retrieve the Sea Bat
when a very large marine animal, estimated to be over fifty feet long,
suddenly appeared in the sonar array's field of vision.

There was no doubt the blip was a biologic. The question: *what
was it?*

The extreme depth eliminated any possibility of the species being
a sperm whale, while the creature's weight—approximated at twenty-
five tons—ruled out a giant squid. The consensus among the three
oceanographers onboard was that it was most likely a very large
whale shark.

Paul Agricola had a different theory. He believed the creature to
be *Carcharodon megalodon*, a sixty-foot prehistoric species of great
white shark whose extinction two million years ago had remained an
unresolved mystery in the paleo-world. Furthermore, Paul intended
to prove the creature was a Meg by using the Sea Bat's electronic
signals to bait it to the surface.

For days the crew of the *Tallman* tried, but the predator, while interested, refused to rise above the warmth of the hydrothermal plume. And then another object appeared on sonar—this one a submersible.

The USS *Sea Cliff* was completing its third and final dive in the Challenger Deep, the deepest part of the Mariana Trench. The mission was top-secret, the three man vessel containing two scientists and the United States Navy's top submersible pilot—a thirty-year-old commander by the name of Jonas Taylor.

Exhausted from his third dive in eight days, Jonas was struggling to maintain the *Sea Cliff*'s position just above the hydrothermal plume when a strange glow appeared to be circling below the mineral clouds directly beneath the sub. A skipped heartbeat later a monstrous albino head rose majestically from out of the plume, its eight-foot-wide jaws hyperextending open to take a bite.

It was Paul Agricola's actions that had led the Megalodon to the *Sea Cliff*, forcing Jonas Taylor to execute an emergency ascent that had killed the two scientists on board. Dishonorably discharged, his career over, Jonas would return to the Mariana Trench seven years later—this time as a marine biologist intent on clearing his name.

As for the marine biologist who had actually discovered a Megalodon alive in the abyss, Paul Agricola was forced to take a vow of silence by his father, who feared his son's involvement with the U.S. Navy could lead to lawsuits against Agricola Industries by the dead scientists' families. Seven years later, Jonas Taylor's exploits in the trench would cause the disillusioned Canadian scientist to hang up his lab coat and move to San Juan Island to live off his father's hush money.

Thirty-five years ago Paul had missed his opportunity to land "the big one."

Late last night, the charter boat captain had caught a beauty.

Paul Agricola's guest was a retiring executive from BP oil—a personal friend of his father. The *Tallman-II* had picked him up in Vancouver yesterday afternoon, along with one of his local vice presidents and two female "escorts" in their late twenties. The plan was to spend the day sport fishing in waters not affected by the quarantine—although most of the action had taken place in the yacht's private cabins.

The fish had been hooked last night while en route to San Juan Island. Unaware his guests had been troll fishing in quarantined waters, Paul wanted to cut the line, but the oil executive had insisted on hauling in the catch so he could mount it in his game room. And so, under cover of darkness they had dropped the nets and dragged the fish on board.

The moment Paul saw the six-foot shark he knew it was Bela's offspring.

————

By the time the *Tallman-II* cruised into Friday Harbor, the docks by the yacht's assigned berth were swarming with news crews and locals. Thrashing in a net along the starboard side of the sixty-foot boat was a shark, its weight estimated by the fishermen in attendance at three hundred pounds.

Paul Agricola waited in the bridge while his crew secured the *Tallman-II* within its berth, mentally rehearsing the speech that would begin his long-overdue fifteen minutes of fame.

Upwards of a thousand people were standing on the wharf in front of the bow of the docked yacht, Terry and Jonas among them. They couldn't see beyond the wall of reporters and film crews, nor could they identify the game fish splashing about inside the net.

They were about to leave when the yacht's captain climbed down from his bridge, armed with a bullhorn. "For those of you who don't know me, my name is Paul Agricola and I'm the captain and owner of this yacht. Last night, while returning from a fishing trip outside the quarantined zone, we hooked a species of fish that has no business being in our waters . . . a predator whose presence proves that we've been lied to by the authorities and the man responsible for the two monsters that killed Captain Lebowitz and those two young women . . . God rest their souls."

Jonas pulled down the brim of his hat, his heart pounding rapidly in his chest.

"Before I became a fisherman, I was a marine biologist and a damn good one at that. I know why Bela and Lizzy came to these waters . . . they came here to give birth!"

The blood rushed from Jonas's face. He could feel Terry staring at him, her words lost in the din of the shouting crowd.

Paul Agricola raised his hand for quiet. When none came, he blasted the crowd with the shrill sound of his megaphone. "Shut your yaps and I'll show you. Behold . . . one of Bela's pups!"

Two deckhands leaned out over the starboard rail to steady the net now rising out of the water. A winch secured to a rope separated the catch from the net, revealing a six-foot shark with an albino head, dangling over the deck by its tail.

The crowd's reaction was eventually quelled by the S.O.S. leader, whose retort was amplified by his followers. "It's a great white . . . let it go!"

Paul Agricola responded with a megaphone screech that quieted the crowd. "It is *not* a great white! I checked its teeth. Meg teeth have a raised chevron on the back."

A CNN reporter called out, "How could Bela have had babies? There were no male Megs at the Tanaka Institute. Was this an immaculate conception, captain?"

Paul waited until the laughter and catcalls subsided. "For your information, more than five hundred different animal species reproduce without sex. Female greenflies birth exact replicas of themselves; same with the whiptail lizard. Hammerhead sharks have given birth in captivity to genetic clones of the mother. I have a friend . . . a fellow colleague who told me that he performed genetic tests on Angel's offspring six months ago; the results showed the three runts were Angel's genetic clones, indicating her eggs had been self-fertilized in her womb. Bring in an expert and have him perform a DNA test on this shark and if this female isn't a genetic match of Bela, I'll sell my yacht and give the money to Captain Lebowitz's family."

The crowd reacted, field reporters shouting over one another to be heard.

The shark arched its back, its upper band of pink gums exposed as it began suffocating. Paul signaled for his men to lower it back into the water.

"Jonas!" Terry grabbed his face between her palms to get her husband's attention. "Is this true?"

He nodded, his eyes focused on the baby Meg as it was lowered back into the bay.

The bay . . .

Sweet Jesus.

He grabbed Terry by the elbow and dragged her through the crowd, clearing a path with his cast.

"Jonas—stop!"

People were looking at him now; they had heard his name. A hand reached out and plucked the hat from his head. A pair of fishermen, both bearded and beer-bellied pushed through the throng and grabbed him.

"Here he is, the sum bitch that caused all the problems!"

The mob pressed in, the scent of body odor and alcohol filling Jonas's lungs as he was physically separated from Terry behind a tidal surge of prodding flesh and sweaty T-shirts, the locals driving him back toward the news crews.

Microphones were shoved in his face; artificial lights blinded his eyes. The shouts were deafening, the chaos igniting his primordial instinct to survive. He swung his cast and connected with a few heads, but he was a lost soul fighting an army . . . and suddenly he was underwater.

The ghost-white dorsal fin cut across the brilliant blue shallows of Friday Harbor, blending in with the sailboats docked like sardines around the perimeter of the Yacht Club. Moving in formation beneath Lizzy's pectoral fins was her darker sister, Bela, the two creatures swimming in a symbiotic defensive posture forged from having spent four years living in a tank where they perpetually sensed the presence of Angel, their overbearing mother.

The Megalodon siblings had homed in on the vibrations of Bela's distressed offspring when the yacht had traveled southwest past Shaw Island. Entering the bay, the sisters' sensory array had lost the female pup's distress signals when it had been hauled onto the boat.

When Paul Agricola had returned the juvenile Meg back into the water, he had forgotten that the shark needed to swim to breathe. This had been achieved en route to San Juan Island by the yacht's forward motion. With the boat docked, the shark quickly became entangled in the net and was unable to force water into its mouth to engage its gills.

The suffocating newborn thrashed along the side of the boat, its rapid heartbeats and desperate flailing actions immediately detected by sensory cells embedded in the lateral lines located along the sisters' flanks.

Bela shot past her sibling, homing in on the yacht and her dying offspring. With her belly pressed against the muddy bottom, she approached the net cautiously, her forty-six-foot girth barely squeezing between the starboard side of the yacht and the maze of pilings supporting the wooden pier.

The Meg nudged its dead pup with her snout, her left pectoral fin slipping beneath the *Tallman-II*'s keel, the right coming to rest between two pilings.

Sharks do not have a reverse gear. Wedged in too tightly to turn around, Bela was stuck.

With their attention focused on Jonas Taylor, the members of the media and the riled up locals never noticed the dark sickle-shaped caudal fin slapping at the back of the yacht. It wasn't until the *Tallman-II* began rolling to port that Paul Agricola and his crew suddenly realized they had an uninvited guest.

The water frothed as the twenty-one-ton Megalodon panicked like an angry bull stuck in its paddock. Repeatedly bashing her ivory-colored head from side to side, Bela dislodged a row of pilings, collapsing a city block-size section of Friday's Wharf.

One moment Jonas was being jostled by the crowd, the next he was sliding on his back amid an entanglement of bodies and camera equipment. A shock of cold whitewater blasted him in the face, then his feet struck something solid and he was driven underwater through a maelstrom of human shrapnel and splintered boardwalk until his body was pinned against the muddy bottom.

Bela twisted so that her tail now occupied the real estate vacated by the fallen pilings. Squeezing her head beneath the *Tallman-II*'s keel, she whipped her caudal fin into a frenzy as she lifted the yacht's bow onto her back.

Freed from beneath the Megalodon's right pectoral fin, Jonas fought his way to the surface. He wheezed several precious breaths of air, then kicked and paddled until he found himself straddling a dark island of flesh that felt like sandpaper and sliced through his jeans like barbed wire.

Gripping Bela's dorsal fin like a windsurfer, Jonas stood upon the deranged creature's back as the Meg plowed the *Tallman-II* sideways into the next dock over. He leaped off as the shark finally muscled its way free, swimming out to join its albino sibling.

Jonas grabbed on to a floating plank and held on. After a moment's rest he looked up, a strange sensation coming over him.

Lizzy was spy-hopping in the middle of the bay . . . *staring* at him. *Oh God . . . no.*

Slipping beneath the surface, the ghostly shark disappeared—

Jonas's heart pounded wildly in his chest as the albino monster's massive head rose before him, her gray-blue left eye gazing at him less than a body length away.

Sheer terror subsided to a sense of awe as the creature seemed to size him up.

You recognize me, don't you? You should know me; I'm the one who cared for you since the day you were born.

The weight of the moment intensified as the survivors ceased splashing and the sound of three hundred emboldened onlookers edged their way onto the decimated wharf in muted curiosity like Roman spectators, divided over whether to root for the Christian or the lion.

"You were always the clever one, Lizzy. You know I'm not fattening enough to qualify as a snack, let alone food. What are you thinking? Am I a threat to your young? Is that what your instincts tell you?"

Another twenty seconds passed between man and beast before the Megalodon's mammoth head slid back into the sea.

Jonas squeezed his eyes shut and waited to die.

The force of the blow shocked the survivors in the water out of their lethargy; the onlookers to let out a collective yell as Lizzy struck the *Tallman-II*'s starboard bow with the force of freight train hitting an eighteen wheeler. The yacht rolled hard to port and kept rolling, its flying bridge crushing the small dock separating it from the next berth over before coming to a ninety-degree resting place, its starboard rail high out of the water.

Paul Agricola fell feetfirst through the collapsing dock into the bay, the former marine biologist managing to swim between pilings to reach the next berth over. He surfaced in time to watch the *Tallman-II* sink another twenty feet before she rolled belly-up, the net holding the dead Meg pup surfacing beside her.

9

||||||||||||||||||||||||||||||||

Taiji, Japan

Hiking up Takababe Hill beneath a predawn sky, activists and foreign news crews trained their cameras on the secret dolphin killing cove where a beached submersible remained entwined in a fishing net. The protestors had organized within hours after links featuring the Manta's live video feed had gone viral on Youtube.

Kenney Sills knew the Manta and its pilots would be held captive indefinitely by Taiji authorities, so he convinced the Crown Prince to release the footage as a way to prevent their detention, under the guise of promoting the upcoming Dubai Aquarium reality show. Though the story had broken in 2009 via the Oscar-nominated documentary *The Cove,* very few people were aware of the film or the annual Taiji slaughter responsible for brutally killing 20,000 dolphins each year.

Taken from a dolphin's perspective, the Manta's footage shocked the world, forcing Japan's Chief Cabinet Secretary Yoshihide Suga to issue a hastily prepared statement via Twitter.

"Taiji fishermen are conducting a legal activity. Dolphin meat is part of Japan's diet and economy."

Activists responded immediately, stating that the justification of butchering these intelligent mammals as food was as dangerous to the Japanese public as it was cruel to the creatures themselves. Dolphin meat, often falsely packaged as whale meat, was neither an Asian delicacy nor was it nutritious; furthermore it contained toxic levels of mercury—a result of the species' diet. Consuming mercury damages the human brain and nervous system, affects eyesight, hearing, and motor skills. Mercury also harms fetuses, leading to birth defects.

The cabinet secretary was instructed to stop tweeting and address the public at a ten a.m. news conference, attempting damage control in what was becoming a public relations disaster.

Meanwhile, the confrontation between local police and the Manta's two pilots remained at a standstill. Each time authorities attempted to hook a tow line to the sub's exterior, David Taylor countered with an electrical discharge through the outer hull, effectively tasering any unlucky fisherman or policeman within two feet of the sub.

By nine-thirty a deal was struck; the reality show producers agreed not to air footage of the dolphin slaughter during the season, in return for the release of their submersible and its crew.

David Taylor was furious when informed about the arrangement by text. He and Nick Porter watched and waited while the netting was cut and the sub pushed backwards into the water by six angry fishermen and a police officer, all of whom were cursing at him and spitting on his cockpit glass.

David gave them a farewell *zap* that had them screaming in agony. Executing a tight 180-degree turn, the pilot raced the Manta out of the bloodstained waters of the cove to cheers from activists poised on the hillsides.

Any good feelings were quickly quashed by the radio transmission.

"Mr. Taylor, I am sending you the *DB-II*'s coordinates. You will plot a course, engage the autopilot, and return to the trawler immediately."

"Kenney—"

"Those are your orders, Mr. Taylor. Commander Sills out."

Damn, he's pissed. David turned to his co-pilot, who was listening intently on sonar. "What is it?"

"Banger boats. They're driving another dolphin pod inland."

"Sonuva bitch! Give me the bastards' heading."

"No way."

"Nick, all I'm going to do is chase the dolphins back out to sea using our active sonar. A couple dozen pings should do the trick."

"David, we're already in enough trouble."

"We're not in trouble; we're history. What are they gonna do? Fire us twice? Now give me the damn heading."

"One-three-seven, just about six miles out."

Diving the sub, David adjusted his course, accelerating to thirty knots. He was feverishly exhausted, desperate for sleep, but there'd be plenty of time for that on the ride home. *Cargo plane, no doubt. Or they could just drop us off in Tokyo and force us to pay for our own return tickets. I think Mom has an aunt living in Kyoto . . . maybe Monty and I can—*

"David, didn't you hear me? You're heading straight into the dolphins' path! Two hundred yards and closing fast."

David switched the sonar from PASSIVE to ACTIVE, instructing Nick to continuously hit the switch. A series of piercing *pings* reverberated from the Manta, creating a wall of sound.

They heard the squeals first and then out of the deep blue appeared dozens of frightened dolphins, the mammals zigging and zagging, their internal compasses gone haywire. Chased from one echolocation-maddening sound into the next, the pod broke away from the sub, scattering in multiple directions.

Sixty feet overhead, the fleet of approaching fishing boats slowed, their captains unsure of what had just happened.

David cheered, pumping his fists.

Nick Porter signaled for quiet. "There's something else coming at us . . . something really big. You need to get us out of here—change course!"

David veered hard to starboard as the adult male shonisaur suddenly appeared off their port wing, the seventy-five-foot ichthyosaur's dolphin-like mouth snapping at the sub's tail.

His heart pumping with adrenaline, David shot to the surface, the sub launching out of the water between two banger boats.

The ichthyosaur attempted to follow, its immense girth—wider than that of a sperm whale—striking one of the boat's keels as the creature leapt from the sea like an oversized humpback whale.

The Manta's wings caught a thirty knot headwind and the craft went airborne, gliding over the water like a flying fish before skidding upon its belly.

David executed a quick surface dive, keeping his head on a swivel as he attempted to relocate the big male ichthyosaur—nearly running head-on into its mate and her young.

"*DB-II* to *Manta-Two*: Mr. Taylor, you were ordered to rendezvous with the trawler."

"Kenney, we're being chased by the shonisaurs!"

"Okay kid, we're on the way. Can you lead them toward us?"

The two pilots gasped as the big male's open mouth suddenly bloomed in front of them, forcing David to pull into a one gee reverse loop and dive—the female's jaws snapping at him from above.

Swooping up and away from the sea floor, he raced the Manta past the fishing boats into open water.

Nick continued pinging the active sonar with his prosthetic left hand. "They're following us, only you're going the wrong way! The tanker's to the east; course zero-eight-zero . . . six kilometers!"

"Stop using the metric system!" Stealing a peek at the sonar monitor, David executed a long, sweeping turn, fearful he was offering one of the adults an angle to eat him.

Sure enough, the male shonisaur made a bull rush at the portside wing. For twelve frightful seconds it was a dead heat, the twenty-one-year-old pilot pushing the Manta beyond its limitations as it veered away from the beast in a wide counterclockwise turn, the ichthyosaur keeping pace, its open jaws so close that David could see mangled bits of dolphin flesh caught between its eight-inch conical teeth.

"One-four-zero . . ." Nick yelled out, wedging his prosthetic arms beneath his seat, bracing himself against the torque of the wide 180-degree maneuver. "One-two-zero . . . one-zero-zero. Almost there . . . Zero-eight-zero—go!"

David pulled out of the turn, the sub jumping out in front of the ichthyosaur—as the rumble of the trawler's engines grew louder overhead.

"*DB-II* to *Manta-Two*: Trawl net float depths are set at two hundred and two hundred fifty feet. Ascend to one hundred seventy feet; maintain course and speed. Two hundred yards . . . one-fifty . . . Passing over you now."

The trawler's twin blades spewed two lines of whitewater beneath the surface as the keel roared past them.

"Eighty yards . . . fifty—brace for impact!"

The Manta sub soared three feet over a horizontal line of floats which marked the top of the mouth-like opening of the trawl net.

The male shonisaur went straight into the steel mesh trap until its snout struck the cod end marking the tip of the triangular enclosure. The net quickly tightened around the creature, pinching its four limbs to the side of its body.

The enraged ichthyosaur twisted and shook—to no avail; the bridle having been pulled closed, sealing the opening.

The trawler captain veered hard to starboard, the deeper trawl snagging the ichthyosaur's mate. The female attempted to spin around within the net, only the steel cables had been pulled tight.

The two trapped shonisaurs thrashed and fought until near exhaustion, their thirteen-foot offspring darting between them, refusing to abandon its parents.

Two hundred feet overhead, the *Dubai Land-II* circled in five-foot seas, its elated crew celebrating the culmination of their six month hunt. The *Mogamigawa* approached in the distance, its deckhands preparing the supertanker's crane that would hoist the captured sea creatures out of the water and into the ship's hold.

Jacqueline Buchwald paced excitedly by the starboard rail, debating whether to keep both ichthyosaurs in the same pen.

———

David circled the two nets, giving the captured creatures and their anxious young a wide berth. Coming down from his adrenaline high, he edited his mental "to-do" list. *Can't dock the Manta until the trawl nets are secured . . . that'll be another hour. Figure twenty minutes to net the little guy. Dock the sub, board the supertanker . . . grab some food and a hot shower, then eight hours' sleep. By that time Jackie should have the creatures secured in their pens and we can be together.*

"David—"

Better yet, maybe I can pull her away for a quickie and then get some sleep.

"Active sonar was left on. There's something out there, circling along the periphery."

"Another shonisaur?"

"I don't think so."

"Probably an orca waiting for its opportunity to grab junior. How big is it?"

"Fifty-two feet."

The blood rushed from David's face. "Where is it?"

Nick pointed.

David reduced his speed to three knots. In the distance he could see something ominous circling back and forth, its features becoming more distinguished as they approached.

It was a sleek creature, as quick as it was massive, weighing in excess of fifteen tons. Crocodilian jaws were lined with five-inch teeth; four short fins steered a hydrodynamic body powered by a thick, long tail.

David's pulse raced as he hovered the sub seventy yards from the creature, which was clearly growing more agitated as he neared. Now he understood why the family of shonisaurs had fled the Panthalassa Sea—the species sizing him up had been responsible for the ichthyosaurs' demise ninety-eight million years ago during the late Cretaceous. For the next thirty million years their kind had ruled the seas—until an asteroid had impacted the planet, leading to the extinction of the dinosaurs.

"*Dubai Land*, this is Taylor. How soon can you have another net in the water?"

"David, it's Kenney. What's wrong, pal?"

"Oh, nothing much. I'm just staring at the business end of a fifty-foot mosasaur and she looks seriously hungry."

10

Captain Steven Beltzer stood in the *Mogamigawa*'s bridge, his binoculars focused on the horizon. He was emotionally spent, having been up all night worrying about whether the Taiji fishermen would harm his son, Nick. In truth, he was angrier at David Taylor and his refusal to obey orders than he was at the Japanese.

And then, in the last forty minutes everything had changed; the capture of the two shonisaurs altering the pilots' status from zeroes to heroes. All that was left to complete the amazing turnaround was for divers to attach cables running from the supertanker's crane to the trawl nets. Once the two beasts were loaded into their pen, Steven would place a call to the boy's mother back in the States and bask in the afterglow of his decision to override her maternal fears and bring Nick along on the voyage.

Beltzer waited while his executive officer, Craig Myrick, systematically shutdown the supertanker's engines, beginning the ten-mile "braking" process calculated to bring the massive vessel's forward inertia to a stop in order to rendezvous with the trawler.

"All engines shut down, skipper."

"Full reverse, all engines."

"Full reverse, all engines, aye sir."

The radio crackled with static, drawing his attention. "*DB-II* to *Tank-II*, what's your ETA?"

"Seventeen minutes. Is there a problem, Commander?"

"Call it an unexpected challenge. The ichthyosaurs were being stalked by a fifty-foot mosasaur. It's circling the perimeter in full attack-mode. I can't risk putting divers in the water to connect your cable."

Beltzer's gut tightened. "Is the Manta docked?"

"Negative. We need the Manta to keep the mosasaur away from the two netted ichthyosaurs or we'll lose them."

"Dammit, Commander, my kid's on that sub!"

"Which is why we need the tanker. David feels the mosasaur will interpret the *Mogamigawa* as a far larger predator and back off enough to allow us to send down a diver."

"What diver would be crazy enough to get in the water with a fifty-foot mosasaur?"

"We're asking for volunteers. The Crown Prince is offering ten thousand per dive. Check with your SCUBA teams. If no one goes for it, I'll make the dive myself."

———

It had become a dangerous game of cat and mouse.

Three times the mosasaur had broken from its holding pattern to make a run at the juvenile shonisaur. The first two times the Manta had swept in and cut off the beast, the sub's pinging sonar enough to chase the creature back to where it had been circling. The last time the mosasaur had snapped at the submersible before it had finally backed off, blinded by the vessel's exterior lights.

David feared what the emboldened predator would do next.

"*Tank-II* to *Manta-Two*, do you copy?"

Nick switched his headset to the radio setting. "Manta here. Dad, where are you?"

"Less than half a mile to the east."

The massive keel could be seen in the distance, displacing the surface like an ominous dark iceberg, the supertanker's forward momentum reduced to two knots.

The mosasaur sensed the larger challenger and retreated another hundred yards before continuing its frenetic figure-eight pattern.

A dull whine reverberated through the sea as the trawler reversed its engines and began taking up cable, hauling the net containing the male ichthyosaur to a more accessible eighty-foot depth. The forty-ton shonisaur thrashed within its bonds, the strain on the steel cables causing the trawler to tilt astern and the winches to shudder.

David gave the approaching *Mogamigawa* a wide berth. The supertanker's port flank moved into place thirty yards away from the trawler, the massive vessel's presence agitating the four prehistoric sea creatures.

The tanker's crane operator lowered a hoist line composed of eight four-inch-thick steel cables attached to a three-foot-wide U-shaped shackle. Minutes passed, and then a lone SCUBA diver wearing a wet suit and facemask fitted with a radio entered the water. Slipping his right arm inside the shackle, he signaled to the crane operator to release slack, hitching a slow, steady ride to the trawl net holding the male shonisaur.

The Manta ascended, circling the sinking diver, who seemed to be having trouble equalizing. David stared at the man behind the mask a full minute before he realized it was Monty.

"Taylor to *DB-II*; Kenney patch me through to the diver."

"Go ahead, *Manta-Two*."

"Monty, it's David—can you read me?"

"No, but I can hear you. Actually, I can't do that very well either with my ears buzzing."

"Dude, you work in the kitchen; what the hell are you doing in the water?"

"Cooking sucks. You can't get face time slicing veggies."

"Do you know you're diving with a mosasaur?"

"Sure. What's a mosasaur? Is it that big flounder with the four flippers and beak?"

"That's the baby ichthyosaur. Never mind. Just stay close to the sub; I'll lead you down to the bridle."

"What's the bridle?"

"It's the thing that pulls the net shut. There's a big O-ring next to it. You need to attach the shackle to the O-ring. As soon as you do, I want you topside in the trawler while they haul the ichthyosaur out of the water."

"Did you know forty-one million Americans drink tap water that contains sex hormones and anti-seizure medicine. Maybe I should drink more tap water—"

"Monty, watch out!" David accelerated, blasting his lights at the curious juvenile shonisaur, chasing it back to its hiding place between the two nets.

———

A hundred and sixty yards to the south, the mosasaur descended. Blue water quickly melded into curtains of gray, the creature's dark dorsal pigment disappearing in the black depths.

———

It took Monty several minutes to secure the U-bolt to the bridle's O-ring, the former soldier unnerved by the size of the animal wriggling in the trawl net beneath him.

David escorted his friend to the surface, his mind easing only after Monty climbed aboard the trawler.

Kenney Sills's voice snapped him awake. "The other Manta has launched. Dock your sub, David. We'll do a crew change while the first ichthyosaur is being moved. You and Nick earned some needed rest."

David's eyes followed the second sub as it slid into the sea, its pilot's hesitation in leaving the shadow of the trawler indicating a healthy fear of their environment. "If it's all the same to you, Commander, I want to be the one escorting the diver on his second dive. Monty's a friend; he'd do the same for me."

———

Jacqueline Buchwald stood by the tanker's port rail, walkie-talkie in hand as she and thirty other crewmen watched the first ichthyosaur rise out of the water. She had converted pens one, two, and three into one large holding area to accommodate the two adult shonisaurs and possibly their young, but she was more than ready to use junior as bait to net the mosasaur. *Shonisaurus* was a sea cow compared to the prehistoric hunter. That it had been stalking the trio of ichthyosaurs was beyond sheer luck.

Metal groaned as the crane's counterweight adjusted to compensate for the 80,000-pound behemoth now rising out of water. Jackie knew the device could handle the weight, though it was not as large as the crane aboard the *Tonga*—that equipment had been specifically designed to wield the *Liopleurodon*'s ungodly mass.

The onlookers followed the crane as it swung the netted creature overhead and lowered it into the tanker's hold. Jackie squeezed through the crowd, taking the stairs down into the ship's infrastructure to supervise the unloading and care of their precious cargo.

———

Matt Evans maneuvered *Manta-One* around the netted female ichthyosaur, marveling at the size of the creature. "Fucking Taylor; six months we patrolled the Philippine Sea and you know he's going to get the full bounty on both of these monsters."

Eric Stamp fumbled with the settings on his headset. "Don't forget Nick Porter. Talk about luck. The guy wasn't even on the active roster before the 'Boy Wonder' arrived."

"You realize what we have to do, don't you, E?"

"Capture the *Shonisaurus* runt."

"Screw the runt. I want that mosasaur. That fish is worth both of the Ickies combined."

"Marine reptile."

"If it evolved gills like the rest of the Panthalassa species then it's a fish. Where is it anyway?"

"About two thousand feet below us. I don't think it'll come up with the tanker in the area. The only reason it's still lurking is because it wants the runt."

"Then let's bring it to him. The Manta is equipped with a net. The moment Big Mama leaves the water we'll capture junior and use him to lead the Mose into the *DB*'s trawl net."

"I don't know, Matt. The sub's net is made out of nylon; it may not even hold the runt."

The radio chirped. "*DB-II* to Mantas: *Tank-II* reports the big male is safe in its pen. Trawl net is back on board and is being readied for deployment. We're going to begin taking up slack on the female. *Manta-Two* will escort the diver to rig the net; *Manta-One* will maintain a defensive position sixty feet below the trawl net's cod end."

"*Manta-Two*; acknowledged."

"*Manta-One*; acknowledged." Eric turned to his pilot. "If we're going to do this then you'd better grab the runt while its attention is still focused on its mother. Once she's out of the water junior's going to go ape-shit."

The trawler's winch engaged, gathering up slack on the net holding the female. The ichthyosaur thrashed about for twenty seconds and stopped, conserving its energy.

The fifteen-foot juvenile flitted about nervously, following its mother to the surface.

———

The sun was setting, the weather picking up. Having survived his first dive, Monty was shaking considerably less as he secured his swim fins to his bare feet and made his way down the trawler's stern ramp to the crews' applause. Knee-deep in the water, he turned to James Gelet and offered the reality show camera man a thumbs-up, then jumped awkwardly into the sea.

The O-ring swung several feet above the five-foot waves like a pendulum. Monty swam over and reached up but was unable to secure the device.

A Middle Eastern voice crackled in his ear. "Galley-boy, this is the crane operator. If this O-ring hits you in the head it will crush what little is left of your brain. Get out of the way so I can lower the hoist line."

Monty knew several Arabic expressions ripe for the occasion but refrained, knowing they'd be edited out. Instead, he went with an old Paul Simon song, mangling the lyrics. "Just drive the bus, Gus, we don't need to discuss much. Just drop the O-ring, Ali, and I'll hook the fishy."

"You are a strange man." He unleashed the hoist line, sending the O-ring dropping like an anchor.

Without thinking, Monty reached out for it—a frayed edge along one of the steel cables catching his right glove, dragging him by his arm into the depths.

Monty yelled out for help as he fought to free himself, the stabbing pain in his ears unbearable.

Manta-Two swooped in beneath him, David able to catch the O-ring on the sub's port wing . . . followed by Monty, who splayed across the cockpit face-first, staring at his friend on the other side of the bulletproof glass.

"Dude, you okay?"

Monty nodded as he pinched his nose and held his breath, increasing the internal pressure in his sinus cavity and ear canals until his ears popped. Sucking in deep breaths of air, he tore the rubber glove from the cable and pushed the heavy U-bolt over the side.

He gave David a thumbs-up and was about to follow the hoist line down another forty feet when the ichthyosaur's agitated offspring suddenly charged the sinking U-bolt, caught it in its mouth, and shook it wildly before releasing it.

Monty stared at the fifteen-foot, three-ton sea creature and decided not to mess with junior.

"No worries, diver, we're on this."

Before Monty could figure out who was speaking to him, the second Manta rose from the depths and circled Big Mama.

The juvenile *Shonisaurus* charged the sub—only to be enshrouded in a bright yellow nylon net.

The runt darted off, sealing the net and hauling the submersible for a ride.

Matt Evans high-fived his co-pilot, allowing the cable attached beneath the Manta's prow to feed out its full sixty feet.

That was a mistake.

Seeking its mother's aid, the young ichthyosaur circled its trapped parent, entangling its own netting in hers—along with *Manta-One*, which was now pinned bow-first to the mess.

David circled, filming everything; Monty still perched on the sub like a hood ornament. "Kenney, you seeing this?"

"Looks like a major cluster-fuck. Mr. Evans, can you detach your cable?"

"Negative, Commander. The mechanism's jammed."

"Mr. Montgomery, looks like you get to play the hero. There's a red lever located along the underside of the Manta's prow. Pull it toward you and the cable should detach from the winch."

"Hold on, Monty, I'll bring you closer." David maneuvered around the fluttering juvenile ichthyosaur, now hopelessly twisted within its own net. The second Manta was pinned beneath the trapped off-spring like a Christmas tree ornament, its nose buried in the net.

Monty adjusted the pressure in his buoyancy control vest so he floated without having to tread water. Sliding off the wing of David's sub, he skulked over to the other Manta, its two pilots strapped vertically in their cockpit like an astronaut crew awaiting launch.

The sun had set, taking with it the sea's last colors of the day. Using his flashlight, Monty located the faulty winch but could not squeeze his arm far enough between the sub's belly and the creature's left rear flipper that was pressing against the net, to access the red lever.

"I can't reach it; it's tighter than a virgin's twat."

"Mr. Montgomery, can you attach the U-bolt to the O-ring? If you can we'll raise the trawl net and cut the sub loose on the surface."

Locating the hoist line, Monty swam it over to the bridle and quickly attached it to the trawl net, anxious to get out of the water before the gray sea turned completely dark. "Okay, Commander, you're good to go."

Monty jumped as the eight steel cables grew taught and the trawl net jerked to life, sending mama ichthyosaur and her offspring roiling within their bonds.

———

The mosasaur wriggled like a python along the sea floor, its senses registering the distressed movements of its prey. With a whip-like thrash of its thick tail, the creature rose, homing in on its escaping quarry.

———

For the last two hours, Nick Porter had been drifting off into thirty-second catnaps, knowing that his sonar array would alert him if his target closed to within a thousand feet. Now, as a wave of adrenaline washed away his fatigue and the mosasaur rose beneath them on a near-vertical plane, his mind reeled with the possibility that this could be the last few moments of his life.

His voice broke as he blurted, "It's attacking! Eight hundred feet and rising real fast."

David glanced at his sonar monitor, saw the mosasaur's speed and knew this time the cat meant business. "Monty, stay with the trawl net, let it take you to the surface."

Pressing down on both foot pedals, David whipped the Manta into a tight twenty-knot circle around the ascending ichthyosaur and its frightened offspring.

Gripping the steel net, Monty held on, his pounding heart adding to the chorus of dinner bells. Looking below, his eyes fixated on the monster's pale belly.

"Two hundred feet!"

Aboard the tanker, the crane operator's heart skipped a beat as he registered the giant winch buckle beneath him.

"One hundred feet . . . David, get us out of here!"

David waited until the top of the trawl net broke the surface before he accelerated toward the tanker's keel.

Ignoring the fleeing sub, the mosasaur launched straight out of the sea, its outstretched jaws clamping down upon the trawl net, its teeth sinking into the female shonisaur's front flipper—missing Monty by the length of its twelve-foot mouth.

The ichthyosaur jerked in wild spasms. Suspended out of the water by all but the tip of its slashing tail, the mosasaur refused to let go. Shaking its head like a dog in a tug-o-war, the predator's teeth sawed through sinew and bone, sending blood from the gaping wound pouring into its clenched mouth.

Twenty stories above the melee, the operator's cab trembled behind a wave of combative forces as the crane's counterweights and deck rigging attempted to equalize the combined masses of three sea creatures, three humans, and a submersible.

It was a losing battle.

First to go was the winch, which sparked in protest as it ground to a halt. That was followed by the front end of the cab lifting and bouncing on deck, joined by the gut-wrenching sound of bending steel latticework. The crane held, but its floating harness snapped, initiating a chorus of wrenching metal that sent the operator fleeing from his cab.

David surfaced the Manta, its two pilots incredulous. Thirty yards away the mosasaur was suspended vertically out of the water, its crocodilian jaws clenching the gushing limb of the trapped *Shonisaurus*. The writhing movements of the trapped female ichthyosaur were snapping the steel strands of the trawl net while threatening to drag the supertanker's hoist crane into the sea.

Monty hung on to the net by his gloved hands, his back to the gyrating creature. His swim fins dangled just above the mosasaur's snout and within six feet of the suspended Manta sub.

David's headset quickly became a cacophony of chaos as the sub's trapped crew and the panicked diver yelled at one another, drowning out the commands of Kenney Sills, who finally muted both parties.

"David, we've got about thirty seconds until the hoist line's steel cables start snapping. If you've got any ideas now would be the time to share them."

"The tanker has auxiliary nets rigged to secondary winches. Have the crew drop one into the water and I'll try to set it in position beneath the mosasaur."

"Roger that. What about the Manta?"

"Monty can't reach the latch. Tell them to eject the life support pod from the chassis before the cable snaps and the shonisaur sinks to the sea floor, taking them with it."

"Negative," Matt Evans yelled, unmuting his radio. "Taylor, you'll need us to position the net beneath the mosasaur. Have your boy try the latch again!"

Kenney Sills muted David's protest. "Mr. Montgomery, you wanted to be a reality show star—"

"Hell." Kicking off his swim fins, Monty freed his right hand so that he was now dangling by his left. Rolling onto his belly, he worked his way along the steel netting by his toes, the bucking actions of the wounded ichthyosaur rendering the task near-impossible.

The right eye of the mosasaur looked up and caught movement. With its murderous gaze now focused on Monty it wriggled harder, its teeth cutting through the yielding flesh of the shonisaur.

Reaching the sub's port wing, Monty again attempted to reach the latch, only this time he was even farther from the center of the craft. Toes bleeding, his hands numb, he unbuckled his buoyancy control vest, allowing the harness and his air tank to fall into the sea. Wedging his right shoulder beneath the wing, he inched his way toward the manual release, the sub's belly crushing his spine.

David watched helplessly as his friend disappeared behind the sub's wing.

"*Tank-II* to *Manta-One*: Auxiliary net's in the water. The winch should be able to handle the mosasaur—"

A metallic *swish* rent the air as a steel strand separated from the hoist line, whipping across a backdrop of crimson sky.

"Kenney, unmute me or I swear to God . . ."

The radio MUTE icon flashed off.

"Monty, it's David. The hoist line's going, get out of—"

"Got it!"

As David and Nick watched, the Manta fell away, plunging thirty-seven feet into the sea—followed by the mosasaur.

"Oh, shit." David submerged, catching the telltale bubbles of the creature's splashdown but not the mosasaur itself.

"Nick, find that monster. Monty, just hold on!"

"David, I can't."

"*Manta-Two*, watch your six!"

David whipped his head around, saw a mouthful of teeth, and jammed both feet to the floor while executing a hard starboard turn.

The mosasaur flew past his port wing and disappeared into the lead-gray sea.

Dangling forty feet above the surface, Monty closed his eyes and let go, falling through the chilly night air. He was accompanied seconds later by the juvenile ichthyosaur, the loosened nylon net falling away from its body.

Commander Sills's voice cut through the static. "Diver in the water!"

David saw Monty's telltale splash.

The mosasaur felt it.

Igniting his sub's lights, David raced at his friend from the north, the monster from the west, its mouth widening to engulf its prey in one massive bite—

—its jaws slamming shut on empty sea.

Monty flipped wildly in the bright yellow net, towed feetfirst behind the Manta's pump-jet propulsion engines which nearly blew the mask from his face. Seconds later he was bouncing along the surface before skidding painfully up the trawler's stern ramp ten feet behind the docked sub.

Unseen hands pulled him free of the nylon net. Dragging him to his feet, they tugged the dive mask free of his face to allow him to breathe.

Monty inhaled a deep breath, bent over in pain—and puked across the ribbed decking.

A wild cheer surrounded him. His entire body trembled as he looked up, his eyes following the trawler's searchlight cutting through the night.

Rising along the tanker's port flank, writhing like an alligator inside a steel mesh trap, was the mosasaur. Having just missed devouring Monty, the creature had torpedoed snout-first into the open mouth of the trawl net, towed in place by *Manta-One*.

David wrapped his arm around Monty's waist, handing him a bottle of water. "You okay? You look exhausted."

The Iraqi war vet took a swig, pouring the rest over his bare feet. "Did you know that every year about two hundred and twenty-five Canadian men fall overboard and drown attempting to urinate while standing in a boat."

"You just peed in your wet suit, didn't you?"

Monty smiled. "You know me well, *amigo*."

Kenney Sills approached, handing each of them a six-pack of beer. "Helluva job, gentlemen. Grab some food and a shower; you'll bunk aboard the trawler tonight. We've got a lot of work ahead of us. Your girlfriend wants the shonisaur runt recaptured before dawn."

"What about its mother?" David asked.

The former Navy SEAL shook his head. "Wounded specimens don't travel well. We'll kill it, load the carcass on board the tanker, and feed the meat to the mosasaur."

11

|||||||||||||||||||||||||||||||||

Friday Harbor, San Juan Island

By seven p.m. every parking spot located within a mile radius of
Friday Harbor High School had been taken. More than two dozen
news vans were situated on the school grounds, most having arrived by ferry from the mainland.

The bleachers in Turnbull Gym were crammed, the crowd flowing
over onto the basketball hardwood. Standing at a podium located
over the wolverine emblem at center court was Christopher Mull,
San Juan County's elected manager, a position that equated to the
island chain's mayor. Seated behind him were the council board
members.

Occupying the two chairs to the right of the podium were Cap-
tain Michael Royston, the U.S. Coast Guard sector commander and
Nick Van Sicklen, head of the Whale Museum in Friday Harbor.
Seated to the left of the podium were Jonas and Terry Taylor.

Christopher Mull ran a palm across his shaved head before turning on his microphone, the sound system greeting the attendees with
an ear-clenching squawk of feedback. "Sorry. We're going to get
started now, so if everyone can take a seat. We're here tonight to

decide the best course of action in regard to the Megalodon . . . am I saying that right, Professor Taylor? Yes? The Megalodon situation. We'll hear from our panel, then we'll open it up to questions from the audience. Upon concluding the meeting the members of the advisory council will vote.

We'll begin with Nick Van Sicklen. Nick, I know the museum uses webcams and hydrophones to keep tabs on the islands' orca pods, any chance you could use them to locate these Megalodon sharks?"

The University of Florida graduate addressed the crowd using a handheld microphone. "Unfortunately, no. Sharks are silent predators. They are also one of Mother Nature's most adaptable creations. As Captain Agricola rightly stated, some species like the hammerhead and blacktip reef shark can breed using internal fertilization, essentially eradicating the male component from the reproduction process. What you're left with are genetic replicas of the mother. Having examined the remains of the shark netted by Captain Agricola, I concur the juvenile's teeth possess the telltale chevron which distinguishes *Carcharodon megalodon* from *Carcharodon carcharias*—the modern-day great white. I now believe the sisters have turned the shallow waters off the San Juan Islands into a Megalodon nursery."

A loud murmur broke out, forcing Christopher Mull to *shush* the crowd. "Nick, are you saying these two monsters are breeding more monsters in our waters?"

"That's exactly what I'm saying. In time, Bela and Lizzy's pups will produce offspring of their own, and these waters will be off-limits to any craft smaller than a ferry."

Calls of "kill them" egged the crowd on.

The county manager motioned for quiet. "Nick, what do you recommend we do to prevent that situation from happening?"

"First, let's remember that Megalodon ruled the Miocene seas for most of the last thirty million years. What ended their reign was the last ice age and the rise of the orca, which are half their size but hunt in pods. Megalodon were solitary predators. Four to six bull orca can take down a Meg even the size of Angel. Bela and Lizzy instinctually knew killer whales were their enemy—which explains why they've been targeting the pods. The problem is that the sisters hunt together in a symbiotic pattern that has kept the orca at bay. And therein lies both the problem and the solution. All we have to do is to kill one of the Megs and the orca will take care of the surviving sister as well as their pups."

The Coast Guard commander smirked. "You make it sound easy; how do we do that? There's a lot of sea to patrol and these sharks are unpredictable."

"Actually, commander, they're very predictable. Threaten their nursery and they'll show up."

"And where's their nursery, kid?"

Nick pointed to Jonas. "Ask him, he knows. The guy's been their keeper since birth. He understands how the sisters think and react. The only reason we haven't stopped them yet is that he's been withholding information in order to protect them."

A hundred side conversations broke out, forcing Christopher Mull to use his palm as a gavel. "Let's everybody calm down. Professor Taylor, I think the people of San Juan County would like your response."

Jonas took the offered microphone from the high school sound man. "First off, there's no conspiracy on my part to protect the sisters; I want Bela and Lizzy removed from these waters as much as anyone."

The island official attempted to silence the catcalls by holding up his hand. "When you say 'removed' you do mean dead, don't you? Because that's what the rest of us want. We want these monsters and their young terminated."

The crowd applauded.

"Mr. Mull, I came to the San Juan Islands to resolve a problem—a problem created when the sisters were released from captivity by a former employee of mine who was working for a radical animal rights group. Despite everything that has happened, man is not on these sharks' diet. Furthermore, these creatures have demonstrated instinctive intelligence and surprising social skills in both their symbiotic relationship and their obvious desire to protect their young. Am I advocating a resurgence of the species? Absolutely not. I happen to agree with Nick—when it comes to the Megalodon pups, I believe the orca pods will police the Salish Sea; that's Mother Nature at work. But I will not help you needlessly slaughter Bela and Lizzy when other more humane options exist."

The crowd reacted—and so did Terry, who stared at her husband, aghast. "You lied to me. All this time you intended to recapture the sisters."

"The lagoon's empty, Terry. Think about it—we can permanently seal the canal doors and prevent this catastrophe from ever—"

The slap across his face stung, but it was not nearly as painful as having to watch his wife struggle to exit the gym.

Aboard the *Mogamigawa*

Jacqueline Buchwald entered the tanker's command center at eleven-thirty a.m. still wearing her overalls and safety harness. "Captain, I was told there's a call scheduled with the Crown Prince."

Steven Beltzer handed her a key on a rope. "Communication Suite-B. Lock up when you're done. You look tired."

"You try putting in a thirty-six-hour shift and see how your mascara holds up." Taking the key, she exited the bridge, descending one flight to the deck holding the officer's quarters.

The three communication suites were located at the end of the corridor.

She keyed into Suite-B, her nostrils immediately assaulted by the scent of old pipe tobacco. Tossing the entire ashtray into the garbage, she situated herself at the Wi-Fi station and entered her password on Skype.

The host was already logged in.

The Crown Prince flashed a smile. "Ms. Buchwald, so good to see you. Excellent work today . . . excellent. When can we expect the new arrivals?"

"The captain says eight days."

"Give me the status of the captured creatures. Are they in good condition? Will they survive the journey?"

"The juvenile ichthyosaur was in shock but made it through the night and should recover. Same for the adult male, which suffered surface lacerations from its extended time in the trowel. I placed the two shonisaurs in the bow pen, the mosasaur in the stern and drained the central pen between them to prevent the animals from detecting the other species' presence."

"And the mosasaur—how big is it?"

"Fifteen and a half meters; just under fifty-two feet. It's very aggressive; it'll definitely be one of the most popular exhibits. And yes, it's a female, so we can freeze its eggs to breed its successors. Same with the shonisaur runt. We got lucky there."

"I believe preparation and patience fosters luck. Isn't that right, cousin?"

Another caller's face appeared on the screen's left border—a stout man with a thick black goatee and unibrow, his eyes cold and black.

Fiesal bin Rashidi grimaced at his first cousin, the Crown Prince. "I am sorry, Your Highness, I missed the comment."

"I was just telling Ms. Buchwald that preparation and patience fosters luck."

"And this comment you now direct at me for my failure to capture the *Liopleurodon*?"

"It has been six months, Fiesal."

"And it may be six years unless you send me a pilot who has the *baydati* to engage the creature. Bait doesn't work; the monster surfaces only at night and keeps its distance from the *Tonga*."

"Then just use the trawler."

"We tried. Five months ago we managed to entangle the creature's hind quarters in one of the trawl nets. The Lio nearly dragged the trawler underwater with it. You have no idea how large and powerful this beast is. It is almost twice the size of the adult shonisaur your pilot managed to capture."

"Fiesal, the pilot was David Taylor."

Bin Rashidi's dark eyes widened. "David is aboard the *Mogamigawa*? Why wasn't I told?"

"I needed to know if he could be trusted, if he was enlisting on our voyage simply to seek revenge on the Lio for killing his girlfriend."

"And your verdict?"

The Crown Prince hesitated. "Ms. Buchwald, you've observed David's behavior—what do you think?"

"He knows he's the most skilled Manta pilot around, which is why he bucks authority."

Bin Rashidi snorted a sarcastic laugh. "He bucks authority because he is a cocky little shit like his father."

"Easy, Fiesal. Ms. Buchwald, has he moved on from Kaylie Szeifert or not?"

Jackie saw the look in the Crown Prince's eyes and felt queasy. "If you're asking me if I slept with David, the answer is yes. But it was just sex—more recreational than emotional. My role on this voyage is not to be a surrogate love interest for David Taylor."

"But you'll continue to . . . *recreate* with our young pilot if it means capturing the *Liopleurodon* and taking over the aquarium as our new director?"

And there it was—the offer that every female desiring to succeed in the business world feared—the enticement to spread her legs in order to move up in the company hierarchy. Only the Crown Prince wasn't asking her to sleep with him, he simply wanted her to continue to be with David.

Was that so wrong? After all, she was attracted to David and the sex was a welcome diversion they both looked forward to. Only now the Prince had made it a morality issue. But if she would have continued sleeping with him anyway, then what difference would it make in the scheme of things? She was already a candidate for the directorship, if continuing her midnight rendezvous with David helped him heal his broken heart, while solidifying her rightful place in the company, then it seemed a win-win.

"I'm committed to the best interests of the Dubai Land Aquarium, Your Highness. Whether David and I spend time together after hours is no one's business but our own."

"Then I assume you have no problem accompanying him and his associate, Mr. Montgomery aboard the *Tonga* to pursue the *Liopleurodon*?"

"As your most qualified marine biologist, it's where I expected to be."

The Crown Prince's smile did not match the harsh look in his eyes. "Shouldn't your first priority be to the three captured sea creatures aboard the *Mogamigawa*?"

Jackie's heart raced. "Of course, Your Highness. What I should have said is that I'll join David and his friend aboard the *Tonga* once the three sea creatures arrive safely in Dubai and have been stabilized in their new habitats."

"Fiesal, who is the marine biologist assigned to the *Tonga*?"

"Alexander Hardie; a competent scientist who is certainly capable of caring for the animals aboard the *Mogamigawa*. I sincerely doubt he is David Taylor's type."

Jackie felt her cheeks flush. *Assholes. They're playing mind games with me.*

The Crown Prince feigned weighing a difficult decision. "Fiesal, I think it best to have one of your helicopters transport Mr. Hardie aboard the *Mogamigawa,* and then fly Ms. Buchwald, David, and his friend back to the *Tonga*. Does that work for you, Ms. Buchwald?"

Jackie gritted her teeth against the fatigue and frustration, tears of indignity welling in her eyes. "Wherever Your Highness needs me."

PART TWO

THE
LIO

12

|||||||||||||||||||||||||||||

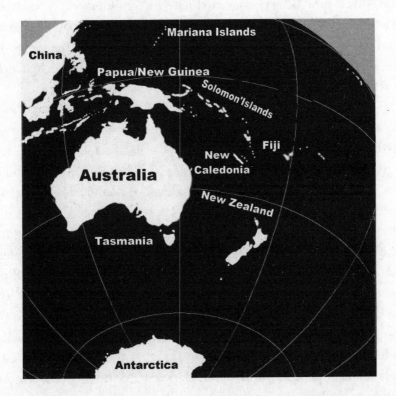

14 Miles Off the Coastline of Brisbane, Australia
Southwestern Pacific

The creature moved effortlessly through depth's darkness, its 200,000-pound frame leaving barely a ripple as it glided above the silt-covered sea floor. Its crocodilian jaws, thirty feet long from snout to mandible, remained open as it swam, channeling water into its gills past a gauntlet of ten- to twelve-inch dagger-shaped teeth, the largest of which jutted outside of its mouth. Every so often its massive fore flippers would sweep the sea, stirring the bottom into swirling eddies.

Liopleurodon panthalassa—the largest and most vicious animal ever to inhabit the planet—was a hybrid of nature, having evolved from a short-necked carnivorous marine reptile into a 122-foot-long gill-breather more than twice the size of its long-dead ancestors.

Pliosaurs first dominated the seas during the Callovian stage of the Middle Jurassic Period approximately 155 million years ago. After a long reign these amphibious air-breathers eventually died off, succumbing to plunging ocean temperatures generated by the ice age—an aftereffect of the seven-mile-in-diameter asteroid which struck Earth sixty-five million years ago.

The geological anomaly that saved and eventually trapped these monsters, along with a thriving food chain of ancient sea creatures, had formed in the depths of the Western Pacific 180 million years ago. Wedged between massive continental plates, the tiny Philippine Sea Plate was driven beneath its neighbors, its boundaries becoming volcanically-active rift zones which eventually forged the world's deepest trenches. Over tens of millions of years the erupting magma cooled into a ceiling above the nine-mile-deep sea floor which spanned hundreds of miles across the southern region of the Philippine Sea. Beneath this false bottom lay an isolated habitat nourished by hydrothermal vents and cold seeps. Stable temperate zones and an abundance of prey lured thousands of warm and cold water species into the abyss. Over tens of millions of years these prehistoric species adapted to life in the perpetual darkness. Marine reptiles like the pliosaurs evolved gills; other predators developed scent and vibration-based sensory systems.

Twelve million years ago volcanic activity sealed the Panthalassa's access points beneath the Philippine Sea. Among the last creatures to seek refuge in this abyssal purgatory was *Carcharodon megalodon*.

The arrival of another apex predator into its habitat had a profound effect on *Liopleurodon ferox*. To combat its new, better equipped rival, the pliosaurs grew enormous.

The female *Liopleurodon* continued its southeasterly trek, shadowing the pod of orca moving along the surface three thousand feet overhead. The killer whales were stalking their own quarry—a mother gray and her calf.

Ordinarily, the *Liopleurodon* would have taken the juvenile from below, but the orca posed a threat and the big female was still recovering from wounds sustained from its encounter months earlier with *Carcharodon megalodon*.

The clash of the titans had occurred in the Panthalassa Sea, ending in the surface waters of the Western Pacific Ocean. The *Liopleurodon* found itself trapped in an alien sea with a higher oxygen content and prey rich in blubber. These two variables combined to increase the creature's metabolism, sending it into a hyperkinetic state which forced it to feed more often. It also affected the animal's reproductive system, inducing the internal fertilization of one of its own eggs.

The *Liopleurodon* was entering its last trimester of pregnancy—the supertanker, *Tonga* shadowing its every move.

Aboard the *Tonga*

Fiesal bin Rashidi was a prisoner of his own ambition.

It didn't have to be this way. There were fifty-three cousins who nursed at the teats of the Crown Prince. Most were useless scoundrels who behaved as if it were their birthright to waste the kingdom's riches.

Not Fiesal. His father, a civil engineer, had sent him to live abroad at the age of twelve, enrolling him at a private prep school in England. With Dubai committed to tourism, Abdul bin Rashidi knew his eldest son would need a western education to stake his claim in the expanding Arab emirate.

Dubai had forged its own path in the Arab world when the Maktoum family had taken power in 1830. Under the leadership of Sheikh

Maktoum bin Hasher Al Maktoum, foreign traders were exempted from taxes, paving the way for the United Arab Emirates to become the leading commerce center in the region. Unlike most of the other autocratic nations, the UAE invested its oil riches back into its economy, transforming the desert into a metropolitan oasis.

Fiesal was a second-year student studying engineering at Cambridge University when al Qaeda terrorists hijacked four American commercial airliners on September 11, 2001. The event ushered in a tide of hatred aimed at all Arabs, the undercurrent of which had always existed. Never mind that al Qaeda had been conceived by the Afghani Mujahideen freedom fighters armed by the United States and supported by Saudi Arabia, in the eyes of most westerners a Muslim was a Muslim and not to be trusted.

Fiesal could register the lingering eyes of his fellow students. Strangers grew bold, questioning his presence at public events. Airport security nodded at him and whispered.

Things grew worse in 2005 after the July 7 bombings in London. Having graduated with degrees in civil and naval engineering, Fiesal could not find an employer willing to hire a Muslim, no matter what his qualifications. A month later Fiesal's girlfriend, Jourdan Coker, under pressure from her parents, broke off their engagement.

Fiesal had sublet his apartment and intended on returning to Dubai, when a friend introduced him to a marine biologist in need of an engineer. Dr. Michael Maren was as paranoid as he was brilliant—an odd chap who avoided eye contact when he spoke and trusted no one. His mother had died recently, leaving him an abundance of wealth to pursue his scientific endeavors. Maren was interested in exploring the deepest ocean trenches in the world and was looking to hire a naval engineer who could design an abyssal habitat and lab possessing a submersible docking station capable of withstanding water pressures in excess of 23,000 pounds per square inch.

The challenge was enormous, the requirement a bit baffling since the Mariana Trench, the deepest location on the planet, possessed a mere 16,000 pounds of pressure. Still, the job paid well and allowed him to remain in England. Over the next three years Fiesal tested a half dozen miniature models before coming up with a design stable enough to flood and drain a docking station nine miles beneath the surface.

Two titanium habitats were constructed while Maren's research vessel was fitted with an A-frame, winch, and steel cable strong enough to lower and raise the enormous weight. After five years of planning and construction Maren was ready to set sail to "an unexplored realm." Fiesal was offered a position on the maiden voyage, but the thought of spending upwards of a year at sea with the volatile scientist and his lover, Allison Petrucci, held no appeal. Accepting an offer from his father's firm, the engineer returned to Dubai to work on the emirate's new airport.

Eighteen months later, Fiesal was contacted by Allison Petrucci. Maren was dead, killed by one of the creatures he had dedicated his life to studying. After coercing the engineer into signing a non-disclosure agreement, the woman presented him evidence of an unexplored sea that dated back hundreds of millions of years, possessing ancient marine life that could be captured and placed on exhibit. For a seven figure sum she would provide Fiesal with maps which showed the access points into the realm her fiancé referred to as the Panthalassa Sea.

The Middle East was a battleground. America's military interventions and a failed Arab Spring had only added more fuel to that fire. Democracy was subverted in Egypt, autocratic rule festered in Syria and Iran, and military uprisings were tearing apart an already toxic situation in Iraq.

Fiesal bin Rashidi convinced the Crown Prince to fund the prehistoric aquarium theme park, believing that the venture would make Dubai the vacation Mecca of the world, presenting westerners with a more positive opinion of the Arab world while inoculating the UAE against the threat of radical Islam.

A high-speed rail would connect the new airport to Dubai Land

and its dozen five-star hotels. The completed aquariums were an engineering marvel—all that was left was the underwater safari required to stock the habitats.

Jonas Taylor was the unanimous choice to lead the mission, only the former navy submersible pilot and marine biologist flatly refused. He and Maren had crossed paths before; the last time culminating in Michael's death. The Tanaka Institute agreed to sell Angel's two surviving Megalodon runts to the Crown Prince, along with four Manta subs.

But there was another Taylor who captured Fiesal's eye—Jonas's son, David. The cocky twenty-one-year-old was not only the most qualified and skilled Manta pilot but seemed fearless around the Megalodons. A lucrative summer job offer in Dubai to stabilize the runts in their new aquariums brought David to the UAE; love would send him into the depths of the Panthalassa Sea.

Locating and netting the Panthalassa life forms proved more than a bit challenging. After several months only four different species were captured, two perishing within their tanker pens. And then Fiesal bin Rashidi laid eyes on the *Liopleurodon*.

The monster was an aberration of evolution; a specimen that Fiesal knew would easily become the identity of the aquarium. While the rest of his crew aboard the *Tonga* remained mesmerized by the surfacing creature, Fiesal fired a transmitter dart into the animal's back, ensuring that they wouldn't lose track of their prize.

That was nearly three months ago.

Half a year at sea changes a man; half a year of failure poisons ambition. The Lio refused to surface, and the *Tonga's* submersible pilots were too afraid to venture close enough to engage the goliath and lure it into the tanker's nets. Compounding the problem was the failure of bin Rashidi's second unit aboard the *Mogamigawa* to capture the three shonisaurs that had escaped the Panthalassa Sea. With only three of the twelve exhibits occupied, the Crown Prince's initial excitement about the aquarium had waned, turning Fiesal's optimism into doubt, his joy festering into resentment, frustration, and bitterness.

As the weeks became months, a sense of gloom seemed to hang over the *Tonga*. Desperate, lacking a game plan and clearly out of his element, Fiesal bin Rashidi lost the respect of his crew. The driving force behind the aquarium spent his days alone in his stateroom, a prisoner to his own ambition. Women no longer interested him, gold no longer shimmered. Stuck on a seemingly endless voyage of damnation, Fiesal bin Rashidi—once the favored cousin of the Crown Prince—had become his albatross.

And then David Taylor arrived on board the *Mogamigawa* and lady luck returned. Three animals captured within thirty-six hours, including a mosasaur!

It was as if the sun had shone for the first time in six months.

The Crown Prince arranged for a helicopter to transport David, his friend Monty, and the female marine biologist to the *Tonga*. Fiesal ordered three of his officers to give up their quarters to the VIPs. A buzz of excitement spread through the crew—the son of Jonas Taylor would take charge of the mission and capture the Lio. The *Tonga* would return home with its prize, families reunited, bonus checks cashed.

Fiesal stood on the bridge, his eyes focused on the transport helicopter approaching from the north, his entire future dependent on the whims of a twenty-one-year-old who either intended to help capture the largest predator on the planet—or kill it.

13

||||||||||||||||||||||||||||||||||

Friday Harbor, San Juan Island

"So here's my advice, J.T.: Kill those bloody Megalodons. And when I say kill, I don't mean you and Mac. Let the United States Coast Guard do the dirty work. Then go find yer son, sell the institute, and live out yer days happy, fat, and stupid."

Jonas opened his eyes, his heart pounding heavy in his chest. The hotel suite was dark, an outline of gray conforming to the top of the bedroom drapes. Turning to his right, he saw the face of the digital alarm clock—7:22 a.m.

He did not need to turn to his left to know Terry was gone.

For a long moment he thought about the dream. He and Zachary Wallace were both marine biologists, but that's where the similarities ended. Jonas was a man of action who was forced to become an academic in order to give his theories credence. Zach was a scientist—a gifted thinker forced to take action in order to prove his theories regarding a legendary life form living in Loch Ness.

Jonas had funded Zachary's energy venture years earlier and the two had become close friends. Still, there was something disturbing about the Highland-born American—at times it seemed he possessed a sixth sense about things that made Jonas feel more than a bit uneasy.

Like his insistence that every Manta submersible cockpit be refitted with pilot airbags. Zachary claimed that for weeks he had experienced a recurring nightmare about an accident involving David and knew the matter needed to be resolved.

That he was now being insistent over killing Bela and Lizzy was no less disturbing.

Jonas sat up in bed, gazing at the empty suite. He felt empty without his wife and he knew she was right. But the sisters were still his responsibility and he was not the kind of person who passed the buck.

The council members had held their vote last night after Terry had abruptly left the meeting. Eighteen votes to kill the sisters, three votes to capture. Nick Van Sicklen was tasked with locating the Megalodon nursery, Commander Royston with taking out Bela and Lizzy.

It seemed everyone *but* Jonas wanted the creatures destroyed.

Fuck it.

Rolling out of bed, he started a pot of coffee and then hustled into the bathroom, his bladder ready to burst. It was yet another "parting gift" of getting older. Shrinking prostate, bad knees, an arthritic back . . . His broken arm itched beneath the cast, agitating his already dour mood.

His morning inventory of ailments was interrupted by a knuckle rapping lightly but insistently on the door.

"Terry?" Flushing the toilet, he hurried to the door and opened it—disappointed to find Paul Agricola standing in the hallway.

"What do *you* want?"

The silver-haired marine biologist-turned-fishing boat captain looked uneasy. "I have a proposal. If I could just have two minutes of your—"

Jonas slammed the door.

Paul knocked again. "Come on, Jonas—two minutes. I brought breakfast sandwiches. Scrambled eggs, ham, and avocado on a fresh bagel." He held the take-out bag up to the peephole.

The door reopened, Jonas snatching the bag. "Two minutes."

Paul followed him inside. "Nice room. Sorry about the blow-up with the missus. I hear she caught the last ferry to Puget Sound. Probably en route to San Francisco as we speak."

Jonas sat at the kitchen table, unwrapping the second breakfast sandwich, having already devoured the first. "Ninety seconds."

"That wasn't thirty seconds. And that other sandwich was supposed to be mine . . . never mind. Listen, I know you don't want to kill Bela and Lizzy. I have a plan that can save them both and get you back in good with the missus."

Jonas chased the second breakfast sandwich down with a swig of orange juice.

"Don't they feed you?"

"I didn't eat dinner. So what's the brilliant plan?"

"You help me recapture the sisters, then sell me the Tanaka Institute for a hundred mill. Ten million dollars due on signing, the balance to be paid in ten-million-dollar installments over the next five years with a forty-million-dollar balloon payment in year six."

"What kind of deal is that? Each of Angel's last four years netted twice that much."

"And you're selling me a facility in desperate need of repair. The canal doors need to be permanently sealed, the Meg Pen Lexan glass has to be replaced. It would be cheaper for me to convert the Wild Coast exhibit over at the Vancouver aquarium—the animal rights groups are demanding the release of their Pacific white-sided dolphins—but I like California. Plus there are three new hotels under construction in Monterey that are desperate to get the institute up and running again—I'm sure I can get them to assist with my up-front costs."

"A hundred and fifty million with twenty million down, and you handle all liabilities, lawsuits, and settlements arising from the sisters' escape."

"Make it fifteen million down and eight year terms on the balance and I'll have my lawyers draw up the papers." Paul smiled. "You think I'm crazy."

"Certifiable."

"Maybe I am. Money . . . it means nothing to me; I inherited more than I can spend. Sure, the venture needs to be profitable, and it will be, but I've been wanting this since the day my research vessel accidentally led that Megalodon into your path."

Jonas gave him a hard stare. "What are you talking about?"

"Seven years before you led Tanaka's kid into the Mariana Trench. You were piloting those dives for the U.S. Navy into the Mariana Trench. My father's research vessel, the *Tallman*, was in the Philippine Sea at the time; my team was collecting water samples from a twelve-story-high underwater volcano using a deepsea drone called a Sea Bat. We were just completing a three-month gig when our drone's sonar detected a fifty-foot biologic circling beneath the hydrothermal ceiling."

"It could have been a whale shark."

"Whale sharks are docile; this thing was a predator. It went after the Sea Bat."

Paul poured himself a cup of coffee. "I knew it had to be a Meg. We tried to bait it with the drone—lead it out of the trench where we could net it. Instead, we ended up crossing paths with some rusty scow-bucket . . . the *Maxine D.*"

Jonas felt the blood draining from his face. "The *Maxine D* was our surface ship; its A-frame was used to launch our three-man bathyscaph, the *Sea Cliff*. Everything was covert; only the scientists on board knew why we were there. I was piloting the sub; it was my third dive in eight days. My job was to keep the sub above the hyrdrothermal plume while they used a remote drone to vacuum manganese nodules off the trench floor. At one point our sonar detected a school of fish, followed by this massive predator—a fifty-footer. We shut down everything until it passed by. Only it returned—you assholes led it right to us!"

"Jonas, we didn't know—"

"The scientists died—did you know that? The navy blamed me; it cost me my career . . . a dishonorable discharge."

"I know."

"You know?"

"I read your story. It should have been my story . . . *my* career. I was the one who discovered Megalodons living in the Mariana Trench, I still have the sonar records to prove it, only my father forbade me to come forward after we learned the *Maxine D* was a black ops vessel. Seven years later you returned with Masao Tanaka and his kids and I had to suffer through your fame and fortune."

"And death. D.J. died in that hell hole. Several dozen people have lost their lives because of these monsters."

"Oh, please. Dozens are killed every day in auto accidents but you don't see people giving up driving. Bees take far more human lives every year than sharks. Face it Jonas, you've lost the stomach for dealing with these creatures. Let me take over the reins while you drive off into the sunset in a Lamborghini."

"And how do you expect to capture Bela and Lizzy? Rod and reel?"

"When you moved Angel last summer, you used a hopper-dredge, yes? Agricola Industries owns two hopper-dredges even bigger than the *McFarland*; we lease them to the city of Vancouver. My crew will convert one of our hoppers into a transportation pen just like you did, only we'll keep the bin drained. When one of the sisters passes beneath the keel, we open up the doors and—"

"And the suction will vacuum the sea and the Megalodon right up into the hopper—that's actually quite brilliant."

"I thought so. And here's the real beauty of the plan—even if we only manage to capture one sister the other will follow the ship straight into the Tanaka Lagoon. The key is to bait the ship's keel doors with something that will bring the sisters in real close."

"One of the Meg pups. Do you know where the nursery is?"

"I have a pretty good idea. So? Are you in or out?"

Jonas shook Paul Agricola's thick, calloused palm, ignoring Zachary Wallace's warning. "Let's do this. Let's bring the sisters home."

14

||||||||||||||||||||||||||||||||||

Aboard the *Tonga*
17 Miles Off the Coastline of Brisbane, Australia
Southwestern Pacific

David awoke to Jacqueline Buchwald's naked torso curled around him from behind, her lips working their way down his neck as her left hand stroked his groin.

He rolled out of bed. "Sorry, I gotta pee."

"And here I thought you were enjoying my company."

"I was . . . don't move." He hustled into the water closet and closed the door.

The private head was small but a luxury afforded to only a few. Standing over the toilet, David relieved himself, gazing at his reflection in the bathroom mirror. *What are you doing? You came here to kill that monster and here you are, falling for another chick. What are you going to do when she wants to co-pilot the Manta with you? Act all chivalrous like you did with Kaylie? How'd that end up?*

"David, did you fall in?"

"Coming!" He washed off, rinsed his mouth with a dab of toothpaste, and then exited the bathroom.

Jackie pushed past him, squatting on the toilet. "What's wrong? Haven't you ever seen a woman pee before?"

"How's this going to work?"

She smiled. "I thought I'd wash up and then we'd screw each other's brains out."

"Do you talk like that because you think it turns me on or because it keeps you from connecting emotionally with me?"

"Wow. Where's all this coming from?"

"Just answer the question."

"I thought I was clear about this. Love isn't on my agenda; it's a commitment that steals focus and time from my career. Sex is sex; it gives me something to look forward to. But if you can't handle it—"

"I can handle it. But what if I start caring about you? What if I'm not ready to walk away after this hunt is over?"

"I don't know." She flushed, then washed up. "I work in Dubai, David; I'm vying for a huge promotion. I'm sure bin Rashidi would hire you full-time if you wanted to stay. But don't do that for me. You have to find your own path."

He watched her brush her teeth with his toothbrush. "Maybe. Or maybe you'd want to work at the institute?"

"Doing what? Overseeing your jellyfish exhibit?"

"What if the sisters returned? Angel came back."

She approached, nuzzling his neck while her hands explored his groin. "Megs are great, David, but we already have one. I want the Lio. Get me that monster and I'll make you a very happy man."

———

The setting sun hung like a burning orange ember over the western horizon, its blinding brilliance forcing the captain to draw the shades over the bridge's starboard bay windows.

The *Tonga*'s command center was identical to her sister ship, the *Mogamigawa*, with the exception of an oval Formica table and eight matching chairs, which occupied the aft half of the mostly empty room. Fiesal bin Rashidi occupied the seat at the head of the table, David on his right, Jacqueline Buchwald on his left. In the chair at the opposite end of the table, his back to a wall chart tracing the *Liopleurodon*'s movements, was Liam Molony, the mission commander. In his late thirties, the red-haired former submariner could be identified by the Ocean City baseball cap he wore every day to protect his fair complexion from the sun.

The other four chairs were occupied by the *Tonga*'s submersible pilots.

Rick Frazier was half Lebanese, half German-Scottish. In his early forties, the pilot had dark, wavy hair and a ring-shaped scar under his lower lip. His co-pilot was an Alabama boy named Gregg Hendley who seemed enraptured by Jackie.

Jacqueline was more threatened by Captain Tina Chester. The lone female pilot in the group had blond hair, intense green eyes, and the self-confidence that comes from being a trained U.S. Air Force fighter pilot. She was paired with a sonar operator whose lack of discipline openly grated on her nerves. Kevin Michael Pulaski possessed surfer-boy looks and a keen sense of hearing, but suffered from Tourette's Syndrome. Every few minutes the sonar specialist would blurt out, "Taco," which drove Tina Chester insane and added an absurd, humorous element to Fiesal bin Rashidi's heavy-handed attempt to impress his guests.

"David, you were able to get a good night's sleep in my first officer's cabin?"

"Yes, thank you."

"Good. We need you at your best. And our chef's buffet was to your liking?"

"I couldn't eat another bite."

"Taco!"

Bin Rashidi's dark eyes sought out Kevin Pulaski. "Mr. Pulaski, is that really necessary?"

"Taco! Sorry."

"It's reflexive," Commander Molony interjected. "We're all excited to have the Manta sub's best pilot joining us on the hunt to capture the Lio."

"Taco . . . yes."

David covered up his grin as Tina balled her fists. "Damn it, Pulaski, did you forget to take your meds again?"

"They make me drowsy."

Fiesal bin Rashidi turned to David, exasperated. "We interviewed over seventy qualified applicants, trained twenty pilots and ten sonar operators—and no one has ventured within a kilometer of the creature."

Gregg Hendley snapped. "Ya'll can sit in your bunker all day and brood, Mr. bin Rashidi, but I didn't sign on to this crazy venture to be eaten. Your subs are fine machines, kid, but that monster's twice as fast and feisty to boot. Damn near bit off our starboard wing before we could figure out where the hell she was—ain't that right, Fraz?"

Rick Frazier nodded. "The active sonar irritates her. The passive sonar . . . it doesn't give us a reliable bearing. She's so fast. And she can maneuver like a seal. Three hundred meters is the threshold. You need that cushion to get away."

"Taco!"

Tina Chester closed her eyes, summoning more patience. "David, you'll need a co-pilot—I'm volunteering. I flew twenty-two missions in Afghanistan and finished with the highest marks in our submersible training exercises back in Dubai. I'm like you—fear is not a factor with me."

David noted Jackie's irritation aimed at the retired Air Force pilot. "I appreciate that, but I'm confused. I was told Mr. bin Rashidi nailed this bitch with a tracking device. Passive sonar should be all you need to lead her to the trawl net."

Fiesal nodded. "I did this, yes. Now all I hear is excuses."

Liam Molony stood. "With all due respect to Mr. bin Rashidi, the tracking device's batteries have been petering out for months. Range is limited to within sixty meters of the surface. Each evening before dusk we send out helicopters to deploy sonar buoys in a 360-degree pattern at a ten-mile radius around the *Tonga*. We then activate the tracker and pray we get lucky. The Lio's a night stalker; she'll only surface after dark to feed, usually closer to midnight when the deep dwellers rise to bask in the moonlight. That's another thing that irritates her. She won't feed two days before or after a full moon, which leaves us blind for the better part of a week. Back in October, we lost her for damn near two weeks; fortunately she left a trail of dead humpbacks and we were able to reestablish contact."

The redhead paused as a heavy airship rotor beat the air. "There goes the first chopper."

"When's the last time the Lio fed?" David asked.

"We came out of a full moon cycle two nights ago but haven't picked up her trail. Assuming she didn't surface . . . five days, maybe a week."

"Contact your chopper pilots. Have them deploy sonar buoys only on southern bearings; skip everything to the north of zero-nine-zero through two-seven-zero. That will allow you to double up on the buoys and save deployment time."

Commander Molony's expression soured. "And if she heads north, then we've lost her forever. I'm not willing to take that risk."

"Which is why you'll never catch her. When I crossed paths with this monster she was inhabiting near-freezing waters."

"I thought the Panthalassa Sea was heated by hydrothermal vents."

"Not all of it. Some areas were warm water habitats, others were nourished by cold seeps, the water near-freezing. The variations in temperature combine with the minerals in the water to form a circular current; warm leads to cold, cold feeds to warm. The Lio and her Panthalassa lineage have spent the last sixty-five million years living in sub-freezing temperatures. If you were trapped in our tepid surface waters and you needed to cool your hot-blooded, over-oxygenated, bigger-than-a-blue whale mass down, what would you do?"

The commander and his submersible pilots looked at one another, perplexed.

David shook his head. "Look at the chart. She's been following the warmer currents to the south, which will eventually lead her to . . ."

"Taco!"

Tina turned on her sonar operator and punched him in the arm.

Jackie looked at David as if seeing him for the first time. "Antarctica?"

"Yeah. And we'd better flush her to the surface soon, because it's gonna be a bitch netting that monster if she's under the ice floe. Fortunately, it's late spring in Antarctica so the sea ice is melting. Still—"

Fiesal bin Rashidi stood, pointing at David. "You see? This is what we've been missing. Mr. Molony, who do you have teaming with Mr. Taylor this evening?"

"Tina's our most experienced pilot—"

"He needs a sonar operator," Jackie interjected, "not another adrenaline junkie. You need to be focused on the Lio's whereabouts, not trying to impress David with your piloting skills."

"You don't need to remind any of us of that," Gregg stated. "We've been at this a lot longer than you have."

"David and I are here to bag that Lio."

"You're wrong," Tina spat back. "Our job is to net the creature, yours is to keep it alive."

"Enough." Commander Molony said. "I'll set up a rotation so that everyone will have a chance to work with David. Tonight is Tina's turn—assuming we get a hit on the sonar array. As for this new sonar buoy alignment, Mr. bin Rashidi, that's your call. But if we lose the Lio—"

"Contact the helicopters, Mr. Molony. I trust David's instincts."

15

IIIIIIIIIIIIIIIIIIIIIIIIIIIIIIIIIIII

Port Metro Vancouver
Vancouver, British Columbia

Located in the Salish Sea where the Fraser River empties into Vancouver Harbor, Port Metro Vancouver is the largest and busiest port in Canada. Each spring when the snowpack melts, millions of tons of water, sand, and silt drain into the lower Fraser, rendering the riverbed shallow. To maintain the deepwater shipping channels for commercial vessels, the excess silt must be removed through the process of dredging.

A hopper-dredge is a large ship which incorporates two suction drag arms to inhale slurry—a water and sand mixture—off the river bed. The slurry passes through pipelines where it is collected in a massive hold known as a hopper, which runs through the middle of the ship like a giant Olympic-size pool. Once the ship reaches its designated dump site, the slurry is released through giant steel doors located along the bottom of the keel that open outward to the sea.

The hopper-dredge *Marieke* was a 5,005 ton steel behemoth with a white superstructure and a hull painted bright green. The lip of her hopper rose ten feet higher than the main deck like an above-ground swimming pool, the empty tank almost two hundred feet long and five stories deep.

Under the direction of Chief Engineer Michael Tvrdik, the slurry pipes were now angled horizontally at the level where the silt line stain had left its mark. The inward flow would be used to forcibly channel seawater and a mixture of animal sedatives into the tank once one or both of the two sisters were captured.

Jonas stood by the hopper rail, gazing into the empty tub. Almost seven months had passed since he and Mac had used the institute's dredge to transport Angel to the Philippine Sea. That voyage seemed to bring with it a dark cloud over his life. His son had attempted suicide, his marriage had fallen apart, and the sisters were loose, responsible for three more deaths.

The stress was taking a toll on his health. As bad as he had it, he knew it was worse on Terry.

Call her. Tell her you accepted an offer to sell the institute. No more liabilities, no more stress, with enough money to take care of our future grandkids.

The iPhone in his jacket pocket rang, beating him to the punch.

He checked the caller ID, recognizing the United Kingdom country code. "Zach? Do you have an update on David?"

"He's aboard the *Tonga*. Yer son believes the Lio is heading fer Antarctica, and his instincts are correct."

"How do you know that?"

"The Panthalassa pliosaurs prefer colder waters—now jist listen. You need tae contact Mac and have him pick up a set of *Valkyrie* laser units from Bill Stone over at Stone Aerospace before he sets sail fer Antarctica in the *McFarland*. The lasers were fitted fer yer Manta sub; I ordered them two weeks ago."

"Whoa, slow down. Why would you order a pair of lasers for our Mantas?"

"Are ye going after David?"

"Yes."

"Is there ice in Antarctica?"

"Yes, but—"

"Butts are for crapping, J.T.; no more dumb questions. Mac needs tae be under way by tomorrow night in order tae be in Antarctica in time tae rendezvous with the *Tonga*."

"Why would we need the dredge to bring back my son?"

"Ye don't. Ye need the *McFarland* tae capture the Lio."

The conversation was making Jonas dizzy. "Who said anything about capturing the Lio?"

"How the hell else are ye going tae convince David tae leave money, stardom, and steady sex with his new girlfriend? Threaten tae put him in timeout?"

"Why does it seem like you're always two conversations ahead of me?"

"Because I can see the entire forest while ye're still lost in the woods. Speaking of which, why are ye still in the Salish Sea?"

"I'm concluding a business deal with the future owner of the Tanaka Institute."

"And who might that be?"

"Paul Agricola. He's a fisherman from a wealthy family."

"Agricola Industries?"

"You know them?"

"Let's jist say our paths have crossed. Whit's their offer?"

"We settled on a one-hundred-and-fifty-million-dollar buyout."

"J.T., why would a private Canadian firm specializing in tar sand technology buy an empty aquarium for one hundred and fifty million dollars?"

"Well, ah . . . part of the deal is me helping him recapture Bela and Lizzy."

"Let me understand this great deal; ye're essentially risking yer life so this energy mogul can leverage yer assets tae buy yer facility. With the sisters recaptured he could easily mortgage the property fer fifty million. Whit's he putting down? Sixty million? Seventy?"

Jonas felt his face flush. "I just want out, Zach. No more lawsuits. No more people being eaten."

"Don't sign anything until ye hear back from me. And don't do something stupid."

"Define stupid."

"Ye'll ken it when ye're doing it. I'm emailing Mac a 'tae-do' list. Oh, and J.T., Megalodons and *Liopleurodons* don't get along. Keep that in mind. Wallace out."

Jonas clicked END, shaking his head. *The guy tells me to kill the sisters but prepare to capture a 120-foot* Liopleurodon?

"Who were you talking to?"

Jonas turned to find Paul Agricola dressed in a navy-blue sweat suit with the logo of Agricola Industries over the heart.

"That was my attorney. He says you're low-balling the down payment."

"With a dozen lawsuits pending? If he can do better, let him. The fishing trawler's waiting. Are we doing this or not?"

"Fishing trawler?"

Paul pointed aft. Two berths behind the ship was a sixty-six-foot fishing trawler.

"You're kidding, right? Bela and Lizzy will crush that into kindling."

"We're after one of the pups; the presence of the hopper-dredge will keep the sisters out of our way. Don't worry; between the dredge's sonar and the trawler's fish finder we'll know when the sisters are in the area. By that time we'll have netted a juvenile and baited the *Marieke*'s keel doors."

Aboard the *Dubai Land-I*
25 Miles Off the Coastline of Brisbane, Australia

The trawler maintained its southeasterly course at a modest eight knots, its captain keeping his vessel within a quarter mile of the *Tonga*'s portside bow. Thirteen sonar buoys were now deployed over a surface area covering 126 nautical miles. Without a confirmed hit on the Lio's tag, forward speed meant nothing.

Poised atop the trawler's slanted stern ramp, ready for launch, were the two Manta subs, their cockpits open and empty. The four pilots were dressed in their neoprene jumpsuits—everyone waiting to hear the horn blast that signaled a sonar surface contact with the *Liopleurodon*.

David was in the bow, leaning back against a canvas drop cloth covering one of the two trawl winches. The night was still young; the stars sprinkled between patches of white clouds, the temperature a balmy sixty-six degrees. Situated between his knees and laying back against his chest was Jackie. The marine biologist was text-messaging, her thumbs resembling a crab's twitching legs as she worked the touch screen.

David found himself drifting in and out of catnaps, his eyelids heavy against the steady headwind. He could sense Michael Mitchell, the reality show's blogger lurking by the rail, taking photos. The Brit's presence was intrusive, though not enough to disturb his rest.

What was preventing David from moving into REM sleep was an uneasiness bordering on fear.

The difference between traveling aboard the tanker and trawler was palpable; the *Tonga* was on the water, the *Dubai Land* was *in it*. Somewhere within the dark ocean that surrounded them was a creature that could easily sink their vessel and devour the entire crew. The anxiety came in waves and was similar to the fear of flying—the threat of dropping out of the sky summoned by a sudden bout of turbulence, or a strike of lightning, or . . .

Stop thinking about it and get some rest.

Adjusting Jackie's weight distribution, David rolled onto his left shoulder and closed his eyes, his inner thoughts forming a gauntlet against the solace of sleep.

The marine pelagic environment or open-ocean zone is situated between the surface waters and the abyss and constitutes the largest aquatic habitat on Earth. Each night trillions of small forage fish such as herring and sardines are drawn to the surface, their presence sending off dinner bells to the largest migratory feeding event on the planet. In the waters off Australia schools of krill attract pelagic fish like the southern bluefin tuna, which in turn summon sailfish, whales, sharks, and other predators to the moonlight rise.

For five nights the *Liopleurodon* had remained deep, its eyes sensitive to the brilliance of the full moon. Now, as the nocturnal orchestra assembled and the predators swarmed into the first overture, the monster rose to join the feast.

Forelimbs beat the sea, back muscles arched as the creature ascended, its senses sifting through the chaos overhead. Adjusting its vertical trajectory, it homed in on the mother humpback whale and her calf, the pliosaur's formidable presence scattering predators and prey alike. Those that could not move quickly enough were swept into its vacuous gullet.

The two cetaceans sensed the creature coming, but there was no sanctuary in the open ocean.

Widening its crocodilian jaws, the *Liopleurodon* launched its entire upper torso out of the sea, its mouth snapping shut over the adult humpback's midsection, its fourteen-inch stiletto-sharp teeth puncturing blubber and sinew.

With several shakes of its thirty-foot skull the Lio split open the belly of its catch, eviscerating the whale's insides across the surface of the South Pacific.

He tugged at the number 85 visitor's jersey, the sweat causing it to cling to his shoulder pads. His high school football team was trailing by four late into the Friday night contest and his quarterback had just changed the play at the line of scrimmage, noticing the defensive back cheating up a step, looking to jump the slant route.

At the snap, David faked a cut and sprinted down field, wide open. Turning, he looked up into an ebony sky framed by a periphery of lights, the football high and deep—a brown object falling surreally . . . his outstretched hands reaching up to grab it over the free safety's lunge.

His legs were churning somewhere beneath him, only his muscles seemed filled with lead as he strode toward an end zone that seemed far away.

The siren sounded, ending the game before he could cross the goal line—awakening David from the dream.

Jackie Buchwald was standing over him, shouting over the noise. "Did you hear me? The Lio surfaced! Twenty-three kilometers to the south—about fourteen miles. They want you to occupy it while we set the nets. David, are you hearing me?"

He struggled to his feet, his mind still lost in the dream.

Grabbing his hand, Jackie led him past a maze of crewmen and equipment to the two submersibles. Gregg Hendley and Rick Frazier were already sealed inside *Manta-Five*, Tina Chester was in the starboard cockpit of *Manta-Six*, her patience waning.

"I already performed the pre-dive check. Do you want me to take her out?"

"Sonar." David climbed into the portside bucket seat, his heart racing as Commander Molony leaned in over him.

"She surfaced twenty-three-point-six kilometers to the south; stay on course one-one-four until we can get another fix. Keep her on passive sonar but maintain a three-hundred-meter cushion. Whatever you do, do not go active. Is that understood?"

Tina turned to hear David's reply.

"Just get those trawl nets in the water, Red. Low bridge, watch your head!" David lowered the cockpit's Lexan dome, knocking Commander Molony's baseball cap from his head in the process.

He adjusted his seat, snapped his harness into place across his chest, then took a quick look at his instrument panels.

"I told you I already went through the pre-dive. Just because I'm a woman—"

"You're a woman?" David looked her over, feigning surprise. "Hope you brought your own urinal."

Tapping the cockpit glass, he gave a "thumbs-up" to the pit crew.

Four men tethered to the main deck walked the submersible on its dolly down the stern ramp. A swell caught the Manta's wings and lifted it, allowing the crew to heave the neutrally buoyant sub into the Pacific.

David adjusted the tint on the cockpit's night-vision glass, causing the dark sea to glow olive-green. Powering up the engine, he pressed both feet to the two foot pedals, the twin propulsion units responding to his touch. Using the center console joystick, he dipped the port wing and accelerated into a shallow dive, taking a position off the trawler's starboard bow as he waited for the second Manta to join them—his mind's eye wandering back to the last time he had seen the *Liopleurodon.*

———

"Earth to David, everyone's waiting." Tina shook her co-pilot by the shoulder—jumping back as he lashed out.

"David, get your head in the game!"

"Huh? Sorry." Looking to port, he saw the second submersible's exterior lights. Pressing down on both foot pedals, he accelerated away from the trawler, adjusting his course to the southwest.

He guided the sub through the olive-green void at thirty knots, descending to six hundred feet to avoid a ballet of krill. After a few minutes of silence he spoke, registering his co-pilot's eyes on his wrists.

"Something on your mind, Captain Chester?"

"Molony ordered you not to use the active sonar."

"Was that an order? Sounded more like a tip to me."

"Either way, pinging is very dangerous."

"Why don't you ask me what's really on your mind—am I suicidal? Do I still have a death wish?"

"Do you?"

"No. But if I tell you to ping, I expect you to comply without hesitation."

"You've never seen the Lio move through surface waters. The prudent move would be to gauge its speed before you start screwing with its auditory senses."

"Fine."

He checked his sonar monitor. The white blip on the oval smart screen represented his sub, the yellow—*Manta-Five*. The blinking red dot was the *Liopleurodon.*

"Captain, why is the red dot blinking?"

"Call me Tina, I'm retired from the Air Force. The red light is blinking because it represents the Lio's last confirmed location. Notice the sonar buoy is no longer actively pinging—that's because the creature destroyed it. Like we said, it's very temperamental when it comes to loud, vibratory sounds. Range to target . . . ten kilometers."

"Tina, go active on sonar. Six pings a minute."

She stared at him. "I thought we just agreed—"

"We're six miles away and I need an accurate fix. You wanted me to gauge its speed, I'm doing it. Unless you'd prefer I let it get closer."

She hesitated. Then she began pinging the sea every ten seconds.

Rick Frazier's voice came over the radio on the third auditory blast. "Hey, guys, we were ordered not to go active."

"Rick, take up a position five hundred yards off my port wing. When she closes to five hundred yards, I'm doing a one-eighty to lead her north. Loop around behind her and start pinging. The moment she chases you, head south. I'll chase her and pull her back to me."

"What's the end game, Mr. Taylor?"

"The end game is to wear this bitch out."

Tina shook her head. "This is not how we were trained. It's also extremely dangerous. We're not dealing with a sixty-foot Megalodon. This creature is twice the size and extremely agile—"

" 'If your opponent is temperamental, seek to irritate him.' Sun Tzu; *The Art of War*. This is war, Tina, not hide and seek. Rick?"

"Okay, partner, we're in. Better check your screen, she just moved into range."

David glanced at his sonar monitor. The blinking red dot was gone, replaced by a solid blue dot that was advancing steadily from the southwest.

Jesus, she's fast.

Tina continued pinging, recalculating distances with each sonar blast. "Range, four kilometers. Speed . . . thirty-seven knots. At our present combined speeds she'll be deep-throating us in about two minutes."

David eased up on the foot pedals, reducing his speed to twenty knots.

"Two kilometers. Just a reminder—our safety zone is three hundred meters—about three football fields for you dumb jocks who don't like the metric system. If you're going to attempt a one-eighty moving at our present speed she'll have gained fifty meters on us before you can accelerate out of the loop."

David gripped the joystick tighter.

"Six hundred meters . . . Five-fifty—"

I want to see her before I turn and run. I want to see the monster that ruined my life!

"Four hundred meters. David, make the turn."

Rick Frazier's voice cut in over the radio. "Kid, ease up, you're too close."

He saw the creature's enormous head materialize from the olive-green ether, its monstrous crocodilian jaws widening enough to bite down on a two-story building.

Ugly bitch. I could fly down your esophagus and tear you open from the inside.

"Three hundred meters! David, what are you doing?"

"Keep pinging until I say stop." David accelerated to thirty knots, aiming dead-center of the *Liopleurodon*'s mouth.

"Oh God, David, don't do it!"

One hundred meters . . .

Fifty meters . . . thirty—

"David!"

"Stop pinging . . . now!"

The muscles in the Lio's neck and back flexed to engulf its prey—its jaws snapping together on empty sea as David rolled the sub to port, shooting sideways past the creature's lower jowl and fluttering gill slits.

Before he could catch a breath the pliosaur's left forelimb occupied his entire field of vision, forcing him to continue the barrel roll until they were inverted, soaring over the creature's tail.

David righted the sub.

Tina leaned over and punched his right shoulder. "You sick son of a bitch. You actually had me thinking you were going to pull a move like your old man."

"Maybe I was."

She checked her sonar, then quickly spun around, looking behind them. "Oh, hell."

David turned around—shocked to see the *Liopleurodon* had already reversed its course and was in pursuit less than fifty yards behind them.

Ping . . . ping . . . ping.

The disturbance was coming from the north.

Confused, the Lio snapped its jaws to the right and left, then arched its back into a rapid turn, homing in on the other Manta.

———

Gregg Hendley continued pinging, each acoustic blast repainting his target, which was closing fast. "Nine hundred meters . . . seven hundred—come on, kid! Where's the reciprocation?"

Ping . . . ping . . . ping.

The infuriated animal snapped blindly at empty sea before contorting back to the south.

———————

David banked into a tight 180-degree turn and roll to the south while Tina worked the radio. "*Manta-One* to *DB-I*; we've engaged the Lio . . . where's the goddam nets?"

"This is Molony. First trawl net has been deployed. Net float depth is set at two hundred feet. We are six minutes away on course three-five-two."

David jammed both foot pedals to the floor, maintaining his four-hundred-meter lead over the Lio.

"David, she's slowing. Twenty knots. Fifteen."

"Blast her again."

Ping . . . ping . . . ping.

The pliosaur made a brief rush in the direction of the sub, then turned away, heading southeast.

David went after her, coming up on her right hind flipper doing twenty-two knots.

"One ping . . . now."

"You're insane." Tina pressed the button.

The acoustic blast sent the Lio's head twisting around, its jaws snapping blindly at the annoying creature, which was already darting over its left hind flipper, sending it into a painful contortion.

The Manta raced to the north, David matching the fatigued monster's speed, keeping its interest by maintaining only a thirty-meter lead.

"Tina, where's the net?"

"Two-point-seven kilometers on this course." She read his expression. "Sorry . . . a little over a mile. But we're still too deep."

"I don't want the trawler scaring her off. We need to keep her attention while ascending to the mouth of the net, while giving us enough escape room so we don't end up getting trapped in there with her. Start calling out our depth and distance . . . in *English*. My brain can't handle the metric system."

Unbuckling his harness, he sat sideways in his seat, piloting the sub while facing backwards. Alternating foot pedals with his right foot, he sent the Manta lurching from port to starboard and back again while easing up on his velocity, allowing the Lio to close the gap to twenty meters.

The *Liopleurodon* snapped at its prey, too preoccupied to be distracted by the surface ship approaching from the south at three knots.

"Two hundred yards, depth is four hundred and twenty feet."

David focused on the creature's mouth, noting how the Lio's jaws widened prior to each lunge.

"One hundred and fifty yards, depth is three-zero-five feet."

Pulling back on the joystick, he increased his angle of ascent—his right foot slipping off the starboard propulsion pedal, the port engine sending the sub slicing sideways toward the pliosaur's open mouth!

Tina screamed as David stamped down hard with his right foot, managing to catch the edge of the pedal just enough to send the ship whipping back to port a split second before the creature's fourteen inch fangs could close on the Manta's acrylic skin.

"What the hell?"

"Sorry." Facing forward, David targeted a faint outline of floats, which marked the trawl net's upper lip.

"Seventy yards. Depth is two-two-seven feet. Thirty yards, two-zero-nine feet. Pull up!"

He pulled back on the joystick—momentarily forgetting about the Lio, which bit down on the Manta's tail assembly, snapping its antenna like kindling while altering the sub's trajectory.

The vessel's wings cleared the top of the trawl net by four inches, the cockpit's belly smashing into a float. The glancing blow caused both pilots to jump. Having shed his harness, David was propelled out of his seat, his skull smashing hard against the Lexan glass as they soared over the net.

The *Liopleurodon*'s snout caught the inside edge of the net, sending its head and upper torso torpedoing inside the steel mesh until its head filled the cod end, causing the bridle to seal the trap.

The net pulled tight, sheering barnacles from the pliosaur's back while pinning its fore flippers to its side. The creature went berserk, rolling and twisting its body against its unseen foe.

Aboard the *Tonga*

Fiesal bin Rashidi paced before the command center's forward bay window, his nerves on edge as he and the tanker's officers waited to hear from Commander Molony aboard the trawler.

"Fiesal, we bagged her! She's in the net."

The Dubai engineer's dark eyes widened. He managed to mutter, "Praise Allah" a second before his men swarmed upon him in a celebratory embrace.

"Enough! We'll celebrate when she swims inside her pen. Captain, how far are we from the trawler?"

"Just under seven kilometers. Not to worry, sir. I began our braking procedure two kilometers ago." The skipper turned to his executive officer. "Mr. Saxe, reverse all engines."

"Reverse all engines, aye, Captain."

Aboard the *Dubai Land-I*

Commander Molony stepped out on deck to a cloudy midnight sky backlit by an intense waning moon. The wind was gusting at thirty knots, churning seven-foot seas that lifted the trawler from port to starboard.

Molony worked his way to the gantry where the trawler's chief engineer was standing by the winch drum, engaged in a heated argument with Jacqueline Buchwald.

"Is there a problem?"

Jackie held on as another swell lifted the boat. "Your engineer is threatening to free the Lio."

The Arab pointed aft to the boom, which was feeding steel line into the Pacific, spinning the winch eight revolutions per minute. "Your fish may be in the trawl, but it is still able to swim. There is less than two hundred meters of cable left on the line. You know what happens when it runs out? The gantry, the boom, the deck . . . *bit-tawfig*—good luck."

Molony removed the radio from his belt holster. "Patch me through to *Manta-Six*."

"Sorry, Commander, we still haven't been able to raise them."

"Then put me through to *Manta-Five*."

Aboard *Manta-Five*

Rick Frazier continued descending, keeping pace with the netted *Liopleurodon*, which was dragging the trawl line seventy meters off his port wing. Trapped from head to hindquarters, the creature was propelling itself through the water by wriggling its body like a crocodile.

"Depth . . . seven hundred meters. They better do something soon or . . . stand by." Gregg Hendley switched his headset from sonar to radio. "Hendley here. Go ahead, Commander."

"What's the hell's going on down there? How the hell is the Lio still taking line?"

"She's in the trawl but her tail's free. Where's the *Tonga*?"

"Four minutes away, but we'll be out of cable long before she arrives. What happened to *Manta-Six*?"

"They lost their radio antenna when the Lio was netted. We've got a visual off our port wing."

"Commander, this is Frazier. The Lio can swim but she isn't generating a lot of torque. If you reverse the winch I don't think she'll offer much resistance."

"Stand by."

Aboard Manta-Six

Tina stared at the creature descending off her starboard wing, mesmerized by the monster's size, grace, and ferocity. "It's so massive. How did it get so big?"

"Cold water and competition; multiplied by sixty-five million years of adaptation."

They both grabbed at their headsets as a bone-chilling *screeeech* filled their ears.

"David, what was that?"

"The steel cable went taut. The trawler's going to try to reel her in." Pressing down on his starboard pedal, he veered to port, giving the Lio a wider berth.

The *Liopleurodon* stopped descending, its whipping tail and snake-like movements no match for the 196-foot, 280-ton fishing trawler. Twisting within its bonds, the beast was dragged backwards toward the surface at a steady sixty feet per minute.

As David and Tina watched, the 122-foot pliosaur pitched and pulled itself into long, wide arcing pendulum-like movements, battling to find a direction in which it could escape the unyielding force.

On its next easterly swing it succeeded.

Using the taut line to generate torque, the creature found itself arcing beyond its 180-degree loop. As its head pointed toward the surface the tension suddenly eased.

Whipping its tail into a frenzy, the *Liopleurodon* rose to attack its enemy.

Aboard the *Dubai Land-I*

Commander Molony stood by the stern ramp, one hand gripping the starboard rail, the other holding a pair of night binoculars to his face, his eyes focused on the approaching *Tonga*. The supertanker's forward momentum had dropped to three knots. The trawler was matching its speed, waiting for the massive ship to stop.

A whirring sound caught Molony's attention. Lowering the binoculars, he turned to the boom. The steel cable had gone slack; the winch was rewinding too quickly, causing the line to tangle.

Molony's initial thought was that the cable had snapped. Disgusted, he retrieved his radio to confirm his fear—only to realize he had the volume turned down and *Manta-Five* was on the line.

"Repeat, the Lio's surfacing! Move the trawler—"

Liam Molony felt the boat's thrusters rev beneath his feet a split second before the deck was pulled out from under him and he found himself sliding face-first down the stern ramp—which suddenly exploded beneath his chest!

The breath was driven from his lungs as he flailed through the night air, landing hard on his back.

Jacqueline Buchwald pulled herself off the main deck, her jaw dropping as she looked aft. The *Liopleurodon*'s upper torso was out of the water, towering three stories above the stern ramp. The incensed slime-coated creature was whipping its head back and forth in a furious attempt to shed the cod end of the trawl net from its snout.

The boom became an airborne missile which struck the masthead. The winch drum was uprooted, shearing wood slats from the main deck.

The cable finally snapped, causing the bridle to unthread, easing the tension on the net.

The beam from a powerful spotlight reached down from the supertanker, placing the creature in a surreal heavenly glow as it continued to fight to free itself from its bonds.

A fore flipper popped loose. The appendage flopped down onto the stern deck, the Lio's 240,000-pound girth sinking the aft end of the boat at a forty-degree angle.

The sea rushed at Jackie, sweeping her up in its cold embrace. Covering her head, she was blindly carried across the main deck, her knees and back abused by unseen equipment before she was able to grab the rung of the ladder leading up to the navigation bridge. Clinging to the aluminum slat, she saw the monster slip free from the shredded trawl net and heave itself back into the ocean, causing the boat's submerged aft end to pop out of the water.

Fearing the nearing presence of the *Tonga*, the *Liopleurodon* dove beneath the trawler, the creature's back arched as it circled the keel in full attack mode.

Detecting familiar vibrations, the pliosaur went deep, its senses homing in on its prey.

Aboard *Manta-Six*

David never had a chance.

With two powerful strokes of its fore flippers the monster was upon them, its jaws crushing the Manta's chassis, separating it from its Lexan bathyscaph like an avocado pit.

Tina screamed.

David winced as a dagger-shaped tooth the length of a football struck the escape pod above his head—and snapped in half upon impact with the thick Lexan glass. For an insane moment he actually laughed—until the mouth closed around them and the creature's tongue lifted them, propelling them backwards down its throat.

"David!"

Tina screamed again as the spherical cockpit became an amusement ride through a hell revealed in terrifying glimpses behind the night-vision glass.

David frantically tore open the panel to the sub's fuse box as they slid past two-story-tall fluttering gill slits. He reached for a luminous red toggle switch as they teetered between the esophagus and the trachea, seconds from plunging into the monster's stomach.

"Tina, don't touch the glass!"

A blinding burst of blue current short-circuited both control panels as ten thousand volts of electricity was redirected from the sub's batteries through a latticework of microwires set within the cockpit glass.

The shock stunned the *Liopleurodon*'s nervous system, triggering a powerful gag reflex that caused the creature to regurgitate the sphere. One moment David and Tina were about to be swallowed, the next they were being propelled through the open sea at sixty knots, rising to the surface.

Tina gripped the edges of her seat, her eyes wide as her mind tried to grasp what had just happened. "Oh my God, oh my God, we could have been . . . I mean we were—"

The blood rushed from her face. Fumbling through her storage panel, she hurried a seasickness bag to her mouth and vomited.

16

Tanaka Institute
Monterey, California

James Mackreides sat in his office easy chair, staring out the bay windows overlooking the institute's man-made lagoon. Beyond the southwestern bleachers, anchored at the institute's pier was the *McFarland*, a 319-foot-long hopper-dredge Jonas had purchased in a government auction and converted to a Megalodon transport. Mac had spent three long weeks on the rusted monstrosity of steel, hauling Angel to what turned out to be her final resting place, and now Jonas was asking him to ready the ship for a ten-thousand-mile voyage to Antarctica.

His wife entered, carrying their son, Kyle, in his car seat. "Well? Are you going with him, or are you staying here with your family?"

"For right now I'm staying. There's no reason for me to travel with the boat, the captain said he'd pick me up in Santiago, Chile. That buys me two weeks to make a decision."

"As far as I'm concerned . . . well, you know my opinion."

"Trish, he's my best friend and he's my partner."

"A partner in what? A bankrupt business? I'm supposed to be your best friend; I'm supposed to be your partner. And why Antarctica?"

"I told you; David is hunting the Lio and the Lio is headed for Antarctica."

"According to who? The last reality show episode we watched had David capturing those creatures off the Japanese coast."

"The reality shows are taped. David's aboard the *Tonga* now and the *Tonga* is searching for the Lio in the waters off East Australia."

"Then why go to Antarctica?"

Mac sighed. "I told you this last night; Zachary Wallace said—"

"How the hell does Zachary Wallace know where the creature is headed? Is he psychic? He's not even a marine biologist anymore; you told me he's involved in some covert energy scheme."

"It's not a scheme. We invested in his company years ago, and since then Jonas takes what he says as the gospel."

"Then let him risk his own life."

"Enough. If it were our son out there hunting that creature you could bet the farm Jonas would be by my side." Mac stood, moving to his desk to retrieve a flight itinerary for Danielle Taylor. "Dani's plane arrives from London in three hours. Terry's seeing her doctor; she asked if one of us could pick her daughter up at the airport."

"By one of us, you mean me."

"I'm ordering supplies for a three-month trip to Antarctica, refitting the Mantas with lasers, and recruiting a crew. Think you might help me out on this one?"

"Sure. And you can breast-feed your son."

She snatched the itinerary and left.

"Trish, come on—" Mac winced as she slammed the door. "And that, Kyle, is why God made Adam before Eve; He didn't want a woman nagging Him about the specs." He checked the diaper bag, making sure his wife had left him a bottle of milk. Propping the car seat in front of the flat screen television, he fished through a stack of *Barney* and *Sesame Street* DVDs. Tossing them aside, he selected a *Three Stooges* short from his book shelf.

"We'll begin your formal education into manhood with the classics. . . ."

Obstruction Pass, Salish Sea

There are over two hundred species of kelp growing in the waters surrounding the San Juan Islands. These algae stalks, attached to sea bedrocks by "holdfasts," are an essential part of the marine food chain, attracting crustaceans and snails, salmon and orca. Clusters of kelp appear as algae forests, their floating canopies forming vegetative rafts that provide rest areas for seals, sea otters, and the occasional kayaker.

Paul Agricola squinted into a blinding sunset as he guided the sixty-six-foot fiberglass fishing trawler west through Obstruction

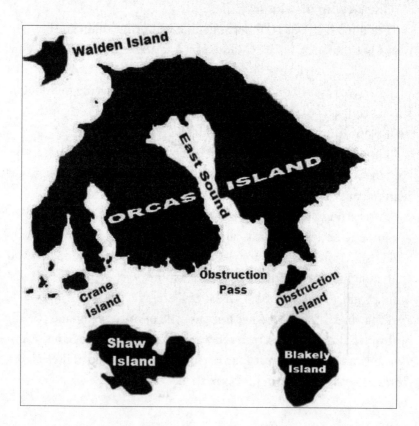

Pass. The channel's current picked up as it swept the boat past Obstruction Island, driving them toward Orcas Island's East Channel. The hopper-dredge *Marieke* remained in the deeper waters of Rosario Strait a half mile away, her superstructure disappearing from view behind Obstruction Island's tree-covered highlands.

Jonas Taylor sat in the bridge hunched over a rectangular computer screen, his eyes bleary from almost seven hours of staring at the fish-finder.

"That's it Paul, I've had enough for one day. My back is breaking, that lunch made me queasy, and whatever your crew has covered beneath that tarp stinks to high heaven. Take us back to the *Marieke*, we'll get an early start in the morning."

"Morning is for catching salmon; we're after night stalkers."

Jonas's adrenaline kicked in, his heart pounding heavy in his chest. "That wasn't our deal. When the sun goes down you agreed we'd be in port or aboard the dredge."

"The dredge can't enter the passes around Obstruction and Blakely Island and there's a kelp forest up ahead I wanted to check out."

"And if we spot one of the sisters? What then?"

"Then we hightail it back to the dredge. Stop worrying; I've got a plan."

A muscular man in an Army Strong T-shirt entered the bridge. "Cheney and Rumsfeld had a plan, and look where that got us." He extended a callus-covered palm. "Presley Gibbons, part-time grease monkey, full-time sport fisherman. So how big are these sisters? I was in the *Tallman-II* asleep when your beasties decided to sink the yacht. From the newscast I'd guess they're about thirty-five feet."

"Forty-six feet and twenty tons of nasty."

"Ouch. At the risk of over-abusing the phrase—I think we're gonna need a bigger boat."

"We have a bigger boat; we need to be *on* the bigger boat."

"Relax, Jonas. Presley is the one who caught Bela's pup. Lured her to the surface with a bloody burlap bag of salmon and netted her for one of my guests. Of course, once I saw her markings I knew what we had."

"Is that what's in the stern attracting all the flies?"

180 ||| STEVE ALTEN

"Not this time," Presley said. "Last night the boys and I went hunting for Columbia black-tail deer; got us a big buck. Just an appetizer for your sisters, but it's a nice meal for a six to eight footer. We'll gut it and drag it around the surface. Last time the entire procedure from cast to capture took less than ten minutes. The key is to net her and get her out of the sea into one of the saltwater holds before momma and auntie get close enough to catch a vibration."

Jonas slid his sunglasses back over his eyes and squinted against the late afternoon sun. Obstruction Pass was bringing them to the spot where Orcas Island's East Sound waterway emptied into the Salish Sea. "You're heading for the site of the charter boat attack?"

Paul nodded, pointing out the spot on his chart. "It's shallow water with a big kelp forest and some major rock formations—perfect for a Megalodon nursery. The diver you rescued can't remember much of anything. But I have a good feeling about this one."

Paul slowed the boat to three knots. "Take a look off the starboard bow. Can you see the kelp canopies? I'll circle the mat; Pres, take over for Jonas at the fish finder."

Jonas relinquished his seat to the fisherman, who adjusted the range finder. "It's a kelp forest all right . . . I'm guessing bull kelp. A few nice sized salmon moving among the stipes. Wait, I see seals in the canopy. I don't know, Paul. If there are seals hanging out I doubt the juvies are in the area."

"Keep watching. The diver swore he saw at least one six-foot albino great white."

Jonas looked up. "I thought you said he couldn't remember anything?"

"That was before I paid him five hundred bucks. Pres, tell your guys to drop the bait in the water. Let's see if we can flush them out."

The fisherman reached for the two-way radio clipped to the back of his belt. "Rod, we're a go. Gut her and drag her."

———

It took Rod Larrivee three attempts to suck in his belly enough to shove the radio back into its belt holster, during which time the wind shifted, blowing a cloud of blue-gray carbon monoxide in his face. Cursing under his breath, the big man turned away from the engine exhaust and reached for the red kerchief dangling from his shirt pocket, mopping sweat beads from his receding hairline.

The deep guttural sounds of the twin outboards reverberated beneath his feet, mixing with the "Moves Like Jagger" lyrics pounding from fifteen-year-old Matthew Dunn's iPod.

"Hey kid, it's show time. You want to gut Bambi or me?"

Matthew held up the sheathed Bowie knife to his uncle. "Can I use this?"

"Sure you can handle it?"

"No problem." The teen followed his uncle to the gray tarp. Rod pulled back the covering, revealing the dead buck. The smell was gamey and rancid, tufts of white fur lifting into the wind. A one-inch-thick braided rope was already tied around the animal's neck and attached to the stern winch.

"Give me a hand." Rod grabbed the deer by its antlers; Matthew the hindquarters—the two Canadians half wrestling, half dragging the carcass on top of the transom.

Matthew inspected the buck's bloated belly. "So . . . do I just slice it open?"

"Not in the belly. Shove the knife in its asshole and work your way up."

"Are you serious?"

"What's wrong, eh? Afraid you're going to hurt it?"

Matthew gripped the knife with one hand, the buck's left leg with the other.

"Sometime today, kid."

"Maybe you ought to do it, Uncle Rod."

"Gimme the knife, Davy Crockett." In one motion the big man shoved the tip of the blade into the dead animal's anus, working his way up its belly as he eviscerated the deer.

Matthew gagged at the sight of the intestines as they oozed from the wound.

Rod pushed the carcass overboard. The buck fell into the emerald sea, twisting on the line. Moving to the winch, the big man released forty feet of rope. "Okay, kid. First one who spots a dorsal fin gets a beer."

––––––––––

The moon rose amber to define the dark horizon, splaying a funnel of lunar light that seemed to follow the fishing trawler as it circled to the south.

Jonas stood in the bow, the crook of his casted left arm wrapped around the support of a searchlight, his right hand free to hold the night-vision glasses to his face. The neon-orange life vest was secured around his chest, the precaution drawing laughter from the crew.

Jonas couldn't care less what they thought. The Canadians' bravado was forged on a confidence that came from years at sea and an ignorance regarding the sisters' ferocity. Paul Agricola was the biggest offender, his attitude toward Jonas a mix of cockiness and judgment. Jonas Taylor had led the life the former marine biologist coveted, only *he* would have done it better.

"No offense, Jonas, but Angel escaped twice on your watch. How many innocent people died because you neglected to permanently seal the canal doors? Even when she was in captivity she still managed to kill four or five people. Now the sisters are on the loose, spawning genetic clones . . . You can bet the down payment that my team won't be making the same mistakes yours made."

"We got sharks, boys!"

Jonas's heart raced as he made his way back to the bridge, where the crew had gathered around Presley Gibbons and his fish-finder. The screen showed five sharks circling beneath the boat's keel and the bait.

"One minute the screen was clear, the next—there they were. I dunno, Paul, maybe there's a trough or an underwater cave down there . . . something that concealed them."

"It doesn't matter; what matters is that we net one of these bitches and get her on board as quickly as we can."

"We're on it." Presley led Rod and his nephew outside to a thirty foot trawl net supported by a central mast.

"Matthew, man the winch; I want the bait no more than ten feet behind our wake. Rod, let's get the net in the water."

Jonas watched as the two men released the net over the starboard side, allowing it to sink forty feet before maneuvering it into position beneath the deer carcass, which was being dragged along the surface just behind the boat's white water wake.

The boat turned ninety degrees to port, Paul Agricola pointing the bow east. The *Marieke*'s captain had moved the hopper-dredge farther south so that its lights were now visible in the distance, the four-mile stretch of water framed by Obstruction Island to the north, Blakely Island to the south.

The presence of the ship gave Jonas a false sense of comfort.

Facing the stern, he focused his night glasses on the bait. Within his olive-green vision the ghostly head of an albino Meg pup suddenly appeared, the six-foot predator gnawing at the carcass with the right side of its mouth before submerging.

Jonas was about to shout out to Presley when he saw something cut across the moonlit sea farther behind the bait, and by the way these fins were rolling along the surface he knew they were not sharks.

"Orca!" He pointed to the west where eight to a dozen tall blade-shaped dorsal fins were moving in formation—only to disappear.

"Shit." Presley moved to the aft spotlight. Powering on the beam, he aimed it behind the boat, sweeping the surface.

Paul's voice called out from the two fishermen's radio. "What the hell is going on out there? There are more sea creatures on the monitor than I can poke a stick at."

Presley reached for his radio—then turned to his left as the surface erupted sixty yards to starboard.

The twenty-eight-foot, eight-ton orca breached, the adult bull flinging an albino Megalodon pup clear out of the water. Before the shark could recover from the bite and toss another killer whale was on it, heaving it sideways like a rag doll.

Presley directed the beam of his light at the onslaught—then pivoted around to port as an even larger eruption of sea and foam obliterated the night.

The orca was a twenty-foot mature female. It emerged horizontally from the sea, its fluke wriggling violently as Bela's jaws pinned it just above the surface. The killer whale thrashed violently, its high pitched cry renting the night as the Megalodon's five-inch serrated teeth sunk deeper into its thick blubber.

Exhausted from the effort to complete the bite, Bela took advantage of the mammal's buoyant carcass to rest.

Jonas stared at the surreal scene through his binoculars, his body trembling. He wondered if the rest of the pack would attack—Bela was clearly vulnerable—then he saw the ghostly-white dorsal fin.

Lizzy's circling the kill, preventing any interference.

He expanded his field of vision and saw the black dorsal fins organizing along the perimeter into two distinct groups—adults and females with calves.

They're going to attack; they're making a stand.

The adults went deep.

Bela released the dying orca and submerged.

———————

Lizzy joined her sibling as both Megs went deep to confront their challengers.

There were two mature bulls leading the charge, followed by an adult female and two twenty-foot juvenile males. The big males raced in at the Megs, then abruptly broke to either side, attempting to separate the siblings.

The sisters refused to take the bait. Remaining in formation, with Lizzy on top and Bela below, the Megs chased after the bull breaking to the west. Lizzy ended the conflict with one gargantuan bite, severing the orca's fluke from its tail, rendering it helpless.

Bela circled back to confront the three charging adults.

When a pack of orca attack a larger whale, they use their superior speed and numbers to distract and disorient their prey, inflicting bite wounds on the cetacean's baleen and pectoral fins while avoiding devastating blows from its tail.

With the Megalodon, the orca had to avoid both tail and head in order to attack the shark's pectoral fins . . . only first they had to slow the predator down.

Like its modern-day cousin, the great white, Megs preferred an assault from below. Descending to the sea floor, Bela rose after the orca trio, targeting one of the juvenile males—missing her prey as the three killer whales broke formation and separated.

Bela turned and chased after the fleeing juvenile bull—joined by Lizzy. Faster than the orca and more than twice the young male's size, the hunt quickly turned into a tug-o-war between the two Meg siblings.

The surviving pair of killer whales joined up with the other bull. The battle was lost, the safety of the pod at stake. Clicking and squealing, the trio signaled to the rest of the pack—only the sisters were far from done.

———

Twelve minutes had passed since the battle had gone deep. Jonas, Presley, and Rod had returned to the bridge but were able to follow very little on the fish finder as the Megs chased the orca to the west and out of range.

Paul Agricola was angry; the appearance of the killer whales having chased off the remaining Meg pups, ruining his plans. Refusing to accept defeat, he circled back around to the nursery, hoping to lure one of the sisters' offspring to the surface.

Jonas had had enough. Stepping out on deck, he debated his next move.

This guy's dangerous. Insist he drop you off at Orcas Island or there's no deal. Then leave in the morning for home.

"Excuse me, Mr. Taylor, but I think I saw another fin." Matthew Dunn was leaning over the transom, pointing to the west.

Jonas pressed the night-vision binoculars to his eyes, scanning the sea.

The tall black dorsal fin identified the orca as a mature bull. It was streaking just below the surface a hundred yards behind the trawler. *Was it after the bait? Another pup?*

Then Jonas saw the two dorsal fins chasing after it.

For the killer whale there was no escape, no shallows offering refuge, no land on which to beach.

Why was it following the trawler?

"Oh no . . . no!" Jonas hurried back inside the bridge. "Paul, get us out of here—full speed!"

"Listen to this guy. Who died and made you captain?"

"The sisters are after another orca; they're right behind us!"

———

Matthew Dunn leaned against the transom, watching the orca race after the trawler at twenty knots.

When it passed the bait, he stood up, his pulse racing.

When it closed within twenty feet of the outboard, he started backing away.

When it leaped out of the water, he screamed.

Thirty-two feet and ten tons of cetacean landed on the aft end of the trawler with the impact of a sledgehammer, crushing the stern deck.

Sprawled on his back, his feet only inches from the orca's mouth, Matthew crab-walked as far away as he could, taking cover behind the winch as a chorus of creaks and splintering fiberglass reached a crescendo—the deck and the orca collapsing ten feet into the fish hold below.

Rod lifted the shocked teen by his armpits. "You okay? Holy Jesus, Pres, look what that orca done to your boat."

Jonas exited the bridge, followed by Paul. "Like I said, asshole, we need to get out of here."

Presley Gibbons moved to the edge of the twenty-foot hole. The orca squealed in pain below deck, the hold taking on water. "We're sinking, fellas. Paul, get on the radio to the *Marieke*. Tell the captain he needs to get here pronto, shallows be damned."

The boat shifted as the bow rose, the stern sinking three feet, the sea only inches from washing over the transom.

Jonas climbed atop the bridge, scanning the surface. Bela circled to port, her freakish albino head leading her five-foot black dorsal fin.

He found Lizzy spy-hopping thirty feet off the starboard bow. The Meg was staring at him with her remaining good eye, the left having been reduced to an infected hole by buckshot from the late Steven Lebowitz's shotgun blast.

Looking down, he saw small waves lapping over the transom.

This is a nightmare.

A horn blasted in the distance. The hopper-dredge was approaching, announcing its presence.

Six minutes . . . ten tops. Not good.

––––––––––

Bela could smell, taste, and feel the trapped orca bleeding and thrashing about in the flooding vented hold. Unable to reach her prey, the Megalodon descended thirty feet, banked away from the bottom, and rose to strike the keel.

The impact opened the floodgates.

Within thirty seconds the hold was underwater, sinking the boat while sending Matthew, Rod, Paul, and Presley rushing up the ladder to join Jonas atop the bridge. By the time they reached higher ground the main deck was two feet underwater.

The five men looked at one another, wide-eyed with fear.

Matt turned to face the hopper-dredge, still a mile away. Waving frantically, he yelled, "Come on! Move your ass!"

Rod and Presley joined him.

Paul Agricola looked at Jonas, then below. Four feet of water covered the main deck, but the sinking trawler seemed to have found its equilibrium. "We'll make it, no worries."

"Right. Because you have a plan."

"Uncle Rod, look at the size of her!"

All eyes followed Bela, everyone struggling to deal with their fear.

As long and as wide as an eighteen wheeler, the Meg was swimming slowly along the surface, making her way aft along the port flank.

Below deck, the trapped orca panicked. Flipping over inside the flooding fish hold, it slapped its tail in an attempt to escape.

With a double slap of her caudal fin, Bela propelled herself over the sunken main deck and headfirst into the hold.

The Megalodon ravaged the orca like a hungry pit bull tossed inside a rabbit's cage. The keel split apart, buckling the main deck, taking the bridge with it.

Five terrified humans fell into the sea to meet their fate.

Jonas was the first to surface, his life vest keeping him buoyant. He remained as still in the water as he could, his eyes locked on the bow of the *Marieke*. A football field away, the hopper-dredge had reversed its engines in order to slow its forward momentum.

Jonas jumped as a something massive grabbed him from behind.

It was Rod. The big man was hyperventilating. Struggling to stay afloat, he lunged at Jonas, using his body as a floatation device, his powerful grip pinning him underwater!

Naval training took over. Ducking his chin, Jonas used his arms to sink himself deeper, taking Rod underwater with him.

The big man let go, allowing Jonas to escape. He surfaced two body lengths away, then stripped off the vest and tossed it to the fisherman.

The ship was less than fifty yards away. A rope ladder unraveled along the dredge's port side, illuminated by a spotlight.

Presley and Paul Agricola reached the ladder first, beginning their climb to safety.

"Come on." Jonas grabbed onto Rod's life vest and dragged the big man with him.

Matthew Dunn swam past them, his churning legs a beacon of vibration. Reaching the ladder, the teen suddenly found himself levitating. He laughed at the bizarre sensation, until he looked down and realized where he was.

The scream never made it past his vocal cords. Rising beneath him, the teen's feet on her tongue, Lizzy's jaws snapped shut, puncturing his chest as the vice-grip squeezed the air from his lungs.

Blood poured out the teen's throat a second before his cervical verte-brae snapped, his detached head falling backward into the sea.

Rod screamed and didn't stop until the medics sedated him.

For a surreal moment Lizzy's triangular head remained upright in the water, her cold blue-gray eye trained on Jonas as Matthew Dunn's blood dribbled down the corner of her mouth. The night had cost her an offspring—now they were even.

Message delivered.

Message received.

17

||||||||||||||||||||||||||||||||||

Aboard the *Tonga*
16 Miles Off the Coastline of Brisbane, Australia

At 3:12 a.m., the Manta's escape pod breached the surface, its batteries shot, its life support unit running on emergency power. David estimated the *Tonga* to be three miles to the northwest, the trawler too low in the water to see. Having been forcibly separated from its chassis, the Lexan sphere lacked any means of propulsion. When their air ran out David knew he and Tina would be forced to pop open the hatch. Waves would sink the unstable pod and they'd have to swim for the ships—an eventuality he hoped to avoid.

Fortunately, every Manta sub was equipped with a homing signal. Fifteen minutes after they surfaced, the trawler's lights appeared on the dark horizon.

It was nearly dawn by the time the two Manta crews had finished briefing bin Rashidi and Commander Molony. Having captured the *Liopleurodon*, the trawler's crew had failed to keep tension on the net; the tanker was too late to the scene. Bin Rashidi vowed that changes would be made to insure these mistakes would not happen again—his rant done as much for the reality show cameras as for the Crown Prince.

Exhausted, David disappeared immediately after the meeting ended. Unable to sleep, Tina Chester, Rick Frazier, and Gregg Hendley reconvened in the rec room. They were joined by Kevin Pulaski, who brought two bottles of Jack Daniels.

The chamber that served as the private domain of the *Tonga*'s submersible pilots was more of a counselor's hangout at an overnight camp than a modern-day entertainment center. There were two antiquated pool tables with scuffed felt surfaces, a ping-pong table but no ping-pong balls, a kitchenette that looked like something out of a two-star motel, and a broken video poker machine. The only modern upgrades had been arranged by Liam Molony during the ship's last port of call, when he insisted Fiesal bin Rashidi purchase a horseshoe-shaped leather sofa, a seventy-inch flat screen television, a blu-ray player, and a small library of English-language movies.

The four pilots splayed themselves across the couch and passed around the first bottle of vodka.

Kevin Pulaski took a small gulp before handing it off to Tina. "Be honest—were you really inside the Lio's mouth?"

"Not only were we inside its mouth, we slid down its throat. Another thirty seconds and we'd have been on our way to the intestines." She took a long drink, draining a third of the bottle. "I was so scared I peed my pants."

Gregg took the bottle from her. "The escape pod's too thick to digest. You would have eventually passed out it's rectum like a giant enema."

"Or you could have ignited the hydrogen tank; turned the pod into a rocket."

"The chassis was gone, Kevin. The emergency burn wasn't an option. Face it, David saved us. Who even knew you could electrify the Lexan glass? I didn't know; I doubt Molony knew."

Rick took the bottle from his co-pilot. "So where is the Wonderboy now?"

Tina scoffed. "Probably in his luxury suite banging the marine biologist."

"Je . . . je . . . jealous?" Kevin asked, opening the second bottle.

"No."

"Je . . . je . . . jealous?"

"I said, no. Are you deaf?"

"Easy, it's his Tourette's."

"Je . . . je . . . jealous?"

"Jesus, take another drink. And don't backwash."

Rick drained what remained of the first bottle. "So what happens now that we're down to one sub? You know David's got the pilot seat locked up. Who's turn is it next to ride shotgun with Mad Max?"

The three other pilots remained silent.

Rick looked at Tina. "Two hundred grand. Is it worth the risk of being deep throated again?"

She wiped away tears. "I don't know."

"David's aggressive, and maybe that's needed to capture this monster. But he takes unnecessary risks. When the Lio surfaced we backed off. When it tore itself free of the net Gregg and I were three meters off the *Tonga*'s bow. That's standard operating procedure during a surface confrontation. What did Taylor do, Tina?"

"He didn't listen. We all tried to tell him how fast the Lio is, but he's—"

"Je . . . je . . . jealous?"

"Cocky." Tina took one last swig and resealed the bottle. "To answer your question, Rick, I'm done. My nerves are frayed and I know I'll be seeing that monster in my dreams for years to come. I'm asking for my funds to be wired and then I'm going ashore in Brisbane. Anyone else care to join me?"

Rick nodded. "Gregg and I talked about it; we've had enough. Kevin?"

"I'm ge . . . ge . . . gone."

San Francisco International Airport
San Francisco, California

Danielle Taylor slowed the black Lexus-JX sedan, attempting to time her arrival outside Gate-C. The Cambridge graduate student was forced to circle the airport one more time before her father emerged from the baggage claim exit.

Jonas Taylor climbed in the passenger seat. Dark circles framed bloodshot eyes. Two day stubble was coming in white, matching his sideburns. An ace bandage was wrapped around his left forearm.

"Hi, sweetheart."

"Hey, Dad." She leaned over for the kiss. "What happened to you? You look like hell."

"Been there enough times to collect frequent flyer miles. How's your mom?"

"Better. The doctor changed her meds. We haven't told her about David; we thought it would upset her."

"What about David? What happened?"

"He's fine, don't have a heart attack. He had a run-in with the Lio. They air the show tomorrow night but the Crown Prince e-mailed Mac a preview just to prepare us. You can't see him actually being eaten, but he talks about it during the reenactment."

"Good God."

"He's fine. He electrified the escape pod and the Lio regurgitated him. Like father, like son, huh?"

Jonas laid his head back, closing his eyes. "This has got to end."

———

An hour later they exited Cabrillo Highway, heading south on Sand Dunes Drive. Jonas stared at the concrete and steel bowl in the distance—wishing he could turn back the clock on his life.

Mac's car was the only vehicle in the parking lot. Jonas found him seated in the west bleachers, watching the ocean run up through the lagoon's canal.

Groaning with the effort, he sat backwards on the grooved aluminum bench next to his friend. "Hey."

"Hey yourself."

"The *McFarland* en route?"

"As of noon today. Two Mantas on board, along with four *Valkyrie* lasers, courtesy of Bill Stone at Stone Aerospace, arranged a month ago by your spooky pal, Dr. Zachary Wallace. Oh yeah, he also delivered thirty-five sonar buoys, God only knows why. Does this guy use a ouija board or does he have crystal balls?"

"I have no idea. But he tends to be right. Who's rigging the lasers to the Mantas?"

"Cyel Reed, and he's not a happy camper. Hopefully he'll have field tested them before you arrive in Chile."

"Anything else?"

"You mean, am I flying down with you? To be honest, I hadn't made up my mind, though I was leaning toward staying here. Then I heard what happened to that kid. Fucking Lizzy; she's as mean as her mama and a lot smarter."

"So then you're going?"

"I was . . . until I got bumped."

"Bumped? By who?"

"By me."

Jonas turned to see his wife making her way slowly up the bleachers.

"I'm going with you to bring back our son. I'm going to Antarctica."

PART THREE

ANTARCTICA

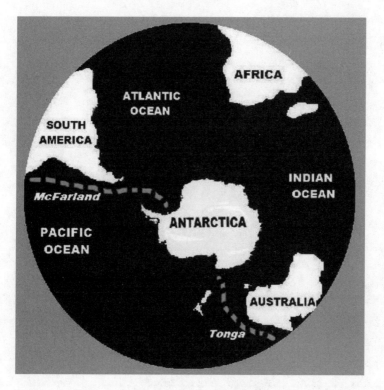

18

||||||||||||||||||||||||||||||||||||||||

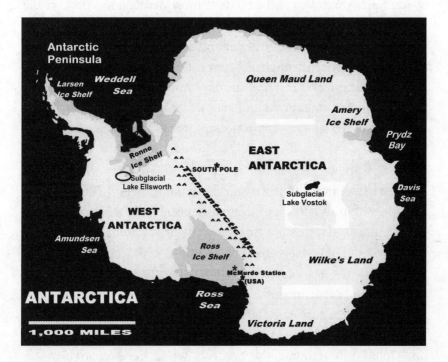

Antarctic Peninsula

Larsen Ice Shelf

Weddell Sea

Queen Maud Land

Amery Ice Shelf

Prydz Bay

Ronne Ice Shelf

SOUTH POLE

EAST ANTARCTICA

Subglacial Lake Ellsworth

Transantarctic Mts.

Subglacial Lake Vostok

Davis Sea

WEST ANTARCTICA

Amundsen Sea

Ross Ice Shelf

Wilke's Land

ANTARCTICA

1,000 MILES

Ross Sea

McMurdo Station (USA)

Victoria Land

Weddell Sea, West Antarctica

At just over eight million square miles, Antarctica is bigger than both Australia and the United States, with ninety-seven percent of its land mass covered by an ice sheet that averages two miles thick. The continent is divided into three distinct sections: its east and west regions and the peninsula.

The Antarctic Peninsula, nicknamed the "Banana Belt" for its less frigid temperatures, officially begins with the outlying South Georgia and South Sandwich Islands. The peninsula itself encompasses a five-hundred-mile stretch of mountains, the peaks of which tower over 9,000 feet. West Antarctica occupies the land mass located directly below the peninsula and is separated from the larger eastern region by the Trans-Antarctic Mountains. East Antarctica is the largest of the three regions and spans two-thirds of the continent from the Trans-Antarctic Mountains clear to the eastern coastline. A desert of ice, East Antarctica is the coldest, most desolate location on the planet.

Antarctica's spring and summer and its extended hours of daylight run from October through February. Darkness arrives in March, with temperatures dropping another forty degrees. The coldest temperature ever measured on Earth was minus 135.8 degrees Fahrenheit, recorded in East Antarctica at Russia's Vostok Station.

———

At only three hundred feet and displacing a mere 4,500 tons, the passenger ship *Ortelius* had originally been designed as a research vessel built for the Russian Academy of Science. Reflagged and out-fitted with luxury suites, the cruise ship could accommodate one hundred passengers, serviced by a crew of fifty-eight on its twelve-day Antarctic excursions.

Captain Christopher Rafalski sat in his chair in the oversized bridge, pretending to read a daily weather bulletin. Seven crewmen on Alpha shift manned the controls while his executive officer scanned the Weddell Sea for ice. Milling about the command center were half a dozen passengers—the cruise line offering its guests un-restricted access to his bridge. After nine years of splitting his year between the Arctic and Antarctica tours, the captain still struggled with his social skills, though he did perk up when the two Swedish women entered his domain.

After several minutes he realized they were a couple and went back to "reading" his daily report.

The voyage had begun five days earlier in Ushuaia, the capital of

Tierra del Fuego, Argentina, the southernmost city in the world. Sailing south through the Beagle Channel, the captain managed to cross the Drake Passage seven hours ahead of a nasty weather system, sparing his passengers and crew a rough trip. A solitary tabular iceberg greeted them on day four as they entered the Weddell Sea, the Antarctic Sound as free of sea ice as Captain Rafalski could ever remember—the realities of global warming in full display, despite the ignorant rants of the dozen or so climate change deniers on board.

For the passengers, less ice meant greater access to Emperor penguin colonies. This afternoon they would come ashore on Brown Bluff, a flat-topped, steep-sided volcano known as a *tuya*. Formed when lava had erupted through the ice sheet, Brown Bluff featured an easily accessible cobble and ash beach, its photographic red-brown tuff cliffs towering in the distance.

Rafalski's executive officer scanned the deserted shoreline as the *Ortelius* navigators slowed the ship to anchor. "Captain, conditions appear ideal for landing. No tidewater glaciers, no brash ice present."

"Alert the passengers and the expedition staff. Everyone desiring to come ashore is to report to the main deck in fifteen minutes wearing life vests."

———

It was late in the afternoon by the time the motorboat carrying Jennie Bachman and her partner, Marie, landed on the ash-covered shoreline. This morning's events had been derailed by Jennie's migraine. Medication and two hours of sleep left her with a hangover, but the crisp Antarctic air had cleared her head, enticing her to come ashore. While the late afternoon sun kept temperatures tolerable, the ship's staff warned them that the evening would bring conditions approaching zero.

A drop in temperature did not scare off the two thirty-five-year-olds, both of whom were born in Stockholm, Sweden, and could tolerate the cold. Bundled in layers beneath their matching fur-lined neon-orange ski jackets, they trudged ashore in their rubber-soled boots to check in with the staff.

A fire pit was stacked ten feet high with wood, folding tables set up to accommodate a dinner buffet. They approached a Russian officer who located their names on a passenger list. "Sorry ladies, you missed the last hike to the volcano, but the shoreline makes for a nice walk. Sunset is in an hour; we'd like everyone back before then to work on your group's skit."

The women scanned the coast in both directions. To the north, a family of four could be seen and heard a quarter mile away.

They headed south.

Small waves lapped along the beach. The Weddell Sea was calm and disappointingly ice-free. In the distance they could just make out the towering white rise that marked the Larsen Ice Shelf. The women paused to take a few selfies with their iPhones, then locked arms and set off at a leisurely pace.

They had walked just under two miles when they heard a haunting cry coming from the south.

"Jennie, what was that?"

"I can't be sure, but it sounded like a whale."

Breaking into a jog, the two women followed the shoreline around a bend to the west which concealed a small cove. A pod of humpback whales had stranded themselves in the four foot shallows. The haunting cries appeared to be coming from an adult, its right flipper slapping weakly along the surface, the cetacean's head propped along the beach.

Jennie, who volunteered at Animal Rights Sweden when she wasn't working as a film critic, gazed into creature's half-open eye. "Marie, we need to call the captain . . . get some rope and a few boats. The tide's rising . . . with a little effort we can still save—"

"Jen, stop! Look at the water—it's not red from the volcanic ash . . . that's blood."

"Blood?"

Marie led her to the other side of the stranded humpback. From their new vantage they could see a ten-foot-long, three-foot-wide wound along the whale's partially submerged belly.

"Oh my . . . what could have done that?"

"Probably a pod of orca. We saw a bunch of them on the way here."

"Marie, look at the size of that bite—that wasn't an orca. It had to be a Megalodon."

"Maybe it was Angel?"

"Angel's dead."

"You don't know that. According to two different Angel websites, Jonas Taylor lied about her death in order to deal with pending lawsuits from . . . Jennie, what are you doing? Are you crazy?"

"I need a picture of that wound." Jennie stepped onto the back of a dead whale, cell phone in hand. Stepping carefully, she made her way along its barnacle-encrusted blubber to get a closer shot of its mate's gushing belly wound.

She managed a dozen shots and three selfies before the sun dipped below the volcanic rise to the west. She continued snapping photos using her flash.

"Jennifer, enough! It's getting dark and I'm cold."

"Two minutes." She shot a short video, describing how she and her life partner had found evidence proving that Angel was still alive.

It was dark by the time she finished. The tide was coming in fast now, lifting the whale carcass beneath her.

The loud *ka-chauwff* sound startled her.

"What was that?"

"I don't know." She aimed her flash out at sea.

The beached humpback began thrashing its fins, attempting to climb farther out of the water.

"Jennie, your whale's panicking. Come in!"

"Marie, there's something out there!"

Ka-chauwff.

"Did you see that? It's a whale spout. Maybe it is an orca; I can see black and white markings. Walk back around the cove and see if you can video it."

"Not until you come ashore."

"I'm coming. Go now, before you miss it."

Marie jogged around the mouth of the inlet to where the deeper waters entered the cove. She saw the beast lurch forward as she reached her best vantage.

It was a gargantuan bull sperm whale, its enormous blunt head straining in the rising tide to reach the remains of the meal it had returned to claim. The size of the creature startled her—from the top of its skull to the tip of its slapping fluke the creature had to be eighty to ninety feet long.

Aiming her iPhone, Marie snapped a few photos.

With a sudden *ka-chauwff* from its blowhole, the bull breached the shallows, its head rising two stories as it forcibly chomped down upon the carcass of the female humpback. Rolling onto its side, the sperm whale attempted to tow its meal out to sea, in the process revealing a bizarre alabaster-white underbelly and a wide lower jaw that was more orca than sperm whale. It was as if the two species had mated to produce a monstrous offspring.

A scream—followed by a splash!

Jennifer . . .

Marie sprinted around the inlet, her heart racing as she reached the shallows where her fiancée was trudging out of the water, dripping from head to toe.

"It pulled the dead whale out from under me. I dropped my phone in the water."

"Forget the damn cell phone; we need to warm you up before you freeze to death. Switch jackets with me; here, take my hat and gloves."

Marie helped her shivering partner slip on the dry jacket, then led her back around the inlet. The two women jogged in the direction of a distant bonfire—the wounded humpback crying out in the distance.

19

║║║║║║║║║║║║║║║║║║║║║║║║║║║

Aboard the Supertanker *Tonga*
Tasman Sea, 28 Miles NW of the Coast of New Zealand

Jason Montgomery opened the watertight door, releasing a blast of cold salty air. Sealing the interior hatch behind him, he descended two flights of rust-covered steel grated steps to a narrow catwalk overlooking the very bowels of the ship. The immense space, situated five stories beneath the underside of the main deck and originally designed to hold three million barrels of crude oil, now held sea water. Divided into two large holding pens, the tank was lined with a rubber sealant and contained a simplified filtration system.

Monty followed the catwalk to a circular stairwell that lead down to a porous steel deck.

Seated on the edge of the walkway was David Taylor.

The distraught twenty-one-year-old looked up as Monty joined him. "How'd you find me?"

"I was a former Marine Recon medic." The barrel-chested, tattooed man half sat, half collapsed onto his buttocks next to his friend, wiping moisture from his shaved head and six-inch "devil's" goatee.

"Actually, Jackie told me. She's worried about you. She says you've hardly slept in three days."

"I'm afraid to sleep. Every dream is the same. I'm alone inside the escape pod . . . trapped in the creature's belly. In the darkness I hear Kaylie calling out to me, calling my name." David pounded his right fist against the grating, his knuckles covered in blood. "I keep searching, only I can't find her . . . I can't make her stop—"

"David, it was just another night terror, triggered by what happened the other night. Kaylie wasn't in there. Even if you had allowed the Lio to swallow you, she's long gone."

He watched David continue to pound his fist, then reached out and grabbed his wrist, holding the bleeding knuckles up to the light. "This isn't who we are. Flesh and bones—it's just a wrapper the soul lugs around while we're stuck in the physical world. Kaylie's soul is where it's supposed to be. She's safe. You're the one who needs to be rescued."

David nodded, his eyes welling with tears. "I do. I need to be rescued. I don't want to feel like this anymore. I'm tired of being scared."

"When I got back from Iraq, I was the same way. You need to exercise; maybe think about getting back on the meds. You'll get better, I promise."

David wiped away tears—streaking his cheeks with blood. "I'm not used to you being so coherent."

"I've been getting laid on a regular basis. Probably raised my serotonin levels. But you, my friend, need to sleep. There was a Russian scientist—Marie Mikhailovna de Manacéïne. She conducted one of the earliest experiments on sleep deprivation. She found that when she deprived puppies of sleep, they all died within four or five days. Fucking Commie bitch, testing her theories on puppies . . . like they didn't have lab rats back then. Now giraffes are different. Giraffes only sleep about two hours a day in ten minute sessions. Koalas, on the other hand, sometimes sleep twenty-two hours a day. I think my roommate back in college was part koala."

"Douche bag, you never went to college."

"I didn't?" He smiled. "I think you're right. By the way, I heard bin

Rashidi had one of his engineers devise a way to capture the Lio directly into the *Tonga*'s net. With the other pilots gone and only one Manta available, who do you think they'll assign as your new co-pilot?"

"They've already started bribing me to solo. The Crown Prince offered me a hundred grand for every reality show episode I appeared in the water with the Lio; with a two million dollar bonus once it's captured and loaded in the tanker."

"Fucking Arabs; they think they can just bribe people to get what they want. You turned it down, I hope."

"I told them I wouldn't do it unless they offered you the same deal."

"Wait, what?"

"Whatever I earn they have to pay you as well. They agreed."

"The Crown Prince . . . salt-of-the-earth. And Mr. bin Rashidi—say what you will about him but the man grows on you. Where's the Lio now? I bet you knocked some of the fight out of it."

"The sonar buoys picked up a surface signal last night about twenty miles off the west coast of New Zealand, so it's still heading south."

"Don't decide anything until you get at least eight hours of sleep. Fortunately, your old pal Monty brought a bottle of whiskey, just in case of emergencies."

Aboard the Hopper-Dredge *McFarland*
Drake Passage, 525 Miles East of the Antarctic Peninsula

The Drake Passage is six hundred miles of open water, 11,000 to 15,600 feet deep, situated between the southernmost tip of South America and the South Shetland Islands, which are located a hundred miles northeast of the Antarctic Peninsula. A combination of factors make this stretch of sea the most treacherous on the planet.

Three oceans converge upon the waterway—the Atlantic, the Pacific, and the Southern Ocean. Within this climatic boundary cool humid, sub-polar temperatures meet Antarctica's frigid weather. This draws cyclones and other low pressure systems which sweep in from the west, churning up waves that can surpass sixty feet. During winter months, sea ice can extend as far north as Cape Horn, adding to the dangers associated with the crossing.

———————

The hopper-dredge *McFarland* was forty nautical miles south of Cape Horn when ominous gray clouds appeared over the western morning skies. By noon winds began gusting at thirty-five knots, the seas turning into white-capped peaks.

Two hours later the storm's full fury was upon them, with swells reaching sixty-five feet.

The captain ordered the hopper filled with sea water to increase ballast and the ship trimmed so that it was listing fifteen degrees to starboard. This raised the port side, reducing some of the pounding, but the continuous rolling over mountainous crests into steep valleys was exacting a toll on both the ship and its crew.

Jonas and Terry Taylor held onto one another as they made their way down a slanted passageway that rolled beneath them like something out of a carnival funhouse. Seasickness had chased them from their cabin, now they sought a view of the horizon, hoping to anchor their lost equilibrium.

Accessing an interior stairwell, they began the long seven-story ascent to the bridge, each step precarious as the claustrophobic corridor heaved from zero to thirty degrees. After several minutes and assorted bruises, Jonas hugged his wife to his right hip, gripped the rail with his left hand and practically carried her up to the command center.

Reaching the bridge, they quickly realized the higher the vantage, the worse the pitch. With no empty chairs available, Jonas made his way with Terry to a support rail situated before the forward bay windows. Hugging her back from behind, he gripped the rail with both hands and held on as the bow plunged into the sea, disappearing underwater, only to burst free once more, sending plumes of spray across the main deck.

Turning to his right, he saw a flat-screen monitor bolted to the navigation table. The animated map showed their position, course, and speed. A Beaufort Scale categorized the storm conditions as a twelve—the highest rating on the chart.

The captain made his way over to the couple, one hand holding the support rail, the other a cup of coffee held inside a non-spill container. "You folks really don't want to be up here. Best place to ride out the storm would be in the galley on Deck-2. It's lower, it has interior windows, and it's more centrally located. Up here—it's a friggin' rollercoaster."

Jonas looked at Terry, whose Asian complexion had turned a whiter shade of pale. "It's your call."

She nodded weakly.

"Speaking of calls . . ." The captain reached into his jacket pocket and removed a folded slip of paper. "This transmission was received about an hour ago."

Jonas opened the message.

TO: Jonas Taylor
FR: Zachary Wallace
RE: <u>URGENT MATTER</u>
Meet me in Grytviken in 48 hours. Will join you
and my fellow Scot to locate your son.
—Zachary Wallace

"Grytviken? Never heard of it."

The captain moved to his navigation station, typing a command on a computer keypad. The monitor showing their position widened to encompass a tiny island cluster lying between the southernmost part of the Drake Passage and the Antarctic Peninsula.

"Grytviken is an old abandoned whaling station located on South Georgia Island. It's on the way, but why your friend would want to meet you on that rust bucket makes no sense to me."

They held on as a six-story-high swell lifted the *McFarland*'s bow toward the lead-gray heavens before plunging it three stories underwater.

Terry held on to her husband. "What did Zachary mean when he said he'd join you and his fellow Scot in finding David?"

"He must think Mac's with me. Come on, let's get you down to the galley before I hurl up a lung."

20

|||||||||||||||||||||||||||||||||

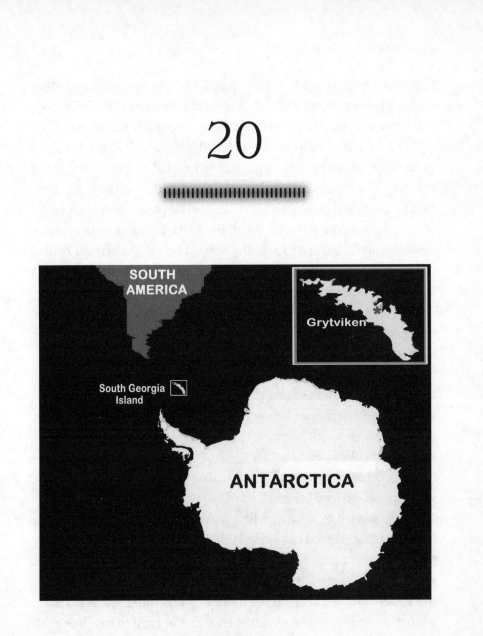

Grytviken
South Georgia Island

Erected along the anchorage in King Edward's Cove at the foot of the snow-capped peaks of South Georgia Island lies the remains of Grytviken, Antarctica's first whaling station. Established in 1904 by a Norwegian whaling captain, the commercial enterprise not only hunted the beasts, they also sliced up the blubber and cooked the oils to produce meat, soap, fertilizer, margarine, nitroglycerin, and other oil-based products. By the time it was shut down in 1965, Grytviken and other stations like it had slaughtered over two million whales.

The *McFarland*'s captain anchored the hopper-dredge a hundred yards offshore, wary of the graveyard of rusted vessels listing along the quay. The storm that had battered the ship during the Drake Passage crossing had yielded to blue skies and sunshine. Jonas helped his wife into the motorized rubber raft, the *McFarland*'s executive officer, Leslie Manuel, assigned to pilot the boat. The crew lowered the Zodiac into the bay using the starboard winch. Releasing the cable, the XO started the outboard, guiding the raft past several rusted whaling vessels, their deck-mounted harpoon guns a stark reminder of the violence the ghost town's occupants had once inflicted upon nature's largest sea creatures.

Dozens of prefabricated steel buildings lined the deserted wharf, their rusted exteriors sharing the same burnt-orange look. Close by, a herd of sea elephants sunned themselves on the shoreline. King penguins stood watch on grass-covered knolls, while unseen fur seals barked out calls to one another.

The XO beached the craft, not trusting the century-old dock. "Are you sure your friend is here?"

Jonas pointed to a small white A-framed chapel, one of the few buildings that seemed habitable. A fit man in his forties was making his way down a path leading to the water, his brown hair long and pulled into a ponytail. He wore a ski parka and jeans, and a five o'clock shadow. An army-green duffle bag was slung across his back, a large object the size of a kitchen trashcan hugged to his chest with both arms. It must have been heavy because it forced him to stop every twenty paces.

Dr. Zachary Wallace set down the item encased in thick plastic, handed his duffle bag to the woman in the raft and embraced Jonas. "J.T, thank God. My chopper dropped me off yesterday; one day in this ghost town is enough. Terry, whit a nice surprise; I wasn't expecting tae see ye here."

She offered her cheek for a kiss. "No, apparently you were expecting your fellow Scot."

Zach seemed surprised. "Mac's not here?"

"He's back at the institute with his family." Jonas saw the perplexed look. "Is something wrong?"

"Wrong? No, I . . . of course not." He picked up the heavy object and carefully passed it to the female officer in the raft. "Please be careful with this, lass. If ye could have yer crew bring it tae my quarters I'd be grateful. If ye could return for us in an hour, that would be most appreciated as I need tae show the Taylors something before we leave the island."

The XO handed Jonas a two-way radio. "Call me when you're ready."

Jonas waited until the Zodiac pulled away. "So what's so important that you had to meet me on this Club-Med for penguins, and what does it have to do with David?"

"I'm going tae show ye, only I can't explain everything right now. Ye have tae trust me on this . . . for David's sake. Agreed?"

"For now. Only I don't like mind games."

"This isn't a mind game, J.T., it's more like one of those sliding block puzzles where ye can't lift the pieces off the board; you have tae manipulate them around a track until everything aligns tae form an image."

"Sounds like a mind game to me."

Zach led them up a dirt path cutting through the heart of the station. "Grytviken isn't as much a piece of the puzzle as it is a clue. A hundred years ago this camp was a slaughterhouse. Boats like those two steam-powered whalers decimated the entire whale population around these islands. The carcasses would be inflated with compressed air and towed back tae Grytviken, where winches would haul the catch ontae work areas. Crews worked day and night using knives on poles tae strip large sheets of blubber, which were then stuffed intae pressure cookers." He pointed to a series of silo-shaped rusted objects. "Each one of those pressure cookers could process twenty-four tons of blubber. The oil was then pumped intae a plant for purification. Meat and bones were dealt with separately."

They passed a blacksmith shop, a barracks for workers, a hospital, library, laundry, bakery, and a building Zach theorized had been a movie theater. A five-minute walk brought them to the outskirts of the station and two white-washed pink-roofed stucco buildings.

"This is the tourist section of town. Believe it or not, Grytviken gets about eight thousand visitors a year."

"To see what?"

"I dunno. Ernest Shackleton is buried in the church cemetery." He pointed at the two stucco buildings. "The caretakers live in that house during summer months when the cruise ships visit. The other building is our first destination—the whaling museum."

They followed the dirt path to the two-story dwelling. On the front lawn was an immense three-thousand-pound steel appendage. "That was one of the claws used tae drag whales, tail first, up the stern ramps of whaling ships."

They entered the museum. Framed black and white photos shared the walls with gruesome saws and cutting tools used by the whalers. Walking behind a glass case, Zach forced open a door swollen within its frame. Locating a battery-powered lantern he had stowed behind the counter, he led them down a set of rickety wood steps into the cellar.

Crates were stacked three and four high along the damp stone walls. An open sea chest had been emptied, its contents organized into piles of leather-bound books.

"These are the original logs of the whalers' captains—at least the more recent ones. Everything prior to 1930 was either donated tae museums or sold tae private collectors. No matter; whit I was looking fer were any unusual events occurring at sea during the years 1940 through 1943."

"Why those years?" Terry asked.

"Good question; I'll answer that right after I read tae ye this passage." He held up the top book on the pile. "This is the log of Captain Klarius Mikkleson, who hunted whales in these waters from 1935 through 1947. The text is written in Bokmål, and my translation of the Norwegian language is a bit rough, but I think ye'll get the basic idea. In most of these entries the captain simply recorded the days' catches. The first in a series of unusual entries begins on January 4, 1940."

He turned to a bookmarked page and translated aloud.

"*4 January: After ten days with no sightings, we arrived in the Weddell Sea. Late afternoon yielded two adult fin whales, a male (18 meters); and a female (12.5 meters). The calf was spared but remained in the area while the carcasses were inflated. At eight bells, first mate reported a whale breach less than one kilometer off the starboard bow. Harpooner estimated the creature at 22 meters and in excess of one hundred tons. Eyewitnesses claim the beast devoured the fin calf in one bite. First mate and harpooner remain divided over the identity of the species. Jaws and black coloring with white belly support the first mate's claim of a giant species of killer whale. Harpooner disagrees; stating the telltale rectangular head clearly identified the creature to be a bull sperm whale. After two hours and no further sightings we continue southeast to the Antarctic coast.*"

"*5 January, 3 a.m.: Second mate reports creature has returned and is following our ship, feeding upon the two fin carcasses from below. This is behavior never before observed in a sperm whale.*"

"*5 January, 7:30 a.m.: Daybreak has chased our visitor away. Having seen its head and spout trail as well as its lower jaw, which enabled it to take great bites out of the fin carcasses, I believe it to be an undiscovered species of sperm whale, perhaps native to Antarctica. Sperm whale oil taken from immense chambers in the beast's head is of the first quality and fetches a much higher price, and the size of this bull could render a yield equal to a month's voyage. Therefore we shall use the day to dismantle the harpoon gun and move it from the bow to the stern in hope the whale returns tonight to finish its meal."*

"6 January, 6:30 a.m.: No sightings. Female fin whale had to be cut adrift as its bite wounds attracted sharks."

"7 January, 3:00 p.m.: Longboats killed three minke whales, all under nine meters. No sperm whale sighting."

"8 January, 1:30 a.m.: First mate informed me the sperm whale has returned."

"8 January, 11:00 a.m.: A long night. The sperm whale was harpooned and dragged the ship aft-first for seven kilometers, nearly to the ice sheet. Longboats finished the beast by daybreak, but at a cost. Three crewmen were lost, along with a longboat which was smashed by the beast's fluke. With our haul we return to Grytviken."

Jonas and Terry looked at one another, sharing the same thought.

"Ye're wondering why I read this tae you."

"Or what a sperm whale harpooned more than seven decades ago has to do with our son."

"Not a sperm whale, J.T., but an ancestor of our modern-day sperm whale—a creature possessing an orca's jaw and fifteen inch teeth . . . a predator that dated back tae the Miocene Period and competed with *Carcharodon megalodon* for food."

Zach removed a folded manila envelope from his jacket pocket, handing Jonas photocopies of an article published in *National Geographic*. "Paleontologists first found the creature's fossils in a dried lake bed in Peru back in 2008. They named the extinct sea monster *Livyatan melvillei*, combining the Hebrew spelling for the biblical Leviathan with the surname of Herman Melville, the author of *Moby Dick*. It's a fitting title for a predator that not only owned one of the most vicious bites in history but the largest teeth."

"As my husband said, what does this have to do with our son?"

"It doesn't . . . yet. But I suspect it may. I ken, I know, I'm babbling like an idiot, but pieces of a moving puzzle are sliding intae place very fast now. David's part of it, so is the *Liopleurodon*. I thought by having your engineers install air bags in the Manta subs it would be enough. Now I'm not sure . . . not after whit jist happened."

"What just happened?"

He took out his iPhone. Scrolling through a series of photos, he held one up for them to see. "These pictures were taken along the Antarctic Peninsula four days ago. Here's a better shot, you can see the creature's lower jaw as it bites down on the humpback's fluke. That's definitely not a sperm whale . . . agreed?"

Jonas widened the screen. "Kind of hard to tell. What did you call it?"

"*Livyatan melvillei.*"

"I don't understand," Terry said. "Where did this extinct creature come from?"

"A subglacial lake. There are hundreds of them concealed beneath the Antarctic ice cap. These are saltwater lakes that have remained liquefied because of the immense pressure generated by the ice sheet. Many of them are heated by geothermal vents, which reside above the continent's crustal plates. The ice age that froze Antarctica fifteen million years ago happened very quickly, trapping its inhabitants. Chemosynthesis replaced photosynthesis and new food chains replaced the old. *Livyatan melvillei* was one of the predators that survived."

Terry nodded. "The years 1940 through 1943—I'm guessing these were unusually warm years?"

"Yes. Global temperatures spiked. Antarctica shed massive tabular bergs, many as large as Texas. There are three major subglacial lakes located along the Weddell Sea coastline, buried beneath a mile and a half of ice. Subglacial rivers connect these lakes tae the Weddell Sea. One of the passages must have opened back in the austral summer of 1940, releasing the whale that Captain Mikkleson wrote about in his log book. Thanks tae global warming, these last five summers have been among the hottest on record. Last summer, a major section of the Filchner-Ronne Ice Shelf collapsed intae the Weddell Sea. This summer a passage leading from one of the subglacial lakes may have opened up, allowing at least one of the trapped Miocene whales tae escape."

"And what are we supposed to do about that?" Jonas asked.

"Capture it. Or help me hunt it down and kill it, I don't really care which. As long as we maintain secrecy in regards tae where the whale came from."

"Why?" Both Taylors asked the question at the same time.

"Because a discovery like this will bring scientists and money to Antarctica in droves; everyone vying tae explore these subglacial lakes. Before long, they'll be constructing submersibles that can burn through the subglacial rivers, upsetting the delicate balance of nature that is already being threatened by climate change. We can't allow that tae happen."

"Don't bullshit a bullshitter," Jonas said, tossing the article back at the marine biologist. "You may have come here looking for evidence to support your subglacial lake theory, but you already knew these melvillei things were here."

Terry stared at Zach's face. "Jonas is right. You had an ulterior motive in bringing us here. Who are you protecting?"

"He's protecting himself," Jonas said. "You managed to access one of these subglacial lakes, didn't you?"

Zachary looked away. "Jonas, this isn't about me."

"Answer the question, or you'll be spending another night on this godforsaken island."

He hesitated. "Yes. I was in one of the lakes. Yes, I crossed paths with a pod of these whales, jist as you crossed paths with *Carcharodon megalodon* all those years ago in the Mariana Trench. And jist like yer naval dives, my mission was also top-secret, so don't ask me why I was there or whit we found. All I can tell ye is that it's very important we keep this hundred-ton genie in its bottle, or the repercussions down the road will be catastrophic."

Terry cut off her husband's reply. "You mentioned placing air bags in the Mantas. What does that have to do with any of this?"

"Nothing. It was jist a precaution; inspired by a recurring nightmare."

"Did this nightmare have something to do with David?"

"David was piloting one of the Mantas. In the dream, he crashed intae the side of a ship and broke his neck. I phoned Jonas and asked him tae put the air bags in, jist for my own peace of mind. Again, it was jist a dream."

"Which subglacial lake did you access?" Jonas asked.

"I'd rather not say."

"You want us to capture or kill this prehistoric whale of yours, but you won't tell us which lake it came from?"

Removing a laptop from his backpack, Zachary opened a file, then pulled up an image and showed it to Jonas and Terry.

"These images of the Filchner-Ronne Ice Shelf were taken by an Earth Remote Sensing satellite using synthetic-aperture radar. The image on the left reveals rifts forming beneath the ice shelf, caused by melt water originating from ice streams and possibly Lake Ellsworth. The post-collapse image on the right shows jist how close Lake Ellsworth and the Ellsworth Trench are tae the Weddell Sea. Again, this was taken last summer. The appearance of that Miocene whale indicates a connecting passage may have opened."

Jonas studied the images. "I've never heard of the Ellsworth Trench."

"It's a subglacial canyon that was discovered a few years ago.

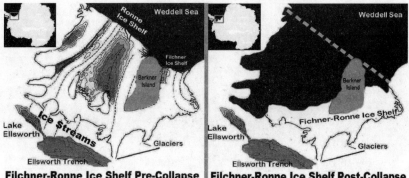

Filchner-Ronne Ice Shelf Pre-Collapse | **Filchner-Ronne Ice Shelf Post-Collapse**

The trough is located a mile beneath the ice shelf. It's fifteen miles wide, runs east for more than one hundred and eighty miles, and probably flows intae Lake Ellsworth. Geologists believe the trench was formed about 80 million years ago when Antarctica broke away from the rest of the planet's super continent."

Zach powered off the laptop. "Whit I want . . . whit I *need* is for us tae acquire blood and tissue samples from the *Livyatan melvillei*. Each subglacial lake possesses a unique mineral content. I need tae ken if the whale inhabited the lake I was in. I brought a variation of a harpoon gun used tae tag great whites in the field. The dart's sensors will analyze blood gases and tissue samples and download the information tae me laptop. We can rig the device tae one of the Manta subs. One shot from a safe distance and we'll ken where this whale has been."

"That's all well and good," Jonas said, "but you still have to find the damn thing."

"These creatures have spent the last fifteen million years living in darkness. The whale will hunt by night and return tae Lake Ellsworth by day in order tae avoid the light. Mac loaded thirty-five sonar buoys aboard the *McFarland*. We'll deploy them around the Ronne Ice Shelf, locate and tag the *Livyatan melvillei,* and then we can be on our way."

21

Macquarie Island
807 Nautical Miles from the Coastline of Antarctica

Macquarie Island is located approximately halfway between New Zealand and the Antarctic coast in an area of the Southern Ocean known for its gale winds and stormy seas. The landmass was discovered by an Australian seal hunter in 1810. For the next hundred years the island's vast population of penguins, fur seals, and elephant seals were hunted nearly to extinction. Macquarie became an official wildlife preserve in 1933, ending the trade.

Only twenty-one miles long and three miles wide, Macquarie consists of two volcanic elevations connected by a narrow isthmus at sea level. The only humans on "Macca" today are scientists working at the Australian Antarctic Division station.

———

The *Liopleurodon* was weak; it had been six days since its last feeding. The battle along the surface had taxed its energy, with its reserves going to the unborn offspring growing impatient within its womb.

Like a salmon seeking familiar waters in which to spawn and

perish, the Lio continued its journey into the colder latitudes, struggling in its alien environment.

Moving just above the ocean floor at six knots, the hundred and
twenty-two foot pliosaur remained in a catatonic state somewhere
between sleep and cruise control. Hunger directed its senses, self-
preservation its menu. Whales were out; the effort required to stalk,
ambush, and kill anything larger than a lone calf now beyond its
capacity. Bursts of speed were necessary to chase after schools of
fish; sharks and squid gave it a wide berth.

Too weak to feed, the largest predator ever to inhabit the sea was
slowly starving to death.

Moving south past New Zealand, the pliosaur followed the steeply
descending sea floor into the Puysegur Trench, a 20,700-foot cleft in
the South Tasman Sea. The sudden increase in water pressure eased the
creature's burden, escorting it over the next five hundred miles to the
south where it intersected with an even deeper fissure—the Macquarie Trench.

———

The Australian Antarctic Division's research station on Macquarie
Island consists of more than a dozen buildings of various shapes and
sizes, erected on a quarter-mile-wide stretch of beach bordered to the
east and west by the Southern Ocean and to the north and south by
snow-peaked mountains.

Sharing this small landmass with its human visitors were the Macquarie natives.

Eight hundred thousand royal penguins waded in the surf like
beachgoers on the fourth of July. Albatross occupied the skies, searching the sea for food, their nests sequestered in the crags of the
island's volcanic rock. Fur seals stayed close to the water, ceding the
prime coastal real estate to Macquarie's largest residents—the elephant seals.

Several thousand two-ton females covered the narrow isthmus,
each twenty- to forty-member harem polygamized by a single bull, the
largest of which measured twenty feet and eight thousand pounds.

Shielded from the extreme cold by a thick layer of blubber which held large volumes of blood, the mammals possessed an abundant storehouse of oxygen. Combined with sinuses located in their abdomens, which stored blood and oxygen and increased concentrations of myoglobin in their muscles, the bull elephant seals could remain underwater for up to two hours while diving more than seven thousand feet, their smaller female counterparts a third that time and distance.

———

The thirty-two foot sea craft moved into deeper waters as six-foot swells and thirty-knot winds attempted to push it back onto the narrow stretch of beach. The bone-chilling blast forced marine biologist Brandon Cornatzer to lower his binoculars and remove his wool Philadelphia Eagles hat to pull out its retractable ski mask.

And this is considered summer . . .

The New Jersey native tugged the mask in position over his face and once more looked through the binoculars, refocusing his gaze upon the elephant seals occupying the isthmus to the east.

Most of the plump brown bodies lazing along the shoreline were females. Having given birth to their pups back in October, a new mating ritual had begun. The mature bulls had come ashore first, followed by the cows who were then divided into harems. It had been a week since the orgy had wound down; twenty-three days since the pups had started weaning—activities that kept the cows on land, preventing them from feeding.

Brandon Cornatzer could hear two of the dominant males barking at one another from across the beach head, each bull in excess of seventeen feet and seven thousand pounds. Fastened around the mammals' blubbery chests was an underwater tracking device attached to a neon-orange harness and a series of underwater cameras.

Brandon's associate, Tom Beckendorf, stepped out from the protective confines of the bridge. "Anything?"

"Humphrey and Nixon are still jabbering at each other. The

females are getting antsy; I'd bet my frozen left testicle that today is the day."

As if on cue the mammals rose up in progressive waves and charged clumsily across the beach into the olive-green shallows.

"Here we go!" Brandon followed Tom inside, taking his place at a laptop connected to a bank of computer screens. Typing in a command caused the monitors to flash on, revealing two distinct scenes.

The monitors labeled *Humphrey* were herky-jerky land shots following the chaotic exodus of undulating blubber. The monitors under *Nixon* revealed an underwater ballet of brown bodies dispersing through the shallows. Brandon zoomed in on a cow as she caught a two foot manta ray in her jowls, two other females chasing after a small shark.

With a silent splash Humphrey entered the sea. The forward camera was blocked by a flurry of bubbles and dark flippers moving along the surface, the belly-cam offering a dazzling view of elephant seals torpedoing above a backdrop of white sand which quickly yielded to patches of volcanic rock and the deep blue depths.

The elephant seals continued trekking east to the Macquarie ridge, a volcanic fissure formed twelve million years ago where the region's three tectonic plates converged. The ridge separated the deep waters of the Pacific and Indian oceans, its basalt magma flow responsible for the creation of Macquarie Island.

Over the next three hours the boat shadowed the two bull elephant seals and their harems, the mammals diving eight hundred to a thousand feet to feast on schools of squid.

And then, as Tom watched on sonar, the bottom seemed to drop away, disappearing into darkness.

"Tom, take a look—the bulls are leading the cows into the sea trench. Wonder what they're after?"

"Better switch over to the night-vision lens."

"Humphrey just passed eighteen hundred feet and his cows are staying with him."

"Females usually don't venture that deep, do they?"

"Must be something special down there . . . and there it is!" Brandon zoomed in on a slope of white goo, which hung from an escarpment on the chasm wall like a massive snow drift.

There was no telling what species the baleen whale had been or how it had died. At some point the carcass had sunk, the remains of its fluke catching on a crevasse where it remained suspended, beckoning a feast.

Hundreds of six-foot-long hagfish moved in and out of the cavern that had been the whale's mouth, the eel-like denizens devouring the beast's internal organs from the inside. Dozens more had stripped off the cetacean's hide, exposing thick bounties of blubber.

The elephant seals swarmed upon the carcass, devouring blubber and hagfish like a busload of hungry seniors at an all-you-can-eat Las Vegas buffet.

Tom joined Brandon at the monitors, the two marine biologists mesmerized by the visuals. Over the next hour the elephant seals fed in shifts, the cows returning to the surface every fifteen to twenty minutes to breathe, their spots at the banquet quickly replaced by another female.

The bulls refused to surface, their presence serving to divide the bounty between the harems. Every so often two of the males would fight over a section of meat, one skirmish involving Humphrey and a juvenile bull, the latter quickly ceding its claim to the bigger mammal.

And then a blip appeared on sonar—a gargantuan life form that was rising slowly from the 23,000-foot depths.

"Jesus, what the hell is it?"

Tom stared at the object. "I don't know, but it's as big as a submarine."

"A blue whale?"

"Not that deep."

"A Megalodon?"

Tom looked at his colleague. "Way too big, thank God. It's probably just a school of squid."

"Tom, what if it's a school of Humboldt squid? Those predators will tear the elephant seals apart."

"Christ, you're right. How deep are they now?"

"Twenty-six hundred meters and change. They're coming up nice and slow, hugging the chasm wall so they don't scare the elephant seals off."

"Clever creatures."

"They're also bioluminescent; if they are Humboldts then we should see them soon."

"Two hundred meters."

"Nixon senses something; he's diving to take a look."

The two scientists watched, holding their breath as the bull descended, the camera angles limited to the rock face and the underside of the elephant seal's jowls.

Suddenly Nixon veered away from the wall, swimming rapidly into open water for three chaotic seconds before both monitors were enveloped in darkness.

Nixon's bank of monitors went static.

"What the hell just happened?"

"If I didn't know any better I'd say Nixon was just eaten."

"Jesus, what the hell could devour a four-ton elephant seal in one bite?"

"Tom, maybe you ought to move the boat?"

"Look at Humphrey!"

The bull was ascending fast, the monitors revealing multiple angles of cows fleeing for the surface.

"Start our engines; get ready to haul ass!" Brandon exited the bridge and hurried out on deck. The sun had set, the southern sky laced with emerald-green curtains generated by the aurora australis. The ocean reflected the heavenly light, yielding to dozens of elephant seals, which broke the surface in a state of panic. Most of the snorting beasts headed north, others swam in frenzied circles, more than a few striking the boat.

Brandon leaned out over the starboard rail. What the hell was down there?

———

The *Liopleurodon* had taken the large bull in one succulent bite, the elephant seal's high fat content quickly re-priming the pump of its depleted energy reserves, stimulating its central nervous system. With a rapid sweep of its fore fins it attacked the herd, each furious snap of its jaws catching three or four cows at a time, its six-inch stiletto fangs bursting the mammals' bodies like piñatas filled with hot blood.

The pliosaur went berserk, eating its way to the surface.

Through the haze of its feeding frenzy, it detected a challenger hovering along the surface.

Rapid contortions of its muscular tail powered the enraged creature past the fleeing elephant seals. The Lio's monstrous mouth hyperextended open as it struck the boat's keel, its momentum launching its upper torso and the vessel straight out of the water. Unlike a Megalodon, the pliosaur's jaws were designed to snatch, not crush. Twisting sideways, it fell back into the water, slamming the fiberglass craft bow-first into the sea.

Tom Beckendorf was thrown into the inverted galley, buried beneath a rolling avalanche of equipment.

Brandon Cornatzer was flung overboard, the frigid temperatures shocking his system. He struggled to the surface, his deflated lungs barely able to draw a breath, his tearing eyes widening in time to see what appeared to be the silhouette of an impossibly large crocodile rolling on top of his boat.

For a brief second the aurora's green lights illuminated a reptilian eye, then the boat sunk and the monster disappeared, leaving him treading water among hundreds of baying, snorting elephant seals.

Brandon convulsed in fear and shivers, his muscles turning to lead, barely able to keep his head above water. Seconds later the surface exploded on his left—his heart nearly with it—as the creature once more rose out of the sea, its six-story upper torso blotting out the sky, its jaws opening and closing upon a mouthful of elephant seals. For a surreal moment the monster seemed to defy gravity before falling sideways back into the water—its splash generating a seven-foot wake that rolled toward Brandon.

Before he could scream, something grabbed him from behind and he was dragged backwards onto an inflatable life raft. The wave lifted the rubber craft beneath him, tossing him on board.

The marine biologist looked up at his friend, unable to find his voice.

Tom handed him an aluminum paddle. "We need to get away from the seals. Nice and easy."

Brandon knelt by the edge of the raft, his entire body quivering as he attempted a stroke. Tom took up a position on the opposite side, the two men gradually distancing themselves from the dispersing seals.

The *Liopleurodon* struck twice more, each leap farther to the south.

The men stopped paddling. Tom searched through the vessel's emergency supplies, locating two wool blankets sealed in plastic, a flare gun, bottled water, rations, and most important—a radio that linked them with their base camp back on Macquarie Island.

Aboard the *Tonga*
Sixteen Nautical Miles Southeast of Macquarie Island

David's first impression of the engineer from Qatar was that he was an obstinate man.

"In order to *successfully* capture the *Liopleurodon*, the animal must be sedated the moment it is netted. Even unconscious the creature is far too big for the trawler's winches to handle. As such, I have devised an alternative method of setting the trawl which allows the tanker's winches to already be engaged. This requires Mr. Taylor to lead the *Liopleurodon* between the two ships and into the net."

David stared at the computer-generated schematic. The trawl net was positioned twenty feet beneath the surface, stretched out between the tanker and trawler. "This will never work. The Lio sees the *Tonga* as a larger life form; it will never get close to something that big."

"What if the *Tonga* and the trawler were dead in the water?" Jackie asked. "No engines, nothing for the Lio's senses to perceive. All you'd have to do is get it to chase you—you could lead it right into the trap."

David shot his "sex-buddy" a harsh glance. "If it's that simple, why don't you do it? Just be sure to figure out a way to keep from being netted yourself, because I don't see any place on this schematic for the Manta to go."

Fiesal bin Rashidi smiled. "Come now, David, you are being too modest. Last summer in Dubai, I witnessed you give our pilot candidates a demonstration of what your Mantas could do. Maneuvering within the confines of an aquarium, you accelerated in tight figure eights, then launched the sub out of the water at a forty-five-degree angle, clearing a fifteen-foot-high suspension bridge, nearly striking the duct pipes that ran along the ceiling." Bin Rashidi turned to Jackie. "He soaked everyone there, including our instructor, a no-nonsense American naval officer named Brian Suits. Captain Suits had been putting David in his place all day. Upon exiting the sub, David handed the captain a dollar bill as if he were a valet, telling him to 'park it in the shade.' That was the moment I knew we had found the one man in the world capable of capturing the *Liopleurodon* described by Michael Maren in his field notes."

Jackie winked from across the conference table. "He's something special, all right."

David was about to reply when Liam Molony entered the meeting room, the mission commander out of breath. "We just received a distress call from Macquarie Island. Two of their scientists were attacked by the Lio about eight nautical miles south of our present location. I ordered the *Dubai Land-I* to pick them up, but we need to get there fast before the creature leaves the area."

Bin Rashidi dragged the engineer out of his chair. "Get the trawl net into position; I want your trap set in place the moment we arrive. Commander Molony, David will need a co-pilot."

"I can handle it." The red-haired former submariner turned to David. "There's something else you need to know. The scientists were shadowing two elephant seal bulls mounted with tracking devices. At least one of the two males was eaten. It's possible the tracking device is still functioning inside the Lio.

"We may finally be able to track this monster while it's in deep water."

22

||||||||||||||||||||||||||||||||||

Agricola Industries
Vancouver, British Columbia

The saber-gray S550 Mercedes-Benz sedan followed the two-lane private road to the security checkpoint, which was already four cars deep. Beyond the iron gate lay an industrial campus of sprawling manicured lawns and man-made ponds, all centered around a six-story office complex and a series of manufacturing plants, their matching green glass exteriors reflecting the morning sun. Nicknamed "Emerald City" by Peter Agricola, the company's late founder and CEO, the business park had taken on more of a militaristic feel since the private Canadian firm had been bought out by the defense sector giant, ITT.

Paul Agricola waited impatiently for the drivers in front of him to be individually scrutinized. His dashboard clock advanced to 9:04.

Four minutes late and I'm still not through security. Bad enough the Board of Directors already thinks of me as inherited baggage.

He rolling down his window as the guard approached. "Morning, Mr. Agricola. Can I see your badge please?"

"Oscar, we've known each other since your kid was in diapers."

The guard scowled. "Frickin' ITT, they're watching everything we do. Even if I let you in without seeing your badge, you couldn't get past the lobby."

Paul fished through his glove box, removing the plastic card hanging from a lanyard.

The guard swiped the magnetic strip. "Thank you, Mr. A. Say, how's your sister—"

Paul drove off mid-sentence. *What was the point of schmoozing with the help if you still had to comply with all the rules?*

He followed the private road to the employee lot, parked the Benz in his reserved spot, and headed inside the tower for his "spanking."

———

"What the hell were you thinking? Don't you realize your name still carries weight in the business sector?"

Paul leaned back in his chair at the end of the twenty-foot-long oak conference table, his eyes following the short woman in the gray skirt and cream-colored blouse as she made her way around the crowded room. Tracy Ann King had been a rising executive at ITT when the defense company had taken over; now the auburn-haired CEO, twenty years his junior, ran his father's company.

"Tracy, I feel horrible that the kid was eaten, however—"

"Excuse me, Mr. Agricola, but this is a board meeting. Show the proper respect."

Paul exhaled a long breath. "With all due respect, Ms. King."

"Actually, it's *Dr.* King. I earned my Ph.D."

"Yeah, well good for you, but I'm not calling you Dr. King unless you decide to lead a peace rally through downtown Quebec. As for going after those Megalodons, *my* doctorate degree happens to be in marine biology. I was also the one who discovered those sharks living in the Mariana Trench thirty-five years ago and I'll be the one who captures those two she-devils. Then we'll see how the Agricola name carries in the business community, especially after we rename the Tanaka Institute the Agricola Entertainment Center."

The eighteen board members seemed to turn in unison toward Paul.

"Taylor's selling the institute?"

"Is there a signed contract in place?"

"Dr. King, shouldn't this sale have been brought before the board for a vote?"

Paul held up his palms. "Easy, maggots. This deal has nothing to do with Agricola Industries or ITT. I'm purchasing the Tanaka Institute using my own funds."

Tracy King stood over him. "You have signed paperwork?"

"I have a deal in principle. The attorneys are finalizing the contracts, which will be signed after I recapture Bela and Lizzy. As for the teen's death, that still falls under the Tanaka-Taylor liability section, so stop worrying."

Side conversations broke out.

"Enough!" Tracy King circled the room, returning to her chair at the head of the oval table. "Tell me, Mr. Agricola, after your last disastrous attempt, how do you plan on capturing these two monsters without getting anyone else killed?"

"It's called going back to basics. My engineer is meeting me in Warehouse B in about an hour to requisition a few items necessary to put everything into motion. If all goes as expected the sisters will be back in their lagoon and tourism in the Salish Sea will owe me a debt of thanks."

The female CEO sat back in her chair. "Your new venture will need seed money. Perhaps we can arrange something . . ."

"Forget it. Once the sisters are recaptured the banks in California will be lining up to offer me money."

The suit to Tracy King's right turned to his CEO. "Technically, anything stored in our warehouses remains the property of Agricola Industries and ITT."

Tracy King's eyes widened. "What was it you needed to requisition from *my* warehouse, Mr. Agricola?"

Paul ground his teeth. "You know, Dr. King, if you really want to be a part of this venture then you should be on board our boat when we capture the two Megs."

"And risk being eaten by those two monsters? Not a chance."

"Oh, I guarantee the Megs won't eat you. Call it a professional courtesy."

———

Michael Tvrdik followed the signs to Warehouse B, parking his Chrysler minivan out back by the aluminum bay doors. The engineer found Paul Agricola inside holding a coffee-stained instruction manual while directing a forklift operator where to set down a large wooden crate roughly the size of a golf cart.

"Michael, right on time."

"Paul, why am I here? I told you on the phone that I don't want anything more to do with capturing the sisters."

"You're here because I paid you in advance. As for the sisters, no one else is going to be at risk, thanks to the object inside this crate that you are going to get up and running for me as quickly as possible."

"What is it?"

Paul motioned to the forklift operator, who used a crowbar to pry open a rusted combination lock, breaking the latch in the process.

Michael Tvrdik helped the two men lift the top off the container. Inside the crate was a ray-shaped metal object with a seven-foot wingspan. Peeling yellow paint along its right wing identified it as a Sea Bat.

"What the hell is it?"

"What do you mean? It's a Sea Bat, an underwater drone."

"If it's a drone then why is it attached to a cable?"

"It's not autonomous. We used it in conjunction with a Multi Beam Echo Sounder to map the sea floor of the Mariana Trench. The Sea Bat dropped beneath the hydrothermal plume—it's what attracted the Megalodon thirty-five years ago."

"And what am I supposed to do with it?"

"Get it operational."

"Paul, it's a piece of junk. I'd probably have to swap out every circuit on board. Wouldn't it be easier to simply replace it with one of the newer drones?"

"Sure. While you're at it, why not replace the Mona Lisa with a poster of Kim Kardashian? Michael, this thing worked, and do you know why it worked? It worked because its metal skin produced electrical discharges in the water that were detected by the Meg's ampullae of Lorenzini. The newer drones are plastic; they don't make them like this anymore. Inside the unit is a sonar array—that can be replaced with a new one. Same for the batteries, underwater cameras, and lights. As for the cable—get rid of it, we'll be using the line attached to the hopper-dredge's winch. So? How soon can it be ready?"

"I don't know . . . maybe a month?"

"A month is too late. I want Bela and Lizzy sealed inside the Agricola Lagoon within ten days."

Aboard the Hopper-Dredge *McFarland*
Weddell Sea, Antarctic Peninsula

The ship continued its southeasterly course at fifteen knots, paralleling the Antarctic Peninsula. To starboard were snow-packed cliffs; to port a dark ocean illuminated by curtains of aurora light.

Zachary Wallace crossed the main deck, pausing to look down at the *McFarland*'s massive hopper. On Jonas's orders, the captain had drained the 175-foot long, forty-five-foot wide, fifty-five-foot-deep tub. For several moments the Scot stared at the hopper, confirming a distant memory.

Locating an interior stairwell, he ascended six flights to the bridge.

The *McFarland*'s command center seemed far too big for its solitary row of computer consoles. Large bay windows surrounded the chamber on all four sides, looking out nine stories above the ocean. The boat's captain, a man named Jon Hudson, was at the helm. Terry Tanaka was seated at a chart table studying a map of the continent.

"Hey Terry. Jonas and I were supposed tae meet here tae plot out the drop zones fer the sonar buoys. Is he here?"

"Actually, he told me he was meeting you in your stateroom."

"Me stateroom?"

Terry hid her satisfaction at seeing the marine biologist caught off-guard. "Is that a problem?"

"No . . . of course not. I'd better hurry; he's probably down there pacing around in that damp corridor waiting for me."

Terry smiled. "No worries, he has a master key. Knowing Jonas, I'm sure he's waiting for you inside your quarters."

Zach paled as the blood rushed from his face. Darting out the door, he descended the stairs two at a time.

––––––––

Jonas was seated at a desk in front of Zach's laptop when the Highland-born scientist rushed in. "Dr. Wallace, you're just in time. I've been looking at this file—"

"That was encrypted!"

"My mistake. I was looking at this *encrypted* file and came across a map of Antarctica with a few GPS time codes that require, well . . . a bit of explanation."

Jonas spun the laptop around so the screen faced Zachary. "I see you've got both the *McFarland*'s location and the two Dubai ships David is aboard accounted for. Today is February the eighteenth— no problem there. But somehow you've charted my son's location on March third. Tell me, *professor*, how the hell do you know where my son will be . . . thirteen days from now!"

Zach sat down on the edge of his cot, his eyes focused on the screen. "Jonas, there are things I can tell ye and things I cannae."

"Well, you'd better damn well tell me the things I want to hear or we'll be dropping you off at the nearest research station and you can thumb your way home."

"That would be a mistake."

"For who?"

"Potentially, for a lot of people . . . yer son included."

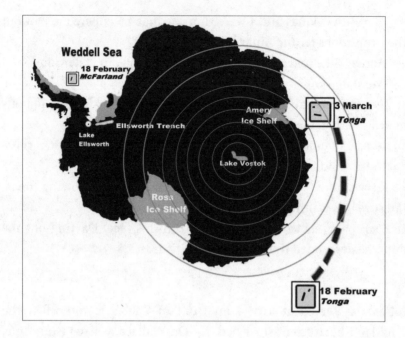

"From this map I can assume the lake you were in was Vostok. How the hell did you manage to access a lake buried beneath two miles of ice?"

"Two and a half." Zachary ran a hand through his hair, pulling out the ponytail. "Seven years ago I was recruited for a mission—a mission to send a three-man submersible equipped with *Valkyrie* lasers through the Antarctic ice cap intae Lake Vostok. The purpose of that mission, as it was explained tae me, was purely scientific exploration. We'd go down, collect microbes, document any life forms we happened across, then pop back up through our own burn hole, riding the pressure generated by the ice sheet. For the record, I didn't want tae go—at least not at first. Eventually my ego saw this as a Neil Armstrong-moon walk opportunity. But I had serious reservations."

"Who funded the mission?"

"I was told it was a U.S., Chinese, and Australian venture, but that all turned out tae be a lie. The mission was a black ops venture, my presence lending credibility tae the story concocted as an excuse tae get surveillance equipment intae Vostok before the Russians."

"Surveillance equipment? I don't understand. What could possibly be buried in a fifteen-million-year-old subglacial lake that would interest the Pentagon?"

"Not the Pentagon—I never said it was the Pentagon. The group in charge was multinational; they play by their own set of rules and essentially run the planet. The banks, the oil companies, the military industrial complex, the energy sector—especially the energy sector. Interest in Vostok began many years ago after SOAR—the Support Office for Aero-physical Research, sent a reconnaissance flight tae conduct magnetic resonance imaging over Antarctica. When they flew over Lake Vostok their magnetometers went bonkers. Scientists from Japan and Germany later confirmed the presence of a magnetic anomaly in the subglacial lake along a rise located in its eastern sector. The affected area packed enough juice tae power every city in the world for the next hundred years."

"What is it? What's down there?"

Zach shook his head. "We're not going tae talk about that. Whit we're going tae talk about is destiny."

"Destiny?"

"Specifically, the potentiality of multiple possible outcomes. The philosopher, John McTaggert, developed two theories about time and outcome. McTaggert's A-Theory stated that the only real time is the present. The past is gone and the future exists only as a probability distribution, a potentiality of the possible things that can happen. Since the future isn't set, it's not real."

"Makes sense. And his B-Theory?"

"That the past, present, and future all co-exist simultaneously. Since the past determines the future, everything that has happened since the Big Bang was predetermined. Quantum physics is based on B-Theory, that everything that could possibly happen has already happened, that time is dependent purely upon the observer. The overriding question—is it possible tae alter the present by changing the past?"

"I don't know. I'm a former phys. ed. major masquerading as a marine biologist; what the hell do I know about quantum physics?"

"Let's go back in time thirty-five years. Whit if this Paul Agricola fella hadn't been in the Philippine Sea the day ye piloted a three-man submersible intae the Mariana Trench? Would ye have still crossed paths with that Megalodon? If not, would your life be completely different right now? Different wife . . . different kids?"

"I don't know. I knew Masao Tanaka, so when his UNIS drones stopped working seven years after my naval dive he probably would have still sent Terry to recruit me to pilot one of their submersibles into the Mariana Trench. If everything is predetermined like you said, then you might board a different train, but all tracks lead to similar outcomes."

Zach nodded, Jonas's words having a deep impact. "Seven years ago I boarded my own train—a submersible that escorted three of us intae Lake Vostok. Seven years later, the ripples from that experience forced me tae return. My family was in trouble, the world on the brink of a disaster—I desperately needed tae change the present by altering the past. I knew the source of that magnetic anomaly would allow me tae do so, if I could reach it. The powers-that-be knew it too and were out tae stop me."

"I don't understand. You're here in Antarctica to go back to Lake Vostok?"

"No, Jonas. That return trip to Vostok already happened. I succeeded in rerouting the past because a close friend of mine sacrificed his life in order tae get me back tae that magnetic anomaly. On March third—thirteen days from now—we began a thirty-six hour marathon through subglacial rivers that led us intae the lake. We reached Vostok aboard one of the Manta subs your engineer is currently reconfiguring in the hold.

"Ye, Jonas Taylor, were the pilot."

23

||||||||||||||||||||||||||||||||

The crew of the *Dubai Land-I* found Tom Beckendorf and Brandon Cornatzer afloat in their life raft, surrounded by a sea of sharks drawn by the blood and blubber of the decimated elephant seal pack. The two scientists were taken aboard the trawler while the ship's sonar operators and lookouts nervously scanned the ocean, fearful of what might lie beneath the dark swells.

The arrival of the *Tonga* eased tensions on the trawler. The scientists were transferred to the supertanker, where they were treated for hypothermia. Fiesal bin Rashidi offered to fly the men on his helicopter back to Macquarie Island—if they provided him with the radio frequencies used to track the two bull elephant seals.

The scientists agreed.

Nixon's tracker had been crushed when the big male had been devoured by the creature. Humphrey had met a similar fate, only the bull's tracker had survived its journey into the Lio's stomach. Its signal was detected moving south on course zero-nine-six at fourteen knots. The depth of the device—at 13,013 feet—indicated the

Liopleurodon was following the Hjort Trench, the southernmost extension of the Macquarie Trough.

———

The eastern sky paled as it gently pushed out the night, dawn's appearance still forty minutes away. Jacqueline Buchwald stepped out onto the *Tonga*'s main deck, the frigid air forcing her to pull her jacket's fur-lined hood over her head. She found David Taylor standing by the bow rail with his friend Monty, the two men looking out onto a black sea specked with ice.

Monty leaned out over the rail and spit. "Did you know that during the first two years of a baby's life the kid's parents will miss six months of sleep?"

David removed a metal flask from his jacket pocket and took a swig. "Was that supposed to make me feel better?"

"Only if you're planning on having a baby." Monty looked over his friend's shoulder. "Speaking of which, here comes your baby mama."

Jackie joined them by the rail. "Monty, would you mind if I spoke to David in private?"

"Why would I mind?"

She waited thirty seconds. When Monty refused to move, she walked away, waiting for David to follow.

Monty winked. "Baby mama."

"Shut up." David joined Jackie, a gust of Antarctic wind forcing them to seek refuge behind a generator.

Jackie huddled next to him for warmth. "You didn't sleep in our stateroom. That's four nights in a row."

"I've been staying with Monty."

"David, drinking until you pass out . . . it's not a good thing."

"Was that all you had to say?"

She looked into his eyes. "Actually, I wanted to apologize. The other day with the engineer . . . I was out of line. Sometimes all of us, myself included, think of you as a pilot version of Superman, that you can pull off any maneuver in those subs—including nearly being eaten. We forget that you're only twenty-one; that just because you pilot the Manta without fear doesn't mean you're not afraid. The whole thing about losing Kaylie . . . I should have been more understanding. The truth is—I really do care about you."

"Really?" David looked at her coldly. "Because you told me our relationship was strictly about sex. No love, no emotion."

"I was wrong. These last few days . . . I've really missed you."

"Don't go there. Kaylie played the same mind games with me in Dubai during the pilot selection process. I was pretty gullible back then, not anymore."

"So that's it then?"

"No." He took another drink from his flask. "We can still be sex buddies."

"I don't think so. If that's all you want then you can hook up with one of those Arabian supermodels."

"I did."

Jackie's eyes teared up. Unleashing the hurt, she punched him in the chest with both gloved fists, pushing him aside as she stormed off, the wind buffeting her as she crossed the open deck.

Monty joined David behind the generator. "First she loves you, then she hates you?"

"Something like that."

"I think I've seen this love story before. Boy meets girl, boy loses girl, boy gets girl back. Girl gets eaten by monster."

"You really are a dick, you know that?"

"Hey, I'm not the one who told my girlfriend I slept with one of the reality show bimbos. By the way, which one did you sleep with?"

"Shut up."

"No seriously, which one—just in case Jackie questions me under threat of torture. Was it Jihan? Zeina? Hoda? It wasn't Nesrin, was it? That girl is crazy."

"It was the one you *didn't* sleep with!" Ducking his head, David jogged across the deck, heading back inside.

"Yeah, well I slept with all of them, Junior, so you're not foolin' nobody!"

Aboard the Hopper-Dredge *McFarland*
Weddell Sea, Antarctica

Jonas Taylor felt like he was having an out-of-body experience, Zachary Wallace's words causing an almost hypnotic effect. "Let me get this straight; you're telling me that, in some alternate reality that no longer exists I piloted the Manta through eight hundred miles of subglacial rivers into Lake Vostok?"

"Don't dwell on it, it'll make ye crazy. Think of it as a dream."

"How can it be a dream? I remember my dreams; I don't remember any of this!"

"Ye don't remember because the event I described was jist one of an infinite number of potential realities. Did it actually happen? Yes and no. Yes, from my perspective it happened because it allowed me tae return tae Vostok and set things right. No, it didn't happen because it was replaced by the reality we're living through right here and now."

"How can you replace a reality . . . wait, you mean time travel?"

"It's complicated. Suffice it tae say that returning to Vostok reset my life tae the day I was recruited for the mission. Instead of accepting the offer, this time around I turned it down, essentially cancelling the mission, and along with it, the potential reality that had ye piloting the Manta intae Lake Vostok. Still confused?"

"Uh . . . yeah."

"Jonas, as far as the world kens there has never been a manned exploration of Lake Vostok. Trust me, that's a good thing."

"What about March third? What happens then?"

"That's the trillion dollar question. The last time we lived through this moment together three distinct events took place, all at the Amery Ice Shelf on the opposite side of the continent. First, ye and Mac arrived in the *McFarland* tae rescue me from some seriously fucked up people. Then the *Liopleurodon* showed up, along with yer son. The powers-that-be then launched a submarine designed by Skunkworks that was equipped with a Europa-class *Valkyrie* laser and bow plates which could be superheated to temperatures exceeding 1,500 degrees—essentially a vessel designed tae move through hundreds of miles of subglacial rivers. We followed the sub's borehole all the way intae Lake Vostok. Again, that was then, this is now. Variables are already shifting between the two realities. For instance, back then Mac accompanied ye tae Antarctica, Terry remained at the institute. It's a small difference, but differences are a good sign that this reality remains independent of that last disaster."

"If that's true and the events coming down the pike thirteen days from now all take place at the Amery Ice Shelf, why are we in the Weddell Sea?"

"Good question. We're here tae insure nothing happens that might cause things tae revert back tae that March third reality. Ye see, altering the past is like diverting a river—sometimes it works and sometimes the river over-compensates farther downstream—in this case from the Amery Ice Shelf in East Antarctica tae the Ronne Ice Shelf in West Antarctica. Whit hasn't changed is that the bad guys still want tae find out whit's causing the magnetic disturbances in Lake Vostok. The difference between now and then is my actions back then led them tae believe Vostok could be accessed from the Amery Ice Shelf. My mission to Vostok never happened, but they're still looking for an access route to investigate the lake. Unfortunately, last summer's collapse of the Ronne Ice Shelf may have provided them with one. The answer lies in that whale's bloodstream."

"Which is the real reason you had Mac outfit our subs with *Valkyrie* lasers and load all those sonar buoys aboard the *McFarland*. It had nothing to do with the *Liopleurodon*, or helping bring David back to California."

"Not true. In fact, both David and that monster may play an important cause and effect role on March third."

"Why? What role did they play the last time?" Jonas felt his pulse quicken. "Your recurring nightmare . . . David died in that alternative reality of yours, didn't he? That's why I agreed to pilot the Manta into Vostok—to allow you an opportunity to reset the clock and alter the present—this present!"

"Stay calm—"

"Answer the question. Am I right?"

"Yes. But we're here now and things have changed."

"Bullshit. You won't know that until after March third."

"True, but I've taken precautions."

"Like what? Having me install air bags in the Manta's pilot consoles?"

"Yes."

"It's not enough. I want my kid off that tanker!"

"Jonas, that's extremely dangerous. These events aren't random, ye have tae let them play out or the butterfly effect can lead tae a hurricane. David's safe for now. We need tae deploy sonar buoys around the Ronne Ice Shelf and hope we can locate and tag that Miocene whale. Meanwhile we'll continue tae monitor the *Tonga*. If they head east after the *Liopleurodon*, then we make way for the Amery Ice Shelf; if they head west then we wait here in the Weddell Sea. Either way, we'll be there when it counts."

24

||||||||||||||||||||||||||||

Friday Harbor, Orcas Island
Salish Sea

Jennifer Marentic, president of the Salish Sea Association of Marine Naturalists took her place at the podium before a small assembly of board members, guests, and three news crews.

"Members of the board, honored guests, and my fellow naturalists . . . I have been asked by Nick Van Sicklen, head of the Whale Museum as well as our county manager, to assess the damage the two juvenile adult Megalodons are rendering unto our southern resident killer whales. The purpose of this investigation will be used to determine if marine sanctuary laws can be bypassed under an invasive species clause, allowing officials to kill the two Megalodon siblings. I asked Seth Bowling to complete this investigation, comparing annual orca sightings over the last ten years with this year's activities, including any deaths directly or indirectly caused by the Megs. Seth?"

The sixty-two-year-old environmentalist and semi-retired aquaculture engineer exchanged places with Jennifer at the dais. "Resident killer whales, known as J-clan, are subdivided into J, K, and L pods. Nine members of K-pod were killed by these two Megalodon sharks six weeks ago. Since the attack the surviving members of K-pod have relocated to the Strait of Juan de Fuca along with J- and L-pod members. Sightings around Vancouver Island are up; sightings around the San Juan Islands non-existent. There have been no other documented attacks by the Megs on resident orca.

"Does this lone attack justify exterminating two juvenile females belonging to a species once believed extinct? An invasive species is defined as an organism, either a plant, animal, fungus, or bacterium, that is not native and has negative effects on our economy, our environment, or our health. There are other people present in this room that are far more qualified to address the Megalodon's negative effect on our economy, so my comments will be restricted to the resident killer whales. The absence of our three orca pods around the San Juan Islands certainly affects tourism as well as the health of the Salish Sea, however it must be noted that the resident orca population has experienced a substantial decline over the last decade. This decline can be attributed to three variables.

"Variable one is changes affecting the orca's local food source. Ninety-five percent of our resident killer whales' diet consists of chinook. This species of salmon, specifically those spawning in the Fraser River area, are in a steep decline.

"The second variable is toxicity passed from the chinook to the killer whales. Chinook feed on Cherry Point herring which spawn at sea in the winter and then migrate in the spring to fresh water estuaries. These estuaries are now being exposed to thousands of tons of coal dust, the poisonous residue of which is being generated by the fifty million tons of coal exported every year from our ports. The coal contaminates the herring, the herring contaminate the chinook, and the chinook poison the resident orca population.

"The third variable affecting our killer whale population is noise pollution. Coal and crude oil exports are expanding rapidly. With upwards of twenty new coal and crude oil terminals and refineries being proposed in Washington, Oregon and British Columbia, the problem will only grow worse. Rapid expansion has led to more tanker and bulk carrier traffic. These immense carriers cruise past the San Juan Islands every day. Orca vocalizations are essential for hunting and the noise generated by these vessels reduces the whales' range of communication by sixty-eight percent.

"It is the shared opinion among Salish Sea marine biologists that the variables of toxicity and noise pollution would have caused the resident orca population to go extinct within the next five to seven years. Ironically, by occupying the San Juan Island shipping channels and driving the pods out to sea, the two Megalodons may have actually saved the local killer whale population from extinction."

Aboard the Hopper-Dredge *McFarland*
Ronne Ice Shelf, Weddell Sea

The sheer white cliffs towered five hundred feet over the Weddell Sea, the convergent point where water met ice bathing the coastline a brilliant emerald green.

The remains of the Ronne Ice Shelf were separated from the Filchner Ice Shelf by a three-thousand-foot rise known as Berkner Island. Together, the two plateaus still accounted for more than 83,000 square miles of ice, but the loss due to climate change had raised global sea levels by a frightening five centimeters.

Jonas Taylor and his wife stood before the starboard bay windows in the control room, gazing at the spectacle of Mother Nature.

"Cyel Reed is rigging Zach's device to the prow of the Manta. It's a powerful harpoon gun that will tag the whale while analyzing its blood and tissue samples. The data is downloaded to his laptop—one quick shot and we're out of there before Moby Dick even knows what happened."

"One quick shot . . . only you have to travel fifty miles beneath the ice shelf to take it. You quit trying to recapture Bela and Lizzy because it was so dangerous, now you're right back at it again."

"What do you want me to do, Terry? Tell Zach I'm backing out?"

"Tell him we came here to find our son, not to hunt whales."

"The *Tonga* hasn't arrived in Antarctic waters yet, and Zach has eyes and ears aboard the tanker. The moment we know where the Lio is headed we'll set sail to intercept. But if what Zach says is true—"

"You don't honestly believe that crazy story about the two of you being in Lake Vostok?"

"I don't know. Zach's admittedly a strange bird—"

"He's certifiable."

"Maybe. But he's also quite brilliant. This entire episode with David—he's always been two moves ahead. And I think it all ties in with Vostok."

Pulling Terry aside, he lowered his voice to a level just above a whisper. "Seven years ago, when Zach came to us asking for seed money to start up his solar energy company, I initially turned him down. I had three experts study his designs and business plan and all three said there was nothing special about his thermal collector specs. Mac agreed. It made no sense to us that one of the world's best known marine biologists would suddenly throw everything away to build a solar plant in the Scottish Highlands, of all places.

"Zach wasn't surprised that we turned him down, in fact he was expecting it. He asked to meet in private, then showed us something else—a small device the size of a hockey puck. He had Mac shut down power to the office complex and then plugged the device into a wall socket. Suddenly everything worked again—at least it did for about twenty minutes until the adaptor short-circuited. The unit was just a prototype for a clean energy technology that channeled negatively-charged electrons in the air into a positively-charged core, creating a magnetic field which spun three sets of internal rotors. He called the technology zero-point energy and said that even a small device like the prototype could provide enough electricity to power the entire institute for a hundred years. He explained that the solar plant was a necessary ruse to keep the powers-that-be from shutting him down."

"You mean the fossil fuel industry?"

"I mean the powers that run everything—the oil companies, the banks, the military industrial complex. A clean, free source of energy would flip the world's economy on its head.

"Zach was extremely paranoid, but the device was impressive and back then the institute had money to burn. Instead of putting up the seed money we decided to fund the entire plant in Drumnadrochit and became his silent partner. Here's the kicker—when I asked him what he was going to call these miraculous new devices, he said the *Vostok*, then quickly coughed and re-pronounced the name as Voltec before asking my feedback on a dozen other names."

"You're saying he slipped up."

"Like a government informant given a new identity who accidentally introduces himself using his old name. Zach's not a guy who makes these kind of mistakes, which is why I still remember it. To answer your question, I don't know what's in Lake Vostok, nor do I want to know, but yeah, I think he was there, which means that maybe I was there, but only because David was somehow involved in the equation. If finding this ancient whale safeguards our son from something that may or may not happen on March third . . . well, then call me Ahab."

Terry eyed her husband. "I know that look, Jonas Taylor. You're thinking about capturing this creature and bringing it back to the institute."

"Terry, we're after a tissue sample—"

"Then why are you tagging it?"

"Okay, fine. If this thing is real, then capturing it serves two purposes—it removes a predator from these waters and resurrects the institute. Think about it—your father's whale lagoon would finally get its whale."

"It does have a nice sense of closure to it. But how would we even get it into the hopper?"

"Paul Agricola showed me a way. By draining the tank and opening the keel hatch above the whale, the suction would inhale it straight up into the hopper. The problem is sedating it. Angel breathed the phenobarbital that was injected in the water through her gills. The whale's an air-breather. We'd have to figure out how to—"

The ship's navigator approached. "Excuse me, Dr. Taylor, but we've arrived at the first sonar buoy drop zone."

"Are there any other ships in the immediate area?"

"No, sir."

"How long will it take us to deploy all thirty-five buoys?"

"Sixteen hours. The sonar array will cover approximately one hundred and eighty miles of coastline along the southernmost tip of the ice shelf that parallels Lake Ellsworth."

"Commence deployment. Oh, and ask the captain to drain the hopper-dredge."

"Yes, sir."

Jonas turned to his wife. "Looks like we have sixteen hours to kill. Any ideas, Mrs. Taylor?"

Terry hooked her arm around her husband's waist. "Why don't we go to our stateroom; I could sure use a back rub."

Coulman Island
Ross Sea, Antarctica

Located in the Ross Sea, Coulman Island is an eighteen-mile-long, eight-mile-wide landmass composed of overlapping shield volcanoes. Flat craters share the geology with cinder cones that rise thirty-six hundred feet. A caldera occupies the southern end of the island, its magma chamber situated more than two thousand feet below the surface.

Emperor penguins inhabit the coast, the curious birds avoiding the northern section of the island where the landmass meets the Ross Ice Shelf. In another month the frozen land bridge would thin and break apart, yielding to the sea. For now it remained thick enough to support a base camp that housed scientists, technicians, and researchers from the International Antarctic Geological Drilling (ANDRILL) Program. A fleet of vehicles and two cranes mounted to tractor trailers had traversed the ice sheet from the American research station at McMurdo Sound, transporting enough equipment and supplies to support a small army. Two platforms towered above the

camp, their hot water drills having melted access holes through the eight-foot-thick ice sheet.

A team of scientists inside a command trailer watched on monitors as the first drill was lowered through the borehole into the 3,115-foot depths. Videotaping the tube's descent was a remotely operated vehicle named SCINI (Submersible Capable of under-Ice Navigation and Imaging). Equipped with cameras, oceanographic instruments, and sensors, the ROV would be used to explore the underside of the ice sheet.

Twenty minutes passed before the hot water drill reached the sea floor, spinning its way through rock and sediment. From this deep hole would emerge a core of strata that dated back fifteen million years to a period just before the climate change event that buried Antarctica beneath two and a half miles of ice.

———

The *Liopleurodon* glided effortlessly along the floor of the Southern Ocean, the thirty-seven-degree water temperatures soothing the hot blood in its veins, calming the unborn young within its womb.

More than a week had passed since it last fed.

The creature had been shadowing the pod of minke whales for the last thirty-two miles. Driven by hunger, the pliosaur arched its back as it rose from the depths, its massive forelimbs requiring but a single powerful downward stroke to streamline its body into a ninety-degree, twenty-knot vertical assault.

Fifteen hundred feet from the surface the black waters turned gray.

At twelve hundred feet the gray became an annoyance that blurred its vision.

At nine hundred feet the blurred vision advanced to a searing burn, the deep blue light casting painful blinding sparks of twilight in its eyes.

Whipping its tail, the Lio rolled away from the sun-drenched shallows, beating a hasty retreat into the depths.

The creature continued shadowing its intended prey as the whales entered the Ross Sea. And then a strange new presence rippled through the Lio's senses. As it entered the Balleny Basin it grew stronger; as it ascended over the Adare Seamounts it teased its hunger with a potpourri of scents and vibrations. The *Liopleurodon* had never experienced coastal prey before, though its ancestors had proliferated in these very seas.

The pliosaur ascended gradually as the sun dipped lower in the late afternoon sky. And then, without warning, the water temperature dropped, accompanied by a sudden darkness.

The Jurassic monster rose warily, the sounds and vibrations of the surface muting in its brain even as a strange glow filled its field of vision.

Whack!

Without warning, the *Liopleurodon*'s snout collided painfully with the underside of the Ross Ice Shelf. Shaking its head, the creature stroked its powerful forelimbs and swam off, its head and back sliding against the ceiling of ice.

Again and again it tried to find its way around the barrier, each failed attempt fueling a growing sense of anxiety. In this muted new world there was an absence of prey. Trapped against its will, the animal drove itself into a frenzy as it zigged and zagged beneath the ice sheet, desperate to find its way out.

At some point its senses latched onto a new vibration—this one coming from below.

Banking away from the ice sheet, the *Liopleurodon* descended into the depths to investigate.

———

Scott McColl, head geologist of the Coulman Island ANDRILL site sat outside his tent before the tripod-mounted video camera. The day was fading, the sun low on the horizon, obscured behind a cloudy haze. He waited for his assistant to take his place behind the camera before logging on to Skype. Checking his image in the reference box, he placed the battery-powered headset over his ear, covered it beneath his wool cap just as the head instructor at New Zealand's online education program, LEARNZ logged on.

Angela Rogers's face appeared on his screen. "Good morning, Dr. McColl. We're very excited to see you again."

"It's actually late afternoon where I'm at, Mrs. Rogers, but I'm excited to be back online for another virtual field trip. How many students are watching our broadcast today?"

"Over four thousand. Please tell us where you are and the purpose of your mission."

"Mrs. Rogers, our team is on the Ross Ice Shelf close to Coulman Island, which is in the Ross Sea. We're here with scientists from the Crary Laboratory at McMurdo station, where we've assembled two drill platforms, one of which went operational a few hours ago. Our ANDRILL team is using a hot-water drilling system that allows us to drill through ice, seawater, sediment and rock to a depth exceeding fifteen hundred meters. The core we'll be extracting and studying will provide our scientists with a geological record from the present to nearly twenty million years ago. This information is important because it provides us with data about past periods of global warming and cooling. Our target date is between fourteen million and fifteen million years ago, the warmest part of the middle Miocene before Antarctica froze. Our goal is to understand how Antarctica's sea ice, ice shelves, glaciers, and sea currents affect the world's ocean currents and the planet's atmosphere."

Dr. McColl nodded to his assistant, who picked up the tripod-mounted camera and followed the geologist across the ice to the first drill site.

"As you can see, the Ross Ice Shelf is very flat. The ice beneath our feet is about eight to ten feet thick . . ." McColl ceased mid-sentence, watching as members of his team raced past him, everyone converging upon the trailer which served as the drill platform's command post.

"Dr. McColl, we seemed to have lost you. Is your microphone still working?"

"Huh? Yes, can you hear me?"

"Yes. Can you tell us what we're looking at?"

"To be honest, I'm not sure. Something exciting seems to be happening. Let's see if we can find out." The geologist jogged across the ice to the trailer and worked his way through the crowd, followed by his cameraman.

One of the techs saw him and frantically waved him over. "Dr. McColl, there's something down there!"

"Down where? You mean the drill site?"

"No sir, the sea floor. It's circling the line; it must be attracted to the drilling."

"It?"

"A biologic," said his friend, Mitchell Friedenthal. The engineer in-charge of ANDRILL's remotely operated vehicle was working a joystick with his right hand, a keyboard with his left. "The ROV picked it up on sonar. I'm sending SCINI down to take a closer look."

Every eye inside the trailer—along with the lens of the tripod-mounted camera—was trained on a row of monitors mounted above the engineer's command post. The multi-angled images were dark, save for a spinning underwater light, the beam of which offered glimpses of the drill line's flex tubing as it descended.

"Seven hundred meters to contact. I'd say whatever it is that's down there is pretty damn big."

"A blue whale?" Dr. McColl asked.

"That would be my guess. Who knows? Maybe the drill vibrations sound like krill? Five hundred meters until . . . stand by." Friedenthal checked the ROV's sonar. "Looks like we got its attention, boss. Whatever's down there is coming up to say hello. Boy, this thing moves fast. Two hundred meters. One hundred meters . . . oh, shit."

For a brief second a monstrous crocodilian mouth was caught in the ROV's spotlight—a moment later all three monitors sizzled with static.

German, Italian, and English conversations broke out at once.

"Quiet!" Dr. McColl turned to his engineer who was frantically punching controls on his keyboard. "Mitch, what just happened?"

"I don't know, but the ROV's not responding."

"Can you replay the tape?"

"The tape . . . right." Checking the time code, Friedenthal reversed the recording, then replayed it on the monitors in slow-motion.

One side of the *Liopleurodon*'s massive head and left fore flipper appeared on screen, its mouth opening beyond the scope of the lens for a few frames before the images went to static.

"What the hell was that?"

Another New Zealander entered the trailer, out of breath. "Dr. McColl, you'd better get out here!"

The geologist and his team rushed out onto the ice to the drill platform. The steel frame was reverberating, the bolts securing its foundation to the ice sheet wobbling loose.

It's got hold of the flex tube . . .

Scott McColl was about to shout an order when the shaking abruptly stopped.

An uneasy quiet took the frozen plain, broken only by a woman's muffled voice coming from McColl's discarded headset. The members of the multinational expedition looked at one another, unsure of what to do next. One by one they looked down, each man's fear shared by all.

Dr. McColl nodded, as if reading their thoughts. "Leave the equipment; everyone in the trucks. We need to get off the—"

The creature's dark head exploded through the ice sheet, rising clear up to its forelimbs. The two enormous appendages flopped free of the sea before sliding outward, effectively pinning the *Liopleurodon*'s upper torso out of the water.

Unable to move or breathe, the monster went berserk. Its lower limbs churned maddeningly beneath the ice as if treading water, its tail whipping from side to side until the pliosaur managed to slide out onto the ice sheet, its entire one hundred and twenty-two foot, hundred-ton girth exposed to the star-filled heavens.

Now it was the humans' turn to panic.

Fifty-three men and two women shouting in four different languages attempted to distance themselves from the unfathomably large creature snapping its jaws and lashing its tail at every perceived movement.

A German geologist took advantage of his spiked boots to sprint to one of the trucks. Climbing inside, he gunned the already running engine—never seeing the appendage that upended the vehicle, tossing him through the windshield.

Dr. McColl's assistant, Dwight Taylor not only saw it but captured it on his tripod-mounted camera, causing thousands of students and teachers in New Zealand to simultaneously whip out their iPhones, taking the frightening images viral. No relation to Jonas Taylor, the Colorado native's last name would nevertheless spin endless conjecture among the media.

Scott McColl was slipping, sliding, and running blindly within a pack of stumbling, panicked scientists and engineers—the size of the fleeing group catching the visually-impaired eyes of the Lio. Unlike its ancestors, the pliosaur had never been out of the water and its limbs were far too weak to support its own body mass. Lunging sideways, it slid across the frozen plain, its tremendous weight cracking the ice beneath it.

The wall of ski jackets in front of Scott McColl stopped without warning as the rock-hard surface beneath their boots simultaneously fractured and compressed three feet into a crater the size of a baseball diamond. A knee-deep tide of frigid seawater seeped through the fragmented surface, creating small floating islands of ice.

Twenty-two men and two women were left in darkness, attempting to keep from falling. Several crewmen ended up in the water, the cold shocking their systems as they fought to climb back up on their frozen rafts.

Scott McColl was less than thirty feet from the monster's open jaws when the Lio flopped sideways into the Ross Sea and disappeared underwater, unleashing a ten-foot wave. The geologist leaped, bounding across fragments of ice after his fellow fleeing explorers as the swell caught him from behind, sweeping him up in its polar embrace, churning him underwater before pile-driving him face-first onto the ice.

Scott sat up, shivering, his forehead bleeding. The wave had carried him and many of his surviving colleagues over the hole in the ice from which the creature had emerged. As he was dragged to his feet a familiar voice called out from the pond-size crater, desperate for help.

Scott stood, spotting his engineer in the water. "Mitch, hang on! Lars, grab the rope out of the Sno-Cat! Mitchell . . . oh, God no."

The *Liopleurodon*'s massive head surfaced, the dagger-shaped eleven-inch teeth jutting out of its upper jaw gingerly plucking Mitchell Friedenthal from the floating mounds of ice, the man's screams piercing the frigid Antarctic air before abruptly going silent.

Tears rolled down Dr. McColl's cheeks, freezing as they fell from his face. Close to passing out from the cold, he allowed his assistant to lead him onto the jacked-up transport known as "Ivan the Terra Bus," where the frightened survivors from ANDRILL team were anxiously waiting, praying to get to Coulman Island before the beast struck again.

25

||||||||||||||||||||||||||||||||

Aboard the Hopper-Dredge *McFarland*
Ronne Ice Shelf, Weddell Sea

It had taken nearly two days to deploy thirty-five sonar buoys along a one hundred and eighty mile stretch of the Ronne Ice Shelf. Thirty-seven miles inland from the Weddell Sea, buried beneath more than seven thousand feet of ice, was Lake Ellsworth, a subglacial purgatory of life kept liquid by pressure, friction, and the planet's own internal heat.

Over the next forty-eight hours three pods of orca, dozens of minke whales, hundreds of emperor penguins, four Weddell seals, and a tourist boat crossed the sonar array.

No biologics were detected moving out from beneath the Ronne Ice Shelf.

Jonas spent most of his free time field-testing the reequipped Manta. With the two bulky *Valkyrie* laser units strapped to its wings the sub's performance was noticeably sluggish. Zachary Wallace had chosen to trade speed and hydrodynamics for the ability to melt ice rapidly and Jonas was having second thoughts about facing an eighty-foot bull Miocene sperm whale in a cavitating vessel with a top speed of only twenty-three knots. In the end he told his engineer to only convert one of the two subs, leaving himself a "game-day" decision.

The incredible news story coming from the Ross Sea broke on the night of February twenty-first. Every person onboard the *McFarland* had their computer and iPhone tuned in to the story—except for Terry. Having finally seen the monster her son was risking his life to capture, she refused to watch anything more, insisting to her husband that he end this Miocene whale nonsense and order the hopper-dredge to intercept the *Tonga*.

One major problem: The tanker was located halfway around the continent. If they chose the wrong route and the Lio headed for the Weddell Sea instead of the Amery Ice Shelf as it had in Zach's "other reality" then they'd never be able to rendezvous with the ship by March third.

Zachary Wallace assured the Taylors that the *Liopleurodon*'s unexpected appearance and encounter in the Ross Sea was a positive sign. The journey from the Weddell Sea to the Amery Ice Shelf would take five days, that gave them four to determine their course of action.

Privately, Zachary feared what might happen if the Lio remained under the Ross Ice Shelf for an extended period of time. According to his contacts aboard the *Tonga*, the thickness of the sea ice had muted the tracking device's signal and Fiesal bin Rashidi's crew were again operating in the blind.

On February twenty-third the Crown Prince of Dubai held a press conference at the entrance of his nearly-completed resort to announce that over a billion people had now seen the *Liopleurodon* footage. He predicted the monster—once captured—would draw ten times the number of guests than the Tanaka Institute drew during its last four years harboring Angel and her pups. For the first time the prince permitted news crews to tour Dubai Land's massive aquariums, allowing them to film Angel's only remaining captive pup— now a thirty-six-foot long juvenile albino adult. As a special treat, he offered an exclusive glimpse of his *Dunkleosteus*, a prehistoric fish that dated back 360 million years to the late Devonian period, then concluded his infomercial by revealing that his two ships had entered the Antarctic Circle and were actively tracking the *Liopleurodon*, although he refused to give out their location. "If you want to know then I suggest you watch this week's episode of Dubai Land: Sea Monster Quest. It is must-watch television."

The sonar array remained silent another thirty-six hours, pushing Zachary Wallace's deadline for the *McFarland*'s departure to its limits.

And then, on the night of February twenty-fifth at 8:52 p.m., sonar buoy number seven detected something immense moving out from beneath the Ronne Ice Shelf.

————

Zachary Wallace descended a steel stairwell into the bowels of the *McFarland*, accompanied by a disturbing sense of déjà vu. Reaching the lowest deck, he made his way aft through a tight corridor, past the engine room to a watertight door.

WARNING: PRESSURIZED DIVE CHAMBER
Do NOT enter when red light is ON.

The light was off, the door open.

Jonas was already inside, speaking with a silver-haired man in his fifties wearing a navy-blue jumpsuit and leather jacket stained with grease.

Perched on rubber blocks above a pair of sealed horizontal doors were two Manta submersibles. Attached to vessel number four's nine-foot wings were two *Valkyrie* lasers. A harpoon gun protruded from beneath its prow.

Jonas was inspecting the unit. He looked up as Zach entered the chamber.

"Zachary, I don't think you've met my chief engineer, Cyel Reed."

Reed snorted sarcastically. "One chief, no Indians . . . and still no

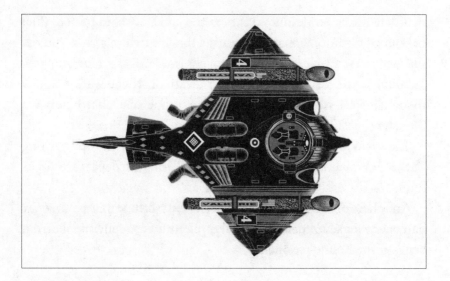

damn heater down here. I had to pour boiling water over the star-board wing just to tighten the support struts on the laser after your last test run."

Jonas examined the *Valkyrie* strapped to the right wing. "It seems pretty tight."

"A virgin's tight until she's been ridden a few dozen times. If I told you once, I've told you a hundred times, you can't fly this albatross like an F-15. Weight distribution's off. You don't put a luggage rack on a Ferrari and expect it to perform. Barrel rolls or the ability to melt ice—pick your poison, J.T."

Jonas turned to Zach. "It's your mission; your call. Or should I say, 'your premonition'?"

"Melting ice is more important than speed."

"Not if we're being chased by a hundred-ton sperm whale with teeth bigger than a Meg."

"True. But these lasers can plow us straight through any blocked passages below the ice shelf."

"Zach, I don't want to be anywhere near the ice shelf. At the brief-ing you said we'd park the Manta along the bottom and wait for your whale to return from his nocturnal feeding. Then, as it passed over us—"

"I ken whit I said, but things can change in a hurry. Whit if it's echolocating and detects the sub's engines before it passes over us? Whit if it takes another route back tae the lake? Having those lasers charged and ready tae go gives us another weapon in our arsenal."

"Weapon? I don't want to kill this thing, in fact, I was toying with the idea of capturing it."

"Out of the question."

"Hang on Zach, I haven't even pitched you my idea—"

"Ye had the captain drain the hopper; I'm assuming ye think ye can create a vacuum effect powerful enough tae inhale the melvillei straight up intae the tank. Forget it. That might work for one of the sisters, but this creature is twice their size and mass. It'll sink us, Jonas, and that's not a premonition, that's simple physics."

Jonas glanced at his engineer, who shrugged. "What do I know about tagging whales?"

Zachary climbed inside the starboard cockpit of *Manta-Four*, stowing his laptop in a side pouch.

Jonas situated himself in the portside command console. Cyel Reed leaned into the open cockpit to point out the triggering mechanism he had rigged to fire the harpoon gun.

"Duct tape? For real?"

"I'm not ruining the cockpit's finish to screw in some lame control; the duct tape will do just fine. Pleasant hunting, Ahab." The engineer sealed the cockpit glass and left the chamber to occupy a small control room farther down the corridor.

Jonas methodically ran through an abbreviated systems checklist. "Hatch sealed. Life-support—go. Batteries—go. Backup systems charged. *Valkyries* charged. Chamber is pressurized." He checked the radio headset. "Terry, are you there?"

"Yes, Jonas."

"How long do we have before first light?"

"The captain says you've got three hours, give or take ten minutes. The *McFarland* will remain in position outside the sonar grid. Ask your friend if he's heard from the *Tonga*."

Zach shook his head.

"Nothing yet."

"Jonas, are you sure about this?"

"One quick shot and we'll be home for breakfast. Love you."

"Love you, too."

"Mr. Reed, *Manta-Four* is ready for launch. Did you remember to release the clamps on our docking blocks before you left the chamber?"

"Kiss my ass."

"Acknowledged, docking clamps released. Seal and flood the chamber, please."

Water rushed into the compartment, lifting the buoyant submersible off its perch. A red warning light powered off, yielding to one in green. Seconds later the sound of rusted metal hinges groaned all around them as the keel's three-inch-thick steel doors opened, venting the chamber to the Weddell Sea.

Jonas waited until the pressure equalized before maneuvering the two-man submersible out of the flooded dock and into the frigid black sea.

"Switching to night-vision glass." Turning a rotary switch on his control console, Jonas changed the tinting on the cockpit glass, the darkness blooming into an olive-green world.

Moving beyond the hopper-dredge's keel, Jonas descended eighty feet, the visibility incredibly clear. The sea floor was a brown nutrient-rich muck carpeted in pink starfish, strange-shaped coral, and colorful urchins.

Ahead loomed a wall of ice, the underside of which was suspended fifty to seventy feet off the bottom—the entire Ronne Ice Shelf floating on the Weddell Sea.

A gentle three-knot current flowed out from beneath the ice sheet, rocking the submersible. Jonas powered on the Manta's external lights, revealing a seemingly endless passage squeezed between the muck and the ice shelf's frozen ceiling.

"I'm glad we're not going in there."

Zachary checked the coordinates on the sonar buoy that had

detected the Miocene whale's emergence. "We're three kilometers too far tae the west."

Keeping the Manta just outside the opening of the horizontal chasm, Jonas headed east.

"Dr. Wallace . . . a question: How long can a modern-day sperm whale hold its breath?"

"On a deepwater dive? About ninety minutes. Why?"

"Lake Ellsworth is located approximately thirty to fifty miles to the south of our current position. Prior to the collapse of the ice shelf last summer the lake was seven hundred miles farther inland. Seven hundred miles is a long journey underwater on a single breath of air. How do you suppose your Miocene whale could have made it this far back in 1940 before the ice shelf collapsed?"

"Good question. The answer is—I'm not sure, although the issue has been on my mind as well. I've come up with three potential explanations."

"I've got all night."

"First, the passage that opened between Lake Ellsworth and the Weddell Sea back in 1940 could have contained air pockets."

"That's a bit of a cop-out."

"Agreed. And even if it turned out tae be true, I doubt any air-breathing mammal would have attempted the journey unless one of the other possibilities were in play."

"Go on."

"Like your *Liopleurodon*, *Livyatan melvillei* could have evolved gills."

"I very much doubt that. *Liopleurodon* was a sea reptile. Gills may have been a natural progression for a pliosaur; not so with a mammal. What's your third theory—and make it a good one because I'm not spending all night waiting for a ghost."

"A ghost? Jonas, you saw those photos, this whale is real."

"I don't know what I saw. The images were blurry and that lower jaw and teeth could have been photoshopped. So what's your last theory?"

Zach exhaled, exasperated. "In studying how sperm whales are able tae hold their breath for so long, scientists at the University of Liverpool recently discovered the mammals possess an abundance of myoglobin, a protein which binds oxygen in the blood. In deep diving mammals like sperm whales the myoglobin becomes electrically charged. The charge causes the proteins tae repel each other, preventing them from forming clumps that could impede their ability to carry oxygen. This innate form of electro-repulsion, combined with elevated levels of myoglobin, prevents the proteins from sticking together, increasing the ability of the sperm whale's muscles tae store oxygen. Myoglobin is found in high levels in meat and is whit gives it its red color. *Livyatan melvillei* is a prehistoric cousin of the modern-day sperm whale, but it's still a different species. While sperm whales prefer tae eat squid and fish, Miocene whales were voracious meat-eaters. According tae Captain Mikkleson's log, the meat taken from the Miocene whale that attacked their ship was as black as the midnight sea, indicating extremely high concentrations of myoglobin in the creature's muscles."

Jonas nodded. "Okay, I'll buy into that . . . for now. How close are we to—"

Without warning the Manta was barreled sideways by a tsunami-like current flowing out from beneath the ice shelf. Before Jonas could react the starboard wing flipped over, the riptide sweeping the inverted submersible out to sea.

Gripping the joystick, Jonas rolled the Manta right-side-up. Banking hard to port, he accelerated out of the intense stream. "Zach?"

"That was a subglacial river."

"I wasn't expecting that kind of intensity."

"It's the ice. It generates thousands of pounds of pressure. That's got tae be the passage the whale followed out of Lake Ellsworth."

"If that's the case then we may have a problem. Your whale wouldn't have battled that head current to re-enter the lake, it would have taken a different route beneath the ice shelf. While we're waiting here, it could be making its pre-dawn return trip miles up or down the coast."

"That's unlikely, Jonas. Whales possess sensory systems that function like built-in GPS units; it'll use the subglacial river as a reference point. No, I think we jist need tae find a place close by, settle in and wait."

With the current fading on his starboard flank, Jonas flew the sub along the bottom, searching for a soft landing spot. Easing up on the Manta's dual pump-jet propulsion units, he allowed the neutrally buoyant vessel's belly to come to rest on an open patch of sea floor surrounded by sea urchins.

The digital clock on his console read 04:36. "*Manta-Four* to *McFarland*."

"Go ahead, Jonas."

"Terry, we located the subglacial river. Any sign of the whale?"

"Negative. It's still off the grid."

"Acknowledged." Settling back in his seat, Jonas closed his eyes, the sound of rushing water soothing his frayed nerves.

"Just came on screen two-point-six kilometers due north of sonar buoy eight. Jonas, do you read me?"

"Huh?" Jonas opened his eyes, repositioning the fallen headset over his ears. "Two-point-six kilometers from buoy eight . . . acknowledged." Turning to Zachary, he punched the sleeping marine biologist on his left shoulder.

"Oww. Whit was that for?"

"You fell asleep."

"So did ye!"

"True, but I'm older than you. Check your sonar, the whale's on the grid."

"Got him. He's thirteen kilometers due west, heading straight for us." Zach pointed to the cockpit glass. "I think we picked up a few stragglers."

Jonas looked up, surprised to find the cockpit's entire field of vision obscured by red and orange starfish. "Damn it."

"Can ye get rid of them?"

"Sure, I'll just roll down the window and pluck them off one at a time."

Zach shrugged. "I thought maybe the Manta had a windshield wiper."

"Just keep an eye on your damn whale." Pressing down on both foot pedals, Jonas accelerated away from the sea floor, attempting to shake the invertebrates loose.

To his horror the creatures remained suctioned to the Lexan glass.

"Son of a bitch, these things are glued on."

"The whale jist passed sonar buoy thirteen. He's less than eight kilometers away."

"Hold on." Whipping the sub 180 degrees to starboard, Jonas listened for the rush of water generated by the subglacial river. Locating the current, he aimed the bow of the sub into the intense sixteen knot stream, the blast of sea prying loose a cluster of starfish, leaving less than a third of the cockpit glass still obscured.

"Jonas, I lost him."

"What do you mean, you lost him?"

"He passed sonar buoy fourteen and disappeared off the screen."

"Christ, he's under the ice shelf." Banking to starboard, Jonas pulled the Manta out of the current and accelerated beneath the ceiling of ice. "So much for your theory about the whale using the subglacial river as a reference point. You Ivy League eggheads . . . you always think you're right."

"For the record, I played Division I football in college, jist like ye did."

"You're comparing Penn State's football program to Princeton? Please."

"Ah yes, forgive me. At an Ivy League school, we actually have academic requirements." Zach winced as the sub barely missed scraping a jutting section of ice. "Okay, so I was wrong about the whale. But if ye stay close tae the river we should run right intae him."

"Let's not take a chance. Go active on sonar."

"Go active?"

"You have a problem with that?"

"No. It's jist—these whales, they become extremely agitated when you start pinging."

"And I get extremely agitated when I have to fly an unstable sub beneath a mile and a half of ice without my anxiety pills. Now do your job and find that fucking fish . . . *mammal*—I know!"

Zach switched the sonar controls from passive to active and pressed a green button, causing a loud sonic *ping* to reverberate from beneath the sub's prow.

"Nothing yet. Wait . . . there he is. Three kilometers tae the southwest on course two-two-seven. He's ahead of us, heading right for the current."

"Continuous pinging. See if you can bring him to us."

Zach started to object, then thought better of it.

PING . . . PING . . . PING . . .

"We've got its attention. He jist altered his course to intercept. Two kilometers and closing fast."

Zzzzzzzzzzt. Zzzzzzzzzzzzzzt.

The burst of sound rattled the sub's cockpit like a giant tuning fork.

"What the hell was that?"

"Echolocation. We're not the only ones that can go active on sonar. He jist closed tae one kilometer. How do ye intend on tagging him now that he kens we're here?"

Jonas reduced the sub's speed to eight knots. "How about one right between the eyes on that big square head of his. Should be like tossing a football through a truck tire."

"Only this truck tire wants tae eat ye. Three hundred meters."

Jonas flipped the safety on the harpoon gun with his left hand, fingering the trigger as he stared into the olive-green abyss.

Then he saw it, and the sheer size of the creature caused his heart to race.

The squared-off head bearing down on them was as large and as wide as a three-story barn. Charcoal-gray on top, it faded into lighter shades of silver; its lower jaw and belly ivory-white. The whale's entire body undulated as it swam, its head rising as its lower torso and fluke completed a powerful downstroke, its skull dropping below the hump midway down its back as its tail rose. From this angle Jonas could not gauge the bull's length, but it was moving at a speed in excess of twenty knots.

Christ, it's faster than the Manta. . . .

Cursing Zachary's decision to use the laser-laden sub, Jonas accelerated at the charging beast.

Sensing its approaching prey, the Miocene sperm whale rolled onto its left flank, opening its formidable mouth to feed.

For a frightening moment the whale disappeared from Jonas's view behind a cluster of starfish. Quickly adjusting his course to compensate, he targeted the gyrating head, allowing the massive skull to fill his partially obstructed field of vision.

"Sixty meters . . ."

"God, what a brute. Hey, that's a good name—Brutus."

"Naming the whale isn't important right now." Zach clenched his arm rests. "Forty meters . . . thirty. Jonas, that's close enough!"

Jonas waited another three seconds before squeezing the trigger and banking hard to starboard.

Twice as thick as an arrow, the barbed spear exploded out of the gun barrel at sixty knots. With a puff of black blood the tag struck the whale two feet below its blowhole, the shaft's remote sensors buried within the thick blubber ten inches deep.

The sting was barely perceived by the enraged cetacean. The eighty-foot *Livyatan melvillei* snapped its lower jaw upon empty sea even as its left eye caught sight of its escaping prey.

Jonas fought to regain control of the sub, the one gee maneuver shaking the Manta while nearly snapping the steel support bands securing the port laser to the sub's wing.

Zachary opened his eyes. "We're still alive?"

"For the moment."

Zzzzzzzzzt. Zzzzzzzzzzzzzzt.

"It's chasing us?"

"And here's more bad news—it's faster than us." Jonas's eyes jumped from the partially obstructed view of the bottom of the ice sheet to the aft camera monitor where the Miocene whale was bearing down on the Manta like a bat out of hell.

"It'll be dawn soon. Can ye make it out of here?"

"We're heading south, the exit's north. Sharp turns are off the menu; I nearly lost one of the *Valkyries* on that last maneuver. Gradual turns and we lose ground—ah, crap, hold on!"

Jonas veered to starboard a heartbeat before the bull whale clamped its jaws on the port wing.

"Ye realize this is a losing battle."

"No shit, Sherlock. I'm open to suggestions."

Zach closed his eyes, deep in thought. "Enter the river."

"The river runs north, I told you we're heading south." Jonas banked hard to port, the gnashing jaws of the enraged whale forcing him into a thirty-degree turn, the sub reverberating behind the torque.

"There, now we're heading east."

"Stay on this course. When you reach the subglacial river, enter the current and head south."

"Into a sixteen-knot current? You're crazy."

"Just listen. The sub's far more hydrodynamic than the whale; the force of the current will not only cut its speed in half, it'll wear it down. We can open up some distance, then double back when we can."

"Okay, that sounds semi-intelligent. Where's the river?"

"Less than a kilometer ahead."

Eying the charging whale in his aft camera, Jonas banked to starboard, resuming his trek to the south.

"Jonas, I jist told ye tae stay on course."

"Let me do the driving, Mr. Peabody. If we enter that river from the east that current will tear us apart. I need to ease my way in."

"Okay, that sounds semi-intelligent—for a Penn State graduate. Jonas, watch out!"

The Miocene whale suddenly lunged forward, its teeth biting down on the tail section of the Manta. For a brief second the sub reverberated and slowed until the radio antennae snapped off in the *Livyatan melvillei*'s mouth.

A *whoosh* of current filled Jonas's headphones. Edging his sub to port, he felt the current rippling along the wing. Continuously tapping the joystick, he managed to immerse the Manta into the subglacial river, its boundary as wide as a six-lane highway.

A glance in the aft monitor revealed the whale had followed them in. Battered by the current, the aging bull had to fight twice as hard just to maintain its pace. As Jonas watched, the creature fell behind, eventually disappearing from view.

Zach turned and punched Jonas on the right shoulder.

"What was that for?"

"That was for all us Ivy League student athletes who had tae put up with comments from dumb jocks like you."

"Hey, I graduated with a three-point . . . oh shit!" Jonas veered the Manta to port, slicing his way across the subglacial river as the left side of the whale's enormous head suddenly appeared outside the current.

Unable to reach the sub, the goliath beast was forced to reenter the river and was immediately pummeled by the intensity of the forty-meter-wide stream.

Shooting out the other side of the current, Jonas maintained his southerly course, distancing the Manta from the still-immersed *Livyatan melvillei*. When the whale left the current to pursue, Jonas re-entered, slicing his way back across the vortex, exiting out the opposite side. This repeated maneuver enraged the beast while wearing it down.

After ten minutes the exhausted cetacean had had enough. Breaking free of the current, it disappeared from view.

Zach continued pinging until the whale was beyond the range of sonar.

Jonas kept the sub east of the river. The starfish were gone, the cockpit view revealing a noticeable narrowing of the gap between the bottom of the ice sheet and the sea floor.

Without warning, the passage dead-ended at a wall of ice.

Jonas eased up on the propulsors. The subglacial river had curved to the southwest, the cockpit's night-vision glass revealing a narrowing passage that faded into darkness.

"Zach?"

"Looks like we've reached the end of the Ronne Ice Shelf. The passage must lead inland until it connects with Lake Ellsworth. I suggest we head east for a while longer jist tae make sure we don't cross paths with Brutus before we exit tae the north."

"Fine by me. Is the tag working?"

"The tag . . . I completely forgot." Removing his laptop from a storage pouch, Zach powered up the unit and scrolled through the data being uploaded by the tag's sensors.

"Well?"

"Good news. The trace minerals pumping out of the geothermal vents in Lake Vostok are absent from Brutus's blood gases. The whale's never been tae Vostok."

"So everything's good?"

Zach smiled. "Everything's good."

The loud warning *beep . . . beep . . . beep* from sonar wiped the smile from the Scot's face. "It's coming at us from the east. Jonas, move!"

Jonas stamped down on his right foot pedal while jamming the joystick hard to the left, sending the submersible into a tight turn to port as the *Livyatan melvillei*'s enormous head bloomed out of the olive-green darkness.

There was no other option. A gauntlet of ice lay before them, with the Miocene whale bearing down on them from the east, its angle and speed cutting off any chance of escaping to the north.

Pressing both pump-jet propulsion pedals to the floor, Jonas aimed the Manta down the throat of the subglacial river . . . into oblivion.

26

||||||||||||||||||||||||||||||||

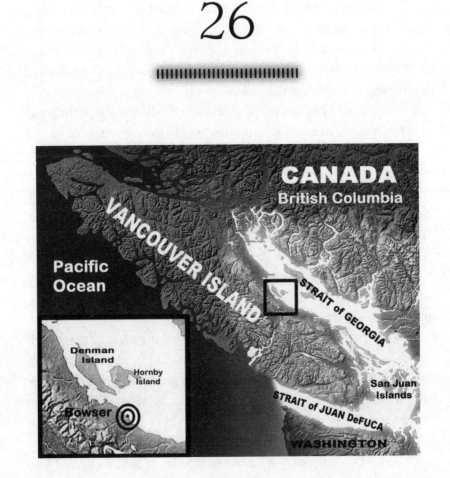

Vancouver Island, British Columbia
Salish Sea

Tim Rehm turned off Route 19 onto Route 19A, an extension of highway that hugged the eastern coastline of Vancouver Island. The thirty-seven year-old strength and conditioning coach at New Jersey's Monmouth College felt his adrenaline pumping as the deep blue waters of the Strait of Georgia appeared on his right. He fought the urge to lose himself in the incredible view—the islands of Texada and Lasqueti looming on the horizon, Hornby and Denman Islands still ahead but far closer to shore.

Approaching the town of Parksville, he debated whether to make a quick stop at the grocery store. Checking the time, he decided against it. Dusk was only four hours away and he needed to catch a few hours of sleep before tonight's festivities began. He hoped Tania had stocked the refrigerator in his rental cabin.

Continuing north, he passed Qualicum Beach and a sign that read *Bowser: 4 km.* Another ten minutes and he turned into the gravel driveway of the Shady Shores Beach Resort and Vacation Home Rental, a little known slice of paradise managed during the winter months by his former assistant in the Monmouth College athletic department. The oceanside property consisted of a two-story, A-frame log home featuring a matching gazebo complete with a hot tub, and seven two-bedroom private cottages. Living on a teacher's salary, Tim couldn't afford to stay in the "big house," but Tania had offered him full use of one of the cottages for the rest of the week, plus air fare to fly him out.

Sixty-three-year-old Tania Cruz was sweeping off the front porch of the log A-frame when the rental car turned in from the main road. The Cuban-born American limped over to greet her former boss, her slightly deformed right foot—a result of childhood polio—swollen from having been on it all day.

Tim gave her a big hug. "Tania, how are you?"

"The foot's a bit sore, but I can't complain. What about you? You look tired."

"I am tired; I've been traveling almost non-stop since last night. But, if what you told me on the phone is true, then it'll be well worth it. So, uh . . . is it true?"

"Come on, I'll show you." Tania took his arm and escorted him down a private path to the rock-strewn shoreline. The sun was strong in a cloud-free sky, neutralizing the winter's chill. The Salish Sea was calm, its surface as glassy as a lake. An unusually large tide pool occupied a huge swath of beach, separated from the Georgia Strait by a sandbar. To Tim's amazement, large salmon were leaping out of the water, attempting to escape.

"Can you believe the size of this tide pool? It's been like this for two weeks. Yesterday I waded in and caught three salmon using only a bucket. Morning's the best time to fish, before the sea lions invade the beach."

"Tania—"

"The high tide brings them in—the fish, not the sea lions. We get crabs and bull heads, and quite a few octopuses. Or is that octopi?"

"Tania, show me where you saw them."

"Everything happened out on the jetty." She pointed up the beach where a wooden pier stretched sixty yards off shore. "We're early, but there's something you need to see; then you'll believe me."

They followed the shoreline past a fire pit and wooden chairs to the eight-foot-wide boardwalk. Tim's heart raced as he followed her out, the water lapping along the pilings beneath their feet.

She pointed to the wooden bench at the far end of the jetty. "I sit out there almost every sunset. You'll see why in a few hours . . . it's so peaceful."

"When was the first time you saw them?"

"Last Wednesday. At first I only saw the white one, Lizzy. Her dorsal fin passed within twenty feet of where I was sitting."

"Did you freak out?"

"Please. I'm a single mother from Havana. I put one daughter through med school, the other through law school. I doubt they even knew I was there. The second night I got a little bolder. I brought a salmon out with me. When I saw the fin I stomped on the deck. The albino submerged, then a minute later her head rose out of the sea maybe ten feet from the jetty—Tim, it was so incredible. I cooed to her, 'Hey beautiful, are you hungry?' Reaching in my bucket, I tossed her a hunk of salmon, only it was a bad throw and it landed behind her. That's when I saw the other one—the one with the white head and dark back. It came out of nowhere and ate Lizzy's fish."

"Bela."

"I don't like Bela. When the albino looks at you, you can see she's thinking things through. When the dark one looks at you, she looks right through you. Got to watch out for that one. Fortunately, Lizzy runs the show."

"How would you know that?"

"Two daughters, Tim. A mother knows which child's the boss. These sharks, they swim in tandem, did you know that? Lizzy's on top. The boss is always on top."

"Tania, the tandem swimming deal—it's been reported in every newspaper."

"I don't read the newspaper, I observe things for myself."

They reached the bench at the end of the jetty and sat. A gust of wind had them adjusting their coat collars, the late afternoon chill accompanied by a strong fish odor.

"Tania, how deep is it out here?"

"I don't know. Pretty deep, I suppose. The tankers come by here every morning. Do you want to hear the rest of my story or not?"

"Please."

Tania took in a deep breath. "The third evening I brought two buckets of salmon with me. I was hoping to get the white one, Lizzy, to catch a salmon in her mouth only she never surfaced, she just circled the jetty a few times with her sister in tow. So I tossed the salmon close by and watched them feed. That was Friday. Saturday I waited until nine o'clock but they never showed up. About an hour later I was taking out the garbage when I heard a haunting sound far out into the strait. It sounded like a humpback, only like it was in distress.

"Sunday morning I came out to fish the tide pool when I noticed blue herons flocking around my bench, a few eagles circling over head. When I came out here, I found something caught beneath the jetty. Take a look."

She knelt down by the edge of dock.

Tim hesitated, then laid down on his chest next to her and leaned out over the edge—gagging at the stench.

The tide had jammed it against one of the pier's cross beams. The remains of a telltale flipper indicated the dead whale had been a juvenile humpback. The head, rostrum, mouth, and throat grooves were intact; everything situated from the small dorsal fin to the fluke was gone, presumably eaten.

"Ugh, it's disgusting. Why are you keeping it around?"

"I'm not; the flipper's wedged between the dock and a support strut. Such a nice gift."

"Tania, you don't actually believe they left this for you?"

"Who's to say? I had a german shepherd years ago that used to leave dead possums on our back porch. Sometimes they weren't dead, they were just playing possum. The point is the dog would bring them to me as a sign of respect."

"This isn't the family pet. These are big, prehistoric sharks."

"Prehistoric sharks raised in captivity. I'm not saying they can be domesticated, Tim, I just don't think they should be slaughtered."

"On that we agree." Tim helped her to her feet and back to the bench. "Tania, be honest; this isn't just about us selling footage of the Megs to the networks, is it?"

"No. I want to free-dive with the sisters."

"Free-dive? With Bela and Lizzy? You're insane."

"Tim, you grew up near water, I grew up on an island. My father taught me how to spear fish when I was six. He taught me to respect the ecosystem and the creatures we share it with. Sharks are not the oceans' bad guys, humans are. I've free-dived with great whites twice in the Farallon Islands and three times in South Africa. We both went cage diving together in Guadalupe. You know me; I'm not a thrill-seeker or an adrenaline junkie. This is purely about teaching people that Megalodons, like great whites, are not simply giant killing machines and that humans are not part of their diet."

"Except that they have eaten humans, and there are two of them. Maybe you think you've charmed Lizzy but Bela has a completely different personality."

"Accidents happen; people end up in the wrong place at the wrong time. Car accidents claim more lives every year than shark attacks. Tim, I can read a shark's body language; I can interpret every twitch and movement. A few swim-bys recorded on your pole-mounted video camera will allow us to gauge their demeanor and whether they just fed. If we both agree it's safe then I'll slip into the water with a snorkel and mask and hang by the jetty. If Bela gets aggressive, all I have to do is duck behind the pilings—they're spaced too narrow for the Megs to slip through."

"Fine—as long as we agree you won't attempt anything certifiably crazy—like hitching a ride on Lizzy's dorsal fin."

"No rides . . . for now. But Tim, imagine the impact that would have among the locals, not to mention the environmentalists and animal rights groups fighting to protect these amazing creatures."

"Tania, no. And there's one other condition you need to take care of before I break out the underwater cameras . . . the dead whale. I don't want it anywhere near you while you're in the water. The last thing we need is a repeat of the Maggie Taylor incident."

Aboard the *Tonga*
Ross Sea, Antarctica

A week had passed since the *Liopleurodon* had crashed through the Ross Ice Shelf, wreaking havoc upon an international team of scientists before a viewership of thousands of high school students in New Zealand—who promptly sent it viral.

While the event promoted the Crown Prince's reality series, the inability of the *Tonga*'s team to track the creature beneath the ice shelf only served to add more gray hairs to Fiesal bin Rashidi's beard. The engineer's task was daunting—locate a mobile creature beneath a hundred and sixty foot thick frozen desert that was roughly the size of France.

To accomplish this feat, bin Rashidi ordered his helicopters to deploy twenty-two sonar buoys along a three hundred and seventy mile boundary where the Ross Sea bordered the ice shelf, hoping to detect the *Liopleurodon* as it exited to open water. The engineer's own experts doubted the plan would work. The array had far too many gaps;

the creature could easily slip out in the depths or remain beneath the ice indefinitely—in the end it was all a matter of luck.

Bin Rashidi had plenty of luck—all of it bad. Compounding his problem relocating the Lio was the health of his crew. Extended months at sea will wear the best sailor down; add eight days in the Antarctic Circle with no end in sight and the mental and physical toll can be steep.

A wave of sickness spread throughout the ship; a third of bin Rashidi's crew had the flu and were confined to quarters. Among the ill was Liam Molony, the mission commander who he was counting on to co-pilot the Manta sub with David Taylor.

———

The heavy scent of disinfectant escorted David Taylor through the deserted corridor. He stopped at the stateroom numbered ST-501 and knocked.

Thirty seconds passed before Fiesal bin Rashidi cracked open the door. "David . . . put this on before you come in, I don't want you to get sick."

The door opened wide enough for bin Rashidi to pass a surgeon's face mask through the crack.

David unfolded it, secured it over his nose and mouth and entered.

The Dubai engineer was dressed in a bathrobe, T-shirt, sweat pants and wool socks, a scarf wrapped around his neck. The heat was turned up to a stifling ninety degrees, the porthole cracked open, channeling a stream of frigid air into the suite.

Bin Rashidi motioned for David to sit. "This fever . . . one minute I'm cold, the next I'm drenched in sweat. Keep the mask with you; we can't afford our only pilot to get sick."

"What did you need to see me about?"

"I spoke to my cousin this morning. He wants you to take the sub beneath the ice sheet and search for the Lio."

"Search for the Lio under a hundred and eighty thousand square miles of ice? I could search for a year and not find that thing."

"Agreed. But the reality show pays for the ongoing costs of our mission and we cannot afford another episode like the one that will air this week. A sick crew coughing on camera while we wait for a sonar buoy to beep does not make for riveting television. Once you launch I'll order the men to prepare the trawl net in the new ready position. Commander Molony agrees we can use the practice, plus it'll look good on camera."

"What am I supposed to do about a co-pilot?"

"Molony has been training one of the crew. Get changed, grab your gear, and report to the trawler, your co-pilot is already onboard."

————

Twenty minutes later, dressed in his neoprene pilot's jumpsuit, gloves, boots, and bundled in an extreme weather jacket, David followed one of the crewmen down an internal stairwell. A gantry dead-ended at a watertight door. The sailor wrenched it open, revealing an overcast day, their perch situated three stories above the waterline. The Arab, who apparently spoke no English, pointed to the rungs of a ladder permanently bolted to the starboard flank. The *Dubai Land-I* waited below.

Securing the hood of his parka, David carefully made his descent, wary of the slippery layer of frost which coated the steel bars. His quadricep muscles were shaking by the time he was helped onto the trawler's stern deck and escorted to the Manta.

The sub's cockpit was open. A crewman was seated in the starboard seat, his head concealed beneath the hood of his parka.

David lowered himself into the vacant bucket seat and sealed the cockpit. "Yo dude, it's frickin' freezing in here; my nipples are hard."

"Mine, too." Jacqueline Buchwald pulled the hood away from her strawberry-blond hair. "All systems are go, we're ready for launch."

"No . . . no way, Jackie. This isn't going to happen."

"Can I just explain?"

"There's nothing to explain. I'm not taking the sub out with you as my co-pilot."

"Because of what happened with Kaylie?"

"Yes . . . no. Yes."

"Yes, meaning you still have feelings for me and refuse to risk my life? Or no, you don't have any emotional ties; you just don't trust me as a co-pilot?"

"Yeah, that one."

"For your information, I've been practicing in the simulator all week. Commander Molony tested me; I graded out a ninety-one percent on sonar and passed all ten of the required maneuvers."

"A simulator's nothing more than a video game, Jackie."

"Agreed. But I'm the only healthy option you have. So stop with the déjà vu. I'm not your old girlfriend and we're not descending nine miles into the Panthalassa Sea. This is essentially a joy ride intended to fill forty-two minutes of a reality show episode. The chances of us coming within fifty miles of the Lio are slim to none, so crank up the heat before both our nipples fall off."

David cracked a smile. "A joy ride, huh? Okay Jackie, let's take a joy ride." He sealed the cockpit and then signaled for the crew to lower the sub down its launch ramp.

"Wait . . . shouldn't you go through a pre-launch checklist?"

"Weren't you just doing that?"

"Yes, but I'd feel better about it if you confirmed everything."

"Nah, I trust you. Besides, it's just a joy ride."

The crewmen pushed the sub prow-first into the sea.

David powered up the twin propulsor engines and accelerated into a thirty-degree descent, the deep blue underworld rushing at them.

Jackie's eyes widened, a smile stretching across her face. "This is incredible—" She grabbed for the armrests as David rolled the Manta counterclockwise into a double wing over wing somersault.

"Stop . . . I'm going to puke."

"Barf bags are in the glove box." Pulling out of the roll, he accelerated to the north. After a minute a soft glow appeared, gradually becoming a wall of ice. Descending to six hundred feet, David soared beneath the frozen ceiling into darkness.

A twist of a dial activated the night-vision glass, turning the sea an olive green.

"Anytime you want to listen in on sonar would be fine by me."

"Sonar, right." Jackie adjusted the headphones over her ears. "Active or passive?"

"We're not going to find the Lio by listening for its farts; go active."

"Right. Let's see . . ." She flipped the toggle switch, then set the acoustic cycle to three standard pings per minute.

The reverberations echoed in her ears, the waves of sound appearing on her sonar monitor. She closed her eyes and listened. "Nothing out there but the ice sheet. Wow, I can hear it crackling. David, are we following any particular heading?"

"North on zero-zero-zero, keeping it simple. We'll go straight in and come straight back out again on one-eight-zero. The last thing we need is to get lost under here."

"Agreed. So, aren't you going to pull another macho maneuver? Try to make me lose my lunch?"

"Lunch was bad enough going down. Want to drive?"

"Are you serious?"

"Not much damage you can do. Strap your feet to the pedals. Remember, you can veer hard to port or starboard using just the foot pedals, but the joystick will feel more comfortable. Switching over to your starboard console in three . . . two . . . one."

"Got it!" The sub's portside wing dipped, followed by its starboard wing before Jackie sent the Manta plunging on a steep descent. She leveled out at twelve hundred and sixty feet. "This is so cool."

"Easy, Maverick. You're flying blind. Check our heading."

"Two-six-six. We're heading west."

"Which means we're off course, and that's not a good thing. The ice is going to play havoc with our radio transmissions; God only knows how it will affect the Manta's GPS. We need to rely on ourselves to find our way back to the trawler."

"Sorry. Returning to course zero-zero-zero. Any particular depth?"

"You've got thirty-four hundred feet to play with and the Lio likes it dark. After nearly suffocating on the surface, I kinda doubt she'll be going anywhere near the ice. Why don't you descend to twenty-five hundred feet; that should give us a clear sonar reading topside and below."

Using the joystick, Jackie dove the sub, this time on a more gradual descent. "Was she a good pilot?"

"Kaylie? Yeah, but her forte was sonar."

"How long were you two marooned in the Panthalassa Sea?"

"I don't want to talk about it." Donning his headset, David closed his eyes and listened to the sea, the rumble of cavitating ice thundering softly in the distance.

An electric charge jolted his eyes open as Jackie squeezed his inner thigh.

"Don't shut me out, David. Teach me how to be a better pilot. Sonar, for instance. How do I distinguish one life form from another?"

"Not everything is a life form. Take the ice. When the ice shelf calves it can sound like a small splash or a distant explosion depending on your proximity. Sea ice whines. A passing iceberg can sound like a scream or cry. Storms tend to hiss, while ships have very mechanical sounds. The simulator has everything in its library."

She held up her palm. "Listen! Do you hear that chirping?"

"That's a Weddell seal. They sound different from Ross seals, which are more like those light sabers in Star Wars. Leopard seals tend to howl."

"What about whales?"

"Whales broadcast over different frequencies. Blue whales register sounds around ten hertz while fin whales are at ninety-eight hertz. Minke whales generate pulse trains between one hundred and three hundred hertz. Orca clicks and whistles are the most sophisticated, coming in between two thousand and twenty thousand hertz."

"What about that gurgling sound?"

David listened, then suddenly sat up. "Check the frequency."

"It's low . . . about five hertz."

"See if you can pinpoint it."

"Hang on . . . okay, I think I have it. It's seven and a half kilometers to the northeast on course zero-one-eight. I can't be sure of its depth. Do you think it's the Lio?"

"I doubt it. Still, you'd better let me take over so you can focus on that sound. If it starts heading in our direction, I want to know about it." David switched command of the sub back to his console, altering their course. He tried the radio. "*Manta One* to *Tonga*, do you copy?"

The line returned nothing but static.

"David, maybe we should stop pinging?"

"Not yet. I don't want to lose it in ambient sound. Do you have a depth yet?"

"It's close to the sea floor, just below three thousand feet. David, if it is the Lio, what's the game plan?"

"The game plan is to lead it to the *Tonga* and pray bin Rashidi's men don't have their thumbs up their asses. How close are we now?"

"Just under three kilometers."

"Jackie, if you're going to be my co-pilot you need to know I can't think in the metric system."

"Sorry. It's a little over a mile up ahead and a thousand feet below us."

David slowed the sub to five knots before executing a steep, spiraling descent. "Visibility's pretty good. I'm going to approach it nice and slow from the sea floor."

Jackie nodded, her limbs trembling noticeably.

"You scared?"

"Yes."

"Relax, it's just a joy ride."

She smiled.

"Just for the record, I didn't have sex with one of the reality girls."

She looked at him. "Why did you—?"

"Because you pissed me off. Quit staring at me and watch your screen."

"Yes, sir."

The bottom came into view, its mud-like surface home to clusters of sea urchins and starfish. David flew the Manta close to the sea floor, his forward speed barely enough to keep the sub on course.

Both pilots jumped as a seven-foot, two-hundred-and-fifty-pound Ross seal shot past them.

"What's his problem?"

Jackie gripped his arm. "David!"

David killed the sub's engines.

The dark silhouette appeared out of the haze, the *Liopleurodon* gliding silently along the bottom. Its four limbs hung limp, the tips of each fin stirring up the sea floor as the hundred-and-twenty-two-foot monster passed overhead like a landing Boeing 747. Looking up, they could see massive teeth protruding from the underside of the creature's upper jaw, its lower jaw yielding to a thick neck and fluttering gills, its belly nearly scraping the top of the Manta. For several seconds the view was obscured behind the mud clouds churned by the Lio's dragging fins, the view clearing in time for David and Jackie to witness the long, rigid tail pass by.

Before either pilot could steal a breath, a miniature version of the behemoth smacked its mouth against the cockpit glass. The newborn *Liopleurodon* was eight feet long and lanky. Attracted to the consoles' LED lights, the curious crocodilian creature refused to leave.

Jackie whispered, "David, we have to get out of here!"

"Shh!" He glanced down at his rear-view camera monitor just as Momma Lio faded into the murk and disappeared.

David was about to power on the sub's engines when Lio Junior opened its mouth and gagged out a crow-like gurgle, alerting its mother.

The *Liopleurodon* immediately spun around, revealing the captured Ross seal held in the tip of the pliosaur's jaws by its tail, the wounded sea mammal reeling in body convulsions.

David didn't hesitate. Powering up the Manta, he gunned both engines and ascended away from the bottom doing thirty knots.

The Lio raced after the sub, all four limbs churning in sync. It closed the gap quickly—until its maternal instincts took over and it circled back to protect its three-day-old offspring.

Biting off the Ross seal's tail, the Lio released the crippled mammal to its young.

One moment the creature was bearing down upon them, the next it was gone. When it was clear to David that the sub was no longer being chased he doubled back, circling four hundred feet above the hyperactive female.

He looked over at Jackie, who was wiping cold sweat beads from her face. "You okay?"

She nodded, fumbling to unscrew the cap on a bottle of water. "Maybe the simulator needs to add a charging sea monster to its program."

"At least we know now why the Lio headed for the Antarctic Circle. It needed the colder waters to birth its young. The question is, how long will it remain beneath the ice? Whales won't venture beneath the shelf, and it certainly can't survive on seals. I wonder if it's lost?"

"David, you do realize that everything's changed. We don't need the adult anymore, only the baby."

"I'm not sure Fiesal bin Rashidi would agree. Even if we could capture the infant, what makes you so sure it could survive the trip back to Dubai without its mother?"

"Let me worry about that. You figure out a way to flush the Lio out from beneath the ice sheet."

"There's only one option—we have to get it to chase us. Since we want it to head south, we should probably get it to chase us to the north."

Jackie capped her water bottle, her hands still trembling. "I'm not crazy about this whole cat and mouse thing. Maybe there's another way?"

"Let me know if you think of one." David circled fifteen hundred feet above the Lio until the sub was hovering north of the creature. "Jackie, count down our distance, I want to know how close it'll allow us to get to its pup before it attacks."

"David seriously, this is not a good idea."

Pressing the joystick forward, David dove the Manta at a thirty-degree angle, maintaining a speed of eight knots.

"Twelve hundred feet . . . eleven hundred feet. David, please don't do this."

The dark four-limbed creature with the white belly gradually became visible.

"Nine hundred feet."

Sensing the approaching threat, the Lio arched its back in a defensive posture.

"Eight hundred feet. David, that's close enough."

Slowing his descent, David hovered the Manta seven hundred and sixty feet above the *Liopleurodon* and less than a quarter mile to the north.

A wave of adrenaline sent his heart racing as the Lio suddenly rose from the sea floor. Stomping down on his starboard pedal and jamming the joystick to port, he banked into a sharp 180-degree turn and accelerated to the north, the creature rising fast in pursuit.

"Five hundred feet . . . four hundred feet—can't this thing go any faster?"

"You tell me. You're the one who was simulator-certified."

"Three hundred feet. Wait, it's slowing."

The intense twenty second sprint wore down the fifty-ton pliosaur, which was still exhausted from having birthed its pup. Warily, it began its descent, its head turning every ten to fifteen seconds to check on the Manta.

Returning to her young, the *Liopleurodon* nudged it with its snout, guiding it to the south.

27

||||||||||||||||||||||||||||||||

Beneath the Ronne Ice Shelf
Weddell Sea, Antarctica

Jonas Taylor banked hard to starboard, sending the Manta submersible soaring through a dark fissure that appeared in the cockpit's night-vision glass like a four-story-high olive-green birth canal. Shooting through the chasm, the sub was slowed by a sixteen-knot current, the Manta's hydrodynamic design preventing the vessel from being pushed backwards.

The Miocene whale followed them in, its fluke forced to work twice as hard just to maintain half its cruising speed.

Zachary Wallace continued pinging, calling out the *Livyatan melvillei*'s proximity. "He jist entered the current. He's definitely slowing down; ye've got about a kilometer on him."

"Zach, there's something up ahead . . . I can't see it, but I hear it. The current sounds different."

The passage dropped like a rollercoaster, an upwelling of current pinning the Manta against the ice ceiling.

Jonas activated his exterior lights, the twin beams revealing a sixty-

degree downward slope. Banking away from the ceiling, he accelerated down the shaft, the whale closing the distance.

"Step on the gas, J.T."

"I can't. The current will catch our wings like a kite if we start wobbling. How deep is this shaft?"

"Maybe a mile. Sonar's bouncing all over these walls; it's hard tae
get a fix. Exterior pressure jist passed sixty-five hundred psi. What
can the sub handle?"

"We'll be fish food long before the pressure gets us. Where's your
whale?"

"He was close, but he's falling behind again in this current. And
stop calling it *my* whale."

"You got me into this mess, that makes it your whale. As for this
current, I think we may be in a bottleneck."

"Are ye sure?"

"Look for yourself. The shaft is widening; our angle of descent is
easing as well. Oh Christ, hold on!"

Jonas pulled back on his joystick as the passage suddenly leveled
out, opening to a vast chasm. The flat ceiling of ice above their heads
spanned beyond the scope of their field of vision, the depths of this
claustrophobic passage less than seventy feet.

Zachary checked a fluctuation on his salinity meter. "Jonas, this is
meltwater. We're no longer in the Weddell Sea."

"Then where are we?"

"I can't be sure, but I think we're beneath the glacier that feeds
intae the Ronne Ice Shelf. Glaciers float along subglacial rivers as
they migrate tae the sea. The ice cap is above us, the geology of West
Antarctica below us."

"In other words, we're between a rock and a hard place. Now how
do we get out of here?"

"I assume we exit the same way we came in."

Jonas glanced at the blip chasing after them on sonar. "Somehow
I doubt your whale's going to allow us to double back."

For the next twenty minutes they trekked north through the

subglacial river in silence, the blip on their sonar screens gradually closing the gap. To Jonas, it was like piloting through a dark, underground tunnel, the Manta's headlights illuminating a brown vortex of emptiness, the only evidence of movement coming from the peripheral glow reflecting off the ceiling, which rolled past them like a conveyor belt.

Several times Jonas caught himself drifting off.

The third time his feet eased off the accelerators.

His eyes flashed open as the sub was nudged from behind by the *Livyatan melvillei.* Stamping down on both pedals, he reopened the gap to thirty feet.

"Damn it, Zach. What kind of co-pilot are you?"

"Ye're blaming me because ye fell asleep?"

"I'm blaming you for being stuck two miles beneath the Antarctic ice, being chased by a fucking whale."

"If ye recall, I was the one who warned ye not tae ping these creatures."

"And if you recall, I came to this godforsaken continent to find my son, not to . . . ah, never mind. Start pinging again; see if you can find a way out of this river."

Zach pinged their new surroundings, watching the acoustic reflections ripple outward across his sonar monitor. "Jonas, don't get yer boxers all in a knot, but this passage narrows significantly in less than three kilometers."

"Meaning what?"

"Meaning in less than three kilometers we'll hit a wall of ice."

"Brilliant." Jonas veered to starboard as the whale attempted to bite the sub's port wing. "The passage can't just dead-end. Where's that subglacial lake your whale was supposedly inhabiting?"

"Lake Ellsworth . . . right." Zach scanned his GPS system. "Crap. We're too deep tae get a signal."

"Then take a guess!"

"Okay, I'm guessing we're too far west. Can ye head east?"

"Not without being eaten."

"One kilometer until impact. Jonas, ignite the *Valkyries!*"

Feeling for the control switch his engineer had duct-taped to the side of his console, Jonas powered up the lasers, the sudden heat and bright light chasing the whale from his port flank. He attempted to alter his course—only to see a wall of ice looming ahead.

Both men let out a yell, Zach covering his face—

The sub shook beneath them like a truck passing over train tracks, the Manta's twin lasers transforming the gauntlet of ice into a melting stream of slush and water.

Shocked to still be alive, Jonas reduced the sub's speed, allowing the lasers more contact time to clear the way, easing the rough ride to a mild turbulence.

A quick glance at the rear camera screen confirmed they had left the Miocene sperm whale behind.

Jonas flipped the monitor the middle finger. "Screw you, *Brute*."

"Unfortunately Jonas, I think we're the ones that are screwed. I have no clue where we are or how tae get back."

"No problem, we'll just go up."

Zachary grabbed the joystick. "Don't! Those *Valkyries* aren't rockets. Ye'll stall us and we'll become stuck inside the glacier."

As if in response, the sub jammed against a rough patch of ice before lurching ahead another six feet, only to stall and lunge forward once more.

Jonas turned to Zach, who shook his head. "The propulsion units are churning slush."

"What were they churning when they managed to take us all the way to Lake Vostok in your imaginary reality?"

"That was different. We were moving through subglacial rivers, not solid ice."

The Manta stalled again. The whirring sound of propellers spinning against air caused both men to look at one another, their situation dire.

Thirty seconds passed.

Another two minutes.

Jonas eased up on his foot pedals, afraid he would burn out the engines.

With a sudden lurch, the propulsion units caught melt water. The Manta shot forward, chunks of ice bashing the exterior of the cockpit—parting to reveal a dark void.

The stunned pilots let out a yell as the sub plunged twenty feet, free-falling nose-first through the air before plunging into a pitch-black alien sea.

Zachary turned to Jonas, his face pale. "Congratulations, Magellan. Looks like ye found Lake Ellswood."

Vancouver Island, British Columbia
Salish Sea

Tim Rehm methodically arranged his video equipment on the wooden deck of the jetty. He attached a small video camera to a fifteen-foot reach pole, allowing him to film underwater from the safety of the dock. While it gave Tim real-time images that were displayed on his laptop, it did not have a night setting like his larger handheld unit.

The buoy-cam had a nocturnal setting, but the weather was picking up, creating a three-foot chop that rendered the device useless. That left the remote camera he would strap to Tania's left wrist and his larger handheld underwater camera, which he could also use for surface shots.

He glanced at Tania, who was in her wet suit, seated in a lotus position. Preparing her lungs for her free dive, she was inhaling deep breaths through her nose, her abdomen ballooning outward with each steady inward gust before exhaling through her mouth.

Tania had spent most of the afternoon trying to convince Tim to join her underwater, even if it was only to film her from beneath the pier. She assured him the remains of the dead humpback had been removed by the resort's gardener, but that wasn't quite enough to change his mind.

Then why was he wearing his wet suit?

Growing up on the New Jersey shore, Tim Rehm felt as at home in the water as Tania. He had been SCUBA diving since middle school and had encountered his share of sharks in the wild, but had never purposely put himself in harm's way just for a quick thrill. His first experience cage-diving with great whites hadn't been planned—he and Tania were attending a coaching clinic in San Francisco when his adventurous assistant convinced him to spend his one free day watching her cage-dive off the California coast.

The next morning at 5:40 a.m., Tim found himself reluctantly boarding a dive boat at the Emeryville Marina in San Francisco Bay. Tania and her fellow adrenaline junkies had paid eight hundred dollars to spend the day cage-diving, Tim coughing up half that fee just to watch the action from the safety of the boat.

The dive site was the Farallon Islands, a protected marine sanctuary located twenty-seven miles off the coast of San Francisco. Nicknamed "the Devil's Teeth" by sailors, the waters off these craggy islands were home to whales, seals, and seabirds and—from late summer through the end of November—a population of great white sharks that migrated annually across the Pacific from Hawaii.

An overpowering stench of sea lion excrement greeted them as their boat circled the rocky landmasses. The captain dropped anchor near Southeast Island, a place he proclaimed to be "a prime feeding spot." He described the Farallon community of great whites as fourteen- to twenty-foot adults, the females easily distinguished from their male counterparts by their larger, bulkier girths.

Four hours passed before the first shark was sighted—a surface kill sixty yards away that sent seal blood spurting into the gull-infested air. The first four divers—Tania among them—quickly scrambled into the submerged cage, where they remained for nearly an hour without a single encounter.

And so it went for the rest of the afternoon. Being a protected wildlife preserve prevented the crew from using chum, forcing them to rely on fake rubber seals to attract the sharks, which the crew futilely dragged along the surface.

Excluding an occasional splash in the distance, the sharks stayed away.

By day's end the passengers were cold and grumpy, ready to head in. The captain offered discounts on a future excursion, and then asked any observing passengers if they wanted to give the cage a final shot in exchange for their vouchers.

Tim found himself donning a wet suit to join Tania on the last dive of the day.

Following the captain's instructions, he laid down on his belly along the bottom of the cage, the air line connected to his face mask a preferred alternative to wearing a bulky SCUBA tank. The water was a frigid fifty-four-degrees and murky, the sea seemingly void of life.

A half hour passed. And then, incredibly, a large female rose majestically out of the mist directly beneath them to investigate the cage. The twenty-foot great white was as wide as Tim's Buick Regal and probably outweighed the car by a good three hundred pounds. It circled the two humans for fifteen minutes, its aura overwhelming, its demeanor non-threatening.

As darkness arrived the female moved off, disappearing into the murk with a final wave of its caudal fin—the predator's appearance having forever altered the destinies of its two transformed onlookers.

———

Tim Rehm stared at the sea, its surface glittering with the golden reflections of the setting sun. He and Tania had bonded over their experience in the Farallons, each together and separately pursuing similar encounters with the sea's apex predators. With his career limiting his free time, Tim still managed to fit in three to four cage-dives a year off the Jersey shore. Two summers ago, he had joined Tania for a cage-dive in Isla Guadalupe, a great white hot spot located a hundred and sixty miles off the coast of Baja, California.

Tania had gone a different route. Accepting an offer of early retirement, she had moved to Vancouver Island to commune with killer whales during the winter months, spending her summers in Mexico where she worked for Big Animals Expeditions, a company specializing in open water encounters with great whites.

Now she was attempting the ultimate big animal encounter . . . and despite his fear, Tim found himself keeping his options open.

Exhaling briskly, Tania stood up and offered him her left wrist to mount the remote camera. "Not too tight, I don't want to cut off the circulation. The girls will be able to detect a throbbing pulse."

"The girls?" Tim strapped the camera to her forearm. "You make it sound like you're spending the evening with your Mahjong group."

"Attitude is everything during these wildlife encounters. If you're calm, the sharks feel no threat. So? Have you decided?"

"For now, I'll remain on the jetty . . . which is where you promised to stay until you got a good bead on these two . . . *girls*. What time did you say they've been showing up?"

"Right around dusk. I think they may be feeding off Hornby Island."

The two divers wrapped themselves in their winter coats and sat on the bench, waiting for the sun to go down. As they watched, the sky over Texada Island turned bright crimson, fading to violet as the landmass gradually disappeared along the horizon.

Tania gripped his arm, nodding to their left.

Tim Rehm's eyes widened. The albino Megalodon was spy-hopping thirty feet from the jetty, its triangular head poised above the water-line just below its gills slits, its gray-blue eye watching them.

Reaching slowly for his handheld camera, Tim adjusted the night lens and began filming.

"Hi there, beautiful. I have something for you." Reaching into an ice chest with her gloved right hand, Tania removed a hunk of salmon by its tail. Whirling her arm, she flung the fish at the Meg, who caught it in its mouth.

"Tim, did you get that?!"

"Got it."

"What did I tell you? These sharks aren't monsters, they were raised in captivity." Reaching for her swim fins, she slipped them on over her rubber boots.

"Tania, wait. Where's Bela?"

"I don't see her. Can you find her on the underwater camcorder?"

Grabbing his reach pole, he powered on the camera and slid it into the water, the herky-jerky live images playing on his laptop. He scanned the area around the jetty, but could not find the dark-backed Megalodon.

Tania spit into her face mask. "Anything?"

"No, but visibility's only about ten to fifteen feet without a night-vision lens. Plus she's mostly black."

"Her head's white, so is her belly. You should be able to see that. If you can't then she's not around, which means now is the best time for me to get in the water with my girl Lizzy."

Using her rubber dive gloves, Tania grabbed another fish and tossed it high in the air at the albino shark. The Meg snapped at it but missed, the effort revealing a band of thick gums and razor-sharp triangular teeth.

Tania sat on the edge of the dock. She positioned her mask over her eyes and nose, allowing the snorkel to dangle by her mouth. "Hand me another fish."

He reached into the chest and removed a twenty pound chunk of salmon, its severed insides dangling.

Tania took it from him and tossed it in the water about fifteen feet from where she was sitting. "Come and get it, sweetheart."

Lizzy's left eye followed the splash. As if beckoned, the Megalodon's head slid beneath the dark waters and disappeared.

Seconds later, the predator's ivory hide emerged from the blackness twenty feet beneath the surface. As she swam past the jetty on her side, her mouth opened to swallow the fish.

Tania waited until she passed, then slipped feetfirst into the sea.

Tim positioned the reach pole underwater, his heart pounding in his chest. Glancing at the laptop's monitor, he saw a flicker of white and aimed the camera for it, managing to film the Megalodon as it turned back toward the pier, moving slowly toward Tania.

Tim's legs shook as he stood by the edge of the jetty, filming the forty-six-foot creature as it passed beneath his friend, towing her in its wake.

"Woo-hoo!" Tania waved as she was carried away from the dock and out to sea. Shoving her snorkel in her mouth, she sucked in a deep breath of air and surface dived.

Tim scanned the dark waters, his pulse quickening. "Tania?" He aimed the reach pole, but the shark had moved out of range.

He glanced at his wristwatch, the second hand sweeping past the six.

Fifty seconds later an ivory dorsal fin surfaced thirty yards away, Tania holding on with her gloved right hand, waving at him with the left.

"Holy shit! Holy fucking shit! You go, girl!" He reached for his handheld camera but by the time he had focused, the dorsal fin had slipped back beneath the waves.

Tim grabbed his fins, hastily working them over his rubber boots. *Stay beneath the pier behind the pilings. Get a few passing shots, then get out.* Positioning his mask and snorkel, he inhaled a quick breath, hugged his underwater video camera to his chest and stepped off the pier.

Tim sank six feet. Before he could surface, he kicked his way beneath the jetty, slipping behind a pair of wooden pilings, each support as thick as a telephone pole.

As luck would have it, the tide was out, providing him with two feet of air space between the waterline and the underside of the jetty. Wrapping his legs around an algae-covered piling, he was able to remain underwater while breathing through the snorkel, safe and secure.

Aiming the camera out to sea, he searched through the viewfinder for the albino shark. *Come on, come on, where are you—there!* Catching sight of the Meg's tail he zoomed in, locating a pair of human legs dangling along the shark's incredibly massive left flank. He stayed with the shot until they moved out of range.

Amazing . . . fucking amazing. I'm underwater, filming a sixty-year-old woman being towed by a Megalodon. Using his right shoulder and the piling like a tripod, he repositioned the camera, readying himself for the shark's next pass.

With his mask pressed against the viewfinder, Tim Rehm never saw the albino head rising from the depths directly beneath him.

Primal instinct caused him to suddenly jerk back as Bela gnawed on the piling. For a moment she remained stuck, until she shook her head, breaking off two of her razor-sharp lower teeth which remained embedded in the wood.

Tim backed away, his heart feeling as if the organ was about to burst from his chest.

Bela refused to be denied. Jamming her snout in the gap between two sets of pilings, she attempted to squeeze her way beneath the pier. When that didn't work, she moved off.

Tim watched the dark-backed Megalodon as it swam around the backside of the jetty. With a burst of speed it rammed the bottom of the pier, the sound of splintering wood sending the cameraman kicking and paddling his way through the corridor of pilings as he attempted to reach the shallows.

A white glow filled his peripheral vision. Turning to his left he saw Lizzy and Tania. The Megalodon was swimming parallel to the jetty. His friend was waving—from inside the creature's mouth!

Tim gagged as he swallowed a mouthful of seawater. Tania was alive, her arms flailing wildly as Lizzy's teeth kept her pinned within its jaws.

He jumped at a resounding *thud*—followed by an ear-splitting *crack* as Bela broke through two rotting pilings, collapsing a twenty foot section of pier above his head.

Dropping his camera, the strength training coach torpedoed through the water, stroking and kicking through the ten-foot-wide channel formed by the jetty's wooden columns—never realizing the gaps between pairs of pilings were progressively widening as he drew closer to shore.

Thirty yards from the beach . . . don't stop!

The blotch of white bloomed in his right eye's peripheral vision, the scorching pain shooting through every nerve cell in his body as Bela's hideous mouth shot sideways beneath the pier, plucking him from his escape route.

For a fleeting moment lying somewhere between consciousness and death, Tim Rehm transformed into the twenty-foot female great white, soaring through the chilly waters off the Farallon Islands.

Bela shook her mammoth head, chasing his soul into another existence.

Lizzy waited for her sibling to join her at the end of the pier. Their prey had stopped thrashing, but the kills were fresh and the pups were still too young to be particular.

Descending into the depths, the albino predator and her pigmented twin followed the Georgia Strait to the deep waters off Hornby Island, where their surviving young waited to be fed.

28

Lake Ellsworth, 2.1 Miles Beneath the Antarctic Ice Sheet
West Antarctica

Jonas Taylor shut down the two *Valkyrie* lasers and brought the Manta to the surface. Zachary quickly switched the sonar from active to passive.

Enveloped in a primordial darkness, the two men simply stared out the cockpit in silence, the sub bobbing gently in waters made olive-green by the night glass.

And then, as they watched, random flashes ignited like puffs of lightning concealed in a cloud bank—each bioluminescent burst from the frozen heavens beckoning a response from the lake's surface until the silhouette of the lost world revealed itself to its mesmerized guests.

The lake was six miles long—an inverted S-shaped topographic hollow with two small landmasses that rose several hundred feet. The ice sheet which pressed against Lake Ellsworth was convex, sagging over the middle of the waterway, where it came to within twenty feet of meeting its surface waters. From here the ceiling gradually tapered back until it reached four to five stories along the periphery, where it buckled against the eastern wall.

An underwater light flashed close by. Curious, Jonas descended the sub, expecting to find a bioluminescent fish. Instead he discovered a pair of plant-like objects, each the size and shape of a surfboard, the anterior surface of which held several rows of barbed suction pads. These objects were not free-floating, they were attached to the underside of the ice sheet by long, vine-like appendages that dangled to the surface in pairs.

As Jonas and Zachary watched, a burst of pink light ignited thirty feet overhead. Like a slow-moving nerve impulse, the bioluminescent flash raced down the limbs to cause the two objects with the sucker pads to illuminate underwater.

"Is it a plant or an animal?" Jonas asked, circling the objects at what he hoped was a safe distance.

"I have no idea, but I need tae observe what's happening along the underside of the ice sheet. Is there any way ye can direct one of the sub's exterior lights directly overhead?"

"No, but I have something else that should do the job." Unbuckling his harness, Jonas turned around in his seat and rummaged through a storage compartment, removing an aluminum lithium-powered flashlight. Ascending to the surface, he pressed the flashlight's lens to the inside of the cockpit glass and turned on the beam, aiming it at the section of ice sheet located three stories above the sub.

Instead of illuminating the bottom of the ice sheet, the flashlight's beam revealed a dense root system, which fanned out from the center of a hole. There were dozens of these strange orifices—perhaps hundreds or even thousands of them—poised over the lake's surface waters, each fifteen to twenty feet in diameter. Crawling in and out of these dark holes and across the root system were thousands of centipedes—each insect three to five feet long.

Dangling from the perimeter of each hole were the two vine-like limbs, which reached beneath the surface waters to illuminate their two plant-like pods lurking underwater.

"Zach, I thought you told me Lake Ellsworth was squeezed beneath a mile-thick ice sheet? This looks more like the underside of a bizarre rainforest. Those holes remind me of the inside of a rotting trunk."

"I agree it's bizarre, and yet I'm not convinced this thing isn't a living, breathing animal. Jonas, can I borrow that light a moment?"

Zach aimed the beam at the center of the hole directly above their heads as a strobe of blue-green light ignited from within the orifice, traveling outward through the roots and down the dangling pair of limbs to the sucker pads.

"My God . . . is it possible?"

"Is what possible?" Jonas looked at his friend, who was using the light to count the number of thick roots originating from the perimeter of each hole.

"Jonas, I dinnae think we're looking at the underside of a tree. Each hole births eight long roots and these two strange appendages that dangle these big sucker pads underwater like bait. Doesn't that sound vaguely familiar tae ye? It does tae me. I've encountered a modern-day relative of this species before . . . in the Sargasso Sea."

"Eight arms, two tentacles . . . you think those things are cephalopods?"

"That would be my guess. Which means each hole is actually a mouth and the squid's head is burrowed in the ice sheet. They're using bioluminescent signals tae lure prey close enough for their two sucker pads tae grab hold so the beastie can feed itself."

"How can they survive out of the water?"

"I don't ken. I suppose it's possible they evolved into ice creatures as a means of survival, especially if *Livyatan melvillei* is the dominant species in this lake. Keep us at a safe distance and let's see what happens."

Jonas circled the sucker pads as he gradually submerged the Manta. In the distance he could see faint sparks of bioluminescent signals, a sight that reminded him of his submersible descents into the bathypelagic zone. Living in perpetual darkness, eighty percent of the sea creatures inhabiting the deep possessed light-emitting cells called photophores that were used to attract mates as well as prey.

At least one of the species in Lake Ellsworth shared these same traits.

"Zach, since you obviously seem to have more subglacial lake memories than me; how do you suggest we go about finding our way out of here to get back to the *McFarland*?"

"I'm working on a few options."

"Anything you care to share while we're sitting here, waiting for God knows what to show up and get eaten?"

"The idea for our escape comes from the mission tae Lake Vostok."

"You mean the one that never happened?"

Zach grinned. "Yeah, that one. To access Vostok our engineers designed a three-man torpedo-shaped submersible equipped with twin *Valkyrie* lasers. We literally melted our way through two and a half miles of ice tae reach the lake. Getting back tae the surface relied on a different strategy that jist might work for us."

Zach pointed to the Manta's exterior pressure gauge, which read 3,281 psi. "The weight of the ice sheet causes tremendous pressure within these subglacial lakes—something the Russians discovered the hard way when they drilled their first borehole intae Vostok and unleashed a geyser. Our exit strategy took advantage of the lake's internal pressure. We were instructed tae launch vertically out of the lake with the lasers powered on. Upon contact with the ice sheet our melt hole would unleash the lake's internal pressure and literally propel us up tae the surface, riding a geyser of water."

"Did it work?"

"We never got tae try it. Our targeted extraction point had the ice sheet within six feet of the lake's surface; our actual immersion spot was way off course in an area where the ice sheet was more than a hundred feet overhead. But the theory still holds true."

"Thanks for sharing; now how are we going to leap thirty feet into the air in this weighed-down sub, when we can barely outrun a prehistoric sperm whale?"

Zach pointed to his sonar monitor where a pair of blips had appeared. "Watch and learn."

Jonas stared at the objects which were rising slowly from the depths beneath them. "What are they?"

"I don't ken. Every subglacial lake has its own unique ecosystem. Twenty million years ago, Lake Ellsworth was covered by ocean. Fifteen million years ago an ice age deposited a dome of packed snow over the entire continent. The Ronne Ice Shelf cut off access tae the Weddell Sea, sealing off the lake while trapping whales and other sea creatures within its landlocked boundary. Food chains are only as stable as their microbial foundations. Lake Ellsworth receives deposits of organic materials from West Antarctica's subglacial streams. Geothermal vents replaced photosynthesis with chemosynthesis, preserving the waterway's microbial life forms. We ken *Livyatan melvillei* survived; whit else is on the food chain is jist a guess."

What had been two blips on sonar now numbered more than a dozen. From the circuitous manner in which the life forms rose, Jonas could tell they were not predatory by nature. This was confirmed moments later when the first creatures rose majestically into view, their massive wings flapping gently as they rode an upwelling of current to the surface.

Within minutes the sub was surrounded by a ballet of giant manta rays, the graceful creatures dwarfing the sub, their focus on the bioluminescent mating calls that were being falsely generated by the strange creatures inhabiting the ice sheet.

As Jonas watched, one of the mantas brushed its belly against a flashing sucker pad—foreplay to a primordial mating ritual.

With a heart-stopping reflex, both sucker pads suddenly animated to grab the ray by its wings, the poison-tipped barbed suckers piercing the manta's flesh. The tentacles flexed, lifting the stunned animal out of the water and high above the lake's surface, its wings flapping wildly as it attempted to free itself from its captor's grip.

Jonas surfaced the sub. Zach aimed the flashlight's beam into the dark orifice overhead, illuminating a hideous clawed beak inside the giant squid's mouth.

Two of the eight massive roots animated from beneath the ice sheet. Thick and powerful, these sucker-lined appendages aided the cephalopod's tentacles in securing the three hundred pound manta ray. Gripping the captured animal by its two wings, it tore the creature's torso in half, its bloody innards falling out of its body into the lake, splattering across the sub's cockpit.

Through the blotched Lexan glass, Jonas saw one of the squid's thicker arms shove half its meal into its mouth, the giant squid's beak tearing into the succulent meat.

Hundreds of centipedes scrambled inside the feeding orifice, fighting over the scraps.

Jonas felt queasy. He adjusted his air vent to blow on his face, then reached into the refrigerated compartment beneath his seat for a bottled water and bag of trail mix.

"All right, professor? Did you see what you needed to see?" Jonas turned to Zach, who was staring at his sonar monitor. "What is it?"

"I dinnae ken, but the manta rays are taking off like bats out of hell."

Zzzzzzzzzzt. Zzzzzzzzzzzzzzt.

The burst of echolocation rattled the sub's cockpit, causing both pilots' pulses to race.

Jonas strapped himself back in his harness. "Where is he?"

Zach traced the location of the whale on his sonar array. "He's about a mile tae the southwest and he's not alone—his acoustics painted three smaller adults and two juveniles."

"Sounds like Brutus has himself a harem. You think he knows it's us?"

Zzzzzzzzzzt. Zzzzzzzzzzzzzzt.

"I would say he kens. Follow the mantas. Maybe we can lose him in the crowd."

Jonas submerged, accelerating after the school of rays. "What happened to that brilliant plan of yours to escape through the ice sheet?"

"Take a look around—haven't ye noticed how dark it's become? The ice squid, or whatever the hell those things are, retracted their tentacles the moment they registered Brutus's echolocation."

Jonas looked around. Zachary was right; Lake Ellsworth had vanished into pitch darkness, the bioluminescent impulses gone.

––––––

At eighty-two feet and a hundred tons, the Miocene bull sperm whale remained the unchallenged authority of Lake Ellsworth. Over the last four decades it had sired twenty-three offspring with seven different cows in three subglacial lakes. Adhering to the lake's population limits, it had forced itself into exile, spending the last few mating seasons wandering through subglacial rivers, awaiting death.

The collapse of the Ronne Ice Shelf had opened a new world to the sixty-three-year-old predator. Endowed with the largest, most complex brain on Earth, it had adapted easily to open water and was progressively exploring the Weddell Sea. Sunlight did not affect its eyes—the sub-species of *Livyatan melvillei* that had survived the last ice age had borne their young blind for more than twelve million years, however the ultraviolet rays did irritate its hide, limiting its exposure to surface waters during the day. Having come across a pod of modern-day sperm whales, it had chased off a mature silver-headed bull and supplanted him as the dominant male. Twice in the last week it had returned to its adopted family, impregnating two of their cows.

The Miocene sperm whale's unexpected encounter with the strange life form during its return trip beneath the ice sheet had set the bull off. Instinctively, it had recognized the submersible as a threat. Now, its presence in its own roost was not only a direct challenge to the male's authority, it placed the safety of its brood in question.

Bearing down on the sub, the dominant bull would not allow it to escape.

––––––

"Jonas, the whale's gaining on us; it's closed tae within a hundred yards."

"Go active, ping the hell out of this place. Find me that river, some shallows . . . anything."

Zach hit the sonar array's green button, causing three loud sonic *pings* to reverberate from beneath the sub's prow. "There's some kind of landmass up ahead. Maybe there's a beach?"

"I don't want to beach, I want shallows."

Zach set off three more pings. "Forty yards tae starboard; can ye hear wave variations in your headset? It might be an inlet."

Jonas forced himself to focus in on the acoustics, catching a hollow echo of sound. "You might be right; hold on."

Powering on the sub's exterior lights, Jonas veered hard to starboard, following the targeted area on his sonar screen.

Appearing up ahead was a city block-long gauntlet of volcanic rock—no shallows, nothing resembling an inlet. And then he saw it—a dark crevasse that was either a natural split between two rock formations or the entrance to an underwater cave.

Accelerating toward the fissure, he realized—too late—that the passage was less than half the width of his submersible.

Zzzzzzzzzzt. Zzzzzzzzzzzzzzt.

The strength behind the acoustic barrage ended any internal debate. Rolling the Manta onto its port wing, Jonas shot the sub sideways through the rift, fully expecting to smash bow-first into rock.

The starboard wing scraped basalt, the Manta jarred roughly as one of the pump-jet propulsors was sheared away from the sub's undercarriage—and then night ignited into day as the ship's exterior lights refracted off the walls and ceiling of an underwater grotto.

Jonas pulled his feet away from the propulsor pedals and rolled the sub level again just in time to veer away from a cavern wall.

Before he could steal a breath, a monstrous force struck the cave entrance, unleashing a thunderous reverberation that caused baseball-size rocks to rain inside their refuge.

Jonas banked away from another wall, spinning the sub around so that it now faced the cave entrance—the narrow passage blocked by the Miocene whale's enormous head.

"Don't move, Brutus, stay right where you are," Jonas whispered, powering on the *Valkyrie* lasers.

"J.T., whit are ye doing?"

"Just teaching our friend a lesson on what happens when you mess with the wrong sailor."

Zachary grabbed his right hand as he reached for the joystick. "You'll kill him."

"It's him or us, now let go of my hand."

"Fine, jist tell me the truth so we can set the record straight—are ye a marine paleobiologist dedicated tae preserving extant life forms or are ye still a disgruntled navy submersible pilot with a thirty-five-year-old chip on yer shoulder? Because the Jonas Taylor I thought I ken would find any way he could tae avoid slaughtering a majestic creature like this."

Jonas shut down the lasers. "Listen. Do you hear that cavitating sound? That's what's left of our starboard propeller. Look at your life support gauges; we're down to our last six hours of air. You like this cave? That whale may just end up burying us in here. You want to question my motives, start by questioning your own. Why are we here, Zachary? We're here because you told me some crazy story about a mission to Lake Vostok that never happened. We're here because you needed my help, warning me that my son's life was in danger. If it's between my son and that Miocene nightmare then—"

"Try backing it off. Scorch its hide if ye must . . . give it a painful burn but don't press the *Valkyrie* tae its flesh or ye'll kill it. Trust me on this."

"Trust you? You're a hypocrite, do you know that? Last week you were prepared to kill this animal in order to protect your little Vostok secret. What changed?"

"Ye're right. Having lived through it, I guess I forgot everything I learned." Zachary laid his head back. "The last time we went through this together—ye ken, my crazy Vostok story—the bad guys ended up slaughtering an entire pod of these Miocene whales. Seeing what ye were about tae do, I realized that we're supposed tae be better than this . . . not jist me and ye, but mankind . . . humanity. It's a lesson I had learned before but forgot until this very moment; that at the end of the day our survival as a species may jist come down tae whether or not we respect the rights of other species tae live. God, listen tae me, I sound like a bloody Disney character."

Jonas weighed his friend's words. "All right, Donald Duck, we'll try it your way." Restarting the Valkyires, Jonas rolled the sub onto its port wing and inched forward, guiding the Manta slowly out of the passage.

The heat from the lasers set the water to boil, blistering the whale's exposed hide.

The creature retreated, allowing the sub to exit.

Once outside the cave, Jonas righted his vessel, keeping the Manta's prow ten feet from the bull's silver-gray head. Growing more agitated, but unable to devour its searing-hot prey, the whale swam from side to side like a caged tiger as it attempted to circumnavigate the lasers' intense heat.

Jonas waited it out, refusing to allow the creature to get around the sub's prow even as he was forced to compensate for his damaged starboard propeller.

After several minutes of cat and mouse maneuvers, the frustrated beast swam off.

Zach breathed a sigh of relief. "See now? Dinnae that feel good?"

"It'll feel good when we're back on board the *McFarland*, now stop yapping like a woman and find that river leading us out of here."

29

|||||||||||||||||||||||||||||||||

Ross Sea

A neon-green ribbon of light snaked across the midnight sky, the aurora reflecting off the Manta's cockpit as it was hauled out of the dark sea onto the trawler's stern ramp.

David Taylor opened the Lexan hatch. For several minutes the twenty-one-year-old pilot simply breathed in the frigid Antarctic air, exhausted from having completed a nine-hour game of cat and mouse with the *Liopleurodon* and its offspring.

He glanced over at Jackie, who was being lifted out of her side of the cockpit by two members of the *Dubai Land* crew. The marine biologist deserved credit for having learned how to operate the sub on short notice, but passing a crash course on a simulator and repeatedly being chased by a hundred-and-twenty-foot pliosaur as they attempted to herd it out from beneath the Ross Ice Shelf were two different things. For forty minutes Jackie had screamed and cursed-out David until she was hoarse; twice vomiting into a sea-sick container. After her third valium, she had mercifully passed out.

The experience reminded David of one of his Uncle Mac's funnier military stories. While stationed at the U.S. naval base in Guam, the brash chopper pilot was approached by the pretty aide of a visiting congressman, who was looking to boost her boss's "tough guy" image for an upcoming election. Mac negotiated a date with the woman in exchange for a thirty minute helicopter flight for the politician and his film crew. But the congressman turned out to be a "chicken-hawk," his brash pro-war stances in Washington conflicting with his wealthy family's influence, which had exempted him from the draft. Nothing bothered Mac more than a hypocrite. In David's godfather's words, "on our first aerial maneuver the southern boy screamed, on the second he puked across the dashboard. By the time we landed he was passed out cold. Unfortunately, the aide turned out to be his niece so I didn't get laid, but I did get it on with the Filipino nurse who treated him at the base hospital."

Monty approached, his friend handing him a ski jacket and wool hat as they watched Jackie being led inside. "Don't feel bad; eighty-nine percent of couples surveyed report damaged relationships as a result of insensitive or inappropriate use of technology. From the look of things, I'm guessing you won't be getting laid tonight."

"Nice to see you, too. Where's bin Rashidi?"

"Aboard the *Tonga*, waiting for you to debrief him. Is it true the Lio gave birth to a Lio Junior?"

"It's true. And just like a momma croc, she's extremely protective of it. What are you doing aboard the trawler; I thought you were sick?"

He nodded to a cameraman filming them from across the deck. "Can't afford to miss my reality show bonus. Come, our chariot awaits."

Monty led them to a cargo net spread out across the middeck.

A steel cable rose nine stories overhead, threaded to one of the supertanker's winches. Standing back to back in the middle of the net, they waited for a crewman to take up the slack.

Seconds later they were rising along the *Tonga*'s starboard flank inside their makeshift elevator.

Commander Molony greeted David with a bear hug as he entered the bridge. "Outstanding job, kid. How was Jackie? Rock-steady, I'll bet."

"Absolutely. The last few hours—I barely heard a peep out of her. Where's the Lio?"

"She's moving east, following the coast. We've taken up positions to the south, keeping her from escaping into open water."

Fiesal bin Rashidi entered the chamber, announcing himself by blowing his nose into a paper towel. "Six months we've chased this devil. Today was another wasted opportunity."

"Not at all," Liam Molony said. "In order to have a chance to capture the Lio we first had to locate the monster and then flush it out from beneath the ice sheet. David accomplished both tasks in half a day—tasks that could have taken weeks, perhaps months. Even better news—the Lio gave birth to an offspring. Fiesal, we don't need to capture the monster; only its pup."

"I don't want the pup without the mother!" The tirade sent him into a coughing fit, which ended with the engineer spitting into another paper towel. "David, you know this creature better than anyone. Be honest—can it be captured or are we wasting our time?"

David looked into his employer's dark, fever-ridden eyes. "The adult is exhausted, that gives us a fighting chance. Plus she definitely doesn't like the Manta. If we can drive her into the shallows, I think we can net her."

"How?"

He turned to Commander Molony. "Under the ice, I got a good feel for the momma Lio's speed. When she chased me and I ran fast she gave up the chase pretty quickly. But when I allowed her to feel like she could catch me, I got her to follow me a good mile.

"Working in deep water like this makes it very hard; we need to force the creature into the shallows—find a coastal area that pens them in a bit. We'll set the big nets up between the two ships like we planned, then cut both vessels' engines the moment I make another run at junior. I'll keep the momma's attention by letting her nip on my heels as I lead her into the trap. Between trying to protect her offspring and chasing after me she won't realize the boats are there until it's too late. Once she's hauled out of the water we use the trawler net to capture the baby."

Bin Rashidi moved to the chart table and a map of Antarctica. "Captain, we need to push the creature into the shallows; where do you suggest?"

The captain took a moment, then pointed to a coastal area in the Amundsen Sea. "Pine Island Bay. The depths drop to about two hundred feet, but there's dozens of shallow coves along the Thwaites Glacier to trap your monster in. If she maintains her current speed and heading, she'll arrive there on her own in the next seventy-two hours."

Fiesal bin Rashidi nodded. "Pass the word to everyone on board: we either capture the Lio in Pine Island Bay or I shall terminate this mission, in which case no one shall receive their bonus monies."

Grabbing a fresh paper towel, he exited the command center, hocking up a ball of mucus from his irritated throat.

Vancouver Island, British Columbia

Paul Agricola stood on the shoreline by the decimated jetty, gazing at Denman and Hornby Islands to the northeast while a nervous forensic photographer leaned out over a twenty-foot gap in the pier, snapping photos.

A detective approached, pulling Paul aside. "This stays between us; agreed?"

"Andy, you're my brother-in-law."

"Yeah, yeah, and your tab is getting full." He pulled out a small notepad. "Two people are missing; one the resort's manager, Tania Cruz, the other a guest from New Jersey who checked in two days ago. The groundskeeper claims Cruz had him remove the remains of a juvenile humpback whale from beneath the end of the pier Thursday afternoon. That was the last time he saw Cruz alive."

"You believe him?"

"He was caught breaking into her apartment, so I wouldn't exactly call him a credible witness. We're running a background check to see if he has a history of violence. And yes, his boat is big enough to have taken out that section of the pier."

"You know what I'm going to ask . . ."

"Could one of those mega-sharks have done it? Hell, I don't know—you're the marine biologist. If I was betting the farm, I'd go with the groundskeeper."

A police officer approached, carrying a framed photo. "Sir, we found this inside the woman's apartment. Thought you ought to have a look."

The detective stared at the image. "Ah, geez." He passed it to Paul.

The photo was taken underwater—an elderly woman open water diving with an eighteen-foot great white shark.

———

The islands and islets of the Salish Sea are geological remnants of the last ice age, formed by glaciers which excavated the sandy trenches of British Columbia. Eventually these canyons filled with seawater, creating the Strait of Juan de Fuca and the Georgia Strait.

Located in the Georgia Strait off the east coast of Vancouver Island within miles of the jetty, Denman Island and Hornby Island were each home to about a thousand residents, including artists and Hollywood actors seeking privacy amid the tranquility of nature. Rugged and mountainous, the small islands were covered by a north-west rainforest of Douglas fir and were accessible only by ferry.

Paul directed his helicopter pilot to fly over Denman Island's coastal waters. Half an hour's search yielded no signs of the two missing people nor anything that might render the highly trafficked area suitable as a Megalodon nursery.

Hornby Island was another story. Shaped like a fisted hand with an extended thumb, its geography was dominated by Tribune Bay, a half-moon-shaped white beach overlooking warm water shallows. An extensive flyover revealed several seals and a pod of porpoises, but no sharks.

It was already late in the afternoon by the time Paul finished his search of the bay's emerald green shallows. Nursing a bad headache, he ordered his pilot to return to Vancouver. Heading southeast, they flew over Helliwell Provincial Park, its grassy meadows yielding to stunning bluffs along St. John's Point.

And that's when Paul saw it—Flora Islet, a tiny landmass located just east of Hornby Island. Home to hundreds of sea lions, the deep waters were a favored stomping ground to a species of six-gilled shark. These rarely seen deepwater creatures returned to Flora's waters every summer where they swam back and forth over the ledges and overhangs of a sheer rock wall, its vertical face dropping over seventy-five meters.

The sun dipped below Vancouver Island, igniting a mass exodus of sea lions from the water.

Paul quickly switched to his night-vision binoculars, scanning the sea.

The first Meg pup he spotted was one of Lizzy's, a pure albino that rose from the depths like a submarine-launched ballistic missile to snag an unsuspecting sea lion. A moment later a larger sibling surfaced to challenge her for the kill.

The two juveniles suddenly dispersed.

A moment later, a ghostly white figure came into view as it rose slowly from the depths along the rock face.

Paul smiled to himself. *Peek-a-boo, I see you, Lizzy. And I'm coming to get you, my precious.*

Beneath the Ronne Ice Shelf
Weddell Sea, Antarctica

They had used reciprocal transmissions—sonar pulses emitted in opposite directions at the same time, the shorter acoustical travel time revealing a swift current that led into the subglacial river and the way out of Lake Ellsworth.

Twenty minutes later, the Manta was back beneath the Ronne Ice Shelf, the current driving them south toward the Weddell Sea.

Emotionally and physically exhausted, the two men remained

imprisoned by their predicament. Soaring beneath the unpredict-able contours of the ice shelf, Jonas Taylor could not trust the autopilot to safely guide the sub. Fearful of the Miocene sperm whale, Zachary Wallace remained diligent at sonar.

Jonas popped four aspirin, his lower back throbbing in pain, his legs feeling swollen. "This is it for me; if I never ride in another sub again I'll be a happy man." He glanced at Zach, who was rocking in his bucket seat. "We have plenty of urine bottles, you know?"

"I dinnae have tae pee, I'm jist trying tae stay awake. Maybe ye can engage my brain with some witty conversation."

"Okay. When that bizarre ice squid captured one of those rays and hoisted it out of the water into its mouth—what were you thinking?"

"Whit do ye mean?"

"When I asked you how we were going to get back to the *McFar-land,* you said you were working on a few options. Was one of those options allowing a squid to grab the sub with its tentacles and shove us into its mouth, at which point we'd jack up the lasers and essen-tially burn our way through the animal's mouth and brains and ride the lake's pressure straight up through a mile and a half of ice? Was that your brilliant plan?"

Zach turned to him. "Pretty much, yeah."

"And had that lame-brain plan worked, then what? We'd be sitting on top of the ice sheet in the middle of Antarctica with no radio, fifty miles from our boat."

"That's true. I guess I hadn't thought of that."

Maybe it was fatigue, maybe it was the ridiculousness of their sit-uation, but suddenly Jonas couldn't stop laughing. It was uncontrol-lable, spontaneous hysterics, a release of pent-up frustrations and fears and it was infectious, causing Zachary to burst out laughing. Both men's eyes filled with tears, their lungs and chests convulsing as they gasped for quick breaths, only to break out again.

After five minutes they laid back in their seats, their cheeks numb from smiling.

Jonas downed the rest of his bottled water. "God, that felt good. I can't remember the last time I laughed."

Zach nodded. "Me either. The last seven years of my life . . . all I've done is work and try tae prepare myself for this moment. Before that . . . I was only moderately miserable."

"You have a wife and kids who love you."

"As do ye. So why do ye hate yer life, J.T.?"

"I don't hate it as much as I'm tired of it. When you get older it seems like you're always worried about the next health issue, the next bill, the next doctor's appointment, the next lawsuit. Plus, I worry about my kids. And Terry. And then I do something stupid . . . like letting you talk me into this mission, and now all I want to do is hug my wife and kids and get back to the mundane."

"Yer life is far from mundane."

"You don't get it. I *want* the mundane. I want to wake up in the morning and worry about whether I'm eating enough fiber, not whether my trainer was eaten by an exhibit or if some animal rights group slashed the tires on my Lexus."

"So get out. Sell the institute and move tae a gated community on a golf course, where ye can spend yer days playing with yer putter and balls."

"If it were only that easy."

Before he could get out the words, the ice above their heads became a velvet night sky, the stars sparkling like diamonds, the aurora a neon-green curtain lacing to the west.

Remaining on the surface, Jonas quickly located the *McFarland*, the crew of the hopper-dredge acknowledging their presence with a flare.

———

Jonas waited impatiently for the docking chamber to drain and pressurize. The moment the red light blinked off and was replaced by the green he popped the cockpit hatch and struggled to pry himself out of his seat, his leg muscles weak, quivering with fatigue.

The chamber's watertight door squealed open and the captain entered, followed by Terry, the ship's physician, three crewmen and Cyel Reed. The engineer took one look at the Manta's chewed off tail fin and grimaced. "I'm not fixing that. Not in this igloo."

Two crewmen helped Jonas out of the sub.

Terry embraced him, her almond eyes glassy with tears. "You were gone seventeen hours. So much for tagging the whale and leaving."

"This whale has a nasty temper. It chased us all the way to Lake Ellsworth."

"I know. We were tracking the whale by its tag and the Manta by its homing device."

"See that," Zachary said, climbing down from the sub, "they would have sent the chopper for us."

"What's he talking about?" Terry asked.

"Ignore him. Where's David?"

"They're on the move," the captain said. "We received a transmission yesterday from Dr. Wallace's contact aboard the *Tonga*. They're going to attempt to capture the Lio and its offspring in Pine Island Bay."

"How far is . . . wait, did you say offspring?"

Terry nodded. "It gave birth beneath the ice shelf."

"We're two days out from the Amundsen Sea," the captain said. "With any luck we'll arrive a few hours before them."

Jonas was about to reply when the chamber started spinning.

Terry felt her husband's legs give out. She managed to hold him up long enough for the captain and one of the crew to grab the unconscious pilot before he hit the floor.

30

Aboard the Hopper-Dredge *McFarland*
Weddell Sea, Antarctica

Weak, feeling queasy and light-headed, Jonas looked up at the ship's physician through feverish eyes.

Dr. Tim Goldman connected the intravenous tube to the peripheral cannula protruding from the vein in the back of Jonas's right hand and started the IV bag drip. "The danger in being immobile in a submersible over an extended period of time is that blood clots can form in your legs. This can happen during air travel as well, especially when sitting in cramped spaces with little leg room for more than eight hours. The medical term for this type of blood clot is deep-vein thrombosis or DVT."

"That's why our pilots always wear compression suits," Terry said, her eyes shooting daggers at Zachary Wallace. "Unfortunately, my husband was misled into believing this last dive would be relatively quick and easy."

Zach ignored the accusation. "Doc, if it was a blood clot that caused him tae black out, will it not jist dissolve on its own?"

"Most do. However, a blood clot that forms in the deep veins of a person's leg can detach and travel to their lungs, causing a pulmonary embolism. This can be life-threatening if not treated in time.

"As a precautionary measure, I'm starting Jonas on a blood thinner. After the IV, he'll take a pill a day for three months. We'll do a full work-up when we get back to California. In the meantime, J.T., you're grounded." Dr. Goldman turned to Terry and Zach. "I mean it. No more submersible activities."

Terry nodded. "Jonas, did you hear Dr. Goldman?"

Jonas closed his eyes, the elixir entering his bloodstream cooling off his fever, settling him into a deep sleep.

Aboard the *Tonga*
Amundsen Sea, West Antarctica

The midnight sea, rendered olive-green by the sub's night-vision glass, revealed an emptiness of liquid space that did not jive with the Manta's sonar array. The creature was out there, biding its time, circling along the periphery, its presence unnerving.

David knew the attack was coming, he just didn't know the direction the charge would be coming from. Visibility was thirty feet at best, which meant the monster would be on him almost the moment he saw it.

He turned to Kaylie, seated next to him in the co-pilot's seat. "What do you think?"

She looked at him, her complexion pale, her eyes cold. "Today you'll die."

———

"Ahhhhhh!"

David shot up in bed, expelling a blood-curdling scream. Eyes wide, he flinched and screamed again as Jackie turned on the light.

"David, it's okay, it was just a dream. David, look at me!"

He turned to her, his limbs shaking, his body bathed in a cold sweat. He attempted to speak, but couldn't find his voice.

Jackie brushed aside her strawberry-blond bangs and took his hand in hers. "You're okay. Everything is going to be—"

"I'm going to die today. March third. Today's the day I die."

"It was a dream, David."

"No, it was real. Kaylie was in the Manta with me. She was pale as a ghost, her eyes lifeless. She told me today's the day."

Jackie climbed out of bed, dressed only in David's T-shirt. She walked to the porthole and pulled back the worn curtains to reveal the predawn sky. "Let's get dressed and eat some breakfast, you'll feel better."

"I'm not hungry."

"Then let's hit the gym, a workout will do us both some good."

"No."

She moved to his side of the bed, removed the T-shirt, and straddled him.

"Jackie, what are you doing?"

"Keeping the man I love warm." She hugged him, her bare flesh on his chest generating body heat.

He hugged her back, the warmth chasing away the coldness of death.

Aboard the Hopper-Dredge *McFarland*
Amundsen Sea, Antarctica

Zachary Wallace leaned over the chart table, studying the map of Pine Island Bay. Surrounded by glaciers and ice shelves, the waterway vaguely resembled the coastline of the Amery Ice Shelf—the access point to Lake Vostok he had relived a thousand times in a recurring dream.

He looked up as Terry entered the bridge, limping noticeably.

"Are ye all right?"

"Stress and Parkinson's don't mix very well. We need to talk."

He followed her one flight down to the officer's deck, entering a deserted break room.

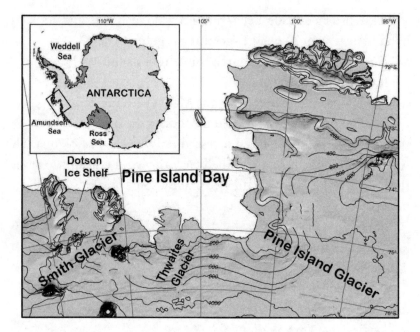

Terry sat on bench, stretching out her right leg. "Today is March third, your big déjà vu day. The last time you experienced this, where was Jonas?"

"With me, piloting one of the Mantas."

"Where was my son?"

"Piloting another Manta, playing a game of cat and mouse with the *Liopleurodon*. He led it away from us and back tae the tanker where it was netted."

"And that's where David died?"

"Terry, it never happened. Everything is different this time around."

"What happened to the Lio after it was netted?"

"The creature was too big and too active. The trawler flipped, the tanker was swaying dangerously. We had no choice but tae kill it."

"And how did you manage that?"

"Jonas struck it in the chest with both lasers. It was a mortal wound."

"So, Jonas saved both crews?"

"Yes."

"And this time around, Jonas is in sickbay, unable to pilot the Manta. Even if my son survives, what's to prevent the Lio from going berserk and sinking both vessels? Who's going to kill this monster with my husband out of commission?"

Zachary felt the blood drain from his face. "I hadn't considered that."

"Of course not. You were too busy with your own agenda to think things through."

"Is there anyone else on board who can pilot the Manta?"

"You're looking at her. Our ETA at Pine Island Bay is sixteen hundred hours. Make sure you're wearing a compression suit, I'd hate for you to die from a blood clot."

She stood, limping toward the door. "If you'll excuse me, I need to wake up Cyel Reed and inform my engineer he has eight hours to attach those two lasers to Manta number three."

Pine Island Bay, Amundsen Sea

The Thwaites Glacier has been heavily studied by geologists because of the rapid flow rate in which it is melting into Pine Island Bay. Researchers at the University of Texas in Austin recently discovered the cause of this alarming phenomenon—magma and related volcanic activity arising from the rifting of the Earth's crust beneath the West Antarctic Ice Sheet. This geothermal dynamic distributes heat across the bottom of the ice like a pancake griddle, threatening to collapse the glacier and raise ocean levels.

The *Liopleurodon* could sense the geothermal activity, the neuromastic cells located along its lateral lines registering the grinding of the ice upon a 2,296-foot-tall ridge located beneath the glacier along the sea floor. It could also detect several pods of minke whales feeding on fish attracted to a stream of warm water flowing out from beneath the glacier into Pine Island Bay.

With its newborn held in tow within the current created by its own

water displacement, the Lio entered a narrow channel leading to the glacier. Remaining deep, it waited for darkness, its primordial senses homing in on the pod of whales feeding along the surface.

Aboard the *Dubai Land-I* Trawler

David Taylor pulled the compression suit into place over his arms and legs, zipping it over his chest.

Monty handed him the matching boots. "It was just another night terror, kid. Don't let it phase you."

"Easy for you to say, you didn't see her."

"What'd she look like? Did she look like a zombie?"

"No."

"Did she look regurgitated?"

"You're an asshole."

"Then how did she look?"

"She looked dead . . . scary dead. I don't want to talk about it anymore."

Commander Molony entered the staging area. "Our luck just turned; the Lio entered a channel that dead ends at the Thwaites Glacier. We'll be in position at the mouth of the inlet in twenty minutes. Are you ready to do this?"

"Yeah . . . sure."

Molony heard the inflection of doubt. "What's wrong?"

"Nothing. I'm fine."

"His dead girlfriend visited him in a dream."

"Shut up, Monty."

"You dreamt Jackie was dead?"

"Kaylie Szeifert. It was just a stupid dream."

Jackie entered, dressed in a compression suit. "Are you ready? Bin Rashidi wants us in the water the moment we arrive at the glacier's inlet."

"Molony, if she goes, I'm staying."

"Sorry, kid, that's not your call."

"The fuck it's not. It's either my call or you can pilot the damn sub yourself."

"David, I can handle it. We're in the shallows; it's daylight."

"Not for long."

"Shut up, Monty."

David sat on a bench by his locker stall, pulling off his compression boots.

"Okay, hold on," Molony said. "Jackie, David's going solo on this one."

"Or you could go with him," suggested Monty. "Think about it; if you're in the co-pilot's chair, his dead girlfriend won't have anywhere to sit."

David started to say something, then thought about it. "That's true."

Jackie looked at the commander, her eyebrows raised. "Well?"

Molony's face flushed, matching his red hair. "Goddam it. Everyone out while I change."

Before they could move, Fiesal bin Rashidi's voice blasted over the intercom. "Commander Molony, report to the bridge at once."

Granted a momentary reprieve, Molony left the room.

Monty shook his head. "Saved by the yell."

———

Bin Rashidi passed the binoculars to the commander, pointing out the bridge's starboard bay windows.

Molony peered through the glasses at the large ship in the distance, a name emblazoned across her stern. "The *McFarland*."

"It's Jonas Taylor's vessel; the hopper-dredge he used to transport Angel."

"What's it doing in Antarctica?"

"Fool! Taylor's after the Lio."

Aboard *Manta-Three*

Terry eased the sub into the crystal-green waters of the bay, the late afternoon sun fading quickly. "Anything on sonar?"

Zachary listened intently on his headphones. "The Crown Prince's ships are entering the bay. David's sub should be in the water soon."

"Where's the Lio?"

"I dinnae ken; it's not showing up on my screen. Should I go active?"

"And reveal ourselves? No, thank you. With these two lasers weighing us down I doubt we could outrun a sea elephant, much less a one-hundred-and-twenty-foot pliosaur. What we're going to do is lie along the bottom and wait until David makes his move."

Pushing down on the joystick, she descended two hundred and thirty feet before leveling out over the sea floor. Keeping her speed below seven knots, she trekked east, moving toward the glacier.

After another minute a series of objects appeared on Zach's sonar screen, his headphones chirping with acoustics.

"Terry—"

"I hear them. They sound like minke whales. Zachary, there's a communication panel by your right foot. Open it, please. You'll see a series of toggle switches set in the OFF position. Is there one with a blinking blue light?"

"No."

"Keep an eye on it. If a light starts blinking that means David's sub is in the area. Flip the switch and we'll be able to speak with him over an inter-sub comm-link."

Zach's gaze shifted from the panel to his sonar monitor, the pod of whales materializing as blips on the edge of his screen.

———

The Antarctic minke is small for a baleen whale. Twenty to thirty feet in length and weighing between seven and eleven tons, the mammal resembles a stocky porpoise with two long flippers and a hook-shaped dorsal fin. Dark backed and white bellied, minke feed on plankton and krill, filtering the small fish through their baleen as they sieve the frigid polar waters.

Seventeen minke whales and three adult humpbacks had gathered within a hundred yards of the Thwaites Glacier to feast on a school of sardines. The cetaceans took turns diving through the swirling maelstrom of fish, their *chuffing* exhalations echoing across the bay, the setting sun reflecting gold off the sheer white cliffs of ice.

As the sun bled into shades of red and magenta the mammals' auras changed. Becoming agitated, the whales stopped feeding. As darkness fell they segregated into two pods, the adults pushing their young into the center.

An immense predator had entered the channel, circling the sea floor directly beneath the panicked herd.

With a thrust of its powerful forelimbs the *Liopleurodon* rose, its hideous mouth opening as it launched itself straight up through the gyrating islands of blubber. The surface exploded in bloody froth as a five-ton female minke was hoisted out of the sea within the breaching monster's jaws, the Lio's dagger-like teeth nearly severing the whale in half.

The pods dispersed—the cetacean stampede fleeing the channel.

———

A bizarre sensation of déjà vu washed over Zachary Wallace as a wall of sonar blips appeared on his screen, converging upon the Manta. "Terry, the whales are fleeing the channel—we're in their path!"

A forty-five-foot humpback materialized out of the olive-green ether, its thrusting gray fluke barely missing the sub.

Two more appeared, followed by a chaotic rush of minke whales.

Terry tried to dive free of the stampede but the cetaceans were everywhere. Powering up the *Valkyries*, she faced the swarm head-on, the lasers' intense heat forcing the whales to give the Manta a wide berth.

"Zach, start pinging. We need to find the Lio before it finds us."

His mind overwhelmed with yet another bad déjà vu, Zachary went active on sonar, sending out multiple bursts of sound.

An immense object appeared on his screen a kilometer to the east, close to the glacier.

And then a second object approached from the southwest. Passing beneath the *Tonga* and the *McFarland*, it was clearly homing in on the Manta's sonar pings.

Zzzzzzzzzzt. Zzzzzzzzzzzzzzt.

Zachary's heart raced, the familiar burst of echolocation paralyzing his limbs.

"Zach, what was that?"

He tried to speak, only the muscles in his throat had constricted in fear.

A blue light illuminated inside the panel by his foot. Reaching down, he flipped the toggle switch on the comm-link.

"Dad, is that you?"

"David!"

"Mom? What are you doing in Antarctica?"

Zachary grabbed Terry's right wrist. "It's Brutus—he followed us here! Ye've got tae move!"

"Huh?" She glanced at her sonar screen, then accelerated the Manta into a tight loop, nearly losing both *Valkyries* as the eighty-foot, hundred-ton Miocene sperm whale shot past the sub.

"Mom, was that a sperm whale?"

"Terry, the whale's too fast for us; ye need tae confront it with the lasers. David, this is Zach Wallace. The whale is a *Livyatan melvillei*, it's a big-jawed—"

"I know what it is. What the hell is it doing here? Mom, above you—watch out!"

The bull had ascended, only to circle back and descend upon the fleeing sub.

Terry and Zach looked up at the charging beast and knew they had no chance. The Miocene whale had the angle and speed, and the Manta's pilot could not maneuver the sub's bow around fast enough to direct the lasers at the enormous square head bearing down upon their cockpit glass.

Soaring through the sea at thirty-six knots, David continuously pinged the whale as he homed in on the prehistoric mammal's left eye.

The presence of another Manta confused the behemoth. Less than two body lengths from the first sub, it veered away from the sea floor to attack the second.

Pulling his craft into a one gee, 180-degree turn, David led the Miocene denizen to the west. He had no desire to net the huge sperm whale; his only thought was to draw it away from his mother's sub. But the creature was surprisingly quick and clearly agitated, and the two cumbersome objects strapped to his mother's sub's wings rendered it vulnerable to an attack. Soaring beneath the *Mc-Farland*'s keel with the whale closing to within fifty yards, he realized the leviathan was not the least bit intimidated by the hopper-dredge, nor would it cease its relentless pursuit until either he or it was dead.

Suit yourself, big fella.

Easing back on the joystick, David began a quick ascent, the *Tonga*'s massive bottom looming ahead.

The two Dubai ships' captains had taken up parallel positions to one another the moment their vessels had entered the channel. Deck hands aboard the *Tonga* quickly lowered an immense trawl net into the water between the two ships. While the trawl remained attached to the tanker's two largest winches, the *Dubai Land-I*'s crew had to stretch and maintain the opening of the trap in order to ensnare the Lio as it swam headfirst into the triangular net.

From his perch inside the bridge of the *Tonga,* Fiesal bin Rashidi stared at the tanker's sonar monitor, his adrenaline pumping as he watched the small blip lead the much larger blip into the alley of water between his two ships.

———————

Jonas Taylor had awoken in sickbay to learn his wife and Zachary were aboard the *Manta-Three,* attempting to help David. Ascending six flights of steps, he staggered into the *McFarland*'s bridge just as his son's sub surfaced astern.

Night-vision binoculars revealed the trawl net stretched between the two Dubai ships. And then the creature chasing after the Manta surfaced, allowing Jonas to identify the species.

Son of a bitch, it's that damn whale!

"Sonar, where's *Manta-Three*?"

"Passing beneath our keel, heading west toward the tanker at six knots."

"And the Lio?"

"Two miles to the east."

"Captain, come about! Get us to the tanker. Sonar, if that Lio so much as farts, I want to know about it."

———————

Sweat poured down David Taylor's face. Echolocating the tanker, the whale had nearly given up the chase, forcing the pilot to cut his speed in half and weave from side to side in order to keep the melvillei interested. Cruising at only eighteen knots, he knew the Manta could not generate enough lift to leap out of the sea in order to clear the trawl net. And yet he had to keep the creature close . . . knowing that if he failed to ensnare the bull sperm whale it would turn and pursue his mother's submersible.

So he took a chance.

Throttling back, he dropped his speed to thirteen knots, allowing the Miocene beast close enough for its open mouth to taste his sub's jet-pump propulsor bubbles.

Incensed, the whale increased its speed as it passed the *Tonga's* bow—just as David crushed the right accelerator pedal to the floor and wrenched the joystick hard to port.

The Manta launched sideways out of the sea. It cleared the steel cables running from the trawler to the net—and smashed nose-first into the *Dubai Land's* bow with the force of a race car striking a brick wall.

One moment David was airborne, the next he was consumed by an explosion of darkness.

———

Unaware that its prey was gone, the Miocene sperm whale swam into the trawl net, stopping only after its massive head became stuck at the pointed cod end. It attempted to turn around, but the crew manning the *Tonga's* starboard winch were already tightening the noose upon the beast's flapping fluke.

A collective cheer went up from both ships as the creature was hauled tail-first out of the sea.

A moment later the *Tonga's* searchlights revealed the catch.

Fiesal bin Rashidi's hands quivered in rage as he stared at the sperm whale thrashing within the trawl net six stories below. "What is this? This is not my monster! Sonar, where is the Lio?"

"Four kilometers to the east, heading this way."

———

Terry Taylor surfaced her sub between the *McFarland* and the two Dubai ships, praying the presence of the immense hopper-dredge and supertanker would be enough to keep the *Liopleurodon* away. She tried to reach her son by comm-link, but there was no reply. Accelerating to twenty knots, she raced for the tanker. "Zachary, start pinging. Find me David's Manta."

"Terry, look."

The two pilots stared at the scene before them.

The Miocene whale was suspended upside-down from a trawl net, thrashing along the starboard side of the tanker as it was hauled up to the main deck. As this was happening, the crew of the trawler were tossing a smaller cargo net into the water, a team of divers jumping in after it.

As Terry watched, her son's sub was hauled out of the sea, the Manta's port wing smashed beyond recognition.

"David . . ."

———————

The *Liopleurodon* had consumed most of the minke whale when it registered the familiar sonic pings coming from *Manta-Three*. Leaving its young to feed on the remains of the carcass, it followed the vibrations, intent on protecting its offspring.

———————

"Jonas, the Lio's on the move; it's heading toward the tanker."

"Get *Manta-Three* on the radio."

———————

"Terry, Jonas is on channel one."

Terry switched her headphones to the *McFarland*'s frequency. "Jonas, David's sub struck the trawler, it looks really bad. I'm going to dock—"

"No! Terry, the Lio's on the way. You need to get out of there."

"David's sub is still suspended along the side of the trawler. I'm not going to allow that creature to grab it."

Zach tracked the *Liopleurodon* on sonar. "Terry, it's moving along the sea floor, it'll ascend directly beneath us."

Terry felt her Parkinson's symptoms kick in, causing her right arm and quadriceps to shake uncontrollably.

Jonas's soothing voice reached out to her. "Terry, listen carefully. In thirty seconds you're going to kill the Lio."

"How?"

"Use the *Valkyries*. Aim for its neck."

Reaching for the makeshift power controls secured by duct tape by her left knee, Terry ignited the lasers, then accelerated toward the trawler, submerging beneath its keel.

"Zach, start pinging."

———

The *Liopleurodon* detected the reverberations, homing in on the irritating sounds.

Terry descended the sub at a forty-degree angle, spiraling into the depths as she searched the olive-green sea for the monster.

And then she saw it.

Its jawline alone was thirty feet, its mouth filled with ten- to-twelve-inch dagger-like teeth, the largest of which jutted outside of its mouth. Its sheer mass was incredible—from its snout to the tip of its powerful stubby tail it was as long as a city block, propelled by forelimbs the size of a school bus—all wrapped around a lead-gray and white hide that partially morphed into the backdrop of the dark sea.

Most frightening—it seemed to be hyperactive, its movements on overdrive as its crocodilian jaws snapped at their approaching submersible.

"Terry, what are you doing?"

She ignored Zach, closing the distance, her strategy based on her own frightful experience with Angel's mother, a predator that had lived its entire existence in darkness.

Not yet . . . not yet . . .

Now!

Flipping on her headlights, she blinded the charging pliosaur as she barrel-rolled away from its outstretched jaws and buried the Manta's bow just above the *Liopleurodon*'s chest cavity, the twin lasers burning matching holes three feet deep into the creature's hide.

Blood spurted across the sub's cockpit glass as the insane beast whipped its upper torso to and fro until it finally tossed the Manta free.

Mortally wounded, the animal sank toward the sea floor, writhing in pain.

———

The captain of the *McFarland* reversed the hopper-dredge's engines, preventing the ship from getting too close to the *Tonga*.

Using his night-vision binoculars, Jonas searched the trawler, locating the damaged Manta. Sealed from the inside, the cockpit was being manually opened using a hydraulic device.

Scanning the crew, he saw a familiar face.

"Captain, I need to reach Mac."

The captain nodded to his first officer, who hustled over to the ship's radio controls.

The *Manta-Three* surfaced and he breathed a sigh of relief.

"Jonas, something's approaching on sonar . . . I think it's the Lio's young."

"Where is it? How deep?"

"Sixty feet. It'll be passing beneath our starboard bow in sixty seconds."

"Captain, is the hopper still drained?"

"Yes."

"Open the hopper doors on my command."

The first officer waved to Jonas. "I have Mr. Mackreides on the line."

Jonas took the headset. "Mac, contact your nephew, Monty. I need to know if David is . . . if he's okay."

"Stand by."

Jonas focused the night glasses on the Manta as the cockpit glass was pried open, allowing a medic and two crewmen inside the sub.

Jason Montgomery hovered nearby. Jonas watched as the war vet answered his iPhone to read the incoming text.

Monty turned toward the *McFarland*.

A moment later he made the thumbs-up sign as David was helped out of the sub, his black compression suit covered in white powder.

Mac's voice came over the headset. "David's a bit shaken up, but Monty says he's fine. The air bag apparently went off, knocking him out."

Jonas bit his lower lip, wiping tears from his eyes. "Thank you, Mac. Stand by please. Sonar, where's Junior?"

"Passing beneath the stern . . . now."

"Captain, open the hopper doors."

———

Situated within the keel, the hinged steel doors of the empty hopper unbolted, the force of the sea driving them inward. Within seconds the vacuous pressure differential sucked several hundred thousand gallons of salt water into the hold—the eight-foot baby *Liopleurodon* along with it.

31

Aboard the Hopper-Dredge *McFarland*
Amundsen Sea, Antarctica

Dr. Goldman finished examining David Taylor. "A mild concussion, other than that no other physical trauma to report. How do you feel?"

"Okay, I guess."

"You look exhausted," Terry said. "Are you still having those terrible nightmares?"

"No, I'm good," he said, avoiding eye contact.

Terry glanced at Jonas, urging him on.

"Listen, David, I know you needed to get away from things for a while, but your mother and I . . . well, we're here to help if you let us. The *Liopleurodon* is dead. That alone should start making things a little easier on you. The question is—where do you want to be? Sure, the Crown Prince has an incredible facility, but do you really want to live in Dubai?"

"Dubai's beautiful. Plus they have one of Angel's pups. She's getting huge."

"Is that what you want to do, David?" Terry asked. "Work with Megalodons?"

"I don't know. Let me process things. What time is the pow-wow with bin Rashidi?"

"Eleven o'clock." Jonas checked his watch. "I've got a few things to do before then. By the way, I met your friend."

"Monty?"

"Jackie. She's very knowledgeable. If we end up keeping the baby Lio, I may hire her to be its trainer."

"Wait, Dad . . . I thought this morning's meeting was about selling Lio Junior to the Crown Prince?"

Jonas kissed his son on the forehead as he stood to leave. "I'm still processing things."

Aboard the *Tonga*

Whomp!

Fiesal bin Rashidi stood on the metal catwalk next to Jacqueline Buchwald, gripping the rail as he gazed three stories below. The immense storage tank ran the length of the ship like a rectangular lake, its fifteen million gallons of sea water divided in half by a three-inch-thick rubber-coated steel gate. The Miocene whale occupied the forward holding area.

As they watched, a dark wake rolled from the bow toward the stern. . . .

Whomp!

The gate shook, the impact of the whale's enormous head upon the steel divider reverberating through the guard rail.

Jackie smiled. "I guess he wants the whole tank."

"Do you find this humorous, Miss Buchwald? Because let me assure you that I do not. I did not spend millions of dollars and six long months at sea to capture a whale."

"This isn't just a whale, sir. *Livyatan melvillei* was a prehistoric sperm whale. Megalodon and melvillei were the two dominant predators during the Miocene era. This creature's teeth are actually bigger than a Meg's, its jaws and bite just as powerful. It's longer and heavier than Angel was, and I doubt there's ever been a bigger Mega-lodon on the planet. The whale would be an incredible addition to the Crown Prince's aquarium."

"I think you've been at sea too long, Miss Buchwald. Besides the fact that this monster would probably destroy its own tank, we are simply not equipped to deal with a mammal of this size. All our aquariums are indoor facilities. This creature requires an outdoor venue."

"Can't your cousin build him one?"

"And what happens when it dies? All our specimens are female, capable of internal fertilization. You know firsthand that we've been storing eggs to maintain our stock. This menace is a male. This creature is not worth the investment."

"Then offer it to Jonas Taylor in exchange for the Lio offspring. The Tanaka Lagoon would be perfect for it."

Bin Rashidi turned to her, his unibrow furrowed. "You think this thought has not occurred to me?"

Whomp!

"The helicopter will transport us over to the *McFarland* in ten minutes. Examine the Lio; make sure it is not injured."

"Yes, sir."

Whomp . . .

Six hundred and seventy feet beneath the *Tonga*'s keel, the *Liopleurodon* lay on its back in a catatonic state, gasping short swallows of sea water. Each inhalation produced soft oxygen-yielding ripples across its gill slits and searing white-hot pain through the damaged nerves in its neck and chest. A burnt scent filled its nasal cavity; fever racked its blood vessels.

The Manta's lasers had melted its hide clear down to its chest cavity, stopping just short of its closest vital organ while cauterizing the wound. The injured creature was in too much agony to use its forelimbs, let alone right itself to swim. And so it remained on its back, paralyzed by the pain, the frigid Antarctic water gradually soothing the damaged tissue.

Aboard the Hopper-Dredge *McFarland*

Fiesal bin Rashidi, Commander Molony, and Jacqueline Buchwald sat on one side of the conference room table, Jonas, Terry, and Monty across from them. Out of respect, David sat at the head of the table in neutral territory.

Bin Rashidi forced a smile. "So, Mrs. Taylor, was it really necessary to kill my creature?"

"Yes. And I don't recall seeing a name tag on the animal."

The smile faded. "Six months my crew and I have been at sea in pursuit of the Lio, the last two weeks in this icebox. My cousin hired your son at his own request and paid him like royalty. Knowing all this you still chose to interfere with our mission just to stock your own facility!"

Terry became livid. "What nerve you have! For your information, we were never after your monster. We were tracking the whale."

Jackie whispered to her boss. "There's a tracking device on the whale's head, three feet below the blowhole."

"The Miocene whale . . . where did it come from?" David asked, the question directed at his parents.

"We don't know," Jonas replied. "There were a few documented sightings . . . we got a tip."

"Then this is a fortunate day for you," said Fiesal bin Rashidi. "We shall trade the whale for the *Liopleurodon*'s offspring. The *McFarland* shall go to Dubai, the *Tonga* to California."

"And my son?" Jonas asked. "Where will he go?"

"Wherever he wishes, of course."

"Dad, I'm not a bargaining chip."

"I know. I just don't wish my legacy to be your nightmare. While you were away, your mother and I agreed to sell the institute. You and your sister will split our share of the proceeds."

Bin Rashidi's eyes widened. "Who are you selling the facility to?"

"At this point I'm not really sure. We have an offer on the table from Agricola Industries, but it's predicated on recapturing Bela and Lizzy. However, having secured the juvenile Lio—"

"Sign nothing," bin Rashidi interrupted. "Whatever Agricola Industries offered, my cousin and I shall best it."

"You want to buy the Tanaka Institute?" David asked.

"Of course. There are two Disney locations in America, plus facilities in Paris, Hong Kong, and Japan. With aquariums, there are strategic advantages in owning multiple facilities. We could use the lagoon to house the whale and the Meg Pen to hold the *Liopleurodon* until it grew too large. By that time the whale most likely will have died, but our Megalodon back in Dubai would be ready to give birth, in which case the adult Lio would take over the lagoon and we'd ship a Meg pup to California. Whatever the case, multiple facilities and a successful breeding program affords us many options."

Bin Rashidi turned to David. "I'm sure your parents and I would be willing to structure the deal so that you were one of the institute's owners."

David looked around the table, all eyes on him. "How long will it take us to get the Lio and the whale back to Monterey?"

"It depends on the *Tonga*." Jonas said.

Fiesal bin Rashidi calculated in his head. "Eight days. Possibly less."

"Dad, is that enough time for Mac to fix the Lexan panel that Bela cracked in the Meg Pen?"

"It's already been repaired. We also installed electrical sensors to prevent any wildlife from charging the glass again."

David tapped his fingers on the tabletop, a life-changing moment staring him in the face. He looked at Jackie. "Want a job in California?"

"With you as my boss? That depends. Does it involve copiloting a submersible?"

"Hell, no."

"Where would we live?"

David turned to his parents, grinning from ear to ear. "Lock it down."

32

|||||||||||||||||||||||||||||||

Ten days.

Three ships.

Two monsters.

And the reality show film crew covered nearly every moment of the return trip on tape. From the negotiations of the sale of the Tanaka Institute, to a rogue wave in the Drake Passage that nearly capsized the trawler, to the daily feedings that drove the weekly ratings through the roof and spurred animal rights protesters across the globe.

What does an eight-foot, two-hundred-and-sixty-pound *Liopleurodon* eat?

A thirty-hour stopover at Grytviken Island stocked the *McFarland* with king penguins, fur seals, and elephant seals, the meat frozen in walk-in freezers.

What does an eighty-foot, two-hundred-thousand-pound Miocene sperm whale eat?

An adult minke will quench the appetite of a full-grown *Livyatan melvillei* for two to three days, a humpback twice that time period— if you can keep the blubber from going rancid.

Of course, audiences tuning in to the reality show never saw the trawler's crewmen netting these sacrificial mammals, nor did they watch the meat being filleted in much the same way Grytviken's whaling community did over seventy-five years ago.

By dawn of day eleven the three ships, crews and two monsters were located ninety miles south of Baja, California, steaming up the coast—unaware that an even larger creature was hitching a ride in the *Tonga*'s displacement current, its wound healed, its senses attuned to its captive offspring sealed within the *McFarland*'s steel hopper.

Flora Islet, Georgia Strait
Salish Sea, British Columbia

Situated off the eastern tip of Hornby Island, Flora Islet was a moonscape of bare rock inhabited by hundreds of sea elephants and seals. The mammals barked and belched and dove in and out of the sea, but none would venture far from land.

The captain of the hopper-dredge *Marieke* positioned his ship to the north of the landmass, then powered off his engines as instructed.

Out on the main deck, Paul Agricola sat on a bench by the empty hopper as his engineer, Michael Tvrdik, used the starboard winch to lower the remotely-controlled Sea Bat into the emerald-green water. Sunset was thirty minutes away, but the skies were overcast and the sisters were never timid about making a daytime appearance.

Opening his briefcase, Paul powered up the drone's remote control console—a laptop with two small joysticks.

The engineer waved from the winch. "You're good to go."

Paul activated the drone's exterior camera, then pushed down on the right joystick as he accelerated with the left, sending the Sea Bat into a steep dive along the vertical rock face.

The monitor revealed a dazzling array of life attached to the volcanic rock. Purple and yellow sponges and pink algae were adhered to the wall, along with bright green sea urchins and orange coral.

Mike Tvrdik joined him, a walkie-talkie attached to his belt. "The captain's standing by at the hopper door controls. You sure you brought enough phenobarbital on board to handle these monsters?"

"We're good."

The engineer watched as the laptop's depth gauge dropped below seventy meters. "You're halfway to the bottom. Where are your sharks?"

"Watch and learn, my friend." Paul hit CONTROL and S on his keypad, engaging the Sea Bat's sonar array.

The screen split, the video camera's images now limited to the left half of the monitor, the drone's sonar array to the right. Small objects appeared on screen, the fish finder identifying each species.

"Rockfish and greenlings, looks like a few longfin sculpins and a bunch of lion's mane jellyfish. Let's see if we can't lure something a tad larger up from the depths."

Paul engaged the drone's autopilot, dialing up a figure-eight holding pattern.

"Thirty-five years ago we dropped the Sea Bat into the Mariana Trench just above the hydrothermal plume. We were pinging the bottom, taking readings when a forty-eight-foot Meg showed up."

"The shark that attacked Jonas Taylor?"

"I had no idea the navy was conducting secret dives into the trench; Taylor was just in the wrong place at the wrong time. It took me a long time to realize it was the frequency of the Sea Bat's sonar array, combined with the drone's metal skin that rendered it a Megalodon lure." Paul pointed to the screen. "And what do we have here?"

A life form measuring 2.45 meters appeared on screen, circling the Sea Bat from below.

"The fish finder identifies it as a great white, but you can bet the farm it's one of the pups. Now watch what happens when I go after it."

Switching his controls from *remote* to *manual*, Paul dove the drone at the eight-foot object, chasing it off to the east.

A moment later a blinking red object appeared on the monitor—a much larger object, listed at 14.32 meters—slightly smaller than an eighteen-wheeler.

"And the first sister has arrived; let's see who it is." Paul zoomed in with the drone's camera as the life form rose silently from the depths, a dark caudal fin appearing on screen.

"Good evening, Bela. Want to go for a ride?" Pulling back on the right joystick, Paul sent the Sea Bat on a steep ascent straight up the rock face—as a second blinking red object appeared on the edge of the screen, moving in from the south on an intercept course.

"Good evening, Lizzy. Catch me if you can." Paul accelerated, forcing the albino Megalodon to alter its angle of pursuit.

"Fifty meters to the surface . . . Michael, get the captain on your walkie-talkie, tell him to stand by to open the hopper doors."

Swooping in behind the drone, Lizzy's snow-white face bloomed on the laptop's screen, forcing Paul to increase the drone's speed.

"Damn, she's fast. Twenty meters—get ready, Michael. Not yet . . . not yet . . . now!"

"Captain, open the doors."

The ship shuddered as a geyser of seawater erupted behind the two men, propelling the Sea Bat up through the flooding hopper and sixty feet into the air, the stunned Megalodon with it.

"Close doors!"

The forty-six-foot-long shark fell back into the overflowing hopper, sending a ten-foot swell rolling over the sides of the tub in all directions.

Seeing the wave, Michael Tvrdik grabbed his boss and held on to the deck-mounted bench as the swell swept over them, blotting out the sky. A long muted moment passed before the wave retreated over the sides of the ship, leaving both men soaked and shivering.

Paul staggered to the hopper's rail and looked down. "Holy shit, it actually worked."

The albino shark was swimming in tight circles in forty feet of water, searching for an exit.

Whomp.

The ship shuddered as Bela struck the *Marieke*'s keel.

Whomp.

Lizzy pounded the hopper's sealed doors.

"Michael quickly, help me with the phenobarbital."

The two men stumbled and slid across the wet deck to where four fifty gallon drums of phenobarbital—a central nerve suppressant—was lined up next to a generator and pump. Tvrdik powered up the machinery while Paul dragged a seventy-foot hose over to the hopper and began spraying the liquid elixir into the Olympic-size tub.

Spotting the human, Lizzy circled the tank, then leaped at Paul, who dropped the hose into the hopper and ran.

Over the next chaotic minutes the captured Meg slapped its half-moon-shaped caudal fin against the sides of the hopper in protest. Paul waited her tantrum out, starting a second fifty-gallon barrel. He drained three-quarters of the container before the shark settled down.

Shivering in the cold dusk, Paul and his engineer crept over to the hopper and looked down.

Lizzy was underwater, barely moving. Her remaining functional eye was rolled back in her head, revealing a bloodshot membrane.

"She's out. Have the captain start the dredgers."

The two massive suction pipes trailing along either side of the ship jumped to life, pumping a river of water into the front of the hopper, providing a steady current for the Meg to breathe.

After a moment Lizzy's gills began to flutter as seawater passed down her gullet.

Paul slapped his engineer across his back. "What'd I tell you? Am I good or am I good?"

Whomp.

"What about the other sister?"

"That's the best part. Bela will follow us all the way down the coast to Monterey."

Grabbing Tvrdik's walkie-talkie, Paul contacted the bridge. "Captain, take us out of the Salish Sea, next stop—the Tanaka Intstitute."

PART FOUR

TANAKA INSTITUTE

33

‖‖‖‖‖‖‖‖‖‖‖‖‖‖‖‖‖‖‖‖‖‖‖‖‖‖‖

Tanaka Oceanographic Institute
Monterey, California

They had begun arriving at noon when the box offices had opened, general admission arena tickets selling for one hundred dollars a seat, the Meg Pen galley for twice that much. Although the schedule was subject to change, the *McFarland* was expected at seven-thirty p.m., the *Tonga* an hour later—all of which left plenty of time for tailgating.

The new owners arrived by four p.m., the Crown Prince on his private jet, Fiesal bin Rashidi by helicopter, the latter accompanied by his marine biologist, Jacqueline Buchwald, who was tasked with making sure the Meg Pen's water temperatures and salinity were suitable for the juvenile *Liopleurodon*.

David Taylor, a minority shareholder, remained on board the *McFarland* with his parents to prepare to move the Lio pup.

Zachary Wallace found David eating in the *McFarland*'s galley with his friend, Jason Montgomery. Grabbing a turkey sandwich and a bottled water from the buffet table, he approached the two young men.

"Mind if I join ye?"

David motioned to an empty chair, his eyes hidden behind dark sunglasses. "Anything for the guy who saved my life."

"And how did I do that?"

"My father told me it was you who insisted the Mantas be equipped with air bags. Something about seeing me die in a recurring dream."

"Something like that. What's with the sunglasses? Are ye making a fashion statement for yer fans on the reality show?"

"Just a little tired."

"I had lots of recurring dreams after my head was nearly blown off in the war," said Monty, spraying particles of his bologna sandwich. "I kept waking up in the middle of the night screaming bloody murder—just like this one did last night."

"David, ye're still having night terrors?"

"Not really. Maybe one or two since we left Antarctica."

Monty held up seven fingers.

"Seven night terrors?"

"I'm sure it'll pass, now that the Lio's dead."

Zach looked worried.

"What?"

"Nothing. Ye're right, I'm sure it'll pass. Just out of curiosity, were these all the same dream?"

"It was confusing, but they all took place at the institute. The Lio was there, but so was Bela—it didn't make much sense."

"And where were you?"

"In the Manta, trying to save my shark."

"Ye say that as if that monster was yer pet."

David removed his sunglasses, revealing dark circles under his eyes. "For the record, I took care of the sisters from the day they were born. I fed them every day after school and on weekends. I even trained them to respond to hand signals. They're not monsters."

"Yeah, they are," Monty said with a belch, "only they're your monsters. You're like the owner of a pair of pit bulls that keep escaping the yard to attack the neighbors. You'll keep defending them right up until the day they eat a member of the fam."

"Every year twenty-five million people die from contaminated water. How many people get eaten every year?"

Monty shoved the rest of his sandwich in his mouth. "In your neighborhood, it's an epidemic."

———

With two captured sea creatures en route, James Mackreides was expecting trouble. Security had been doubled, with Secret Service agents staked out on the floors housing the luxury suites occupied by the Crown Prince and his guests. The media were cordoned off from the main deck by barriers, the police armed with tasers and pepper spray.

On paper, the plan was relatively simple. Upon its arrival, the *McFarland* would sail through the open gates of the canal into the lagoon. A crane was positioned on the expanse of deck separating the lagoon from the Meg Pen's tank and would be used to transport the baby Lio from the hopper to its new home. The *McFarland* would exit, the gates sealed in anticipation of the arrival of the *Tonga*.

The Miocene whale would be sedated an hour before it would be moved. Netting the beast inside its holding pen presented a few challenges; once completed, the tanker's crane would swing the whale over the sealed gate into the canal. Before being released, an organic stimulant would be administered into its gullet using a water cannon, insuring the mammal was sufficiently awake to swim on its own.

Late afternoon quickly turned into evening, accompanied by a gusting winter's wind which whistled through the canal, forcing those attendees who were not sufficiently inebriated to bundle up.

By six thirty, Mac and his assistant, Bradley Watson, found themselves standing by the crane's cab watching the arena's two new Fan-Visions. Located above the western bleachers on either side of the canal the two giant screens had been purchased by the Crown Prince and rushed into delivery.

As they watched the last episode of the Dubai Aquarium's reality show playing on screen, the broadcast was interrupted by a live shot of the *McFarland*, the hopper-dredge passing the Tanaka Pier half a mile to the south.

A collective cheer rose from the crowd.

A moment later, Mac's iPhone reverberated in his pocket. "Jonas, you're early."

"The canal's a tight squeeze, figured it'd be easier with the sun still up. You all set?"

Bradley Watson nodded to Mac, climbing into the crane's cab.

"We're good to go here. Bring the little gal in."

———

Jonas and Terry stood in the *McFarland*'s bridge, the arena filling the starboard bay windows. Three Coast Guard vessels had joined them in San Diego, escorting them up the California coast. The captain and his executive officer, Leslie Manuel, had lookouts posted in the bow, not so much to guide them in—the ship's GPS could handle that—but to make sure there were no telltale air bubbles from divers looking to sabotage the voyage.

Terry squeezed her husband's hand. "Thank you. I know giving all this up wasn't easy."

"After what the sisters and that whale put me through over these last few months, it was actually quite easy."

The captain checked the alignment of the *McFarland*'s bow with the center of the canal a fourth time. "Jonas, we're set."

"Take us in, skipper. Ms. Manuel, what's the *Tonga*'s ETA?"

"Eighty-two minutes. Their captain will begin braking procedures at seven twenty."

"Very good. Terry, I'm heading down to the hopper to help David, want to join us?"

"It's too cold and windy; you know Northern California winters never agreed with me."

"Maybe we can find a nice condo in San Diego?"

"Actually, I prefer Boca Raton."

The crowd stood on its feet and cheered as the *McFarland* moved through the canal. Entering the lagoon, it turned right, following the man-made waterway in a long counterclockwise loop so that its starboard flank would align with the Meg Pen and the crane.

The presence of the cargo net at the edge of the *McFarland*'s hopper agitated the *Liopleurodon* pup. Swimming in tight circles, it kept to the far end of the tub—exactly as David had anticipated.

He waved to his father, then spoke into his radio. "Start the winch."

Anchored at the far end of the hopper, the portable winch began gathering up the cargo net, sweeping up the baby Lio in its grasp. Two members of the crew quickly fastened loops situated along the open end of the net to a hook attached by steel cable to the institute's crane.

David spoke into his radio. "She's all yours, Mac."

"Roger that, Mr. Taylor. We'll try not to drop her."

The image of the baby *Liopleurodon* within the net appeared on both big screens. The creature was hoisted above the deck of the *McFarland* and gently lowered into the pristine waters of the Meg Pen.

The applauding crowd watched the big screens as the image changed to an underwater view taken from inside the gallery.

Ten minutes later Jonas, Terry, and David exited the *McFarland* to their own standing ovation. Zachary and Monty were the last ones to disembark.

Retracting its gangway, the rusty ship made its way out of the canal into the Pacific. Heading south, it anchored at the Tanaka Pier half a mile away.

Mac joined his best friend by the Meg Pen rail, where they watched the Lio circle its new home. "The monies were wired last night from Dubai; we're officially unemployed."

"Thank God." Jonas pointed to the taser hanging from Mac's belt. "Since when do you carry a weapon?"

"Some tree-hugging, slug-loving jackass shot holes in my tires this morning using a nail gun. A note was left on my windshield about cruelty to animals. If I catch the sonuva bitch—"

"Dad!"

Jonas turned, shocked to find another hopper-dredge entering the facility through the canal. "What the hell is this?"

Believing the Miocene whale had arrived, the crowd rose to its feet.

"Mac, I know that ship; it belongs to Paul Agricola."

"Jesus, you don't think . . ."

"Dad, what's going on?"

The *Marieke* entered the lagoon, its bow stopping ten feet from where they were standing. Paul Agricola emerged on deck, holding a bullhorn. "Good evening, Jonas. As promised, I've fulfilled my end of our arrangement. All I need is your wiring instructions for the down payment and I'll officially take ownership of the institute."

"Dad, what's he talking about?"

Jonas was about to respond when a huge roar filled the arena. With the *Marieke* blocking their view, he had to cross the deck to see the nearest video screen.

The FanVision showed an immense shark with a telltale snowy-white head and six-foot-tall black dorsal fin moving slowly through the canal. The moment it entered the lagoon the crowd began chanting, "Bel-la . . . Bel-la . . . Bel-la!"

The Meg's white head surfaced to spy-hop, Bela's hazy-blue left eye staring at David.

"Good God, look at her, Jonas," Mac said. "She must have gained three tons over the last two months."

Terry shook her head. "Just remember some of those calories came from people."

Paul called down to them from the hopper's port rail four stories overhead. "I've got another Meg inside the hopper who's anxious to be reunited with her sister. Come aboard and we'll sign the papers."

Mac pulled Jonas aside. "We got a real problem here. Even if we refuse to sign, by accepting delivery of the Megs we may legally be forced into completing Agricola's deal."

"We're not accepting anything."

Mac's iPhone buzzed, the caller ID recognizing his wife's number. "Trish, I'm really busy—"

"Mac, wait! I'm seated in the west bleachers with my sister. Something massive just entered the canal."

"We know, hon. It was Bela."

"I can see Bela! Mac, I think it was the Lio."

The *Liopleurodon* moved warily along the bottom of the canal. As it entered the lagoon its olfactory senses detected the lingering scent of the Megalodon that had nearly ended its life in the Philippine Sea, along with the familiar smells and vibrations of its young filtering out into the lagoon.

As it homed in on the Meg Pen, the creature sensed the presence of another Megalodon.

Bela's back arched as she sized up the threat. At just over forty-six feet and close to twenty-five tons the Meg was still only a third the Lio's size and a quarter its weight—no match for the massive pliosaur.

Sensing the Megalodon was just a young adult, the *Liopleurodon* ignored Bela to address the real threat to its offspring—the hopper-dredge. Picking up speed, the creature charged the ship—her presence chasing Bela out from beneath the keel and into the middle of the lagoon.

The pliosaur's tail struck the *Marieke* along its starboard flank. It was a glancing blow, a test to evaluate the unknown animal poised between itself and its newborn.

Bela interpreted the Lio's actions as an attack on her captive sibling. Like a hungry tigress enticed by a competitor's kill, she swam back and forth with quick, rigid strokes of her caudal fin, growing more agitated as the Lio circled the northern end of the lagoon.

With a sudden burst the Megalodon attacked, her outstretched jaws barely wide enough to latch onto the pliosaur's thick muscular tail.

The confrontation was more of an annoyance than a threat. The Lio shook the dark-backed Megalodon loose, then spun around and punctured the shark's left pectoral fin with her fang-filled mouth, drawing blood.

Bela twisted in pain, snapping at its enemy's nearest body part—the pliosaur's left gill slits.

Forced to release Bela's pectoral fin, the *Liopleurodon* chased the Meg clear across the lagoon before turning back to relocate her young.

The energized crowd loved it. Dozens of inebriated patrons rushed to the lagoon's rail to snap a selfie with their iPhones of the historical death match, only to be chased back by the police.

Jonas, Terry, Mac, and Zachary Wallace huddled by the Meg Pen's rail, joined by Bradley Watson, the crane operator out of breath. "Hendricks sealed the canal doors, but I don't think they'll stop a monster that size. We might be able to brace the gate from the outside using the *McFarland*."

"Good idea," Jonas said. "Mac, contact the captain—"

"Maybe we ought to ask the new owners—here comes one of them now."

Fiesal bin Rashidi and a small entourage of armed bodyguards exited to the main deck from an interior stairwell.

"Jonas Taylor, this is incredible—how did you manage it?"

"I had nothing to do with it. As far as I knew the Lio was dead."

Terry looked for her son. She found David standing by the lagoon's rail, staring at the dark dorsal fin which was now fleeing across the lagoon, chased by a seven-foot wake. "Bela won't last long."

"We do not care about Bela," bin Rashidi stated. "The only thing that concerns us is the *Liopleurodon*."

"I care about Bela," David said, approaching the group. "Fiesal, we need to open the gate and let her out."

"Unfortunately, that is far too risky. We could lose the Lio."

"As long as we have the baby, the Lio's not going anywhere," Jonas said. "Bradley, have Hendricks open the gate."

"No! Mr. Watson, the Taylor family no longer owns this facility—I do. Do not open that gate or you'll find yourself looking for employment."

Another roar went up from the crowd, this one more of a collective gasp as the *Liopleurodon* breached—Bela caught within its jaws! The Meg thrashed wildly, and then both monsters fell sideways back into the water, their splash creating a two-story-high wake that rippled outward before rolling over the lagoon wall to soak the patrons sitting in the first four rows.

Mac quickly led his group behind the medical pool as the swell rolled over the northern lagoon wall and rail and flooded the deck, washing over the Meg Pen.

Jonas grabbed Terry and lifted her as high as he could as the chest-high wave drove him backwards into the grandstand.

As the backwash rolled back into the lagoon, a bizarre gargled chirping sound cut through the din of the crowd.

Zach pointed. The juvenile *Liopleurodon* was sprawled out on the flooded deck, calling for its mother.

"Oh, geez, we need to move!" Carrying his wife, Jonas led the others into the northern bleachers as the thirty-foot-long crocodilian head rose out of the lagoon, its lower front fangs dripping water and blood from Bela's impaled hide, its upper torso sliding halfway out of the lagoon onto the flooded concrete deck, crushing the guard rail and knocking the crane sideways against the *Marieke*.

The crowd seated in the northern bleacher's lower seats rose as one and rushed to the nearest exits.

Terry looked around, frantic. "Where's David?"

Soaked from head to toe, David had his back to the Meg Pen's rail and was looking up at the reptilian nightmare.

The slime-coated monster stared at him, sea water oozing out its gills. Hissing phlegm, it shifted it weight over its forelimbs and lurched at David—

—only to be forced back into the lagoon by Bela. The Meg had a hold of the pliosaur's left hindquarters and was shaking her head like a dog in a tug-o-war, her five-inch serrated teeth sawing through muscle and sinew, her powerful jaws snapping bone.

Spinning around underwater, the Lio bit the Megalodon on the left side of its head, its dagger-sharp teeth raking Bela's left eye clear to her nostril, forcing the shark to release her grip on its broken limb.

The wounded predators retreated, the Lio circling beneath the *Marieke*'s keel, remaining close to the lagoon's northern wall, the Megalodon seeking refuge in the canal.

David saw the *McFarland* moving into position outside the canal's sealed doors. Sprinting across the arena, he made his way to the steel security fence guarding the canal's paved maintenance walkway. Punching in his security code, he unlocked the gate and raced along the narrow path. Bela moved slowly through the waterway on his left, the wounded Meg watching him with her remaining good eye.

Back on the north deck, Fiesal bin Rashidi ordered his guards and Bradley Watson to lift the stranded Lio pup over the Meg Pen's rail and back into its tank. The juvenile pliosaur squawked and snapped at the men, who finally managed to secure a canvas drop cloth over its head before they carried it through an open gate and tossed it back into the tank.

Jonas pulled Mac aside. "Contact the *McFarland*'s skipper and have him move the hopper-dredge. Then have Hendricks open the canal doors."

Mac tried his radio, getting only static. "Too late. Bin Rashidi must have changed the frequencies."

Zachary pushed his way into the conversation. "Did David tell ye about his latest night terrors?"

"Zach, can this wait—"

"He dreamt this very scenario! I think he's going tae try tae use the Manta tae save Bela."

"Oh, shit." Jonas and Mac left the bleachers, both men hobbling as they tried to keep up with Zach.

Jonas grabbed Mac's arm, pointing to the *Marieke*. "I know a better way to save Bela."

Mac smiled. "Get in the cargo net."

Jonas secured his waist inside one of the net's thick loops and held onto the pulley's large hook as Mac climbed inside the crane's cab. Backing it away from the hopper-dredge, he raised the net, lifting Jonas forty feet in the air before swinging him over the ship's main deck.

Jonas climbed down, quickly getting his bearings. He was standing in the stern, the hopper taking up most of the mid-deck, the bridge and its hopper controls towering before him. As he hurried past the tank Lizzy's head rose out of the water, the albino shark watching him.

"Give me a minute, girl."

Reaching the ship's infrastructure, he started the four-story climb along the outer stairwell to reach the bridge.

———

The last scarlet speck of sunset had disappeared on the western horizon by the time David reached the end of the canal. The tide was out, the top eight feet of the steel doors poking free above the surface. The *McFarland* was stationed directly outside the gate, the ship's stern resting within three feet of the metal barrier, preventing it from opening.

Bela was spy-hopping close by, the left side of her head streaked with blood, her eye hanging from its socket.

"Jesus, girl, it looks like you got into a fight with Freddy Kruger. Stay here, we're going to deal with that bitch one way or the other."

Stepping carefully out onto the top of the right door, David jumped into the ocean. Swimming against the incoming swells, he located the steel ladder embedded along the ship's starboard flank and began climbing.

———

Jonas was winded by the time he reached the bridge. Pushing his way inside the control room, he confronted Paul Agricola and two members of his crew.

"Jonas Taylor—right on time. Our ship's captain and my engineer have volunteered to serve as witnesses." He pointed to several thick contracts laid out on a map table.

"I'm not here for that. The Lio's on the rampage; people's lives are in danger." He scanned the ship's command center, searching for the controls to the hopper-dredge.

Paul moved to a panel located next to a spiral stairwell running to the deck below. "Looking for this? Forget it. Lizzy's not going anywhere until you sign off on our deal."

"You're too late. I sold the institute last week to the Crown Prince and his cousin. Guess you'll have to negotiate a new deal with them."

Paul's expression soured, but he recovered quickly. "No matter. I still have a few bartering chips left."

Jonas moved toward the control panel as Paul reached behind his back and greeted him with the business end of a 9 mm Glock.

"Come on, Paul. Are you really going to murder me in front of two eyewitnesses?"

"No, but I will shoot you in the knees. Now leave my vessel and have the Crown Prince contact me with an offer for the sisters or I'll bash the *Marieke* through those pathetically thin canal doors and release all his sea monsters back into the wild."

———

It was dark by the time David pulled himself over the *McFarland*'s starboard rail. He quickly made his way past the hopper to the ship's infrastructure. Ducking inside the stairwell, he descended into the bowels of the ship, then raced down a steel passage to the submersible hangar.

Manta-Three was perched on its launch pad, the two *Valkyrie* lasers still strapped to its wings.

Damn it, Cyel! You were supposed to remove that luggage rack last week.

Moving to the hangar's control panel, he set the automatic timer to flood and open the chamber in three minutes. Returning to the sub, he popped the cockpit, climbed into the port seat and sealed himself inside.

———

Jonas felt the heat rushing to his face, his heart pounding rapidly as his blood pressure soared. "You pompous ass. My son's out there, he's going to try to kill the Lio using one of the Mantas. At least allow me to contact the *McFarland* to prevent him from—"

"No. First you'll speak with the Crown Prince. You can radio the *McFarland* after he and I negotiate a—"

Paul Agricola suddenly flopped onto the floor, saliva drooling from his mouth, the gun falling from his twitching hand.

Mac ascended the spiral stairwell, brandishing a taser, the two prongs protruding from Agricola's back trailing wires. "Yak, yak, yak. All this guy does is give speeches."

"Thanks, Mac. As always, your timing is impeccable." Moving to the control panel, Jonas opened the hopper's hangar doors.

———

The *Liopleurodon* registered the vibrations overhead. Circling back toward the sound, it charged the hangar doors just as Lizzy shot through the opening—the pliosaur's open jaws biting down hard on the Megalodon at the base of her caudal fin.

———

The hangar doors opened.

David accelerated the Manta into the Pacific. Passing beneath the *McFarland*'s keel, he surfaced on the port side of the ship and headed south a hundred yards before circling back. Descending to forty feet, he raced toward the canal wall and pulled back hard on the joystick.

The sub launched out of the water and cleared the wall by mere inches before landing in the canal.

There was no sign of Bela.

A yellow light blinked on his console—the Manta's batteries were running low. Cursing aloud, David followed the channel into the lagoon, the arena's lights turning the dark waters an azure blue.

That's when he saw Bela. The dark overlord of the Tanaka lagoon was circling over Lizzy, her sibling wiggling along the bottom of the tank trailing a stream of blood—the albino predator missing her entire tail!

Before he could react, the *Liopleurodon* bull-rushed Bela, the pliosaur's monstrous jaws clamping down over her head.

Bela convulsed in spasms as she attempted to roll herself free. But the Lio was far too big and now it had both leverage and the Megalodon's jaws under control.

Blind with rage, David powered on the *Valkyrie* lasers and accelerated at the beast.

Seeing the familiar sub and its two glowing red-hot eyes, the Lio released Bela and circled back beneath the *Marieke's* keel.

"You can run, bitch, but you can't hide!" David went after the creature as the yellow warning light abruptly changed to red, the sub stalling out.

Powering off the lasers chased the blinking red battery light back to yellow. Stamping down upon both foot pedals, David accelerated away from the charging creature, its enormous skull blooming on his left, its snapping jaws just missing his portside wing.

Limbs shaking, David accelerated the sluggish sub into the southern end of the tank, realizing the additional weight of the two lasers made it impossible for him to leap over the high guard rail surrounding the lagoon; the dying battery giving him barely enough power to make it back to the canal.

Remembering the sub's hydrogen fuel tank, he checked the gauge.

Seventy-two percent . . . that's about an eight-second burn. Leap out of the lagoon using an eight-second hydrogen burn and you'll end up buried nose-first in the seventh row of the bleachers, killing yourself and God knows how many innocent people.

No choice. Pray there's enough juice left in the batteries to get back to the canal, then use the burn to vault the wall. . . .

Executing a tight 180-degree turn along the southern end of the lagoon, he headed back toward the center of the tank—shocked to find the Lio blocking his path, the monster's nightmarish jaws now hyperextended wide to engulf him in one hellacious bite!

Fuck it . . .

Twisting the dial to the hydrogen tank, David ignited the fuel using his right hand even as his left searched blindly for the power switch to the *Valkyrie* lasers.

What happened next happened in the blink of an eye.

David's head was flung backward into the seat cushion as the Manta shot through the pliosaur's dark gullet like a missile, the twin lasers scorching the Lio's gills and throat, the sub shuddering as the pink flames burned through the creature's digestive tract, the hydrogen burn propelling the vessel deeper, refusing to allow it to stall as the *Valkyrie*s melted tissue and internal organs like fat off a hot barbeque spit.

David held on in the chaos and screamed—a scream he had bellowed a hundred times before from the depths of his darkest nightmare—a scream that ended with brilliant blue water and laughter as the Manta escaped the *Liopleurodon*'s internal anatomy by opening up a second anus.

The azure waters quickly turned into a lake of spreading crimson as the dead pliosaur bled out across the lagoon.

Powering off the lasers, David directed the submersible to the bottom of the northern end of the tank.

Lizzy lay on her side along the bottom. Unable to swim, the dying albino predator eyed David as she gasped her last breaths. Bela's lifeless body rested beneath her—the Meg siblings inseparable in life, together in death.

EPILOGUE

It had taken two divers, a crane operator, and a driver operating a flatbed truck four hours to remove the two Megalodon carcasses from the bottom of the Tanaka Lagoon. Conversely, it had taken several days for the *McFarland* to haul the eviscerated *Liopleurodon*'s remains out to the Farallon Islands and its great white shark population, and another thirty hours of vacuuming the ravaged pliosaur's residual body parts into the ship's hopper in order to ready the tank for its new occupant.

The Miocene whale known as Brutus did not take well to its new habitat. By day it remained on the bottom of the canal, seeking refuge from the sun's ultraviolet rays; by night it rammed the lagoon's northern wall with its formidable head as it attempted to get to the Lio pup.

———

Jacqueline Buchwald escorted her boyfriend through the institute's exhibit hall and down a corridor that led to the aquarium gallery, a three-story-high underwater viewing area that ran along the entire width of the Meg Pen.

The brilliant aqua-blue backdrop illuminated the dark promenade, the brown and white specked baby Lio moving back and forth along the tank's thick Lexan glass.

Seated in the fifth row were Fiesal bin Rashidi and his cousin, the Crown Prince.

The prince gave him a weak smile. "Sit down please, David, we have a few things to discuss. Fiesal?"

Fiesal bin Rashidi stared at the pliosaur, refusing to look at the minority partner he now referred to as "the cocky American son-of-a-bitch that killed my dinosaur."

"The Crown Prince and I are returning to Dubai. We're taking the pup with us."

"Why?"

"Three reasons. First, because the infant's nerves are frayed from that damn whale pounding its head on the lagoon wall. Second, because we can't give away tickets, let alone sell an arena seat so that people can stare at an empty lagoon. Finally, because I hate living here as much as I despise working with the cocky American son-of-a-bitch that killed my dinosaur."

"That would be four reasons, wouldn't it?"

"David!"

He glanced at Jackie, who was burning holes into his skull with her glare.

Burning holes . . .

He smiled to himself.

David smiled a lot lately. Killing the *Liopleurodon* seemed to have lightened a burden on his soul. He slept through the night and spent his days meeting with his new agent, fielding offers from television and movie producers pitching him everything from lucrative cameo appearances and new reality series concepts to optioning his life story.

The freestyle living caused a rift between himself and Jackie, who was struggling to care for a prehistoric animal that refused to eat. They had signed a month-to-month lease on a two-bedroom condo in Monterey, but the couple had not slept together in over a week.

Bin Rashidi stood up to leave. "Forgive me, Your Highness, but I am in no mood to deal with this spoiled child's lack of respect. Perhaps Mr. Taylor will fare better with the institute's new owner."

"Wait . . . you sold the institute? To who?"

"To me." Paul Agricola moved out from the shadows of the promenade. "I bought the institute and the prince's remaining Manta sub. Now you and I need to talk."

"Forget it." He turned to Jackie. "Are you going to Dubai?"

"I think we both know the answer to that question."

"I'll miss you."

She kissed him on the lips and smiled. "You'll get over it."

He watched her follow the Crown Prince and Fiesal bin Rashidi out of the gallery, then headed for the parking lot exit, Paul Agricola cutting him off.

"Give me two minutes, David. If you don't like what I have to say, I'll hand you a check for your share of the stock and we'll be through."

"Talk."

"I'm tagging Brutus and releasing him. That should please the animal rights groups you pissed off when you killed the Lio. We'll announce it was your decision."

"There's no 'we' in this equation, douche bag. You pulled a gun on my old man."

"That was a simple misunderstanding."

"We're done here."

"Do you know where I found the sisters, David? They were in the Salish Sea, guarding their surviving pups."

"The sisters had pups?"

"Your parents never told you? Each pup is a genetic clone of Lizzy and Bela. We can catch them, David. We can turn the Agricola Entertainment Center into a thriving Megalodon exhibit."

David stared at the Lio. The creature was destined to spend the rest of its life in an aquarium. And now Paul Agricola wanted to do the same with Lizzy and Bela's pups.

"I think I'll take the money. Make the check out to my middle name—cash."

David headed for the exit.

"I sold the idea of capturing the pups to the Discovery Channel as a new reality show."

"Good luck with that." David continued walking.

"You're not saving them by allowing them to live in the wild. You're actually condemning them. With the sisters gone the orca pods will return. They'll slaughter the pups, you can count on it. Help me save them and I'll up your share of the institute to twenty percent."

"Thirty."

"Twenty-five, and we'll hire you a beautiful secretary."

"No. Maybe. But only if we keep my grandfather's name on the marquee."

"Absolutely not. The Agricola Entertainment Center was the name stipulated by our board of directors."

"My grandfather sacrificed everything he had to build this place. He lost his son, D.J., to one of the Megs. The Tanaka name remains; that's a deal breaker." David headed for the exit.

"Wait." Paul Agricola's face turned red. "We put my family's name on the institute, but the lagoon remains under the Tanaka name. That's as far as I go, take it or leave it."

David gazed around the promenade at the blown-up photos mounted on the walls. There were startling images of Angel feeding, the birth of her five female pups, an underwater shot taken in the Meg Pen of Lizzy and Bela swimming in tandem—a defensive posture forged out of fear of their domineering mother. More than anything, David loved working with the Megs; now Paul Agricola was offering him a second chance.

"We need to hire my friend, Monty. He's a war vet."

"Can he co-pilot the sub?"

"No, but he can run our all-female valet parking garage."

Paul Agricola smiled, shaking his new partner's hand.

"Mr. Taylor, I like the way you think."

The MEG series continues with

MEG

GENERATIONS

Look for MEG movie updates at www.stevealten.com.